love's ineligible receiver
connecticut kings
book five

Love Belvin

MKT Publishing, LLC

by Love Belvin

MKT Publishing, LLC

Copyright © 2018 by MKT Publishing, LLC

All rights reserved. This book may not be reproduced, scanned, or distributed in any printed or electronic form without written permission from the author. Please do not participate in or encourage piracy of copyrighted materials in violation of the author's rights. This book is a work of fiction. Names, characters, places, and incidences are fictitious and a product of the author's imagination.

ISBN: 978-1-950014-41-5 (Paperback)
ISBN: 978-1-950014-40-8 (eBook)

MKT Publishing, LLC
First print edition 2018 in U.S.A.

Cover design by **Visual Luxe**

per young lord...

"Bitches be the set up...get wet up...
Let you nut up...then burn you the fuck up.
They seduce you with that shit...
Stroke ya dick...then have they hands all up in ya pocket.
Shit, I know we all got our hustle and I ain't tryna knock it.
But to the crack bitch, groupie bitch—and corny bitches—y'all be the same...
Stay the fuck out my hustle 'cause, man, all y'all be fuckin' lame."

~ Young Lord

chapter one

March 2018

As Mario held the door open, I rolled the white cloth covered cart into the plush office. No matter how many times I'd been in here, the ambiance and moving energy of the room was no less unnerving. Before this job, I'd never been inside the office of a chief executive officer, much less a billionaire. And my boss' boss was just that.

    I pushed my way to the opposite side of the room charmed with old-world aesthetics. Three-fourths of the galactic space was encased in handcrafted Gothic bookcases built into the walls. The fourth wall, from floor-to-ceiling, was a window with the most incredible mountainy vista behind the building. The carpet was a deep green with labyrinthian designs featuring other bold tinctures.

    As I neared the table set for two toward the floor-to-ceiling window, I could hear the calm rumbling of masculine tones and observe the sun setting over the mountains. When I made it to my destination, I greeted the men with my eyes then quickly retreated down to the cart, careful to hit all the marks Nyree had taught me. Tonight I'd be filling in as Eli Richardson's personal assistant, serving a private dinner to him and his friend, Azmir Jacobs.

"But who is this motherfucker?" Eli posed angrily.

The tall, chocolate—*beyond handsome*—friend of his, sitting across from him shrugged with indifference. "A nobody from Compton," his voice smooth, agitation hidden beneath the surface.

"A damn nobody implicating you as a drug lord!" rushed from Eli's mouth with agitation to a level he couldn't contain. Realizing that colorful slip, his eyes brushed against me as I kept working to gather their salads to be served. "Pardon me." He bowed gracefully as I placed the plate before him. "Thanks, Parker."

I nodded, remembering to remain invisible amongst men like this. The trigger words of drama didn't faze me much anyway. When I was hired, I had to sign a nondisclosure agreement. Working here in the front office of the *Connecticut Kings*, there were loads of grist for the gossip mill. They were a high-profile team, from what I'd been told, before their franchise quarterback had gone to prison. America's attention returned when the player, Trent Bailey, was released and reacquired by the *Kings*. His second season back, Trent led the team to a Super Bowl win. It came with its price, though. Trent's new wife that had been in the media for one reason or another was the latest talk. Ironically, she'd been someone I'd been getting to know recently, too.

Without a word, I placed their silverware before them, taking my time and being meticulous in service. Azmir picked up his phone that had been chirping more than Eli's since I'd arrived. In fact, Azmir had two phones laid out on the table.

"Ain't nothing I'm stressing at this point," Azmir attempted control of whatever the irritating agent was. "I've been talking to Chesney. We got a plan in place if it goes beyond YouTube."

"But I've seen it's already gotten close to a half a million views in less than two days. Azmir, don't make small of a potential disaster," Eli warned in rare unrest. "What's his motive, the guy who produced the documentary? Who does he have behind him? Who's funding this bullshit? How does this kid even know you to include you in that bootleg ass home video?"

"A former associate of mine from out West affiliated with a cat that was good friends with him." Azmir's answer was dismissive.

Azmir Jacobs was a polite man but one of discernable power, no less. I seriously doubted if he welcomed these questions. I'd observed him over the time I'd been on staff here in the executive suite. He moved with an undercurrent of uncompromised authority. I could sense a tinge of a thug in him, but Azmir presented himself with elegant masculinity. And he was *fine* as all hell. Lengthy, filling his clothes well, and exquisitely dressed.

"Was?" Eli questioned as I placed his salad before him.

Azmir shrugged. "We haven't heard from his friend in a minute."

"As in AWOL?" my boss pressed.

Azmir waved his hand in the air. "Street shit. Nothing to stress."

"Street shit? This doesn't sound like a low-level car jacker, Azmir! He's got enough dough to produce a damn documentary!"

Seldom did I hear Eli upset. The subject matter must have been some serious implication with damning consequences.

Azmir Jacobs kept his face toward his plate, turning over salad leaves to blend in his dressing. "No real money. Just an irritant."

Eli scoffed, "You sure know how to let shit fly over your head."

"Or brush it off my damn shoulder." Azmir's eyes drew up to Eli's as I brought dinner rolls to the table. "Now, I know you ain't invite me here to stress over some amateur, indie documentary that won't make more noise than it already has." His bright and well-aligned smile appeared, a move of finesse. "What's good witchu, E?"

"Damn," Eli coughed up a chuckle. "This bullshit's got my head spinning, brother. I done forgot why I wanted to see your smooth ass in the first place."

Both gentlemen laughed.

"How's Mel and the baby?" Azmir asked.

"They're good. She's away."

"Yeah? Where?"

"Wanted to cruise Southern Italy. Soooo," Eli released a dramatic and telling breath, "she and a few of her friends set sail for ten days."

Azmir gave an intense chin dip. "On your dime?"

"Of course!" Eli chirped a laughter. "Gives me baby and daddy time."

"You better than me, fam."

"How so?"

"Mrs. J could have a day or two with the girls. But a few days across the pond would require a pop up visit." Eli chuckled at his friend's boorish admittance. "I ain't never lie. *Shit*. She knows. She'd be dropping the boarding stairs for me after about forty-eight hours."

They both laughed. It was actually adorable to see men being light-hearted at possessive talk where it concerned their wives.

"How's my girl, Rayna, anyway?"

Azmir forked food into his mouth then garbled, "Still stuck to me and my babies. That says it all."

"Cheers to that." Eli raised a tumbler and his friend did the same before clanking glasses.

"Indeed," Azmir proclaimed before swallowing back brandy. "There's still time to get in on 'Project Vegas,'" Azmir goaded before forking more salad into his mouth.

"The casino?"

"Yup. It's been a process, but things are running rather smoothly at this point." Azmir's dark knuckles knocked the surface of the table superstitiously.

Just before turning back for the cart for butter, I caught Eli's forehead stretched with suspicion. "Could it be because of your heavy-handed influence over there in Nevada?"

Azmir sat back, chuckling as he wiped his mouth with a cloth napkin. His spirit seemed anew.

"I'm the master of influence, bruh."

"That you are," Eli muttered before going for the last of his salad.

That was my cue to get their main dishes ready from the warmer on the cart. When that was done, I could leave them to it for a while before returning. Already, I'd been feeling like an interloper. Once Eli laid down his fork, I removed his salad plate and swiftly replaced it with his entrée.

"And I'm sure that's what you did with my staff," Eli croaked with a raised brow.

"What do you mean?"

"Underwood, Butler, and Henderson said you 'conferenced' them to discuss a special recruit before and after the Combine." Eli watched his friend raptly for a reaction.

Unbothered, Azmir cleared his plate and lifted it for my taking. "Oh, that."

"Yeah, *that*!" Eli sprinkled salt onto his plate.

Azmir shrugged with his head and brows. "Those numbers he put up while there were unparalleled. You heard the echoes of his abilities. He broke records in the drills." His lips lifted with wicked pomposity. "I believe Rut would be a great fit for the team."

"Yeah. But a pain in the ass for my brand."

"Not on my watch." Azmir's declaration was delivered with that sound authority.

"Yeah. Let's hope so."

"I can guarantee it."

With a chuckle, Eli grabbed his fork and prepared to dig in. "How so?"

"You know I'm familiar with his family."

"He's a grown ass man."

"He's an unbridled talent. You've dealt with those before."

"Yeah. And the last one did a federal prison sentence, leaving this team in a serious tailspin."

"But Bailey came back and set us straight. He had his wild out period—young and dumb. But I like to think much of his rebounding came from the strong support we were able to offer after his bid was done."

Eli laughed heartily, this time his napkin covered his salt and pepper goatee. "Azmir, there ain't no *we*. You're not on my staff. Shit. You can buy your own team. You got the fucking money." Azmir snickered, but in another non-bothered manner as I set his plate before him. "But no! You won't do that. Instead, you come to your old buddy's and sit in on meetings concerning the team and *League*, even speak directly with my coaches and scouts." An even thicker howl exploded from his belly. "And with no shame!"

Less amused, Azmir forked a glazed carrot spear. "Not at all. I'mma *King*, duke."

Eli shook his head at his friend warmly, his laughter slowing. "That, we know, too."

"I'm fully aware of my passion for this team," Azmir's thick tenor poured. "I'll even admit my expressions of it's been a bit unorthodox, but I'm giving you my word Rut'll work. He's been working hard. Soared at the college level."

"Soared being redshirted, and with gang—"

"Conjecture," Azmir asserted firmly. "I can assure you, Rut ain't in no gang. He may be a product of an inner-city climate and grew up with gang members, but you can't penalize him for something he can't help."

Another round of laughter ripped from Eli as I placed a box of cigars—expensive cigars—on a smaller table a few feet away. Nyree told me the market price for the *Gurkha His Majesty's Reserve*. *My God!*

"What's not alleged because it was, in fact, recorded was that threesome shot in his dorm room the end of his freshman year. What's also real is the police report from the young man he knocked out behind the movie theater. He could have blown his chances then. Lucky for him, the kid didn't want to press charges."

"Because said 'kid' was drunk off his ass that night, taunting Rut and his crew. The kid followed them there after the game his team took an L in back on the field. He squatted for hours just to stalk and harass them. What's a kid from the slums of Trenton, New Jersey supposed to do? Give him a Quran to correct the course the kid had put himself on?" Azmir took a sip of the brandy I poured him earlier. "In fact, that same lil' punk got kicked out of school that semester for sexual harassment."

Eli shook his head as I finished serving dinner.

"Just trust me on this, E."

"It ain't you I don't trust. It's the wild tyke I don't need as a risk this season—or next."

"I got you."

"I hope you do. It may be our luck if no one snatches him up before our final pick on draft day in a few weeks. You know nobody wants him."

"Indeed," Azmir admitted calmly. "But everybody needs his talent level. The kid is skilled. You familiar with his numbers?"

Eli shrugged, chewing. "Mildly."

"Well, let's hope for you he'll be doing more of them with a *Kings'* robe on his back and crown on his head."

"The kid turned down endorsement deals from apparel lines like *Nike* at the Combine!"

"Because," Azmir calmly quantified. "You and I know those offers were a slap in the face. They were trying to bait him with lowball proposals although they're fully aware of his athletic footwear company. That small hustle he started in high school is now a four-million-dollar company with very little overhead. Instead of presenting an equally profitable contract, they'd rather diminish his brand."

"You don't have to sell him to me. I trust my competent staff. If it turns out we acquire him, he walks right or will be on his face. My coaches'll cut his ass before he steps out on the green come the first game day." That was Eli's invisible shrug.

He was unmoved.

I waited for a break in their conversation before speaking. "Mr. Richardson, Mr. Jacobs…" I addressed both their eyes as Nyree instructed during her quick tutorial this week when we agreed I'd fill in for her while she took her grandson to the doctor. "Will that be all for now?"

Eli smiled as kindly as I was accustomed to by this point. "For now, Parker. Thanks."

I turned to Azmir in silent request. His eyes brushed across me, causing me to instantly feel subconscious about my appearance. "I'm good, sweetheart."

I nodded, turned for my cart, and began its haul across the room. Behind me, their conversation continued.

I could identify Azmir's voice. "I can always have Jordan keep an eye on him for me."

"And here you go again on my turf," Eli sighed, good-naturedly. "You forget I'mma boss here, too? This is my arena, Azmir. You're just a fan. I run this multi-billion dollar enterprise."

I was just at the door, wearing a smile from their banter while appreciating seeing Eli lighthearted. He was an older man. I wasn't quite sure how old but he had a very mature air to him. It seemed to me his buddy Azmir Jacobs brought down his guard a bit. Ruffled his feathers.

As I opened the door to push the cart out, I heard Azmir pose with full on swag. "Yeah, but what's better than one billionaire?"

Eli, without delay, uttered a seemingly practiced, "Two."

RUT

Damn.

Her ass jiggled a two count before clapping, lifting in the air, and starting the sequence all over again. Her rhythm was on point as music blasted from wall to wall in a private room at *Arch & Point*. This was why I fucked with the spot.

She craned her neck to look at me over her shoulder and mouthed, *"Fuck 'em then I get some money."*

Aye...

The one a few yards away on the pole was upside down. Her eyes were on me, too. Just the way I liked it. I was glad she got rid of that rhinestone top. Her tits were banging. Fake, but dope as hell. She was the gold standard of the club. I'd been after her since the first time I stepped foot in here two weeks ago. *Arch & Point* had a serious no fraternizing policy here, and I'd been told they highly enforced it...until the kid, Rut, came to town. I wanted her bad, and I knew she'd come around with the money I threw at her four days a week. Tonight, the look in her eyes was darker. Her dips curlier, drops lower.

"You enjoying ya time up here?" My cousin, B-Rocka, to my right with a thick one on him, smiled with tight eyes.

This was his first time visiting since I moved to Connecticut a week ago.

I smacked the dotted cheeks of shawtie on my lap. She was working hard for the bills I wrapped around her bikini string.

"You know I make the best outta every situation," I answered.

"Word." B-Rocka's attention was back on the ass in his face while her face was inches away from the floor as we sat on a cushioned red leather sofa. He loved this just as much as I enjoyed it. When I got drafted, he told me the upshot of it was that we'd kick it at this very spot. "That's what's up. How that nigga, TB, treating you?"

That's what all the homies from back home wanted to know, even the chicks. Everybody wanted to know about the Super Bowl 2018 QB from our home state.

I shrugged. "He chill."

"That's it?"

"Yeah. I only seen him once. Them niggas on vacation—most of the vets are. We ain't have a full practice where everybody's on the field at the same time yet. The first off season workout session's coming up. I'll see them niggas there. I've mostly been with the trainers, keeping in shape. We live in the same development though—me and Bailey."

"The one the *Kings* own?"

"Yeah."

"I thought he got a crib in Jersey. Alpine, right?"

"Yeah. But for convenience, I guess, he rents one of the condos."

"Oh, that's what's up, my G. You think that'll be ya plan, too?"

Honestly, I had no fucking clue what my plan would be. I didn't want to get comfortable here in Connecticut. These fuckers ain't really want me anyway. My plan was to see how they responded when I killed it this season. I'd show all them who the fuck I was.

I nodded my answer to B-Rocka while clutching the thigh rocking against my own. "You like that?" I asked my mans about the chick giving him a dance.

B-Rocka pumped his fist in the air, watching the show in front of him. "What about *The Flash*? I thought he'd be here tonight. This his favorite spot. Right?"

I nodded. "Jordan's cool peoples," I answered honestly over the music. "He 'on't come here like he used to, I hear."

"Why?"

"That nigga got the clanks. You know he engaged and shit."

"Oh, word!"

"Yeah. I 'on't know how a nigga can turn away art like this!" I chuckled. My eyes moved up to Chestnut Cherries on the mini stage in the room. *Damn*. She was a banger! "I ain't never getting caught up in no chick like that. Even if I did find somebody I wanted more than ass from, I wouldn't let them change shit about me. If I wanna come to the strip club to see ass jiggling and titties bouncing in my face, shit, I'mma do it!"

B-Rocka busted out laughing. "What if she said she wanna come, too?"

"*Shiiiiit!*" I felt my face tightening. "Hell no! She wanna see tits and ass she could go by her-damn-self. Matter of fact, get a sucka that'll be a'ight with that shit."

He couldn't stop laughing, which made me crack up, too. I was dead ass serious though.

"I heard Johnson brings his girl here," B-Rocka tried to challenge me as I sipped champagne.

"I 'on't know about all that. Don't really believe it. I been here almost every day since being in Connecticut and ain't seen him here once. Can't lie, I was disappointed. After the draft, I told Divine something similar to what you said. The good thing 'bout getting picked by the *Kings* was *Arch & Point* 'cause I could chill with Jordan 'The Flash' Johnson."

While that was the truth, it wasn't the whole thing. I'd still been fucked up about draft night. It was something I'd been keeping quiet on because I knew Divine, also known as Azmir Jacobs, my father's former General, pulled some strings to get me on the NFL track.

After seconds of consideration, my thoughts went back to the subject. "Plus, that nigga work with ol' girl. Why the fuck would any dude bring his broad to the strip club? This'a chance to get a break from them cuffs. Na' mean?"

B-Rocka kept with his laughing as my eyes roved up to see Chestnut Cherries was strutting my way, thighs wiggling and tits bouncing all the way to my spread knees. She locked eyes with shawtie on my lap then tossed her chin, telling her to scram. My dick twitched in my sweats. We both watched ol' girl twirl on the pole Chestnut Cherries had just left.

"It's almost closing." Her voice was husky, eyes heavy on me. "Whatchu wanna do?"

Yup.

My strongman swelled against my thigh.

Game!

I made a show of caressing her dope ass frame from shoulder to toes in her strappy sandals with mild high heels with my eyes. I sized her up, finally deciding on how I'd fuck her tonight. Chestnut Cherries had to be five feet, five inches, a hundred and forty pounds, and at least a thirty-four G bra size. *Nah. A thirty-two.* I knew how to size a woman. I was taught by the O.G.s.

But I was easy on it, slow with my response and meeting her hungry eyes. I even raised my phone in the air to check the time. She was right. It was close to four in the morning.

I shrugged. "I'm going back to the crib." My index finger led my arm as I pointed to shawtie on the pole. "She coming." My attention went to the right of me where two jawns were feeling B-Rocka up. *Bitches could be like hounds.* They sensed money, even if they were off target a little. "And they coming, too. The fuck you doin'?"

It was finally here. Chestnut Cherries with the smooth glistening mocha skin, a fat ass, and perky tits that could dance a cappella was ready for the kid. *Arch & Point* had the strictest "no fucking the dancers" policy I'd ever come across—and I'd been to the best strip clubs from Jersey to Miami. From the first night I saw her, I asked the girls and one of the bouncers about her. Some laughed, some shook their head in answer; all doubted. It was all good, though. A week and a half wasn't enough to acclimate them to Rut's World. And in my world, if I wanted it, I got it. In this case, I'd fuck it. And I wanted Chestnut Cherries.

I never asked her, though. Nah. I hadn't verbalized shit, but I damn sure expressed it through my eyes. And bills. Bitches could always be bought. As sure as my name was Rut, I knew all women had ulterior motives. And this one was no different from the majority of the chicks I'd encountered over my years. She wanted money.

"Who rolling with you?" she asked, chest rising and falling at a new speed.

My eyes rolled over her shoulder. "I told you. Her." I pointed with my forehead. "Maybe one of them." One of the bitches dancing on B-Rocka caught that and smiled too hard. Then my attention went back to the great dame before me. My prize. "And you."

She didn't speak right away, obviously weighing my command, though we both knew it was a request. I sat patiently as she considered it. The girls stood from B-Rocka, informing they'd meet us in the mall's parking lot down the street—aka sneaking out there because of *Arch & Point*'s policy. The shawtie dancing on me earlier tossed me eyes, communicating the same. I didn't respond. She knew what time it was.

Then it was left to my grand prize in front of me, deciding her fate. I'd make it good to her, too. When chicks made me wait this long, I was sure to take my time and show them why they shouldn't have.

Just when I was about to say "never mind," Chestnut Cherries popped back on her hips and rolled her eyes. "A'ight. I'll meet you with Vanilla Chai."

Her words delivered with attitude were husky. And I was excited out my ass.

Love's Ineligible Receiver

"Search?" one of the dancers from B-Rocka's lap back at the club barked in the dark of the big ass, empty parking lot.

My security, Fats, was patting her down while the one before her hopped in the *Benz* sprinter.

He stood on a huff, patience running short at this hour. "Look, you wanna come or what?"

The other girl who danced for me bounced on her toes and hugged herself, cold as hell in the spring air. Chestnut Cherries stood behind, pouting herself as she rolled her eyes.

Ol' girl holding up the line glanced around, suddenly self-conscious about her hesitation. I was used to this. Fats was used to this. As I sat behind the wheel in my *Ferrari California*, I could see B-Rocka shifting in his seat from the corners of my eyes, his attention tight on what was going on out there. He wasn't used to this in Connecticut. We did the screening process a little different in Jersey.

"I'm just saying," ol' girl argued. "I already gave you my phone!"

"And I gotta make sure you ain't got another," Fats countered. "Ain't nobody trying to fuck you or get free feels, ma."

She rolled her eyes and lifted her arms. Fats finished the pat down and jerked his thumb over his shoulder, directing her into the sprinter. The other walked up and raised her hands automatically. This one was more patient with Fats. Likely because she thought I was the carrot at the end of the stick. When Chestnut Cherries strutted up to him with a tight face and pressed lips and raised her arms without being asked, I smashed down on the accelerator, making the engine roar before taking off with a tire-scream on the pavement.

"Oh, my fuggin' gawd...I'm *cumiiiiiiin'!*" she screamed as I pounded in her ass from the back, smacking into it so hard her fat rippled each time I hit. "*Oh! Oh! Oh!*"

"A'ight, sweetheart!" I yelled to the other chick between her legs, and mine a little.

Ol' girl scooted away then slammed herself against the headboard out of breath. Now I could go gorilla on Chestnut Cherries' ass. With each scream, my ego flared wider than the space between my ears. *I bet she wish she would have fucked with me two weeks ago.* That was what ran through my mind as Chestnut Cherries' shoulders quaked while her little waist, on down, jerked. Then I busted myself, my orgasm not as spectacular as this last one for her. It was all good; it was my third and her second.

I reared on the back of my heels, wiped the sweat from my forehead then peeled off the rubber. After twisting it in a knot, I stood from the bed.

"Shit!" Chestnut Cherries breathed, not hiding her impressed smile. She rubbed the underside of her tits. "I ain't never do no shit like that." Her breathing was getting away from her but that "nut" glow was bright as hell.

"Do what?" the other broad, I now knew name was Brandee, asked as she snuggled onto a pillow, laying on her side facing Chestnut Cherries.

My brow raised in the air in question, too, as I observed them getting comfy. That wasn't going down. I knew then I had to figure out a way to get these bitches out of my crib. I was tired as fuck. They had to go.

"Girl on girl with a dude." Chestnut Cherries couldn't fight that damn smirk.

She closed her eyes, contented as hell, and humming as she licked her lips.

Oh, hell no...

I grabbed my boxers, slid them on while the rubber was still clutched in my hand. Next, I went to the roll of paper towels in the corner of the bare room, dressed with just a mattress on top of a box spring and mirrors on either side. While they exchanged words of sexual satisfaction and exhaustion, I wrapped the used rubber inside a paper towel. I banged on the door just as I did when I held the last used condom. Seconds later, Fats opened the door and pushed his fat ass head in.

I handed him the balled paper towel. He knew what time it was, but I could sense something in his eyes. To confirm it, he hit me with the slight straining of them that communicated the question of if I was done. I tossed him my chin in confirmation.

"Yo," he spoke loudly, voice deeper than usual because of the early hour. Fats hadn't been to sleep yet. "It's after seven. You got a nine o'clock meeting."

Shit! For a minute there, I'd forgotten all about it. Just when I thought I'd sleep late before hitting the gym, I was reminded of the *serious* meeting I had this morning.

I turned to my company. Chestnut Cherries had already begun to nod off, but Brandee kept her tight eyes on me, similar to the way she had when I finished her off first so I could start working on her co-worker.

It wasn't my plan to start with her. After they popped whatever pills they needed to get them straight when we arrived, my idea was to go my first round with Chestnut Cherries. I had more to prove to her. But when Brandee literally dived for my dick before I could step out of my boxers, I went with the flow. She came at least three times this morning. It was because she was one of those hyper-nutters. Very few women, in my experience, were one of those. That's because not all women could achieve orgasms, and I didn't always have the time to help them. But not Brandee. She came on my dick and my hands.

By the time I made it to Chestnut Cherries, she was beyond wet and primed for me. The problem I soon learned was she didn't come easily. I hit her with the trifecta as she lay on her back spread to me earlier, using just my hands. She came. But when I finally put my dick in her, she wasn't revving like I wanted. That's when I thought to invite Brandee in. She looked like the type who liked girls. I was spot on with my suspicion and had Brandee go underneath Chestnut Cherries to lick her pussy and rub on her fat ass mahogany nipples while I fucked her ass. It worked.

She was out like a light on the bed, but it was now time for them to go. I didn't do sleepovers.

Brandee began to spit out something irritating her mouth. "What the fuck?" Her face was balled as she plucked from her tongue. "This your weave shedding like this, Chestnut?"

My cheeks spread as my neck swiveled around to Fats.

He shook his head and snorted. "Y'all need a ride back to your cars at the mall? Let's go."

"Huhn? Already?" Brandee complained. "I need a nap."

Fats swung the door open even more, revealing one of the two chicks B-Rocka brought back with him. She was dressed and wearing a jacket while clutching her bag.

"She been waiting on y'all a long ass time. Need to relieve her baby sitter. C'mon!" he barked.

Brandee gasped. And with a disarming smile, I walked over to the foot of the bed and wiggled Chestnut Cherries' baby toe.

"Time to get up, sweetheart." I kept my voice soothing. "Ya ride's ready."

She stirred a bit, glancing around with red eyes that quickly. Her regard hit Brandee, huffing while stabbing her foot into her panties.

"What?" Chestnut Cherries groaned, not looking at all like the self-assured bronzed baddie she did at *Arch & Point*. Her expression softened into a grin. "You think I can get a couple of hours? Damn! That shit you put on a bitch," she purred, stretching like a cat. "I was peeping what you was giving her and getting mad as fuck." She giggled, eyes closed while she lay back down.

Chestnut Cherries wasn't getting it. She had to get the fuck on.

"Why?" I asked, smile and forehead wrinkled with confusion.

She turned over onto her other side, facing Brandee who snatched down the dress over her head and rolled it down the 'S' of her curves, getting with the program like a good girl.

"I ain't never bust like that in my life!" She broke out laughing like she thought Brandee would join her. "I mean, on the low, I don't bust like that no way."

I cocked my head to the side and stroked my dick through my briefs. "Nah?"

"Nope! I may have two times in my whole life," Chestnut Cherries admitted.

That's when Brandee paused in shock. I wasn't. I knew how to fuck. If I told you you'd have a good time, the only time you wouldn't was if I was being a complete asshole, not giving a fuck. No pun intended.

"Bitch, you serious?" Brandee asked.

Still laying like she had all damn day, Chestnut Cherries nodded as she broke out laughing again. "On god!"

"Well, let's go." Brandee threw Chestnut Cherries her panties and dress. I guessed strippers didn't wear bras. I knew with a good boob job a woman didn't need one. Both these broads had implants, but I was cool with it. "Because he's kicking us the fuck out."

Chestnut Cherries' eyes shot over to me. I deepened my smile. Yes, I was being rude. I was impatient and anxious each time I had to tell a chick to leave after fucking. These two were no different. But I always rocked a smile and spoke in a gentle manner. Shit. They had feelings, too.

"It was fun, Chestnut Cherries..." I drawled playfully.

That softened the muscles around her eyes.

"That's it? I wanna go another round. I could cook us up a nice breakfast," she offered.

My head rolled to the other side and brows met. I sucked in my lips to appear the offer was enticing. Then my face warmed into the smile again and I went for her foot, wiggling it.

"You acting like this goodbye. You know I'll be back at the club. We gone do this again."

She struggled with her smile of understanding, but it eventually came. Brandee passed me from behind, going for the door.

"We gone be compensated?" she asked.

And here's the bullshit...

My smile was still high on my face and bright, even at this crazy hour. I asked, "Compensated?" My eyebrows lifted.

"Yeah!" she spat. "We did all that and—"

"And who you think should be getting paid for that work?"

"You had two of us!" Brandee thought she was reminding me.

"Uhn, uhn!" Chestnut Cherries shook her head. "It ain't that kinda party, Brandee." She was dismissing the stupid ass notion.

But her colleague was still gunning for something.

I stepped closer and dipped my voice a few notches for her comfort. "Brandee, wasn't it you who asked if you could come with me after work last night? Matter fact, you been asking me since last week."

"That ain't the point!" she snapped. "I feel we should get something for this."

I readjusted my stance, rolled my neck, and refreshed my friendly expression. "Thank you, Brandee. Your head game might be in my top ten." I turned for Chestnut Cherries. "Thanks, Chestnut Cherries. Your pussy gotta be in my top three." Top fifty, but I was trying to make a point here. Then I turned back to Brandee, whose eyes blew the hell up. "Sweetheart, I don't do prostitution."

And I'd never guess any of the dancers at *Arch & Point* did either. They made more money than most in the game.

"I ain't no fuckin' prostitute, Rut! I'm just sayin—"

"You just saying what?" My harsh delivery of that was notification of my patience running low for this shit.

Brandee backed up, eyes blinking rapidly. "I'm just saying I ain't got no gas money to get home," her voice was small—mousey even, but that whorish persona was still strong.

I pushed my smile out again then tossed my chin to Fats. "Give her something for gas, seeing she would have needed it whether she rolled with me or not."

Brandee seemed too shocked to speak, as Fats pulled out a roll of cash and peeled off a Benjamin. Brandee took the bill and clomped to the door, ego deflated as it fucking should have. Chestnut Cherries, on the other hand, rounded me, being sure her tits were on my bare abs as she beamed. There was definitely a glow about her I'd never seen. Good dick would do that to you.

"Am I gonna see you tonight?" She was referring to the club.

I scratched the back of my head, thinking about this meeting I had to catch and the long day after that.

"Nah. Not tonight, baby." I pinched her chin lightly, careful not to get close enough to make her think I was going to put my mouth on hers. "But we gone get you right again."

The smile that spread on her face made me feel something I was too familiar with: emptiness. If I had a penny for each time a shawtie looked at me with hopes in her eyes I wouldn't need as many hustles as I had. Hopes I didn't share and hopes I'd soon shatter. But it was all good. It was in these moments I, at least, felt human because I knew what was going down.

But Chestnut Cherries was a strong one. She was fighting to not let her feelings get ahead of her, and that relieved me.

"Okay. I left my number on the bed," she informed. My eyes brushed over to the business card next to the pillow. "Hit me when you ready."

I winked and nodded. When the door closed behind them, I turned and slowly dropped my head and arms toward the floor until my fingers touched my toes. I felt and heard my back crack as I moaned. Slowly, I stood and headed for the bed then snatched the sheets off, tossing them to the floor. Then I went into the closet for the *Lysol*. After spraying the mattress and pillows down, I applied clean sheets and pillow cases. By the time I grabbed the old ones and opened the door, Sharkie was pouncing on me.

All one hundred and forty-five pounds of him slamming against me had me swaying a bit at first.

"Hey, baby!" I massaged his head with my free hand. "I know you be holding me down, letting me use ya room for fun and shit, but you think you could chill on the shedding? This the third time this week a chick done complained about hair in their mouth—and it ain't Daddy's, ya dig?"

His response was a big, stinky swipe of a kiss against my chin.

chapter two

"Yeah, but I'm good," he spoke evenly into the cell phone—one of the two he always carried. His eyes squeezed close in irritation as he used his other hand to pinch the area between them. "I'll be boarding in about thirty minutes."

I sat back and downed the rest of my drink as I waited on him. *Shit.* I had to be back at *Hotep Black Financial Bank Stadium* soon. One of my coaches recommended I do some stretching techniques with a trainer there. I didn't want to miss her and lose an opportunity to get on her schedule this week. Then I had a dinner meeting with the charity department of the *Kings*. They were supposed to share with me a list of legitimate charities. I had a few of my own, but they were grassroots level. One of the things I wanted to do when I made it to the *League* was establish a strong leg in my brand for charities.

"Nah, ain't no need for all that. You gotta believe me when I say I'm good." Divine brought my attention back to the table. We were in a small bar in the private hub of the airport. "I'm coming straight to the crib. You gone be up?" That question mixed with the way he pushed his tongue into the back teeth, hiding a sensual ass smirk, clued me into who he was talking to. "If you know what's good for you..." he threatened.

Taking a deep breath, I sat up and toward the table as he was ending the call.

"Tell Ray I said waddup."

"Rut says hello, Brimm." His smile faded when his eyes landed on me. That gaze of intimidation had worked since I was a damn pup and hadn't lost its potency. "She says hey and wants to know if you're enjoying the *Ferrari*."

"Enough to drive it all the way out to Cali," I joked about the model of the car the two of them gifted me draft night.

He repeated my words to her and it was clear she found them funny. I nodded and averted my eyes to the screen playing over the bar across the room. There was a highlight on of a game the *Sixers* played last night.

Alton Alston still ain't loose that speed with that damn chest pass!

"You should be meeting with Melanie Ruiz."

My eyes swung back to the table. "Huhn?"

"President of Charitable Foundation and Social Responsibility. Your meeting this evening." *Oh.* "Mrs. Ruiz is the president. I had my assistant call to be sure she was heading this meeting."

"Why?"

"Because she gets shit done, and charities can be your ally in sports. America likes do-gooders. In our minds, charitable givers are synonymous with wholesomeness and moral soundness. You need to give that impression."

I didn't respond even though it reminded me of this fucked up situation I was in.

"And don't try to fuck her—or your new coach."

My eyes blew the hell up. His finger was pointed toward my face, an act no other man would live to get away with. But more than that, I saw something else. I saw exhaustion I'd never seen from him before.

Then my eyes quickly tightened as I glanced away. "C'mon, man," I breathed. "You know me better than that."

"Nah. I know *you*. I know you believe the rules set for everybody don't apply to you. Well, this one does. Be professional at all times with your *Kings* family. I don't give a damn if a woman throws her panties at you, you dodge them shits like you swing bats."

Dodgers.

I snorted, swiping my nose. "I'm good, big homie. I'm actually excited about the meeting."

"Yeah?"

"Yeah. You know I got the lunch, sneaks, and backpacks giveaway going on every year. I want to expand on those and got a few more ideas to run pass them."

Divine nodded, calm returning to his demeanor. Something was off.

"You hitting up Eli's annual party next weekend, right?"

"Of course."

"You taking Emily?"

I shook my head, eyes going into the distance. "Nah."

I was hoping he wasn't going to tell me I should.

"Good. Don't show up stupid late and don't bring more than one person. And not a woman. As a matter of fact, take Fats."

That offended me. It was one thing to have me in an arranged hook up with a celebrity, but another to think I didn't know how to handle my B.I.

My forehead tightened. "What I look like bringing a bitch to work?"

With his eyes closed, Divine shook his head. That was new. I've known dude just about all my life, he was direct and forceful when speaking to me. Divine had played the role of surrogate father to me for years. He went hard, but he had to with me.

With his face toward the wooden booth's table top, he spoke sharply. "What did I tell you about referring to women as bitches, Rut?" I swallowed, temper swelling in my gut. Balls flaring, too. Divine was the big homie, but, shit, I was a man, too! His eyes rolled up to mine. "Answer me."

Taking a deep breath, I explained, "I don't say it to a female's face, Divine."

"But you deem them as such in your mind, it comes out when you're speaking. Don't matter if you don't say it to a woman—something I find hard to believe—it's in your heart. You ever heard of Luke chapter six, verse forty-five—the Bible?"

Love's Ineligible Receiver

I hadn't been keeping up on my *120 Lessons*, but I knew he recently denounced the Nation of Islam and was now a Christian. We hadn't spoke about why, but my pops put me on to it. It hurt him that Divine was now calling a blue-eyed, blond hair devil his savior and master. That didn't sit well with me either, but I respected him way too much to question it. For the most part, he was the same ADJ to me, even though he'd spit shit like this out of nowhere.

"It says, '*A good man, out of the good treasure of his heart, bringeth forth that which is good; and an evil man, out of the evil treasure of his heart, bringeth forth that which is evil: for of the abundance of the heart, his mouth speaketh.*' You know what that means, son? It means someone like you, who talks so damn much, can't hide what you really believe and what you really love because it's stored in your heart...in your belly, and it'll shoot up like vomit." He inched over the table more. "Women are not bitches, Rutledge. They're no more than men are. And even the ones who you believe are, don't need to be reminded by you. Be a fuckin' gentleman."

"For what?" I covered my face, groaning as I stretched my legs under the tiny ass table I shared with a man just as tall as me. "For these broads to take advantage of me? Nah, B."

"You know it's because you pick *sea* level..." His eyes locked on mine.

A nervous laugh pushed from my nostrils. "Fuck you mean?"

"What I mean is you continue to entertain women who are morally and culturally beneath you. They don't challenge you in the least. I've been telling you for years to start picking eye level."

"You told me to pick friends from the top of the tree. How that sound? Me picking chicks on a lower level than my friends?"

"Two different relationships." He shook his head with a cocky ass smile on his face. "To keep it a buck, you couldn't maintain a woman from the top of the tree. Probably wouldn't attract her the moment you open your mouth. Real women have this amazing intuition and can sniff immaturity out of men a mile away. And, bruh, yours is fragrant."

I chuckled dryly. Divine was old, outdated, and cuffed. What the fuck did he know about women anymore? He only fucked one nowadays.

His attention went to both his phones as they started blowing up on the table. Again, he closed his eyes and pinched between them.

"You good, D?" It was a sincere question.

He waved me off, tone gentler when he breathed, "Yeah. Just some shit I see is getting outta hand."

"That bootleg ass documentary?"

He answered with a hard stare.

Yeah, I've heard about it...

The *YouTube* link was sent to me a few months ago. Now, bloggers were picking up on it, nibbling on its truths from fiction. It was crazy. *And true.* Divine may have kept me from joining a gang back home, but it was easy to seeing he damn near was one himself. And even though I never in my life met Divine, the hustler, I knew him. I was introduced to him the minute I learned why my father was sentenced for such a long time and who his General was.

Azmir Divine Jacobs was black market famous. To the unknowing world, he was nameless, but not powerless. He made lots of power moves for the celebrities we loved and now he was a legit businessman with more companies and investments than I could count. Keeping it trill, Divine was the reason why I had a million-dollar company while in college. I had the passion and desire, but he gave my partner and me the tools. I couldn't begin to describe my gratitude to this man.

"Ain't nothing I ain't taking care of." His usual voice of persuasion was missing but not the swagger I'd tried emulating since I was kid.

"If you want me to look into it, just say the—"

"And you're going to your required therapy session, right?"

That swerve kicked me in the damn gut. It was more than the "no" to my offering. It was him possibly agreeing I needed mental help.

"You think I need therapy?"

His face was blank but eyes hard when he firmly answered, "Therapy ain't a diagnosis. It's a tool. Healthy people benefit from it. Consider it free mental organization."

"I can organize my own mental." I swung my wrists, flashing my palms. "I work hard every day to adjust to this shitty contract, D. I swallow my pride every time I start earlier than my teammates and end later. I'm even hitting up more than one of the off-season workout sessions on top of rookie minicamp this week. And that's *on top* of training five days a week while everybody—rookies and vets—are out here vacationing it up in the off season! That don't sound like no weak ass muthafucka needing a head doctor."

Taking another deep breath, Divine leaned over the table and pointed that finger again. "Indeed. You've worked damn hard to make it to *League* level but don't fuckin' forget my contribution to get you here. You ain't no fuckin' knucklehead, Rut. You're of royal priesthood. You're built different, but I don't mean entitled." His voice deepened and that Brooklyn accent coated his tongue. "You fuck this up, I'm whoopin' ya ass. That's how personal this thing is to me. For the first time in your life, you gone walk right. You'll be silent in practice, meetings, at social functions, in the faces of your superiors, and paparazzi's camera—hell, any camera. The only noise you will make is on that field where you'll show you're the greatest at the game. Am I clear on that, duke?"

I felt like that kid getting scolded at night when his pops came home and found out he showed his ass in school. I ain't know what the hell was going on with the big homie, but I could sense the stress he'd never cop to. I could also feel he was dead ass serious and I got it. Yeah, I busted my ass to make it to draft night, but he was the sole sponsor and biggest advocate in getting me here. I was now a member of the *Connecticut Kings*, Divine's favorite football team. He didn't take this lightly. And to be real, I could respect why.

If there was anybody who could speak to me this way and toss a threat I wouldn't pursue, it was Azmir Divine Jacobs. For me and him, I had something to prove. And not just to myself and Divine, to all those not believing. I was meant to be here.

I'll show 'em all...

RUT

The whistle sounded and, again, I pushed from my toes and powered off to hit the *Quick Out* drill. But damn if again, Stroy, the defensive back, was playing tight bump and run coverage, knocking me off my route and I missed the pass. The whistle blew again.

"Again, Amare!" Coach Underwood shouted.

I grunted, frustrated as fuck for not being able to get this down, but I couldn't let them see me sweat. There were too many people out here and most of them likely counted me out. *Never.* I would never fail. It was rookie camp. I had to show these motherfuckers what they paid for.

I had something to prove, so I quickly moved into position again. This time, I tried to focus hard on my internal foot counts and gradual speed. The whistle blew. I growled and took off.

Shit!

Stroy clipped me again, and right off the fucking line!

"You're not exploding off the line!" an unfamiliar, very curvy voice barked.

My head jerked to where Underwood last stood. Next to him was a…female. Mocha skin with facial features I couldn't see behind her shades but her body was a ten: tiny ass waist, curvy hips in khaki shorts, and her tits sat *nice* even in a loose-fitting T-shirt. As feminine as her figure was, she wasn't your average sized female. This one was hella tall, but well proportioned. With one hand on her hip and the other arm gripping a football at her thigh, something seemed off about her presence.

"Is there a problem?" her edgy tone snapped me out of my head.

I looked around the field and saw everybody staring my way. A few snickers could be heard and I knew what they were about. They thought the broad was about to son me.

I gave her another look over as I tried to even my breathing from the back to back plays.

Then I hit her with the sleek grin, flashing just my top teeth. "Yeah. My dick feeling kinda dry, and I 'on't see nobody else out here who could help. Unless you ready to drop down on ya knees to handle that, you can get the fuck off the field and let me do what I'm getting paid to do."

A few coughs and sputters from muffled laughs cut the air. Coach Underwood changed stances, crossed his arms while holding a clipboard. I knew he wasn't happy, but I didn't give a shit. I was frustrated and trying to focus. This bitch needed to move the fuck on.

But she didn't. She had the nerve to step closer to me. Her perfumed proximity made me sick to my stomach. It wasn't the type of thing you were used to smelling on the green unless it was a celebration hug from family after a W.

"Considering that sucker ass contract you signed, I doubt your dick is much for me to work with, rookie. Besides, your young and dumb ass probably just learned how to hold it to pee." She stepped closer and my face got tighter. "Instead of you talking about the needs of your undersized dick, how about you master this play, and while you're at it, learn my name."

If she 'on't get the fuck outta here...
I scoffed. "Ya name?"
"Yeah. And especially my damn title."
"Which is?"
"Coach. Sloane Brooks. As in *Coach* Brooks." My neck whipped over to Coach Underwood and the other guys. Coach nodded, telling me to take heed. A few of the others around snickered. *Bullshit!* My eyes rolled back to her. "Mmmhmmm," she hummed, dripping too much arrogance. "Now you ready to get this knowledge or would you rather start with the twenty laps your misogynistic tongue just earned you?"

My eyes rolled away and I backed up to give her the floor. After a long stare down, Coach Brooks stepped over to the line.

"You need to explode to make the DB think you're running a *Go Route*. Instead, what you're doing is picking up gradual speed at the line."

"Yeah, easy for a fanatic to say. But the players need practice to get it," I tried making clear. "That's what we doing here. Practicing."

"Some need practice, some just have it." *What?* Then she jerked her neck. "And where the hell you see a fanatic out here?" She looked around the field, trying to play me.

"Oh. My bad," my tone was dry. "Let me keep it politically correct: Someone who's 'passionate' about the game."

Brooks backed up again. "I'll do you one better." She swiped her nose and got into position at the line.

Brooks gave Underwood the cue and, a few seconds later, the whistle blew. I couldn't believe the speed this broad detonated with. She plowed ahead and Stroy, in front of her, went for her. Brooks blocked Stroy's grasp as he turned his hips to bump her. Instead, she broke to the right and caught the ball from the QB standing near the sideline. She was swift, agile with it.

Of course! She's a fucking light ass female!

Brooks jogged over to me again, nothing girlie about her posture. "If you don't explode off the line and you're slow, the DB is going to move slow, too. That gives him time to think about your play. And if he's fast...faster than you..." She shrugged.

So damn heated, I just looked at her like she was an idiot, but there was something in this chick's eyes telling me she was unbothered. She was a tough girl, so what? Maybe she coached some high school kids. That didn't make her suitable for the NF-fucking-L!

"You gonna try it again or start your laps?"

I heaped mucous from the bottom of my throat and hog-spit on the green. After shooting her another look of disgust, I began my run. No way was I going to fucking tuck my tail for no female. Coach or not, she would not be bossing me the hell around.

Fuck. That.

Powerless in telling her to kiss my ass, I ate the laps.

One down...
Two down...
Three...

I trained my thoughts when I ran, letting my mind run, too. I could conceive ideas and dream up next level goals. Around lap five is when I thought to do a block party for my boutique opening in my hometown, Trenton, NJ. *Yup. Make it a city celebration.* I would hit my business partner, Jeremy, up tonight with details.

Yeah...

I was on my fourteenth lap when my thighs felt like weights getting off the ground. Then something played back in my mind from my conversation with Divine the other day after we talked about my meeting with Melanie Ruiz.

"And don't try to fuck her—or your new coach."

I was so fucking heated about him implying I'd try to fuck Ruiz that I missed the new coach mention.

Ain't this some shit...

I met with Ruiz and had no wish in the damn world to lay a finger on her.

And ain't no way I'd even look twice at this Sloane bitch either...

Parker

"May these words of my mouth and this meditation of my heart be especially pleasing in your sight, our sovereign Lord, my faithful Rock, and holy Redeemer," he rasped with passion. "And let the tabernacle proclaim..."

"Amen," I murmured alongside the entire congregation of

Redeeming Souls for Abundant Living in Christ, creating a strong shout across the two-story sanctuary.

The soft keys from the organ created a peaceful backdrop to close the service.

"It is well with my soul," were the last words he spoke before lowering his outspread arms and leaving the podium.

The church was still on fire. As with any other service, Pastor Carmichael left the room wanting more. The man could orate like no one else. His message this morning was of "The Race."

"Guuuuuuuuurl," a rumbling caused me to shift in stance and look to my left. Jade was packing up her baby's bag. "That Pastor is anointed! Did you hear how he compared trials in life to a runner's race? And when you think about it, it's true. You get so tired of going through the same thing."

"It becomes exhausting," I sighed.

Man, did I have loads of experience with fatigue and weariness: literally and figuratively.

"It does! And especially like he said, when you don't know when your break is coming. I've been there." She stopped, facing me.

A smile lifted on her face and those hazel eyes glittered my way expectantly. When she glanced down, I realized what she was asking for. Her baby girl.

"Oh!" I grumbled, handing over the seven-month-old, sleeping infant.

Jade laughed. "Thank God you were here to rock her. The only person she behaves with in church is her father."

I smiled. "Nothing wrong with a daddy's girl."

Jade returned a wry smile. "You're right. I'm grateful for their already bond."

Those words packed more than the sum of their quantity, Jade and I both knew. Other than our meager heights and similar frames, Mrs. Bailey and I had a thing or two in common. One being the absence of our fathers. Another common experience was having never known them.

I met Jade about a year ago in the front office. Her name had been getting around as Trent's one-man—or woman—management team.

Love's Ineligible Receiver

The weird thing about it was Trent Bailey had an agent, attorneys, and a full staff, but Jade was very much involved in the administration of his business. I was working in payroll one day when she came in to drop off paperwork for him. We sparked a conversation and that led to exchanging telephone numbers.

We didn't hang out much, but she told me about her challenges in Trent's world and how even the football wives' club didn't really accept her. That was crazy considering Trent Bailey was the *Kings'* star quarterback and therefore franchise player. In one of our conversations she mentioned the church she recently joined, the one Trent had been a member of for years. One Sunday she invited me, and I was so moved by the aesthetics, atmosphere, and speaker I came again. I'd been coming for months now, driving all the way down from Connecticut to Harlem, New York...just for church. The inspired condition of my spirit each Sunday after leaving justified the nearly hour and a half commute.

"Are you cooking today?" I grabbed my things as the second-floor balcony cleared out.

"Girl, yes." She strapped little Ava Nese in her car seat. "April's making a few desserts and I already marinated my turkey wings." She laughed to herself. "You're about to head up to Connecticut, and Trent and Ky'll be headed down."

"Oh, they're up there today?"

"Yeah, Trent took some things up there for the season. He's moving into a three-bedroom condo at *Kings Court*. You know he had a two bedroom but now with Kyree and Ava Nese he says he needs the space for when we come up." She shrugged.

"I'm surprised you guys haven't bought a house like the other players who commute."

Shaking her head, Jade rolled her eyes while grinning. "The man's cheap, Parker. People find that hard to believe because of his age and lifestyle, but it's true. Not for nothing, I can understand why, but I try to inject my two cents when I feel he's going overboard. Maybe I can do a little more pushing when we come up on Saturday." She winked.

"On Saturday?" My brows met. "For what?"

Jade froze hunched over Ava Nese's car seat. "Eli's annual season kickoff party." When I was sure my eyes appeared gazed over, she added, "The one at his mansion?"

I shook my head and stretched my lips. "No. Didn't know about it this year."

"Have you ever been?"

"No."

"Are you serious, Parker?" She stood straight to face me. "You have to come."

"I wasn't invited," was the excuse I settled on. I had no interest in going.

"It's a *Kings* family event. It happens every year!" Her eyes almost popped out of her head. "Oh, my god! You have to come, Parker!"

"Nah. I'm lucky enough to get help with Jimmy on Sundays to come here, but I doubt I would outside of that."

"You doubt it? Ask his daughter. When was the last time she's been to see him...to help?"

Although an argumentative question, my eyes rolled off to the side as I considered that.

I shook my head. "Doesn't matter. She wouldn't know the first thing to do if something goes wrong."

Rebutting, Jade shook her long and straight hair that was natural from side to side. She once said she had been weave-free for quite some time now. "You're coming."

I snorted. "Jade." My head shook, overwhelmed already with trying to convince her I wouldn't be going. "I can't—"

"Parker, you're twenty-eight." Her eyes narrowed into angry slits. "Twenty-eight and you don't party, socialize, date or let your hair down outside of coming here on Sundays. Your only other outlet is making homemade cosmetics. You're aging yourself prematurely." That made me swallow hard. Jade stepped closer to me for privacy though the balcony was mostly empty at this point. "You've given Jimmy more time than he gave you before all of this. Don't feel guilty about getting out and being around lively people. It's not that far from the house. Make it happen."

I stood there, eyes shifting away from her. A million and two thoughts shot across my brain. I knew she was right but the decision didn't feel that way. I was never the one to be pushed into a corner or have my hand forced.

I sucked my teeth and my eyes squeezed closed. "I forgot…" I bent over the pew to search my bag then I pulled out the small paper shopping bag I managed in there this morning. "I forgot I packed this for you." I handed it over to her.

Jade and Ava Nese arrived a few minutes late this morning, causing me to forget I had it. Since Jade introduced me to *Redeeming Souls*, I'd been allowed to sit in the balcony I eventually learned was reserved for celebrity members. There weren't a gang of them but enough to cause a disruption of the service if members got out of hand with pictures or wanting autographs. Luckily, the ushers assigned to this section recognized my face and would let me in if I arrived before the Baileys. This was what a chance meeting in the front office had evolved into. Social advantages and unsolicited yet interesting truths of my life.

Jade sniffed the bag, eyes rolling to the back of her head to express her delight.

Then they narrowed *again*. "Don't try to distract me with smell goodies, Parker!"

I scoffed, rolling my eyes as I stepped off. "Come on, Jade. I'll walk you two to your car."

RUT

I walked the carpeted hallway, looking at the nametags on all the office doors.

Tamika Barrington.

Nope.
Dontay Lewis.
Uhn-uhn.
Nicole Richardson.
Wrong Richardson.
Nathan Rich—

I stopped and cut a right into the small cove where his receptionist, a dude, was at his desk.

"Mr. Amare, I'm Elliot, Mr. Richardson's assistant." He smiled too fucking bright and his lineup was fucked up. Dude needed to fire his barber. "Mr. Richardson is available. Go right in."

Without unneeded words, I helped myself to the door and pushed it open. My eyes scanned around and found Nate, my *Director of Players' Success*, looking up from his computer. I went straight to one of the two chairs in front of his desk and plopped down.

"This shit ain't working."

Slowly, he shifted from his desktop and sat back in his seat. "What happened?"

Like he ain't know. Today was the last day of rookie minicamp and it didn't end much differently from the first day when I met that bitch, Sloane. They all probably called him while I was on my third lap around the practice field. They all talked to each other. My *DPS* here, therapists, coaches—every-fucking-body. Divine made that clear. None of them believed in me, but I felt different about Nate.

Right after draft night, I was told my mandatory therapy had to begin right away, so I packed my shit up and moved to Connecticut. The first person who reached out was Nate, telling me he was my assigned *DPS*. He scooped me up, took me out to dinner, then we hit up *Arch & Point*. That's when I knew his role was more than a dog and pony act for the organization. From our conversation that night, it was clear Nate took time and researched me. He knew my numbers and focused on my success as part of his orientation. He asked me questions and waited for answers. Applauded my side business and knew my public relations team's plan to develop me as a brand.

This cat knew his shit. Nate understood the business. He didn't come off as a pompous ass, who wanted to judge me on the bullshit of my college years. To keep it a buck, he won my respect before we watched tits and ass in art form. So when that Sloane bitch tried my gangsta on the field and Underwood or Henderson didn't step in, I knew where to come.

"Man, that bit—*broad* is always on my ass about little shit that don't matter. '*You're putting your arms out too early.*' '*Why you jumping for the ball?*' '*Quit the false steps.*' '*Don't catch the ball against your chest,*'" I did my best to sound like a bitchy female. "I'm here to play football, not have her micromanaging every little thing I fuckin' do."

Nate shrugged. "Those all sound like solid tips for a pro-level wide receiver. You're coming to this team out of college; there's going to be a transition."

"I ain't stupid, I understand that. What I don't understand is why this...female, who don't get me or what we're even doing out there gets to nag me about dumb shit."

Nate scratched his chin then sat forward, propping my elbows on his desk. "You didn't read the welcome packet, did you?"

Huhn?

"Welcome packet? I 'on't know what you talking about, man."

"Last week, when we met, I personally put a welcome packet into your hands: a front office roster, a coaching staff roster...among other things. *Important* things."

"Oh. Yeah." I remembered. "You said there wasn't anything in there I needed to sign."

Why the fuck would I look through a bunch of papers? I got lawyers for that...

He scratched his forehead, trying not to laugh. "That doesn't mean you weren't supposed to read it. If you had, you would've known that the team had a new position coach. Your position; wide receiver."

I looked away, annoyed as fuck by the news, all the revelations coming in too late. "Man, Divine threw that lil' mention in there when I met up with him last week. But, shit, I ain't catch it until she jumped in my face the first day of minicamp. I ain't wanna believe the *Kings* were on that feminist bullshit, too."

"She wasn't hired because of an agenda. She was hired because she had the qualifications."

Shiiiiit... "A fat ass and nice lips?"

Nate's eyes rolled to the corner of the room somewhere. I knew that was fucked up, but I ain't give a shit. The bitch had to go.

"A winning record at *BSU*, a reputation for building excellent wide receivers, and experience on the field – with phenomenal personal stats."

I snickered. "Experience on the field? On what field?"

"The football field. She played semi-pro, played in college, played in high school. She's been dominating in this game since before you were born."

What?

I leaned back in my chair. "I see you're on the same exaggerated facts she's on. Before I was born? Really, nigga?"

Nate smiled and frowned at the same damn time like the joke was on me. "She's forty-three years old. So yes, before you were born. And there's no need for exaggeration here. The facts are what they are. Let me give you another one. Coach Brooks is proven. Her place around here is secure, unlike yours."

I sat up in the chair, looking at this cat like he'd lost his damn mind. My stats secured my place on this roster. "The fuck does that mean?"

"It means that your position on this team is still probationary—contract or not. When we start training camp in a couple of months, there's going to be more than eighty men vying for a position on a fifty-two man roster. Most of our vets are already guaranteed. We have, maybe, *six* positions to fill between rookies, free agents, and those who simply didn't perform up to par last season. Coach Brooks isn't going anywhere. But if at the end of training camp she declares you unfit for this team, you will not be wearing a *Kings* jersey come September."

He had to be fucking kidding me. No way was I going to get cut before the season. I earned my spot in the *League*.

"You can't be serious, man. I thought you were supposed to be like my advocate or something?"

Love's Ineligible Receiver

"*Director of Players' Success*," he made clear. "And that's exactly what I'm trying to ensure here, but it requires your participation. The *Kings* already have two game-winning wide receivers: Jordan Johnson and Terrance Grant. The reality is that you're disposable. It's up to you to change that perception."

"So I'm supposed to go out there and kiss her ass? Bring flowers to the fuckin' field for her?"

Nate shook his head. "Nobody is asking you to do that. Go out there and give Coach Brooks the same respect you'd give her if she was a man. Listen to her because she knows what she's talking about. And fucking perform. That's it. Your shitty ideas about women and their place and whatever else? Leave that shit in your car when you come onto *Kings* property and any time you're representing this team. You're here to play football. Conduct yourself accordingly." He took a deep breath. "You've been seeing the therapist. Use that as a—"

"Don't!"

I stared at him, not believing he'd bring that bullshit up. I was a fucking black man, the original man. Of course, I was misunderstood by most. My plight in America was different. My start in life was fucking impossible. So what, I had a few bad moves coming up? I'd more than established myself as a righteous man. I made good decisions. I made it to the fucking *League* with an absent father and a mother, who fought her own demons to survive. It would've been nice to have that shit acknowledged once in a while instead of being misunderstood all the goddamn time.

Nate made his stance clear. I stood to leave, not having shit else to say.

Parker

"Here you go, Ms. P." He stopped right in front of me, bent his knees to meet my reach, and handed me a glass of wine.

Bodies moved casually around the packed and cosmic-sized, palatial home of the Richardsons.

"Thanks, Trent." I took a sip right away, peering over the rim, not quite understanding the root of my nervousness.

"No problem." He lay a clear tumbler down on the coffee table in front of us. "I see you're nothing like my lil' one. She only does the heavy stuff." He referred to the double shot of whatever he'd brought to her from the bar outside.

I smiled as he sat down and noticed Trent scratching his dusted chin. The music was nice and mellow, mostly old school records my mom would jam to. Frankie Beverly and Maze, Koffee Brown, The Roots, Mary J. Blige, and a gang of other tunes I was proud to be familiar with. But that didn't ease my anxiety as I people watched.

"Yeah," Trent brought me back into conversation. "That lil' lady turns her nose up at wine. She calls it 'cute.'"

I began to crack up as Jade walked toward us, strutting in high heels. Trent smiled and his eyes narrowed more when she grew closer as he slowed his humor with me.

"What's so funny?" Jade asked as she fussed with the waist of her fitted pants.

Trent went to scratch his lower face again. That made me curious and something dawned on me.

"Why did you cut your beard?"

Trent's eyes shot over to Jade, and I could tell the direction of his humor had changed. Jade rolled her eyes and sat between us in a huff. Trent kneed her then playfully buried his face into the crook of her neck and nuzzled.

"Yeah, whatever." Jade tried fighting her appeal to his affection.

"This man went and cut his beard without consulting me, Parker." She reached for the drink her husband brought her.

"Oh, wow! Really?" I more or less stated rather than asked.

Clearly, Trent Bailey was without beard. He'd cut it two seasons ago only to grow it right back.

"Yup." Jade licked her lips and took a swig of her liquor. "And he's been in the dog house since."

"A dog house you creep into errrr night," Trent joked and I spit out a cackle.

His brawny arm circled her tiny waist and he kissed her neck. "I'm just messing with you."

"*Mmmmhmmm...*" She playfully rolled her eyes again.

From my peripheral, I could sense heavy eyes on me. I glanced toward my left and saw a guy that had been ogling me since I walked in, gaping again with a clever smile.

"So, how long are you keeping it off this time, TB?"

He sat back on the sofa with a hard sigh. His hand went to scratch again. "I 'on't know. Been thinking about it."

"What?" Jade whipped her neck his way. "What do you mean, you don't know?"

Ignoring her invitation to battle, Trent began to rub her back while staring ahead. "There's nothing wrong with change. I'm just switching it up."

"And you can switch right back to the beard," Jade pushed.

"So you're a lifetime member of the beard gang fan club?" I asked her, teasing.

"No. Just of this guy's. When I met him, he had a wild beard, trying to hide from the world. I managed to break down walls no one else could, so I have a special affinity to his facial mask. It makes him look handsomely mysterious. *And sensual.*" Jade's eyes rolled to the back of her head while her lips were parted. "God, this man had me wound so tight until he *finally* broke!" Her head swung around and back for dramatic affect.

My head fell back as I howled. These two were more colorful outside of church. I'd hung out with them a couple of times before and each time I learned something new about their relationship.

"Jade..." Trent warned as he covered his face.

Jade grabbed her glass again and tossed back what was left. "What? It's true. I was sick with need and you knew it."

Trent's affected grin was the most adorable. I could tell two things in that moment: he was uncomfortable and he dared not refute her claim.

"Hey, guys!" That chirp caught my attention. Mel, Eli Richardson's wife, stood holding a tray with one arm. Her smile was as charming as ever. "I was trying to make it over here before they were clear gone, but I guess you guys are going to have to wait for the next batch of Richardson Punch to be made."

"What's that?" Trent asked.

"My cocktail." Mel lifted a brow and one side of her mouth. "It ain't for the faint of heart so don't sleep on it thinking it's a girlie drink."

Trent kicked out his leg and sighed playfully. "I'll be the judge of that."

I swallowed the last of my wine. "I don't know about that, Trent. Looks like my girl, Jade, here would be the better judge." I winked.

Trent and Jade laughed as I stood.

"Mel, could you show me to the restroom?"

"Sure, but I thought you were standing to help out with the next round." Mel had a saucy sense of humor.

She didn't come into the front office often, but when she did, her energy was always on ten. It made me wonder if that was her "wife of the boss" face or her natural vibe.

I smiled. "Bathroom first. Bartender right after."

She snickered at that. "Come on, girl. I'll be back, Baileys!"

Mel led me out of the festive sunroom where some had gathered, but there were folks all over. I couldn't begin to estimate how many people were here at Eli's "Welcome to the Season" bash. Bodies spilled from the back of the mansion out to the deck that was heated by tiki torches. There was a deejay out there spinning records that bled from the speakers all throughout the rear interior of the place. Red jacket servers made rounds with all types of food. Traveling through the house behind the host allowed me to appreciate the size and plush décor of the place.

"Here you go!" Mel swung her arm to the ajar door along the dark mahogany raised panel wall. "I'll be in the kitchen when you're done. That's straight ahead to your right, the first door on your right there." She pointed before taking off.

I stepped into the bathroom to handle my business. I was on my second glass of wine and my bladder had grown sensitive at this point. After washing my hands and checking my makeup, I sent Mandee a text to check in. Stepping into the hall, I hit send and bumped into a plank of muscles. My phone fumbled in my hand then fell to the floor.

"Shit..." I heard mumbled over me as I reached for my cell.

Quickly examining it, I was relieved to see it uncracked and still lighting properly.

"My bad, baby girl. I hope it's okay," that voice sounded again, pricking my nerves.

Finally, I peered up and found those eyes that had been practically drilling me since I entered the Richardsons' gates. There was a perceptible flip in his pupils. His expression turned hooded, but not with natural propensity. It was forced. Practiced.

That's when I realized the derivation of my anxiety from being here. I hadn't been out socially in years—three to be exact. And the last time I was among people of this caliber, at an event, it was with Jimmy. I had no idea who I was anymore. Was I single? Engaged? Spoken for? I knew what my heart said but what was the label hanging from my forehead for guys like this one to see?

"Yeah." I blinked excessively, mentally stuck. "It's fine. Thanks." I turned to leave, but he grabbed me by the wrist.

"Hey...that's not all I want."

"Huhn?"

"I came looking for you to introduce myself." He proffered his palm. "I'm Terrance. Grant, that is." His smile was corny but his teeth straight and white. "I'm a wide receiver."

The blinking wouldn't stop. This time it was because my brain began to think. I'd heard of Terrance Grant. He'd been having a time with a few guys on the team last season. I didn't know the details behind it, but it had spilled into the media and the big wigs didn't like it. And to think, it had been him checking me out all this time.

"Nice to meet you, Terrance." I nodded like dork. "I'm Parker."

This was awkward already. Mel was waiting on me and I was ready to go.

"Well, Ms. Parker, I think you're beautiful." His smile wouldn't fade. "And if it isn't too much, I'd like to call you sometimes. Maybe even send you 'Women Crush Wednesday' pix throughout the week."

My forehead lifted. "Of who?"

He chuckled, eyes swiping the area behind me as he switched stances. "If I'm sending WCW pix, it would only be of the one I'm crushing on. The woman I'm sending them to."

My eyes fell as I snorted. I didn't have a lot of time. I had to quickly decide if I would give him my number or use more time to come up with a polite reason as to why I couldn't.

I unlocked my phone and tapped my way to the contacts app. "I'll exchange numbers if you agree to me sending you my 'Man Crush Mondays.' *And* you can't get offended if they aren't always photos of you."

The gleam in his eyes faded as they locked on me for countless seconds but his grin remained. His lips pouted then eyes fell as he looked down to take my phone.

"Alright. But I have to warn you, it'll be my sole mission to be your only MCM on every day."

"How old are you?" I quizzed.

His focused remained on my phone. "Twenty-nine."

"You have a girlfriend, wife, fiancée or baby's mother you kiss goodnight?" I mean...those were the appropriate questions.

He handed me back the phone when done. "I haven't had the fortune of kissing my kids goodnight in three years so ain't no way I'm kissing their mother. No wife, girlfriend or fiancée either. Just on the hunt for a WCW."

For the first time, I smiled with Terrance.

"See you around." I turned to head toward the kitchen.

Hopefully he would stop making me the object of his gaping now that he at least had my number. Just as I was nearing the door Mel directed me to, she appeared. Her steps were halted immediately when we met eyes.

"Oh!" She laughed. "I thought you got lost. Come on. I got everything laid out for us."

And she did. Stretched over a mile long island in the center of her lavish kitchen were dozens of coupe cut martini glasses with the *Kings'* logo engraved into them. The style was subtle, even with the colored logo, yet elegant. What a fine touch by the missus. Next to them were bottles of citrus-forward gin, sliced cucumbers and limes, fresh chopped basil, and purple peppercorn.

"Hey, Nate!" I greeted my boss, Eli Richardson's, son.

Nate was also an executive in the front office and brother of Cole Richardson, Jordan Johnson's fiancée. I saw him often at work and even covered for his assistant several times over the years. He was lining up the last of the chic martini glasses.

He smiled, greeting me in return then whispered, "Don't let her work you too much."

I snickered as he finished his task and took off quietly and speedily.

The kitchen was hyperactive with serving staff running in and out with foods, and cooks going between the stove and fridge. Alongside Mel and one of her girlfriends, I grinded, mixed, pureed, and splashed until we filled sixty glasses and loaded them onto festive trays to be served to guests.

"I think this is the fanciest martini I've ever made," I marveled out loud.

"Wait till you taste it." Mel filled a glass with the leftovers from one of the many pitchers and pushed it my way.

I swallowed back one gulp then another. My god, the concoction was light and burst with hidden flavors on my tongue.

"Good god, this is the bomb!" I could hardly breath while declaring.

The girls laughed from across the counter. From my peripheral, I could see Eli strolling toward them. His arm immediately went around Mel's waist and he kissed her affectionately as Trent did Jade earlier.

"Be careful, Parker. That's how she got a proposal from me and a baby in my advanced age," Eli warned with flirtatious humor as his nose grazed the side of her face.

If I were light enough, the busy kitchen would see my blush. My boss had effectively stunned me into silence. Mel was able to wiggle from Eli's hold and we each grabbed trays topped with martini glasses. I was last in line to file out of the kitchen, thankful I chose a crossbody purse to wear tonight. We passed through the vibrant sunroom first and while Mel ventured left, her girlfriend remained straight ahead for outside. I decided to go right. The place was huge and folks were grabbing drinks from my tray almost right away.

I was threading through the sea of bodies, feeling the alcohol hit my blood stream and giggling with light delirium when my feet stopped. My lungs filled and nostrils flared at the sight ahead. *Sherry*. Why was she here? Her presence was just as jarring as the guy she was speaking to.

He stood against the wall, one big hand holding an unlit cigar and a brandy glass. But his posture didn't fit the accessories. His stance was built with confidence and extremely relaxed. One leg, clad in denim, was hiked behind him while the other foot rested on the floor. He was a warm hue of russet with a red undertone and...defined shoulders expansive in distance and globular. His waist was narrow and hidden under a *Rubber Soles* -shirt. His chin was toward his chest as his eyes peered under the rim of the *Connecticut Kings* baseball cap sitting low on his head, but I could catch those eyes. They weren't on Sherry, who practically stood in our line of sight. His attention wasn't on her as he held a phone to his ear while the other held the glass and cigar. Was he on a call?

His mouth moved intermittently. His lips... Goddamn, they were full and perverse...wicked. I couldn't explain how I knew this, but in that fleeting moment, I couldn't be convinced otherwise. This... *This!* It was now clear to me why I didn't get out much. It had taken years, but it happened. I'd come across a man I found grossly attractive. This wasn't good. Neither was his inconspicuous gaze on me. It was entrancing.

One of those eyes winked at me.

I felt my bottom lip hanging.

Goddamn sinful.

chapter
three

I SAW HER BEFORE SHE SAW ME. She could be no more than five feet tall with cinnamon brown skin that looked like it was baked to the perfect shade.

And the weirdest shit happened. As she pranced around the room in sexy ass booted heels with her black toenails out—a long fitted green skirt draping around her hips and exposing her right thigh when she put that one forward, a black tank that laid out the contour of her fucking tits, and a short blue jean jacket revealing her dope ass, baby-making shape—I'd been watching. She wore a tweed newsboy cap that gave her a little swag. Jeremy was in my ear, going on and on about two store openings and some old, corny ass broad was in my face, yapping about fundraising. But beyond all that—no lie—I slipped into some kind of trance where I saw...*us*. Me and this girl smiling as she strutted with a tray full of drinks.

In the first vision I caught, we were on a private plane kissing, tonguing each other down. Then we were on an exotic island, holding hands as we jumped from a ledge into serene blue waters. Next we were on a helicopter with me wrapped around her, starring down the black mouth of a volcano. A volcano! *I ain't never been to see no goddamn volcano.* In another flash, we were on a glossy cobblestone road in France. I was bent down on one knee, fixing the buckle of one of her high heeled shoes. Seconds later, in the next vision we were on our backs in the St. Anton am Arlberg snow, laughing our asses off about the fall we'd just taken together. The last was us at *Madame Tussauds London*, posing next to the newly added wax figure of Ameerah, the black cellist.

"I can give you my number, but I think if you give me yours it would be better. I can make sure you get the information right away," the lady in front of me with the dark ass penciled in eyebrows pushed.

The fuck?

I'd been to Paris once, about a year ago, but I only knew about the Austrian village in the Tyrolean Alps since last week when StentRo posted a pic of him and his wife on *IG*. That aside, why the hell did I just take that head trip like that? That had never happened to me. I felt a little dazed.

"Rut," Jeremy called into my ear. "You there, Rut?"

My eyes blinked away the fog, but I didn't lose sight of her. She stopped in her tracks, gripping the tray with her tiny fingers. Why? She stood there, eyes bouncing between me and the lady smiling in my face.

"Yeah, Jeremy," I finally answered after what I knew was an eternity. "Make the deal. And make sure that nigga cut the check for no less than three hun'ned K." I kept my voice low and eyes on the deer ahead of me caught in my headlights. "They may be coming to the underdogs, something unprecedented, but a lot of the appeal is they ain't paying us what they would a major. Don't get shit twisted."

When her eyes rolled down from my head to the one foot I stood on and rolled back up to my mouth, I winked at her. She liked what she saw and that was cute. That's when her jaw dropped and she looked like she'd seen a damn ghost. Right after that, she took off.

"Alright," Jeremy was finally ready to drop the call. "Don't forget to call me first thing in the morning."

"You got it, playa." I was ready to hang up.

And I did, dropping my phone in my pocket right after.

"Maybe we can find a private room to speak freely," the broad in front of me, who had to be close forty suggested, licking her lips.

When my eyes fell to her, she giggled…hard. Her chest lifted and hand brushed against it. I peeped the wedding band on her left hand she kept low. That quickly, I was irritated. She needed to go away.

Trouble…

Something I didn't need. I came tonight to show my face and nothing more.

I pushed from the wall. "I'm signed to *Love In Action*. You can hit them up for everything you need."

I walked off, not giving a fuck about her feelings. Females could be trifling as fuck. Nobody was beat for a thirsty one like her. She didn't even have game.

"Rut!" I heard call from behind me.

When I turned over my shoulder and recognized him, I forced a smile.

"Eli!" I turned completely to face him. "How are you, sir?"

This was it. This was why I came. Now Fats wouldn't be the only person telling Divine I came to this "work" event.

"Sir?" He scoffed, chin snapping back before he gave me dap. "Don't remind me of my age in my own home," he joked.

I did the laughing thing with him, just not too hard.

"Thanks for the invite." My eyes circled around the room. "This shit is proper."

"The soiree or my home?"

My tone was calm when I answered, "Both."

I didn't really know Eli but didn't want to give the impression I was a sucker, so I kept the humor to a minimum.

"Well, I'm glad you're enjoying it. It's my way of welcoming in new family like yourself and greeting the ones returning for the season. Last season was exceptional and my expectation is no less for this one."

It was a silent warning. Nothing out of pocket, but definitely a clear one.

"It's my plan to be a part of that." I offered my hand to close this awkward conversation. "I have a lot to prove to the organization. Looking forward to doing it."

His face loosened as he shook my hand. I gave a bow, wrapping up this chat before stepping off. I'd be damned if I didn't lose the chick holding the tray. Not that I was pressed. Like I said, this was just a business function.

"Anybody see Parker?" Eli's wife came out of nowhere looking to be in a rush as she held a tray in one hand and cell in the other. "I think this is her phone. She left it in the kitchen earlier when she helped me with the last round of drinks."

"I think I saw her headed out to the balcony a few minutes ago." Eli pointed in the direction I was going.

My quick thinking never failed me. "Shawtie with the tweed newsboy cap?" My brain coughed. "Parker?" I added the name she just gave for familiarity.

"Yeah. She just got a text, but I have to get back to the kitchen for more drinks."

Eli's hands slapped my shoulder. "Rut was just going that way. He can take it out to her."

Without a question, I was handed an iPhone.

love ∞ belwin

Parker

"I like mountain climbing." My eyes rolled up to him again. I couldn't believe he was still talking. It had been at least fifteen minutes with no breaks. "When I moved out here, I had to find spots. So far, Ragged Mountain seems to be my go to place. It's my therapy. You know?"

Leaning over the white stone, pillar balcony railing, I glanced up again to see if he was waiting for an answer. It was clear he wasn't when he didn't look my way. Terrance's eyes stayed out on the garden. Very few people were on this side of the expansive balcony.

"I thought about starting a company to teach young kids how to mountain climb." He finally met my eyes, but I could tell he wanted me to react to that. "Like...take them out of the city and bring them into nature, go over gear and safety." He shrugged. "You know, I know all that. And I'd do it for free. Wouldn't even charge them."

With wide eyes, a baffled mind, and parted lips, I nodded hesitantly. I honestly had no idea what he expected me to say or do.

"Hey, Park!" I glanced behind me. Jade stood at the door waving me on. "Trent's about to teach us the BlocBoy JB."

I nodded before my regard shot over to Terrance in an apologetic moue. Jade was providing me a save from this dry conversation with him. A part of me felt bad because he was nice...and kind of cute. But I saw Trent was uneasy when Terrance came to talk to me while I was sitting with them a few minutes ago. That was unusual but weird. Terrance must have noticed it, too, which was probably why he invited me out here.

"How do you know Trent and Jade?"

Finally!

He asked me a question.

"I met Jade in the front office, but I got to know them at church."

"Church? Don't TB go to church in New York?"

I nodded. "Mmmmhmmmm..."

"How long does it take you to get there?"

I pouted, quickly calculating it. "About an hour and a half. Honestly, less than that. It doesn't seem long at all to me."

"An hour and a half?" his aghast tone told me he couldn't believe it. "They must be serving caviar with their communion down in Harlem."

I laughed, my eyes perusing the lit garden ahead, admiring the various colors and sizes as the sun set.

"It's definitely something in the water," I sat up and placed my palms on the wide railing. "just not nothing in the luxury sense."

As I made my way back into the sunroom, Terrance was right on my heels. There was a burst of laughter in the corner Trent and Jade occupied and now more people with them. Jordan Johnson centered the crowd, doing the BlocBoy JB dance. He wasn't graceful with his moves, making it clear to me he was just in entertainment mode. When Jade noticed me, she patted the empty space next to her. I plopped down and found myself chuckling, too.

"I thought Trent was giving lessons?" Everyone who followed Trent Bailey or the *Kings* knew Trent loved to dance and was actually good at it.

In a hushed tone, Jade shared, "I just wanted to get you away from Grant. He's so annoying."

I laughed hard at that. "He's harmless."

"Aye... Aye!" Terrance shouted toward Jordan as he went into a new dance move. "Let's save all that agility for the field. We don't need to break anything at the welcome back party." He began to laugh and reached his fist out to Jordan for a genial bump as though the humor was mutual.

"And you say he's harmless," Jade groaned in my ear, rolling her eyes.

Jordan stopped, the mirth from his face drained. His fiancée, Cole, grabbed him by the arm and pulled his big body into hers. She pushed from her toes and kissed his lips, quickly murmuring something no one else was to hear but him. I couldn't be sure of it, but I was confident she was encouraging him to ignore Terrance's statement.

Trent re-navigated the conversation, sharing about rumors he heard regarding training camp this year. I sat back and played the fly on the wall as I sipped wine Jade had gotten me while I was out talking to Terrance. I wasn't sure how long I sat listening to the players speak when *the* guy strolled into our small corner. His casual saunter was with grace and confidence as he was followed by a beefy unsmiling man.

"Hey, ol' Rut-Rut!" Jordan playfully called out to him. "I thought you were here."

"Rut" didn't return the jovial energy but definitely accepted his handclap with a sleek grin.

Trent stood to give him the same manly greeting and as he did, he asked, "You came through, huhn?"

"Yeah," Rut returned. *What type of name is Rut?* It sounded more appropriate for a dog. "Been here for a minute. 'Bout to go, though." He stood back while in the center of our unofficial circle. "Got something waiting on me down the road."

"That's what's up," Jordan commented. "Glad you came through to say hello, though."

"No doubt," Rut assured. "I came to bring *Parker* her phone." His long and thick arm pushed toward me.

My ability to answer was delayed because my brain was stuck from the way he uttered my name. It danced on his tongue with lecherous familiarity. It was as if he'd said it a million times, in a million ways. Aroused. Depleted. Satiated. I knew it was senseless to gather that from a simple mention, but my god, it was true. And to corroborate my claim, the devilish gleam in his pupils as he held my eyes made my heart stop and nether region pulse.

"You left it in the kitchen when you made the drinks," he further explained.

And while that wasn't a big deal, the fact that he shared what I was doing as though he'd done it with me didn't go over my head either.

A rash bump at my knee snapped me into action. My eyes blinked excessively as I finally lifted my hand to retrieve my phone. How could I have left it?

"Thank you..." Another brain hiccup. "Rut," I whispered with less confidence than he'd pronounced my name.

"'S'all good, lady," dropped from his lips at the same time his masculine scent enveloped me.

He smelled earthly delicious. It was wrong...provocative. Captivating. I'd been in the presence of men and their cologne for a couple of hours now. Heck, even Trent had a pleasant fragrance about him. But none of theirs spoke to me instinctively and appealed to me. My body's reaction to his odor alone was animalistic.

Quickly feeling disheveled and awkward, I averted my eyes below. *My phone!* That's when I realized I hadn't heard back from Mandee.

Guilt coated my chest. How could I be so irresponsible? It was another reminder of how much of an outsider I was to this crew. How impossible having a social life was for me.

Her response was sent some time ago.

Mandee: *He's perfectly fine babe. We just finished a game of Twister! Please... Have fun!*

My head flew back and I guffawed something hard. One hand held my wine glass in the air and the other, holding my phone, went straight to my belly. Only Mandee could have a sense of humor like that.

"You okay?"

My head finally straightened and I saw Jade's half grin. Her hazel eyes were pink and half-masted. I laughed again.

"What?"

"You got a sitter for my Ava Nese?"

"She's with April. Why?" My humor was lost upon Jade.

"Because..." I was sure to keep my voice controlled. "Poor thing. Trent's going to inhale you in your inebriated state."

Jade shifted closer to my person, eyes even lower. "Poor Trent, you mean. I'm going to ravish every inch of him," she growled, which caused both of us to cackle deliriously.

A mocking tone brought me out of my humor with Jade. Terrance now centered the group, taking everyone else's attention.

"I'm just glad I got my draft experience being number two. I know it was a few years back, but that's a once in a lifetime experience, bro!" He swiped his nose. "It gives me this secure spot on the roster. But you know...I feel bad for these rookies that have to come in here and adjust."

"What you mean?" Jordan asked.

Terrance shrugged. "I mean that justifies my first team spot on the roster. Those last draftees have to sit on the second team."

I didn't know the terminology, but I gathered first teams were for starting wide receivers, something Terrance and Jordan were. Jordan was the team's franchise wide receiver, which meant he was the man as far as that position went. Trent Bailey was the *Kings*' first tier quarterback, so Terrance's ranking didn't affect him at all. Then what was Terrance referring to? My eyes swept the group.

Oh, gosh...

He was still there, situated against the wall while balanced on one foot. His posture and aura was cool. Unaffected.

"Yeah, but we got a sound team again this season. Ain't nobody trippin'. Just make sure we support our QB here." Jordan's arm swept over to Trent, who sat one body away from me. "That's all. It's all about the team." I caught the warning in his undertone.

"Yeah, I'm with it but..." Terrance hesitated. Then he snickered. "I'm first team!" He slapped his chest with his free hand then cracked up. "Get it? First team..."

A few people snickered and I noticed eyes shifting over to the Rut guy.

"Nah mean, Rut?" Terrance's tone was mocking.

Rut's head slowly rolled up from his phone he held waist level. His smile was slow and deliberate.

It all now made sense. Rut was the butt of Terrance's arrogant rant.

"No. No, I'm not trying to put you on the spot here or embarrass you." Terrance lifted a defensive palm in the air. "I know how it is. As a second draft pick, I'm only the second starting receiver so I get it. But if you keep working hard and stay out of *Arch & Point*, you'll be fine. That place may've worked for *The Flash*, but it won't guarantee you yards."

What does that mean?

Several people sighed and pushed out angry breaths at the same time. It was clear to me Terrance was not in concert with his beliefs or opinions. The odd thing about it was the Rut guy's expression remained clever and unmoved.

"Yo, Grant," Trent began on a groan. "why you always gotta bring this negative energy? We at a team event and you wanna single out the rookie..."

My phone vibrating on my lap robbed my attention.

It was from an unprogrammed number with a 609 area code.

+1 (609) 555-8427: *U shouldn't put your phone down at parties*

My face folded and before thinking, I reacted.

Me: Who is this?

My eyes scanned the room as though I'd find my answer there.

"Yeah, Grant. Where in line you got drafted don't matter, bruh," Jordan's deep vocals argued. "Look at Heath Shuler, Ki-Jana Karter, Jim Couch—"

"Nah!" Terrance argued. "Those're all QBs. I'm talking about receivers..."

My phone vibrated in my hand.

+1 (609) 555-8427: *Somebody advising you to password protect ya phone*

My eyes shot up again. This was getting creepy. Scouring the area, my eyes landed on the only thick, lanky figure composed and detached from the heightened emotions this conversation was stirring.

His head was low, the brim of his cap hiding much of his face as he peered down into his hand where he held his phone. Slightly, the brim lifted and those disarming eyes swept my way. They narrowed, causing mine to do the same as my pulse raced and clitoris throbbed.

"Why y'all tripping if what I said had nothing to do with y'all?" Terrance's tone was now crude. His attention went to Rut. "You know what I'm saying. Right? It was no disrespect to you...directly."

Rut stood straight and dropped his phone is his pocket. "I could give a shit if it was," voice controlled, low yet clear. "You couldn't fuck with me on my worst day."

And then he was off.

And my phone vibrated again.

+1 (609) 555-8427: *You coming?*

"Ahhhhhh..." Terrance cried patronizingly with his arms in the air, ever dramatically.

Trent, Jordan, and Cole began speaking at the same time. All chiding Terrance Grant for his asshole-ish behavior.

So many things ran through my fogged brain in that moment. That guy was hella fine. Too fine—dangerously fine. He was the first guy I'd found remotely attractive in years. And craziest of them all, he went into my phone to steal my number. That was the hottest thing a guy had ever done to grab my attention—*and I'd had my fair share of admiring men*. However, there was a shortage of them who wanted more than what I knew Rut wanted of me.

In that chaotic trice, I found courage and stood to my feet. I straightened my skirt as my eyes traveled to the other end of the sunroom where Rut and the big beast trailing his every move were headed. Then my regard descended to Jade who was leaning into Trent, rubbing his arm and whispering something in his ear.

This was it. It was now or never. Act now and brashly or remain dull and unadventurous.

My feet began to move in hurried strides. I tried telling myself to calm down and approach this with experienced know-how. My heart raced, nipples tingled, and body heated with need all over. I passed semi-familiar faces in my hasty exit, offering a faint smile and speed of determination. When I made it to the front foyer, I saw the back of the burly guy lingering after Rut. They moved through the door coolly, so unlike me. By the time I made it out there, a black *Yukon* SUV had pulled up and Rut moved to the backdoor. The beefy guy went to the front driver's door as a valet was stepping out. My eyes swung toward the back where Rut was already inside but the door was still open. I froze. Who was he waiting on?

My phone vibrated again.

+1 (609) 555-8427: *How long you gonna wait?*

My eyes grew wide. Then my feet began the hike down the stairs. After looking left and right to the moving bodies of guests and valets of the Richardson home, I slipped inside and quickly closed the door.

"Just to be clear," his velvety chords trickled and head shook faintly as his eyes cast me into a trance. "I ain't invite you to talk about strong password combinations...or mountain climbing."

My belly leaped.

"Not even about me climbing your mountain?" Her face was straight as a lineup and she didn't blink.

My forehead lifted. I was impressed, even though I could see the pulse in her neck beating fast as hell. All ready to go, I tapped the back of the headrest in front of me and Fats pulled off.

The thirty minute ride to my crib crawled by. I played my phone heavy and she sat statue still, attention to the darkness out of her window. I don't know what I expected of her; didn't really think past the funny texts I sent. But this was me. I cast my net and never came up empty. The problem was thinking of what I wanted to do with her now that I had her.

I made sure to send Fats a text, telling him what to do when we pulled up to the crib. As soon as we made it to my condo at *Kings Courts*, he hopped out of the truck, mumbling to give him a minute. Her neck rolled around until her eyes landed on me with question.

"I'm just giving you another chance to back out of this," was my lie of an explanation.

Her brows met. "Deal's off if I get in there and see one eight-legged creature."

"Just eight?"

"Anything more than two is a deal-breaker." One arched brow raised.

"Then we gone have a problem."

She warned, "I got my Uber app ready…"

I chuckled as I scratched the tip of my nose, my eyes going to the front seat. "Two things: I got a dog. Sharkie. He's being put away now."

"And the second?" she reminded me.

My phone chirped. Fats was telling me the place was clear.

I lifted her soft hand to my mouth, feeling my dick stiffening.

"Me." I kissed her fingers individually. Her jaw fell again. Those damn eyes locked on to me and I caught another flash, some type of leap in time or some shit. She was blasting off. Her head was back, face tight, and mouth open as she came for me. "I got three legs with you this close to me."

Her eyes dropped to my lap. To keep from laughing I tossed my chin toward her door which was closest to my unit.

"C'mon." It sounded like a groan, and I probably had. "Let's do this."

Without much hesitation, she opened the door and scooted out. There, laying on the middle seat, was her phone. Under normal circumstances I would have taken that opportunity to tease her again about leaving her phone around but tonight it worked in my favor. So, I quickly snatched it up and when I was out of the truck, slipped it into my pocket before crossing the SUV, and grabbing her hand. She followed me silently as we hopped up a few steps for the cracked door.

Once inside, I closed and locked the door behind her and tossed my phone on the counter. Music was playing lowly...purposely. She walked in a couple of yards before stopping. With her back to me, I could tell she was scoping out the place. I spotted the stereo remote as I waited. Tapping a button, I increased the volume as she spun around.

She sucked in a nervous breath. "Protection! Please tell me you—"

I deaded that nonsense by dipping toward her little frame, taking her at the sides of her face, and pushing my tongue in her mouth.

Fuck...

She tasted sweet. My tongue swirled through the coat of wine she drank earlier and eventually was able to get to her natural flavor. I wasn't big on putting my mouth or tongue on just any woman, but this one had me curious in more ways than one. For starters, as quick as she decided to come here, her nervousness wasn't like a thot with experience. Her hands that now covered mine on her were misty just like they were when I walked her inside. She was edgy.

By the way her mouth moved and her legs damn near gave out from under her, I knew she was game. It was even more evident from the way her hands dropped and found my belt buckle. With slight but obvious trembling, she tried to undo it. It was another time I wanted to laugh at her but not in a mean way.

I lifted from her face. "What're you doin'?"

Out of breath with her voice as low as a growl, she challenged, "What're *you* doing?"

"Trying to loosen you up." I smiled, holding her face in my hands. I could feel the heavy pulse of her neck.

"And I'm tryin—" She swallowed hard. "to loosen *you* up."

"How 'bout you make sure you ain't too loose for me?"

Her mouth dropped but before she could clap-back my lips were on her again. She moaned. Greedily, my hands fell to grab her ass.

All real...

Her shaky hands grabbed my shoulders, squeezing as though she needed me to keep upright. And that worked until my fingers pushed between her legs and found that sexy black tank was a body suit. I unsnapped it and found her slit warm and glossy. With one finger, I plunged into her cushiness and stirred. She moaned again and this time her legs did give out. I caught her, keeping her mouth on me.

Wanting that reaction again, I pushed into her. Her swollen walls swallowed me as the tips of my fingers pushed until they were deep inside her. Her one hand dropped down and cupped my dick. Then her pussy pulsated and her legs gave out on her again. My body lunged and I was able to catch her with one arm, but I pulled my fingers out, afraid I'd hurt her before we got started. My thumb circled her long and puffy clit instead. And again, her hand went to my dick. This time she tried for my belt.

I pulled from her mouth and tried focusing on her face through my narrowed eyes. I couldn't help my smile as I peeped her face twisting like she was in pain when I knew she was far from it.

Then it hit me.

"You wanna see what I'm working with." It wasn't a question.

If it was, her answer of "affirmative" came when she didn't speak at all, but those eyes went straight below. I snorted then backed her to the staircase until she walked up a few. I yanked softly at her arms, telling her to sit. My hands covered her kneecaps and I pushed her thighs apart. Her jaw dropped again. I could tell she had no clue what ol' Rut was about by the number of times that had happened since I'd laid eyes on her for the first time.

With my eyes on hers, I began to undo my belt and jeans. In no time, her eyes dropped south. When my dick jutted out, her head swung back but she caught herself and straightened as I dropped to my knees two steps beneath her, letting my cock drop onto the juncture of her legs. She bit her bottom lip. I took myself at the base and smacked the head into her clit. When her eyes rose to my face then her brows fluttered, I knew she appreciated the view and service.

Looking into her eyes, I repeated the act. Smacked and rubbed. Hit and poked until her legs curled in the air and her neck gave out again. She was even more beautiful as she tried hiding her true expressions of pleasure. She had a pride about her that aroused the hell out of me. My hand grip worked up my full shaft at some point. I yanked the left side of her tank down, making her tit plop out. Damn. I wanted to taste that, too, but decided against it. I'd worked us into a rhythm here. My dick was now glazed from her excitement. Her hands balled into tight fists and her pelvis rolled against my rubs. She wasn't a noisy one when she came, but her face told it all as she was coming on my damn stairs.

Fuck...

My body jerked and I'd be damned if I wasn't shooting on her. My cum jetting on her lower stomach and hairs as I grabbed the railing of the staircase to steady myself. When I was done, her eyes were closed. I waited for her. Thinking of how I didn't plan on that happening and how that may have made me look like an amateur, I waited.

Then her eyes opened, but narrowly as her chest rose and fell helplessly. Did she think that was it? I couldn't let it go down like that. I rarely came that fast and never unexpectedly. Now, I had something to prove.

I pulled up my clothes then stood her to her feet. Her body suit was out of her skirt, looking crazy. Without patience, I decided to lift her to my chest, wrapping her legs around my waist and carried her up the stairs. She was so fucking wet with her warm pussy rubbing against my abs. We passed by Sharkie's closed door and had to make a quick call to hurry to my room. I managed to open the door with her in my arms. After tossing her on the bed, I closed and locked the door. Right away, I stripped out of my clothes. She turned and found me in movement to my pocket to grab a rubber. That jaw hit the floor again before she jumped in to action and started to undo her shoes. Her skirt was off and before she could get her top off, I'd pounced on her.

"Uhhhh..." she breathed in my ear.

I shifted to taste her neck, licked and scraped my teeth into her soft skin. Her breathing was rough, hands all over my head and neck as her pulse beat on my tongue. My mouth went lower, tongue trailing until it met the cloth of her shirt. Quickly, I lifted and pulled it over her head. Her fucking boobs were gorgeous. Tan and hard at their coffee colored peaks. I pulled them together, unable to decide which one I wanted to attack first. She smelled so damn good. Felt so soft and feminine underneath me as she squirmed, lifting her pussy to rub against my belly. She needed friction.

I reached over to grab the condom then stood to my knees to roll it on. She was stretched wide for me, breathing hard with closed eyes. She looked nervous but wanting.

"You good?"

She nodded, eyes still closed.

"Aye," I called out in a clearer tone.

Her eyes flew open.

My chin dropped. "You cool with this?"

Biting that lip again, she nodded hard and fast. I crawled up her body, licking from the center of her chest to her plump lips. The way her lips and tongue met mine and face frowned, it seemed she struggled between keeping up with me and her needs of me. They were two different things. She wanted to show me she could handle this. And at the same time, she had her aggressive needs of it.

Her hips lifted and that was my cue. I pushed my hand between us and guided myself to her opening. My usual glide got me nowhere so my next was more forceful. I didn't make much more progress, but her hands brushing up the sides of my face to my head distracted me. Her nails scraped down to my shoulders from my neck made me shiver.

She pulled her mouth from me. "You okay?"

It took me a while to answer, my focus was getting inside of her.

"I'm trying to be..." I grunted. "If you would let me—"

"*Ah...*" she groaned, and I knew it was discomfort from me plunging a little harder.

I bit into the flesh of her shoulder, wanting to keep my mouth on her. Everything about this was unusual. This missionary position, her tightness, her being here in the flesh but in her own head.

Eventually, I was deep enough to work. And I did. I licked and sucked all over her neck and shoulders as I plowed into her. She didn't come like I expected her to, but I didn't let it knock me off my game again. I flipped her ass, bent her over, and banged into her until she clawed my sheets, dripped from my work, and her spine wobbled.

Parker

My eyes shot open so wide I thought I had just awakened from a nightmare. I was still here, in his bed. I turned to my right to find him next to me, his broad back cut in muscular patterns I'd never seen. He was definitely an athlete. It was clear by the way he handled me for over an hour, casting me into sensual delirium and exhaustion from his unbelievable stamina.

I have to go...

My head whipped to the opposite side of the room for the time. There was an alarm clock on the nightstand and I was able to make out it was after two in the morning. My heart began to pound again—it had been all night since running into this *Rut*.

But that was earlier. Right now, my reckless acts of adventure had come to an end. My head and back lifted from the bed and I felt a tightness on my lower abdomen. My eyes fell and saw the strangest crust of dry, clear liquid in a weird web on my pelvis. I had no time to investigate it. I managed to find and slip on my bodysuit. I located my skirt and shoes and put them on, too. Crouched over, a flash occurred in the corner of my eye. My head pushed up. It was...my phone slipped halfway out the back pocket of his jeans. I grabbed it, placed my thumb on the home button, and watched my apps appear before heading for the door. I paid the sleeping giant one last glance before creeping out of his room. Then I found my way to the stairs, trying not to clomp my way down in these heels.

More than midway down, my hat came into view. I rolled my eyes while swiping it into my hand. My purse was on the floor next to the island in the kitchen. I opened my Uber app and requested a ride. Biting my lip, I realized something about this felt wrong. I left him asleep and didn't say goodbye. He may have been a bit churlish with his proposal and "last chance" warning, but he was polite and generous. My eyes swayed left to right as my mind spun. There on the counter was a small notepad with a *Love in Action* logo. I scribbled the only words that came to mind.

Then I crept out into the darkness of the devil's hour, prepared to wait.

chapter four

As I clobbered inside the house, my eyes went straight toward his room. Mandee was stepping out and quietly closing the French doors behind her. I rushed over, nearly out of breath.

Parker

"Again, I'm so sorry about this. I feel like the kid who was finally trusted to go to a school party alone." I dropped my things on a table near the wall. "I swear, this won't happen again."

"Oh, my god..." Mandee stifled a yawn. "I told you, you're totally fine. We had the best slumber party." There she went again with her humor. Humor I was grateful for in the moment. Suddenly, her face opened with excitement then eyes narrowed with mischief. "Please tell me you met a random *Kings* exec and let him have his way with you at a five-star hotel in town."

My head jerked back and muscles in my face tightened. "Why?"

"Because it would have meant this unusual slip up was worth it for the both of us. You know as a student I have no life." She grunted.

Mandee was a nursing student and the daughter of a neighbor. Jimmy and her father, Lee, were buddies for years. Lee was a neurosurgeon, who showed amazing support during Jimmy's diagnosis. He was instrumental in getting Jimmy's at home care set up. Thankfully,

Love's Ineligible Receiver

Mandee was pursuing a career that assisted me with his care, and I didn't want to take advantage of it.

My face fell as guilt returned. "I owe you." I dropped my head into my palms. "Big time."

I felt her hand on my shoulder. "That new cucumber fragrance you're working on will do."

When I raised my face, she was on her way to the front door. "Mandee..."

She stopped with the door open. "You think..." I swallowed. "You think he noticed I was gone?"

Her brows furrowed. "I fell asleep in there. If I had, I'm not sure."

Her answer was dissatisfying, but was damned if she said yes or no. Each day I struggled with the progression of his condition. It had been hard to keep up with.

I nodded, dismissing her. Under normal circumstances, I would urge someone leaving the house at this hour to text or call when they made it in safely, but Mandee was literally crossing the street and nothing extraordinary ever happened in this quiet neighborhood. She'd be fine.

The door closed and I turned in the opposite direction, toward my reality. Behind those French doors was the living room, now converted into a bedroom—or something resembling a hospital room. I squared my shoulders and began my walk in that direction. The moment I opened the doors I heard the sounds of life support.

The room was its usual cool temperature. The machines housed in here couldn't afford to overheat. Rhythmic hums of the ventilator's mechanical breaths filled the room. A two-hundred-gallon fish tank contributed to the soundtrack of the room as well. It was his request to have some other form of life in his room. Jimmy had been keeping an aquarium most his life, I'd been told.

He was awake though his eyes looked tired, strained as they followed me as far as they could while I traveled to his headboard. After checking the machines levels, I pulled his blanket up his chest.

"Are you okay?" I asked softly due to the hour.

I leaned over him, an act of comfort for him—or me—and watched his eyes intently. It was his only means of communication at this point. His was upset. I knew this by the amount of time he deliberately took to answer with one blink which meant *yes*.

Two blinks would have meant *no*.

"Have you been to sleep?"

Two blinks.

I sighed, my heart heavier than I would ever share with Jimmy.

"I never go out, Jimmy." He didn't respond. I sighed as I rearranged the beddings over him. "Well, you can rest now. I'm back."

After a long and clearly contemptuous glare, he closed his heavy eyes.

Stubborn man...

With weighted shoulders, I stood from the bed to flip on the camera. I left his room and took the stairs for my own. The first thing I did once I stepped into my bedroom was power on the corresponding monitor to Jimmy's room. The screen flashed on, displaying his motionless skeleton frame in a hospital bed. The next thing I did was prepare for a needed shower. Whatever it was that had dried up on my pelvis had been catching against my bodysuit, irritating my skin.

The last thought I had before closing my eyes was where was the dog Rut mentioned?

I'd just closed the door to the conference room where the *Director of College Scouting* was hosting scouts for their monthly meeting when Nyree walked up on me.

"And you emailed the edited contracts to Rashad Williams?" Her tone was hurried. Its typical, anxious Monday morning manner.

I moved away from the conference room as I replied, "Yes. And I set up the meeting for Dontay Williams and two of the new vendors selected for next season."

Nyree stopped a ways away from the conference room door and placed a dramatic hand on her forehead. "Shit," she whispered. "I'd forgotten all about that. Thanks so much, Parker." Her expression turned shamefaced. "Call it aging, but I don't know what this feeble brain would do without you. Three days a week just isn't enough for me, I see."

She was referring to the number of days I worked here at the front office. It had been one of the nicest things a manager had ever spoken to me. I was grateful for Nyree's warm spirit.

With a smile of comfort I offered, "I need the tasks to keep my mind. No worries." I began to take off backward. "I have to take notes on that marketing conference call for Eric Young this afternoon. That gives me less than an hour to scarf down this decadent peanut butter and jelly calling my name at my desk." Nyree laughed quietly at my theatrical description. "You have this covered. Right?" I gestured to the scouting meeting.

"You bet." She nodded, dismissing me.

Back at my desk, with half my sandwich clutched in my hand, I scrolled down my Instagram newsfeed and came across a newly familiar face. It was a post from *Spilling That Hot Tea*. Rut—a name I still couldn't digest having for a human being—was posing at a red-carpet event with...Emily Erceg. My heart hopped and I became winded all of sudden.

Emily was the sister of Erika Erceg. They were both earthly gorgeous Syrian-American women, and as a family, along with their brother, Erik, and mother, Ellis, had amassed a multi-million-dollar empire stemming from their reality show *Envying the Ercegs*. Erika had been almost an overnight household name, thanks to a sex tape of her and a rapper going viral a few years back.

My attention returned to the headline: **Emily Erceg's In Love Says Insider**

Again, I gazed down to the image—

"Hey, Parker!"

I jumped around in my seat, dropping the PB&J.

Startled, I breathed, "Richell!" My delivery was too alarmed, but not only was I frightened, her timing was impeccable. I lifted my phone. "Hey, how old is Emily?"

"Erceg?" Her face tightened a bit. "Old. Maybe thirty-one?"

My brows lifted. "Thirty-one is old to you?"

Richell, one of many interns slapped her palms together as she stomped one foot. "Girl, twenty-five is old to..." She slowed, realizing her offense.

I dropped my face, my eyes on her. "You do know I'm twenty-eight. Right?"

"But you're different," she tried cleaning up with a giggle. "I'd die to have your legs, Parker. And that waist is fuckin' snatched." She snapped her fingers and popped her shoulders. "Yessss!"

"Richell..."

"Hmmm?"

"Focus!"

"Oh!" Her eyes lit anew.

"How long have they been..." I couldn't find the right phrase.

"Smacking pelvises?"

"Yeah." I rolled my eyes.

She nodded, understanding I was lost on new lingo.

"For a few months now." Her shoulders drew up. "They're so cute together! Girl, I be out on the practice facility, praying I see him and *The Flash*!"

"Jordan Johnson?"

"Yeah, girl! He can *flash* these damn panties anytime he wants. Big facts!"

She attempted a hi-fived I didn't accept. Instead, I shook my head. My eyes circled the area beyond us.

"You know his fiancée works in this building. Right?"

She shrugged, crossing her arms. The time crossed my mind and I checked my phone.

"Pull up a chair." I tossed my arm to one across from me. "I need to pick your brain about *Spilling That Hot Tea* and the *Kings* players."

Thankfully, Richell quickly acted. I had a conference call to prepare for. Grabbing my sandwich, I began running down all my "circular inquiries" about a Rut before my time was up.

RUT

Clutching the *Gatorade* squeeze bottle as I trekked behind my teammates, headed for the tunnel leading off the practice field, I gulped hard and fast. The more I chugged, my chest cooled from the chilled liquid but my arms, thighs, and feet throbbed from the work I'd just put on them. I could hear Jameson a few feet ahead, leading the group off the field, talking his usual shit.

"Yo, my first daughter was born in that house. My wife is crying her eyes out. But what the fuck am I supposed to do? I need to dump it!"

Because you going broke, buying stupid shit with ya money while getting injured every damn season! Fuck outta here!

But of course, those thoughts stayed in my head. I never paid dude no mind with his corny ass. My mind was on calling Dinky about the water bottle plug for the lunch program back at home in Trenton. That and rescheduling with that fucking therapist for this week.

"Not you, Rut!" A familiar bark ripped across the field from the speakers.

The fuck?

Slowly, I dropped the bottle from my sweaty face and turned toward the green. Underwood, the Offensive Coordinator, held the bullhorn inches from his mouth. His eyes were hidden under the tent of his baseball cap, but I could sketch an image of his scowl, knowing it by heart after all the times I'd seen it since getting drafted. A few snickers could be heard as the team passed me on their way to the locker room.

"You got an extra hour on the field. Run your ass now!"

What? We'd just finished a grueling plyometrics drill. *Hours of it!* More giggling could be heard behind me as bodies practically slogged off the field. Jordan "The Flash's" sleek ass smile drew closer to me. My upturned palm automatically rose in the air, silently questioning.

"The fuck is this? High school?" I grumbled as he neared. "Grant and Thomas came late," I began as he slapped my shoulders heavily with that same smirk. "I get why they have to stay after. But I was here early. Fuck I do?"

Smoothly, and on the low, Jordan tossed his chin, telling me to meet him off to the side of the line filing into the tunnel.

Once out of the way, I turned to him curious as hell. But before uttering a word, Jordan spit a laugh from his belly.

Huhn?

"Yo, Underwood is old school as hell!" He laughed. I lifted one brow to hurry this shit along. Jordan caught on and tried to calm himself. "They all tight, man. Underwood, Henderson, Craig, Eli—Wright."

Henderson and Craig were two of the wide receiver trainers, but—

"What this gotta do with them?"

Jordan shook his head. "You had a plus one when you left Eli's shindig the other night." I cocked my head to the side. "You fucked the wrong one."

"So?" My hand flew in the air. "I fucked a jawn; it's what the fuck I do! What that got to do with me having to stay late at practice to run more drills?"

Mentioning her reminded me of the note she left. Fats showed it to me, confused by it. But when I read what it said, *"Sorry for Uber'ing it out. Thanks for keeping up with my phone."* I knew exactly who had written it.

Jordan's face sobered. "Your plus one is linked to the old-school crew."

"Who?"

"Wright."

"Who the fuck is Wright?"

"James 'The Boulder' Wright.'" His forehead lifted for recogni-

Love's Ineligible Receiver

tion from me. Nothing. "Class of '93, franchise wide receiver." He nodded as my face fell when I finally recalled the name. I hadn't heard about Jimmy Wright in years. Before Jordan and Trent's days as franchise *Kings*, it was Tariq Evans and friends' time. They got the ring and made the *Kings* loads of cash. And before Evans' class was Wright's. He brought the *Kings* more than one Super Bowl win in the late eighties/early nineties. I knew Eli, Underwood, Craig, Henderson, and Wright were old as fuck, but I didn't know they rolled together. Besides, I hadn't heard Wright's name in years. My pops used to go hard for him back in his day. "That plus one you retreated with the other night..." His chin dipped.

"...is Wright's daughter?"

He snorted, face toward the ground. "Go lateral."

Latera—

"I fucked a bitch who cheated on her man?" I yelled, mad as hell over the bullshit. That wasn't my fault. *Here we go...* I came up here for everybody to doubt me. I did the damn required therapy, made sure I didn't give the coaches *too much* flack, stayed low so I didn't hear Divine's shit, and now, because I bumped dicks with a damn old fuck *I'm* the problem? I felt my jaw tighten. "That's the big fuckin' deal, bruh? So I smashed her. You know how many bitches I run through?"

Jordan's eyes rolled over my shoulder to something behind me, his jaw dropping and face going lax. I turned to see what caught his attention and my damn eyes rolled away as soon as they hit their target.

Fucking. Eli. Richardson.

I let out an aggravated breath. The last person I wanted to see was my boss when I was copping to banging out his homie's piece of ass. Eli stood with three other stiffs in tailored suits; one a female. They all looked horrified, as though I pulled out my gat and asked for the goods.

He cleared his throat and motioned for the small group to continue down the tunnel. A part of me—a real tiny part—wondered who his company was, hoping it was no one he was trying to impress. He was Eli Richardson after all, the only black owner in the *League*. Who did he have to impress?

Low key snickering had me turning back to Jordan. Half his face was covered by his hand and he coughed into it, clearing his throat.

"Not a good look at all," I muttered, mad as hell. "I know."

I didn't need a warning. Each day since I signed my shitty deal, it was understood Eli didn't fuck with me. He wasn't the type to have personal relationships with many of the players, but everybody knew he rocked hard with Trent Bailey and Jordan Johnson—before Jordan got with his daughter, Cole. That nipped at my ego too. He and Divine were boys. Divine was my people but that still didn't get me face time with Eli. It was another reminder that I wasn't exactly welcomed here.

"Glad you do." Jordan's face straightened. "Look, playa, you gotta hit that field before Underwood blasts ya ass for real. But I'll tell you this: you leaving with that chick the other night ain't under the big homie's radar."

"Because his boy's fuckin' her?" I asked, mad about that recent discovery all over again. "Okay, I won't touch his groupie again. Shit." I snorted. "I 'on't even remember her name!" My head was still fucked up over her leaving a note.

Jordan shook his head. "She ain't his groupie. Try again."

My eyes blew up. "His main bitch?"

Shaking his head even more, Jordan's humor began to feel like pity. "Stop calling that girl a bitch. Get that outta ya system. I don't know the details of their relationship, but I do know they're legit. So legit she works in the front office. She keeps on the low...don't bother nobody." He began to walk off, amusement playing on his face again. "Matter of fact, she may be known now because she left the party with the new asshole draftee. This may be something you wanna consult Divine on, lil' homie. That's all I got for you." Jordan took off for the locker room and I could swear to hearing him laugh even more.

Oh, so now I'm that asshole?

"Rut, get yo ass out here, boy!" I heard from the bullhorn.

"Fuck!" I turned for the field wondering how in the hell did I get myself into this shit.

I started my jog for the center of the field, grunting underneath my breath. One of many rules I lived by was no pussy was worth trouble. There was too much out here for a man like me.

Too much. But I damn sure wouldn't turn down another opportunity...

RUT

"How long are we going to do this?"

My head rolled over to the left where she sat with a device over her crossed legs. Her head was to the side and nose in the damn air.

"Do what?"

"Ineffectively use the time allotted to us."

I straightened my head to face the ceiling as I lay on my back. "Just an hour a few times a week. Right?" I shrugged. "I actually like the quiet time. It's therapeutic."

"And a waste of my time."

"Hey, I didn't request this. I ain't even paying for it."

"But your employer is. An employer who's expecting my feedback about your participation and progress. It's been almost a month."

"Don't remind me," I groaned, brushing my hands over my face. "A month of wasted fuckin' time. Time I could've devoted to what I'm actually getting paid for." Measly pay. "But instead, I'm here taking advantage of ya plush ass, white sofa."

"I'm not giving you a pass."

That had my neck whipping back over to face her.

She sat forward, brows lifting on her big ass forehead. "No." She shook her head, eyes hard on me but voice calm. "I don't ask many questions when I'm asked to take on a client from the *Kings*. In fact, I don't look at the intake paperwork until I've discerned some things on my own. It's a game I like to play with myself. I like to see how accurate I am."

"So I'm a game to you?"

"No more than what you do on the field."

That went over my head, but I wouldn't let her know that. I wanted to know more.

"So what have you—" I used my fingers in the air. "—'discerned' about me?"

She lay the device on the coffee table and stood. I watched as she strolled to one of the black wooden shelves on her wall and straightened an *Urban Grind* coffee mug. I was familiar with the brand. It was a black coffee company. But why in the hell did she have the mug on display like it was significant? Then she walked over to her bookcase in the corner. She pushed back a big dawg bottle of *Mauve*. There were two smaller bottles on either side of it.

She's fucking weird.

"One of many things I've observed about you is your total disregard to your presentation. What I mean by that is, your behavior demonstrates little etiquette. That could be because it was never required of you growing up in the environment you did. And even when you were in college, your crudeness was dismissed and attributed to your age."

I laughed. My head tossed back on the arm of the sofa and I hollered. "And what about now?"

"Now?" She turned to me. Her face was still blank but her head fell to the side again. "Now you're in the big leagues. You're a brand. A product. And products should be set aside from the rest. You need polishing. A conscience of etiquette helps with that. Clean up your delivery for when it matters."

I was bored with it already. "And why is delivery and presentation so damn important?"

"It speaks to your humility and level of class."

I couldn't help it. Hard air pushed through my lips and I found myself laughing again.

Is this what Coach Lou and them had in mind?

The *Kings* added therapy as a stipulation to my contract. I had to start immediately at a few times a week until the therapist "successfully discharged" me. The stupid ass contract read something like that. They could all suck my balls if they thought this would get in the way of my dreams.

"What about your mother?"

"Ha!" I croaked. "She good."

"But has she mentioned about any of the traits I've named."

"Nah. 'Cause she so good."

"Good how?"

"Taken care of. She wants for nothing, so she don't have nothing to complain about."

"Hmmm..."

"Hmmm..." I mocked, stretched out on the couch.

"What about your grandmother?"

"Same boat. I take care of her, she good."

"Girlfriend?"

"Don't have one." *Try again.*

"Kids' mother?"

My eyes rolled over to her. "I'm a twenty-four-year-old, black, educated, pro football player. Out of all those bomb ass character facts, being a father ain't one." My face went tight as I thought about that. "Kind of insulting, too."

"Please accept my apologies. I'm trying to see your full portrait here."

"You'd see a better one if you left broads out." My laugh was dry.

"What's wrong with calling us women?"

I refused to look at her when I answered. "First, we ain't talking about you or every female on earth. We talking about the ones I run into. They broads—most females are. No matter how old they are, most of them come with the shits." I was using "etiquette" by excluding her, but I was willing to bet she was no different from the rest.

I've seen some quality women in my day. Shit. Divine's wife was one. *A fucking unicorn.* That woman had her own job and education before he scooped her, but that was rare. Even Stenton Rogers' wife came up on him. She got fancy degrees and shit, but StentRo sponsored them. For each example I could think of, of a woman having her own and not in a man's damn pocket, I could call out ten more that was nothing more than a damn humping bag.

Sorry...

"Pussy's good, but good pussy don't make a female a real woman." The therapist's neck whipped my way. The minute I realized those words fell from my mouth, my eyes closed and squeezed in frustration. "I didn't mean to be rude. I—"

"Was giving it to me how you see it. Your perceived truth." Her hands clapped and she shrugged. "I'm big on honesty. You laying in here putting up guards is far more challenging than you giving me your ugly truth."

"What truth?"

"The fact that you have a skewed view of women. Your perception of them is poor but in my line of work I know it's because of a series of experiences you've had with them."

I laughed again. "Man, I ain't got no issue with women. I actually see them in a positive light. I've seen some bangers, doc. Ain't nothing like a beautiful, bangin' female."

"Again." She gave a slight nod. "You referenced female."

"So y'all ain't females no more?" I scoffed. "This new aged bullshit got me confused."

"We're females by distinction of human sex. We're women in the scheme of social humanity. I'm personally not offended by the term female, but your manner of reference implies there's a categorical ranking system behind your wordplay."

"Hell yeah. Y'all all ain't created equal but in general..."

"In general, what?"

Fuck it...

"Females are takers. There's always an ulterior motive for what they do. Most of the time it's money. Sometimes it's for social status."

"Just those two reasons?"

"Nah, there are a few more. Like this one chick in college... She was the president of a female club—all black chicks. They were 'bout it, too. Active on campus, holding fundraisers, having big name activists speak at their events, hosting parties, working with the provost's office and shit." I found myself smiling toward the ceiling. "Julia was her name. She was a banger...Malian heritage, too. She would come at me all the time with the shits. She said I was sexist, misogynistic, and a gang of other shit. I told her I wasn't and would prove it.

"One day I decided to sit in on her meeting. I listened through the whole hour and some change about their agenda. Afterward, I was hungry and invited her to grab a bite. The next day I saw her in the student center and chilled with her between classes, kicking it about the comparison of Kendrick Lamar and 'Pac. Two nights later, she was knocking at my door at one in the morning, wearing a robe and slippers. I fucked her that night and a few more after before she asked could we go without protection."

I sat up, finding the whole situation funny all over again. "This the same girl who had vocal views on women's right to choose and all that bullshit. She wanted me to nut up in her and risk getting her pregnant, all for her to abort the baby? Females be trippin'."

"I can see how perplexing that could be."

"But I ain't finished, though." I laughed again, memories flooding in. "When I told her no, she got mad and that turned me off. I decided not to fuck with her no more. This girl got depressed. Within weeks, she stopped going to class, half ate, didn't do her little all black girl meetings. Then the whole fuckin' campus wanted to blame me for putting her light out. She left school, and the next semester, finished online. It was crazy!"

"Did you speak to her?"

"Nah. Coach told me to leave it alone. The whole campus was buzzed behind it. Her little girl group rallied to get me expelled. I had to sit out two games that we ended up losing behind that bullshit."

"Did you want to speak to her?"

"Nah. Not really. She sounded crazy to me. And please don't try to say it was my fault." I shook my head while looking her dead in the eyes. "I may do my shit, but that girl had issues long before ol' Rut came along. But of course, people wanna blame me when I'm only guilty of not turning down ass."

"Would you do anything differently, in retrospect, if you could?"

I thought about it. "I 'on't know."

"You have to have some position on it now: new or old. You're in the *League* now. Conduct is second only to skill set." She tossed her hand in the air. "You're here because of conduct. To reinforce the importance of it. Surely, you have a position on that experience today."

I shrugged. "I really don't know. Now I'm fighting to prove I'm the shit. I worked hard to get here, got here, and was offered a shitty contract. Everything about it is contingent. Hell, I ain't never heard of that type of deal until the *Kings* gave it to Trent Bailey two years ago. I could've given up there, but I accepted it and showed up to work on the first day. I'm never late for practice, always working out, study old footage the coaches recommend, eat the prescribed diet—I lay low. I got a lot of shit on my shoulders. Even doing all of that, my name gets mixed up in shit."

"Like what?"

I didn't want to go there. I damn sure didn't come here to talk and definitely not about some real shit. I checked the time and saw I had less than ten minutes to go.

"A couple of nights ago, the big man on campus hosted a party at his crib. I came through...not to party, but to be professional and show my face. The last thing I was thinking about was ass." I made sure I caught her eyes. "I mean the *last* thing. My mind was so far from it and to prove it, I'll tell you I had ass waiting for me back at my place."

"Okay..."

"Okay. So I get there and see this chick that kept catching my eye. Obviously, she couldn't keep her eyes off me either. One thing led to another, and we left together. We banged out. She left. *Boom*. It's over. Then I show up to work today and one of the coaches got a beef with me. Come to find out, ol' girl from the party belongs to his boy. Not only is he bangin' her, but they're engaged. One thing leads to another today, and everybody, including Eli Richardson, knows I fucked her. I found out her ol' man is Eli's boy."

I sat back and chuckled. "Once again, I'm the bad guy. Mind you,

I'm not engaged. Ain't in no relationship, but I'm the wrong party. You should've heard them today, raving about how good of a girl she is, how she's not that type to get involved with a dude like me...she's upstanding." I shrugged. "They say she even works in the front office. But again, I'm the bad guy."

Her mouth twisted as she mentally chewed on something. "Another public showing of your bedroom tryst, but now, you're a professional football player. You won't be considered a 'kid, being a kid.' You have a voice in this. How can you turn this situation around?"

I took a deep breath, over the topic already. All day it had been running through my mind. It was only a matter of hours before Eli would run back to Divine about this. I was surprised my phone hadn't been blowing up already.

I dropped my face into my palms with my elbows digging into my knees. "I could go straight to her and her ol' man and try to clear the air."

"Apologizing?"

My head shot up. "Hell no! I ain't apologizing for shit. I'll leave that to her. She gotta apologize to that man. I don't owe them shit."

"Then what will you say?"

"I don't know. Just something to clear up the fact I didn't know her and it ain't gonna happen again."

She stood from the chair and took a deep breath. My session had come to a close.

"Getting ahead of a quagmire like this would only speak to your wisdom and maturity. If that's something you decide to do, I just hope you remember etiquette. Your intent isn't always delivered in just the words you say; it's also in the manner of your presentation."

I stood to leave, pulling out my phone to turn on the ringer and check my notifications. Making nice was not my thing but winning was. I had to do something to get out of this shit I found myself in.

When I made it to the door, I mumbled goodbye, mind already on the email my business partner, Jeremy, sent.

"Amare..." I turned to her with my hand on the knob. She was at her desk, leaning back in her chair but her forehead was wrinkled and mouth pouted. *This lady thinks too much.* "If you had company at your place...in your bed, where was your other guest, who was awaiting you while you were at the party?"

"Where I always entertain chicks: in Sharkie's room."

She blinked. "Who's Sharkie?"

I smiled, not necessarily embarrassed. "My Tosa."

Her eyeballs swung right to left. "A dog?"

"My best friend." I closed the office door behind me.

chapter five

I LOOKED AT THE HOUSE, MILDLY LIT and no movements inside the windows. Then my eyes shot down to my cell in my hand to confirm.

60609...

Those were the numbers on one of the posts on the porch of the white colonial with black trim.

This' where Jimmy Wright live?

Neighborhood wasn't bad. It was quiet, no one hanging out after dark. Far better than the slums I'd seen back home in Trenton. But the way they talked about Wright's legend, I was expecting to see it in his crib.

The hell he do with his bank from back in the day?

Taking a deep breath, I backed up to pull into the driveway. I parked behind an old body *Benz* then walked to the front door. The moment my thumb raised to ring the doorbell, I wanted to leave. I shouldn't have come down here. Who gave a fuck about making nice with a chick I fucked? Who gave a damn about an old head baller?

I took a deep breath, pushing myself to get this out of the way. The problem was, I never pushed myself to do shit like this. The only thing I talked myself into was eating clean and working out harder, but this was related to ball, too. I needed to make this good. I had to squash any expectations my actions the other night may have caused...*him or her*.

That's when I finally pushed the damn button. After a few seconds, I saw the silhouette of a petite body moving hesitantly toward the door through the thin curtain to the left of it. Slowly, she unlocked and pulled the knob back cautiously.

"Hi," she seemed to have breathed out.

I didn't speak at first, taking her all in. Heather gray tights covered her short, toned legs and a tight, braless tank top clung to her breasts. She was barefoot and wore a loose ponytail at the top of her head. And...no makeup.

I felt my eyes blink. That's when it hit me: I forgot what she looked like since she left my damn bed. This chick was faceless after I slayed, just like the rest. But standing here, staring down at her—even without the makeup and thick dark lashes she wore at the party—her features reminded me why she broke the dark mood I was in that night. *Shit...* The dark space I'd been in for weeks. It was that lost look in her eyes. The nakedness in them, telling me everything she didn't want me to know.

"Uh..."

Damn!

I couldn't remember her name and my dumb ass had the nerve to fucking blink again!

My hand went into the air as I tried to resuscitate my damn brain. "I...*uh*..."

"You want to come in?" her soft, girlie voice rushed out. She pointed behind her. "I have something on the stove."

She backed up, widening the doorway. That forced my decision and I walked inside. She closed the door behind me and waved me on to follow her. Of course, my eyes went to her ass that jiggled but I curbed my excitement. Tonight wouldn't be that type of party. *Never again* would it be *that* type of party with her.

The house smelled good and was nicely decorated. It was hella quiet, too. I wondered where Wright was. It would be odd running into him here, but I'd deal with that if I had to. I just wanted to squash this and get on with my life.

"Have a seat." She pointed to the kitchen table when she breezed through.

I didn't want to sit but declining would have been rude. And being rude would have been counterproductive. I pulled out the closest chair to the door and sat with my legs out from under the table. She went straight to the stove and lifted a smoking lid.

"My name is Parker. Parker Grayson," she spoke with her back to me.

I was happy as hell she couldn't see the relief on my face. It would have been hard making good with someone whose name you couldn't remember.

"I know your name."

"No, you didn't." She turned her head to look at me over her shoulder.

"I did," I continued to lie. "I just... It's just been a long day."

"Oh, yeah?" She grabbed a mitt then bent to open the oven door. "How so?"

"Lots I don't wanna get into. But one of the biggest was finding out about you."

"What about me?" She pulled a pan from the oven and placed it on the stove.

"You know..." My eyes swept the room for incomers or lurkers. "You."

"That's not saying much. Remember, you didn't even know my name when you rang the doorbell. So how much did you"—she used rabbit ears for quotations—"find out about me?"

"A lot more than your name. I'm sure you know who I am by now. Know I'm connected."

"I don't know about connected, but I did find out our little rendezvous Saturday night made it all the way to my boss—our boss. By Monday afternoon, clock out time, his executive assistant pulled me aside and shared what our boss had learned about my activities once I left his home." She gave me a long side-eye.

"That ain't saying much about what info you heard about me and if you know about my connections."

"Well, let's unpack this one item at a time. Good information about a person should at least start with a name. Your 'connections' can't be that good if they didn't give you that."

She was being a smart ass but her voice was deceptively soft, girlie...smooth while her small back was to me as she worked over the stove. It wasn't as husky, anxious, and velvet as it was the other night when she was curious about my cock. About me.

"I was told you gotta man you ain't bring to the party the other night. Or should I say, you went to his boy's house party and left with another nigga. That's how you do ya fiancé?"

She paused, elbows in the air from her working on her dinner. Parker's head rotated to look at me over her shoulder again at first. Then she dropped the utensils, switched off the eye of the stove, and turned to face me fully.

Yeah...

I'd gotten to her. I had to pull that information out of one of the assistant coaches this afternoon. I was able to get a lot of information on her, including Wright's address. It still blew my mind that she lived with dude. And not because I hadn't seen or experienced this myself before but because everybody was so uptight about it—about Wright. *Why would she be so reckless?*

She leaned against the stove and crossed her arms. "Is that what you were told?"

"That and more."

"And you believe everything you're told—just like that?" Her forehead lifted.

I shrugged and stretched my arms. "Why wouldn't I? Why would anybody lie on you?" I looked her up and down, not really knowing why.

Parker's eyes mocked my own as she glanced down at herself. Her head came up, face folded, and mouth twisted.

"What about my appearance makes everything you heard believable?" I was stuck on that one. "Okay. We're unpacking. Right?" She sensed my confusion and pushed her palms in the air. "Let's start with what you've been told."

My eyes danced around the kitchen. I didn't come here for this. To keep it a buck, I thought I'd be out of here by now. I was shocked as hell when Parker turned for the cabinet and began to unload dishes. This chick was really waiting for me to answer.

I didn't have time for the bullshit, so I got straight to it.

"I heard you're engaged to dude. You a lot younger than him. Y'all been together a minute." I was stalling. This all seemed stupid now. "He been a little sick and you stay with him."

When I glanced up, she was looking at me with small eyes and one brow in the air. She thought I was bullshitting her. Then she turned back for the stove.

"I've heard things about you, too."

I was checking out her ass when I asked, "Word?"

"Yup. Like how much of a loose cannon you are. That you're in love with an Erceg." *Whatever.* "How you sexually assaulted that girl in college." *What?* "And how violent you are. You knocked that Russian kid out cold for no reason."

"That's some bullshit!" I found myself yelling. Parker leaped in the air, facing me. "I ain't never have to assault no girl to get no ass in my life. That's on god, yo!" I was ready for her to come with the shits so I could set her little ass straight, but she kept quiet and that confused me. "Yo, you can go get Wright or what the fuck ever you want, but I ain't about to have nobody accusing me of shit I wasn't charged with. Matter of fact, go get him. 'Cause if you think you gonna stand here and bring up shit you 'on't know nothing about, I rather take it up with ya man."

Calmly, she began walking over to me. "Oh, you'll see him soon."

Huhn?

Her voice wasn't raised, neither did she appear offended. That wasn't the worst tone I'd ever taken with a female, but it was supposed to sting. For Parker, it didn't seem to faze her one bit. I was so wound up I didn't realize she was holding two plates until she sat one down in front of me.

"Eat first. I would offer a *Snickers* bar, but I don't have any around."

Eat? I didn't come to eat. Was this a set up? My instincts kicked in and I began to think about the worst outcome.

I came here unannounced. What would Wright's reaction be if he found me in here, eating from his girl? The nigga was old—older than my pops, maybe. I could beat his ass.

Damn!

I mentally kicked myself. I should have brought Fats. I didn't because this was supposed to be a quick, in and out mission. She invited me in and was now serving me her man's food, but I'd be damned if my stomach didn't growl the moment my eyes dropped and saw the glazed salmon, sautéed spinach, and quinoa. The quinoa had something green and leafy in it with cranberries. What the hell did she know about clean eating?

Then it dawned on me.

"Ya man eat?" My tone laced with sarcasm.

Her head came up from praying and she looked across the table at me. "He eats first. Every day."

She started digging in her plate. It wasn't enough food for me but after I let go of the quick thought of her poisoning me, I thought, "*fuck it*" and started eating my damn self.

"So what else did you hear about me?" she asked, eyes on her plate.

I waited until I swallowed the food in my mouth. "You was a *League* cheerleader. That's how Wright scooped you up."

"Ahhh." She nodded. "*That's* true."

"And what I say so far ain't?"

"You haven't said much to explain why you're here."

Again, I had no words.

Why was I here *now*?

Then I decided to do what I did best: keep it one hundred.

"I came to make sure we was cool and, if I needed, to make sure you was good with Wright. But now..." I stuffed my mouth with fish that melted in my damn mouth.

"But now you want to judge me the way I refused to judge you when I heard about your undergraduate indiscretions."

Undergraduate...

I only heard that word in college. It was one of those terms educated snobs used to distinguish their accomplishments. *What she know about it?*

"Look, I 'on't know what you done read online, but you shouldn't waste your time with that. I'mma good dude, making an honest living, acting my age. I'm actually considered exotic where I come from...a damn prodigy considering the statistics of my success. I'm sure you didn't *hear* that."

Even though her face was down, her mouth balled as though she didn't believe me.

"I ain't even gonna go there." I scoffed. "No need to explain an environment you 'on't know shit about."

Parker's head finally lifted, her face was blank. It was a "nigga, please" expression; I knew it. "I'm from Waterbury, Connecticut. I wouldn't need a community briefing to understand your hood."

"Word?"

She gave a single nod. "Plus, the growing up in poor, urban USA sob story doesn't justify your recent actions. I heard about your declaration on the practice field earlier today about..." She tapped her chin, pretending to think about her next words. "Running through lots of 'bitches' in a week. That doesn't sound like the works of a prodigy to me. Maybe a hood one, but hey... You don't deny your roots. Right?"

She'd heard about that slip up in front of Eli. *Damn, this team really is small!*

She was trying to play me, so I had to switch it up on her. I took a few seconds to work on my plate while I considered my next words. I peeped an open laptop at the far end of the table against the wall. A data spreadsheet was up, fields filled with numbers.

Excel...

"Look..." I took a deep breath. "A few days ago I saw a beautiful female at a party—a party I didn't *really* go to for social reasons; I went for political ones. My young, ripe eyes saw something that appealed to them and I reacted instead of thinking. And now I'm here to own up to my hasty decision."

"Hasty?"

"Yeah." I licked my fingers then used my other hand to push the empty plate away. "I'm guilty. I'm coppin' to it." I shrugged again.

Wish the good doctor could hear that.

Parker swallowed hard and too fast with strained eyes, impatiently ready to speak. "Guilty of what?" she spat.

"It's obvious I didn't ask the proper questions. That led to me baggin' an old player's jawn. He's a fellow *King*. It goes against the code of ethics."

"You view me as someone's jawn? And is that what you think of this? *That's* what you're guilty of?"

I ain't say bitch! What the fuck?

This etiquette thing was getting old and real fast. I dropped my face and pinched the bone between my eyes. "You're that man's fiancée. You live with him. He takes care of you. What did I say wrong?"

"A lot because you don't know me."

My head flew up. "I know you showed to his boy's crib for a social and slipped out on the low for a private after party."

"Just like I *know* you knocked that kid out after a game in college, broke his jaw, and walked off with his girl."

My face went tight as my head dropped again. The visual she just gave was crazy false. That wasn't what happened. *I didn't leave with that broad.* After the ambulance picked him up, she stayed behind while I gave my side of the story to the cops. Then she crept in the theater me and my boys ended up in that night and gave me neck for the first quarter of the movie. I had no idea that was his girl until the next day.

"Look," I shook my head, stretching my lids. "I ain't come here for all this. I just wanted to make sure everything is good between us. Me, you, and Wright."

She stood from the table, grabbing our plates. "Time for you to see the man of the house," she hummed sarcastically. "Come on."

She lay the plates on the counter next to the sink and headed for the hall. Confused, again, I followed her. We walked toward the front of the house, passing the entrance. The small sitting room we marched past was dark and empty.

Where the fuck we going?

When I decided I wouldn't go up or down any stairs because I drove here tonight without Fats like an idiot, we stopped at a set of double French interior, glass panel doors. She opened both wide then turned to me. Then she waved to gesture behind her. I stepped closer and it wasn't long before I heard him, then I smelled him. Finally, I saw him.

Jimmy Wright's...half dead?

A scrawny body laid in a hospital bed with mad tubes running in and out of him, the biggest was to his throat. It ran into a brace wrapped around his neck. His eyes were closed and the systematic chirps of the machines he was hooked up to beeped to a beat that, that quickly became rhythmic. The room was cold and smelled stale like a damn hospital.

What the fuck, man?

Why was she showing me this? Did my pops know he was sick like this? Did Underwood know? Henderson? Eli Richardson?

Then my eyes shot over to Parker, who stood against one of the doors with her hands behind her. There was something new in her eyes. I couldn't decide between anger and arrogance. She was damn sure making a statement with letting me see this man like this.

My eyes rolled back over to the skeleton laying helplessly in the bed. What was up with him? Did he have the package?

Shit!

Did she? And did she give it to me? Was she a carrier? Them motherfuckers were healthy as fuck, tricking the shit out of innocent asses like me!

"It's time for you to leave now." My fucking heart dropped to the floor when I realized Parker was right up on me, close enough not to have to speak much louder than a whisper.

The expression in her eyes now was hard. Protective. No way I could miss that. I backed out of the room and she led me to the front door. Once again, I couldn't find my damn words. But Parker's quick cold mood made me spit out something.

"What the fuck was all that?"

I was out the door, on the front porch when she smiled for the first time tonight, but slickly. "Me teaching you not to believe everything you hear. You don't know me, Rut. Your sources don't either."

When I thought she'd explain her point, the door was slammed in my damn face.

RUT

"It's bothering you."

"No. It's not."

"I believe it is, Amare."

I sat up from the white chaise and looked at her. "We ain't about to make a big deal out of nothing just because I'm giving you something to talk about."

She smiled the "*I know I'm fucking with you*" smile. Then she took a fake deep breath, trying to hide the cocky ass smirk.

"I applaud you on taking the initiative and going to see her. You got ahead of the situation. It showed accountability and leadership." She ended it with a nod.

A nod that confused me. Was she fucking with me? I couldn't decide and didn't like it. Therapist or not, ain't nobody smart enough to play me. I laid back down.

"I've been trying to find out what he's sick with. At first I thought maybe he had the shit."

"What's that?"

I rolled my eyes toward the ceiling. "AIDS."

"Oh."

"But when I was in the gym today, I asked around. Nobody could give me a complete answer, but I gotta bunch of letters that weren't HIV or AIDS."

My mind began to drift with all the things I'd heard from two assistant coaches and a trainer who had been in the *Kings'* camp for years. I knew not to ask Brooks. My pride wouldn't let me no ways.

"Do you care?" That question snapped me from my thoughts.

"About what?"

"About this woman, her fiancé? Do you care about what's going on with them?"

My face went hard and head pushed back into the cushion of the chaise. "Why the fuck would I care about a nigga and his girl? I couldn't give a flying shit."

"Then why, of all topics you choose to finally share with me since beginning this journey a month ago, would it be of this young woman?"

The muscles in my face hadn't smoothed when I shot back, "Because it relates to why I'm here in the first place. This job. This chick is connected to my boss. Her man is his mans. I gotta make sure this shit don't give the head bosses more of a reason to sleep on me. I fucked up and banged the wrong broad. The last thing I need is for these fucks to think I can't control my dick. Or worse."

"What's worse?"

"That I got issues with women. I heard Eli still be on that bullshit with me and that thot in college."

"Then why don't you change the narrative?" My head whipped to her and found her staring at me with one brow in the damn air.

"I'm a man with pride, miss. Ain't no way I'm going to my boss with my nuts in my hands, claiming to be a sucker. I ain't no pussy."

"I doubt you are. I'm suggesting you start on a micro level and stay ahead of this situation. Use *this* woman as an opportunity to get to know a woman. Understand her needs, position under her circumstances, and who she really is. Try your determined theory of women having ulterior motives out on this one."

"Maaaaan..." I hummed, not with the shits. "I 'on't know. I really don't care to be proven wrong. I accept females for being females. All I ask is for them to accept me for being the man I am when I decide to dodge all their bullshit."

"And if you're wrong?" She lay her tablet on the coffee table.

"Wrong? That ain't possible."

"But if you are? You said she cares for an invalid at her tender age. And one who apparently abused her. That alone is a selfless act of a woman."

He did. My trainer told me he saw the pictures. I Googled Wright's name with the word assault and found gory pictures of Parker's beautiful face unrecognizable. It was crazy.

"But there's more to it."

"How do you know?"

"Because there's gotta be. Females stay with the shits. Maybe she's in his will…got her living off a few stacks he left her before he went down." I groaned, rubbing my eyes. "I 'on't know."

"And you won't unless you talk to her."

"And say what?"

Her hands flipped upward from her tiny wrists. "'*Hi. I'm not the guy you thought I was and I want to give you an opportunity to prove you're not the type of woman I think you are.*'" When I looked at her like she was a fucking mad woman, she kept going. "You know," she sat up, crossing her legs and placing her elbow on her propped knee before laying her chin on her palm. "I believe your perception of women is limited to the ones you've grown up with and others you chose to have in your life. You attract what you are. You attract only what you know appeals to you."

"What that mean?"

"It means you're comfortable with your position on women because, at some point, you developed an armor to that type of energy. You've learned how to identify it and created a buffer to repel a specific class of women. This group of women share unfavorable traits you've come to believe is general for all. I can't guarantee this woman is different from that toxic group, but I have to say you not dismissing her could be an opportunity to learn something different."

"And if I don't?"

"Then I could, at least, include in my evaluation notes shared with your boss you've taken steps toward personal development, corrective actions, and measures toward creating and contributing to a genial environment in the *Kings'* family…" Her shoulders rose and dropped. "Some lengthy verbiage like that."

I lay back on the couch, thinking about it.

"It ain't gone change how I feel about females in general." I wanted to make that clear. But there was also an upside to it. "It could prove my point about them all."

"You'll never know unless you get to know her more. And it'll be a deliverable in terms of your participation in these sessions. Help me earn my pay."

My head swung over to her and she winked. It made me wonder how much head doctors earned. Did she see other *Kings* players?

It didn't matter. I had to do this. If it was a game I'd play to get past this mandatory therapy shit, then I'd play to win. I always did.

"I'm game," I more or less mumbled.

"That delights me." Her tone didn't reflect it though. "One last thing..."

"Shoot."

"No sex."

My head swung over to look at her again. Then I sat up, placing my feet on the floor. Was she fucking crazy? Had to be!

She nodded, confirming what I thought I heard. "That's right. No sex."

"Doc, ain't shit celibate about me and if you think you gonna impose that on my personal life—"

"With her." She made clear without raising her voice. "Your views on women are skewed, too. You only deal with a specific type. You admitted earlier to encountering them online on your social media's direct messages, at the club, and most recently, in the strip club. You target the same type of women you despise: those who are attracted to your popularity. You understand in advance they'd be game for whatever usage you have for them, which is always sex. When you get to know someone, it's a less complicated process when you do it without that intricate element."

She was talking too much now, using too many damn words. At the end of the day, it didn't matter.

"I'm good. Parker's cute...sexy and all that, but I come across bangers every day. She's no unicorn."

Besides, I've already had her.

June 2018

Parker

When I pulled back the door and recognized the uninvited guest, I could feel my face fall. I'd thought last night would be the last time I'd see him here.

Rut didn't speak for a while. His strange regard bounced between my face and the ground he stood on. His nostrils were flared and mouth twisted. Clearly, he was thinking. And hard.

After an impatient twenty seconds or so of waiting, I finally prompted him.

"Are we going to make this thing weird?"

He didn't take the bait right away.

"It just don't make no sense to me."

"What?"

His eyes fixed in the direction of Jimmy's room, though he couldn't see inside from where he stood. I caught on to the subject matter but not necessarily the details of his confusion.

I rolled my eyes and exhaled. "It's been a long day of experimenting with new scents and textures, cleaning a tracheostomy tube, and it took all eleven of my working brains cells to repair a tube for suctioning phlegm after it malfunctioned." My head shook softly, apologetically. "I'm tired and hungry. You're going to have to come in while I finish dinner if you want a coherent explanation on anything from me."

I turned to go back into the kitchen where I was just cutting up the last vegetable for my salad. Unable to explain why I knew he'd be on my heels, I was confident he was. I also couldn't wrap my brain around my comfortable level in letting him into the house. But tonight, I was too tired to deduce why.

I swallowed the last of my unsweetened iced tea with a single slice of fresh lemon and exhaled. My head reared and palms went to my belly for a rub before they rose to my face for a full wipe. I was unbelievably drained.

Sitting up, my attention went across the table to where Rut was clearing his second bowl.

"Good?"

I made a Greek salad with grilled shrimp. It was my second time making this particular recipe and this one was better than the last. Rut didn't meet my eyes when he grumbled something resembling yes. I checked the time on the microwave, knowing I'd have to change Jimmy's urinal before hitting the sack. I also knew I'd have to take out something to cook for dinner tomorrow.

Rut's fork finally dropped in his empty bowl.

Taking a deep breath, I asked, "Okay. So what can I do to clear up your confusion?"

"Huhn?" His thick brows met in bewilderment.

"When I opened the door, you mentioned something not making sense..." I prompted again.

I'd basically silenced Rut the moment we stepped into the kitchen when I began busying myself with cutting the last of the cucumber, plating the salads, and tossing jumbo shrimp on top. Though on my days off like today, I lived in complete silence from not having anyone around other than a muted Jimmy, tonight I was especially bushed and needed the sustenance before taking on a guy like Rut. I was honestly surprised to see him again.

His phone went off *again*. It had been blowing up since he got here. At some point earlier, he silenced the ring tone, but it continued to vibrate. This time, he dismissed it with a push of a button. Then he sat back with his eyes to his lap—*thinking heavily again*.

"I don't get how a woman your age is taking care of a man this sick," he finally revealed his thoughts. "I mean... I know he takin' care of you and got you straight, paper-wise, but..." He hesitated. Then his head shook in frustration it seemed. "I don't get why you doing all this. How much money is worth...this?" One hand flipped in the air.

My lips squeezed together as I considered his curiosity. "I don't get paid to take care of Jimmy."

Rut's head jerked back as though the concept was incredible. "You expect me to believe Wright ain't got you in his will? Put you on a monthly payroll while he's down? I heard he got some bread from the big settlement."

I nodded. "Jimmy was awarded a decent settlement from the *League*'s concussion lawsuit. He was diagnosed with ALS—"

"What's that?"

"Lou Gehrig's disease. It's also called amyotrophic lateral sclerosis or ALS."

"Oh. That's what them people was dumping ice water on their heads for on social media a while back?" It was a sincere correlation on his behalf.

"Yes, but I'm not sure they were all actually donating. But yeah, Jimmy was diagnosed less than a year before the 2014 ruling. It so happened that ALS was assigned one of the highest payouts. He was lucky with the timing of it all, but I wasn't."

"Why you say that?"

"Because, like you said, I was young. Jimmy and I had just gotten engaged and then a shit storm of drama hit us and never stopped."

"How long y'all been together?"

I was curious about his concern. I didn't know Rut, but he didn't strike me as a guy who extended himself past his own issues or desires. Just yesterday, I was another "bitch he fucked" and now he seemed to be chewing on every word I gave him.

I took a deep breath, fortifying myself to go back in time. As I did, my spine curled and chest caved. "I met Jimmy in 2013, months before his diagnosis. Of course, I had no idea of his health—*he had no idea either*. I was twenty-two and just out of college. I'd just started cheering in the *League* for the *Giants*."

"How did you meet?"

"At an event he, Eli Richardson, and few of their friends attended in New York. He asked where I was from, and we made a connection there. Within twenty minutes, he arranged for a private table away from the crowd." I shrugged. "We talked about how I made it down to New York City. I was honest in telling him why." *I had mommy issues and was rebellious.* "He came with good game, asking about my dreams. Because he was a retired player, I was comfortable telling him what my interests were. The cheering thing didn't inspire me. It was just fun...something to escape to after getting a degree I'd never use. The next morning he called saying he was leaving for Connecticut and would like to see me again. A month later, I was here."

"When y'all get engaged?" Rut's tone was suspicious.

It made me wonder if he'd known. Had he heard the stories of that one ugly night that caused me to hit rock bottom?

I took another dramatic breath, unable to look at him, but my words came easy after all these years. "We were never really engaged. Jimmy never asked me to marry him. He told me he wanted to be with me forever and gave me the tool in which he thought would make it happen."

"What was that?"

"A huge rock."

His forehead wrinkled. "And you wasn't happy he bagged you?"

Anger flashed in my chest. "I was bagged all right. But what real woman wants to be bagged?"

His head snapped back and face tightened. "What chick don't?"

I sat up, placing my elbows on the table as I neared him. "Not this woman. I'm perfectly capable of caring and providing for myself." My next words cut at my core. "I'm no damsel in distress. I come from a strong lineage of women who made things happen for themselves."

"But you came to live with him. Took the ring. You still here."

"Because I have commitment issues." His face fell. I knew that went over his head. "I committed back then to the wrong person. Jimmy. And he was an ineligible receiver of...*me*. I was young, rebellious, and full of untamed energy. Instead of focusing on me, I allowed him to play director in my life."

"And what's wrong with that? He's a man."

"There was no one playing producer." That zonked him. "Every human being is born with a director's and producer's gene. Either you're a director calling the shots or you're a producer bringing things to life. It's when you marry that you decide which role you'll serve in that union. When Jimmy directed my world, he told me where to live, what my role would be in his life, and who my social circle would be. I had no idea how to produce. I didn't think about those passions and interests I shared with him that first night we met. To be honest,"—I shrugged with my one shoulder and lips—"I don't think he really cared."

"Cared about what?"

"Cared about who I was. He's twenty-three years older than me. All Jimmy wanted was to find a piece to fit into his world. He had no concern about helping me develop my own." The factor of time still played in the back of my head. I had to close this conversation. "To address your assumption of my compensation of his care, unless you consider me staying here rent free sufficient payment, there is no compensation. I pay for my food and most of the utilities."

"Why?"

"Because it's what's needed around here and what I can afford."

"What about Jimmy? I heard he had a trucking business after the *League*. He gotta be sitting on something after that settlement, too."

I snorted. Like hard. It was so loud and abrupt I covered my mouth.

"Jimmy's condition is draining his finances. That settlement money went to lawyers it cost to get it, loans needed to sustain his quality of life those first few years of his diagnosis when he could speak and clean himself, and to close out his trucking business that was failing."

"You mean to tell me 'The Boulder' is broke?"

I flinched at that assessment. It was none of his business what condition Jimmy's financial portfolio was in.

"My point is, I'm not in *Neiman Marcus* charging up his card. I may not earn the king's ransom, but with budgeting, I make sure those machines stay beeping in there, the place has a regulated temperature, and I eat. Other than that, Jimmy's estate takes care of him."

Silence fell over the room for a while. It gave me time to reflect on this journey. I realized how long it had been since the last time I'd spoken to my mother. Mother's Day had passed and I needed to decide if I'd still send her something. I missed the holiday, struggling with what to get her. Would she like what I'd send? Life had been lived on a treadmill for me it seemed. Those things that seemed unbearable and stifling had faded to not more than minor nuances, differences I could live with.

Conscientiousness of time flashed again. My eyes rolled over to Rut sitting across the table, sporting a strange but perceptible expression.

"Did I address what didn't make sense?"

He shrugged with his eyebrows and his head shook softly as he snorted. Then his eyes rose to align with mine, reminding me of how handsome he was. I'd been too caught off guard by his presence here and extremely tuckered tonight to appreciate what caused me to disappear into the night with him last weekend. Not that it mattered. What happened then, happened then. I had no room for another man in my life.

"So you mean he ain't put you in his will or nothing?" Rut's face was tight with deep confusion.

It was so palpable it was childlike.

My eyes closed in a combination of shock and defeat. My jaw fell, too. I didn't have the energy to do this with him.

"Anybody ever tell you you're an asshole?"

"It's hyphenated in my name," he admitted as one big palm patted the air. "but I swear that ain't what this is all about."

I shook my head and closed eyes heavy from exhaustion. "Doesn't matter no ways. It's been a long day and I have more to do before I hit the sack."

The moment my subtle dismissal registered to him, it was clear from the way his expression fell. Rut dropped his head, conceding. I didn't want to be rude, but here was where my patience had depleted for a complete stranger.

I scooted my chair back from the table. "Like I said, I've got so much to do. I'll walk you out and after I need to remember to take something out of the freezer for dinner tomorrow."

Per usual, Rut was on my heels. He didn't speak all the way to the door. When his big frame stepped outside, his countenance was still ruminative.

I was surprised when he turned back to me. "You cook every day?"

"No. I try to shoot for three days a week. But for the second night in a row, I've had unexpected company with an appetite twice the size of my own."

"Oh. My bad." He reached for his back pocket.

"Good night, Rut." My cheeks managed to lift before I closed the door.

chapter six

SHE OPENED THE DOOR AND, LIKE A drama queen, dropped her head.

"You know, they say when you feed a dog he'll keep coming back day after day."

She was sexy as shit in a skirt hugging her hips, a blouse opening just above her cleavage, and pantyhose without shoes. It was too bad she was now neutralized to me.

But I couldn't help myself.

My cheeks stretched horizontally across my face. "I think the saying goes for strays. A stray dog roams from home to home." I shook my head while I looked her dead in the eye. "Ain't shit domesticated about me, sweet cakes."

"Then why are you back for the third day in a row?" Her eyes dropped to my arms. "And with food?"

"I was hoping to catch you before you started cooking again. Didn't want you to waste your time."

"Why?" With a tight face and her head shaking back and forth, she asked, "Why are you bringing me food?"

"So you don't keep using yours on me. You fed me twice. Thought it was fair to return the favor."

She stepped closer into the door frame and narrowed her beautiful brown eyes. "Why? In case I didn't tell you last night and the night before, it ain't that type of party."

"Oh..." I almost wanted to laugh when I caught her drift. She thought I wanted to fuck. "Trust me, Ms. Parker, if I want ass I know plenty of other addresses I could pull up to."

"Then again, why are you here?"

"Because..." I thought for a minute. "Wright's got kids. Why ain't they helping out? You ain't mention them."

Her head dropped to the side. "You using my personal misfortunes for your entertainment or something?"

My eyes blew the hell up. "No! On god, I ain't. It's just..." I shifted the pizza box in my arm then took a deep breath. "I talked to my therapist about you."

Her chin dropped toward her chest this time. "Your therapist?"

"Yeah, but I ain't crazy or no shit like that. A black man is the most misunderstood species in America, even to other so-called black men trying to keep them down—" When I caught the anger sprouting in my chest, I mentally shook it off. "My point is she challenged me to get to know you...try to understand you."

"*Me*? Why?"

"Because..." I didn't want to go there. "It's all related to my draft. My employment. Me having to see her, my run in with you...her thinking I go too hard on females. It's all related—*in her opinion*," I wanted to make clear.

"So now I'm a part of your therapy?"

I smirked. It was slick but deserved. "Let's just call it an experiment."

Her eyes fell to the food again then she opened the door wider and waved me in.

When she closed it behind me, her arm swung toward the kitchen. "You can set it up in there. It's early and I worked at the front office today. The nurse just left but I need to take care of few things with Jimmy. I'll be a minute."

I nodded, understanding it was more than an hour earlier than I showed the previous two nights. When I took off for the kitchen, I thought about the shit I had to move around on my schedule to be here this afternoon. In the kitchen, I lay the box on the counter near the stove and put the bagged groceries on the table. She said she'd be a while so I unpacked most of the items, putting some things in the fridge and others in the freezer. As I pulled out a chair, my phone pinged.

Lifting it from my pocket, I sighed at the name. I swear to god I was good with the challenge but what I didn't like was paper thin people around me. Nobody answered when I asked how long this would last.

I tapped to accept the FaceTime.

Her alabaster skin appeared on my screen. She sat at a table with a pool serving as the most picturesque sunny Cal background. I couldn't tell if it was her crib, her sister's or mom duke's. I didn't care to figure it out but something about her appearance today did catch my attention. Today her puffy lips were a light brown, outlined beyond the natural lining of them, but she made the look work for her. Long dark lashes sprouted around her lids and I spotted a new mole on her cheek.

"Yeah, shawtie?" I sang dryly.

Her shoulders lifted and eyes squinted. "My Rutty-Putty," she squeaked in the baby voice she used from time to time. It never sat right with me.

"I see your mole's moved."

Emily's dreamy expression went south.

I was being an ass and I knew it, but I couldn't help it most times.

She flashed her teeth, obviously embarrassed. "My new guy suggested I move it a few weeks ago. I finally okayed it." Then she pouted. "You no likey?" That's when the baby voice sounded again.

I chuckled. "You good, shawtie. What's real out there?" I wanted to hurry this call along.

"Oh." She seemed to have awakened. "I haven't heard from you since Saturday." Those tanned shoulders rose again. "Just wanted to know if I'll see you in a few days."

"We're still on. I think my flight leaves Friday night."

"Yaaaaay!" she cheered but not too loud. When I didn't know

how to respond, I could tell it made her feel awkward. "Well..." she pushed. "What're you up to?"

My eyes circled the spotless but plain kitchen. "Just chillin' at a friend's."

"Yeah? Where?"

Emily wasn't being territorial or particularly nosy with that question. She was trying to make basic conversation. I knew the game and understood what we were supposed to do. And don't get me wrong, I liked ol' girl. She was crazy cool and down for whatever, but I couldn't put my finger on what was missing the mark for me.

My eyes brushed from left to right again. "*Kings'* circle. That's all." That reminded me. "I need to go. Don't wanna be rude. I'll hit you tonight when I get in. Don't think I forgot you never told me where that birthmark is." I winked.

A stroke of red grew from her neck to her cheeks like a rash. I enjoyed having that effect on chicks.

"Okay, Rut." She puckered her lips. "I'll be waiting for you."

With a fake chuckle, I ended the call with, "Easy style" and tapped to dead the line.

I sat back, pushing my arms in the air and my legs out in front of me as I stretched. My life was full...blessed, but this *League* business came with a lot more backroads than I cared to take.

My hands drummed the table as I waited. The clock ticked on. I wondered what exactly was she doing in there. I'd never been the patient type of guy. Shit, I'd never waited on a female for nothing. This was different for me but not hard. I had no idea what kept me glued to my seat in anticipation, but it was real. I checked all my social media accounts, responded to two emails, and about six text messages. Parker still hadn't come back. When I checked the time, I'd been waiting for twenty-two minutes. Then my phone rang, ripping me from my curiosity.

I took a deep breath. "Yeah, ma?"

"Rut, I told you I needed the money for the fridge!"

I scratched my head. "I took care of it for you."

"How? When?"

"I paid Leon an' them. Sent them the money last night."

She pulled in a heavy breath. "Rut, how the fuck you pay them?"

"*PayPal*. Like I said, I sent it last night, ma."

"What the fuck is a *PayPal* and since when do we use it to treat our mothers like fuckin' babies?"

I rolled my eyes, stretching my legs out. "Nobody's treating you like a damn baby. You told me you needed the fridge fixed and who was gonna do it, so I made it happen. What's wrong with me taking care of it?"

I knew what was wrong. She wanted the cash.

"How the fuck—" I cringed then looked around me. "—you even know how much to pay?"

"You told me it was three-fifty, so I was goodie," I tried to argue, avoiding the truth we both knew, which was the repair was only one hundred seventy-five dollars.

But I didn't get mad at my mother for being my mother. She always ran game like this, trying to squeeze cash out of me.

After a long pause, she sucked her teeth. "That's fucked up, Rutledge. You always sonnin' me."

"Girl, ain't nobody sonnin' you," I tried with a playful tone. "You know I said we gotta move different now. I may be signed, but the money ain't here this year. We're basically on the same level we was before I got picked up." I had to make my finances seem tighter than they were. And while I wasn't broke, I couldn't give her the impression we'd made it. There was still so much more bread to get. "Just be easy. I got you. The fridge'll be ready for your lil' bingo party."

I knew that was a big part of her social life. She invited her crazy ass circle of friends, and they'd play and cuss each other the hell out as they got drunk. She'd smoke her cigarettes, drink her Henny, and brag about how bomb her life is because her son was on the come up. I wasn't mad at her. She deserved whatever good life she was living but had no clue of what it cost me to provide it.

"Any-damn-way," she dragged out, and I could imagine her rolling her eyes. "you need to call Kim. She been on my last damn nerve, calling me about you."

"What about me?"

"How you ain't calling her like you used to since you been up there!"

"I been working!" I served her the same energy she gave me. "What the fuck she think I'm doing? Up here holding my sacs, waiting for the season to start?"

"I 'on't fuckin' know. All I do know is she a damn Hawkins and them Hawkins can be spiteful as hell. I told you I went to school with her aunts and uncle. Them mufuckas be on their shit. Just call the girl once in a while!"

"I do," I answered honestly. "I called her last week. She ain't even answer. Ain't nobody gone be sweatin' her. She ain't my girl." That quickly, I was mad as fuck.

"Just do what I tell you to do, Rutledge!"

I twisted the base of my palms into my eyes, rubbing away the stress these "women" caused in my life.

"I gotchu, ma."

"Okay," she snapped. "I gotta go. Mommy want me to take her to get some crabs."

"A'ight. Y'all be safe."

"Bye, baby." Her pitch wasn't as soft as it could be, but I understood it was because she didn't get what she wanted.

Money....

I took a long breath, tossing my phone on the table as gently as I could.

"Rutledge?" Her soft voice had my damn belly jumping. When my head shot up, she was gliding past me in sweat shorts, a black tank top, and slippers. She never looked my way when she asked, "Is that one of your many nicknames?"

Dazed for no reason, I mumbled, "Nah. I ain't really big on nicknames."

She turned to me with chary eyes. "You expect me to believe your momma named you Rut?"

A deep chuckle bubbled from my belly. "Nah. But she did name me Rutledge. Took me a few years to grow into it, but I made it do what it do."

That's when she turned her whole body to face me. "Your real name is Rutledge?"

I scoffed, unoffended yet amused. "Hell yeah!"

"Rutledge?"

"Yeah." I gave a firm nod. "Rutledge Kadar Amare. The one and only."

At first she was quiet, obviously thinking as she went back to the stove and slid the pizza onto a metal tray then into the oven.

She walked to the other side of the table. "Kadar and Amare sound like Arabic names…" She left it open for discussion.

"Kadar is. It's got a few meanings: strength, fate, destiny, predestination, to have power, to be master—a whole bunch of shit." I scratched the tip of my nose. "I forgot about 'to be capable.' My pops wanted me purposeful. And Amare is righteous, his last name."

"Righteous?"

"Five Percent Nation." I gave another strong nod then pulled up my left sleeve to show her the inked universal flag. "The Nation of Gods and Earths. But Amare is African. It means possesses great strength."

"Is that his legal name?"

I shook my head, slightly embarrassed by that fact. "He made sure it was mine, though. Him and mom dukes fought over the name. He wanted all my names to reflect destiny and purpose, but she wanted tradition. He fought her all the way till the delivery date and loss." I shrugged. "He thinks he lost. I always thought he came out on top."

"Yeah." She smiled. "He got two out of three."

"Yup."

"Where did Rutledge come from?"

"My grandfather. His pops, too. There's a bunch of Rutledges in my family. I guess my moms thought the first name was stronger than the last."

She didn't speak, just stared at me. It was strange but not uncomfortable for a man like me. It did make me wonder what she was thinking.

"Spit it." I exhaled, sitting back in my chair.

"Nothing!" She kind of giggled, kind of blew me off.

"Nah. I can see it dancing in your eyes. You're thinking and a lil' too hard." Just like she did Saturday night before hopping in the truck.

"It's just..." I could tell her restless legs kicked underneath the table as she repositioned herself in her seat. "I think..." Her head leaned to the side, eyes narrowed, and lips pushed together hard. "Don't they believe the being of God isn't supernatural, but rather a component found in every black man?"

I nodded. "It's true."

"It's also their belief black women don't have the god component in them and are considered subordinates but still hold a higher standing than white people."

I nodded again, agreeing.

"So..." Her head shook. "You find many women aligned in that belief?"

That one threw me. I didn't understand her question.

"Many? There're lots of females in the Nation."

"But any of the ones you pursue?"

My brows shot up when I thought I understood. "I honestly don't know. I don't ask," was the honest to god truth.

Then I caught a faint smile in her eyes that wasn't matched on her face. "Well, I'm sure Emily Erceg wouldn't have the strongest position on it, but what about other girlfriends from the past?"

"Emily ain't my girl, for one. And two, the one girl I used to have ain't active in the organization like her pops is, but she's righteous."

"And okay with being subservient to you and every other 'woke' black man?" She rolled her eyes then stood from the table.

I wasn't going to be baited into a debate about my beliefs, especially not by a corny ass Christian. They may outnumber most groups, but they were dumb as hell for accepting a white savior taught to them by slave masters.

"Let me guess..." I watched her grab a pitcher from the fridge then check on the pizza. "Your grandma, who your childhood pastor would never let step foot on the pulpit, wouldn't approve of men being closer to god than women?"

"My grandmother would burn a pulpit, God rest her soul. But it wouldn't matter what she thought, I could never believe women are inferior to men. We women are equally built and oftentimes lead in intellectual and emotional development, scientifically speaking."

I would have responded but my attention was fastened to her ass as she bent at the waist to pull the pizza out of the oven. That reminded of why I couldn't resist the doctor's challenge.

"Do Wright's kids live in the neighborhood?"

She went for the cabinet to grab plates. "No. The closest one lives about twenty-five minutes away and the furthest is in New York City."

"They come through a lot to see him?"

"The last time Junior was here was Christmas. And his daughter, Sherry..." She froze to think about it. "Maybe the first week of January. I haven't seen Junior's twin since just before Thanksgiving when he was visiting a friend in the area." She shrugged and began fixing our plates.

This started feeling familiar. It was the third day in a row I sat in this same seat and watched her do this very thing.

"So who helps you?"

With her back to me, she shrugged. "We've been blessed with flexible nursing care. It's been a battle with the insurance company, but they do cover in-home care by a licensed nurse for up to ten hours a day. They only allow about forty hours a week, though."

"How do you work then?"

"I only work the front office three days a week. I'm a floater."

"What's that?" I asked as she sat my plate in front of me.

"I'm basically assigned wherever help is needed on the days I work." While going for another cabinet door, she asked, "Tea or water?"

"Don't matter." I stood for the sink to wash my hands.

After pouring us both tea, she sat down with her food. I joined her soon after and watched her pray in silence. Out of respect, I waited until she was done to start.

"Mmmmmmm!" Her eyes went wild and looked sincerely appreciative. "Shrimp pizza."

"Shrimp scampi," I made clear.

I watched her take her first bite. "Mmmmm…" she moaned again and I had to force myself to start even though I wanted to know what she thought of it. She licked her thumb with her eyes toward the ceiling. "Fresh parsley and cherry tomatoes."

I don't know why my dumb ass smiled as I nodded.

"It's my favorite pizza. Can't have it when I'm training. I figured I'd treat you to my goodies for once."

Her eyes blew the hell up. I guessed that was a bad joke; one with reaching arms.

"Where's it from?" Her blinking eyes were to her plate.

"*DiFillippo's.*"

"Sounds familiar. One around here?"

"I don't think they have one in Connecticut yet."

With closed lips, her jaw dropped again. I was beginning to get used to that expression from her.

"Where did this food come from?"

"I had my peoples bring it up from New York City about an hour ago."

"You ordered take out from New York City?"

I had to laugh, but it was a nervous one. "They 'on't exactly make this for takeout. They ain't that type of spot, really."

Her eyes bounced around as her cheeks were packed with food. She was processing what I'd said, but I wanted to get off the subject. It was really no big deal. I figured it was the least I could do.

"I'm glad you like it."

It looked as though she was frowning when she chirped, "I do. A lot. Thank you."

"Ain't nothing." I cleared my throat. "Don't one of his sons work for the *Kings*?"

"Whose?"

"Wright's."

"Oh!" Parker shook off whatever haze she was in then reached for her glass and took a long sip. "Junior—well, James. Yes."

"And he don't help out?"

She shook her head and took another bite. As she chewed, I kept eating.

"Help out? I wouldn't call it that. He's over Jimmy's estate and makes sure his bills are paid, and I guess, I'm still here taking care of him." She shrugged and rolled her eyes.

That told me there was beef. Even though I still struggled to find how she was coming up off this, I didn't think it was cool for me to push the idea.

We finished eating without much more talking. I couldn't find the words to get the information—or confirmation—I needed about her benefitting in some way from doing all of this. But eventually, I had to go. There was a conference call I had to jump on with my partner, Jeremy. One he made sure I understood I couldn't get out of.

When she walked me to the door, I stepped out and turned to her.

"You 'on't seem as cranky as last night." I didn't know why I had to share that observation with her, but it felt easy to.

She chuckled. "That's because I worked the front office today. Believe it or not, my most exhausting days are the ones I'm here with him all day. There's always something to do."

I nodded, mind still going. Then something hit me.

"Three days a week at ten hours a day don't take up that forty-hour allowance a week the insurance company allows."

The smile she gave was...cute. It was shy and soft as her eyes rolled playfully and she could hardly look me in the face.

"I have a few on reserve. Let's say I'm banking them."

"For what?"

She shrugged, still beaming. "I can't really say why. I mean, I could, but it would sound silly."

After a few beats, I encouraged her. "Try me."

Her shoulders lifted again, attention somewhere across the street. "For when I get a life, I guess."

"Like what? A man?"

That's when Parker's eyes were on me again, her glow dimmed. "Thanks for the fancy pizza, Rutledge Kadar Amare."

Yeah. She was being a hard ass again, but her tone was gentle and sweet, and eyes soft as she closed the door.

Parker

"Like what?" My eyes brushed over Jimmy's frail body. He'd had a rough day and was tired. "An infection?"

Her head swung to the side, unimpressed with my guess. "Possibly granulation tissue, which is the developments of bumps. Those would have to be surgically removed before decannulation."

"But he hasn't been on the tracheostomy tube all that long." I didn't understand.

She swung her hand dismissively but with tact. "We don't know yet, Parker. When you take him to the doctor in the morning, we'll know more." Nurse Jackie finished packing up her stethoscope and placed it into her bag. Her shift had come to an end. "You're doing a great job with keeping the area clean and dry. If I didn't know that piece, I'd be panicking. It may not be an infection at all. Maybe a few simple adjustments need to be made, but we're less than twenty-four hours from learning more." She tried to end it on a sweet smile.

Dry, hot air pushed from my lungs as I glanced back over to Jimmy. I didn't want him to consume my anxious energy.

I swallowed back my butting emotions. "I'll walk you out, Jackie."

Quietly, I led her out of his room, wanting to hurry and return. I needed to make sure he was relaxed. This was the part I hated most about this journey we'd been on. There were too many unknowns and unexpected glitches along the way. I understood ALS was a progressive disease—God, I couldn't sleep nights worrying about what I'd wake up to—but the small nuances of new problems, popping up suddenly.

The doorbell rang midway there. Without much thought, I had a confident guess who was on the other side.

"Excuse me," I murmured, getting ahead of her.

When I pulled the door open, my eyes raked up. When they made it to his naturally thick lidded eyes my lungs expanded, taking in more air than I'd intended. Rut was big. Colossal. Oh, so robust. And I happened to know all that mass of muscle was agile too. The sight of him in sweat shorts, a long sleeve shirt, and shower shoes increased my exasperated state, but his presence neither surprised or annoyed me.

"Hey, Rut."

Uneasily, he let out a breath, too. "Whaddup, P?"

I moved back, welcoming him in. "There's leftovers in there. If you could, wash your hands and get it started?"

His head dipped to greet Nurse Jackie then again to confirm my invitation. When Rut strode off for the kitchen, he left a trail of masculine fragrance behind him.

Heavenly...

I turned to finish seeing the nurse out, only she had her eyes glued to Rut's glutes.

"Nurse Jackie?" I extended my arm out the door.

"Oh!" She jumped into moving as she giggled. When outside, she turned to me. "I know who he is. I follow the *Kings'* nation." Her shoulders lifted in merriment and cheeks shaded pink. "I'm so happy for you, Parker."

My face opened in understanding. "Oh, him?" I shook my head. "Oh, no! Just..." I couldn't stop rocking my head side to side. "It's not that type of party: trust me. He's..." I couldn't find the words and realized nothing I said could explain an appropriate picture.

Jackie nodded, face red and cheeks stretched a mile wide from east to west.

"Enjoy your weekend, Nurse Jackie."

"See you Monday!" She tittered shyly, turning to skip down the stairs.

After closing the door, I took a deep breath. My head dropped and I rolled it on the base of my neck to loosen the tension I began feeling there. I could do this. I could do this.

I turned for Jimmy's room and found him dozing.

"Hey there, Boulder." I measured the faux excitement in my voice as I took to the foot of his bed. He used to get a kick out of hearing me refer to him by his field moniker, James *"The Boulder"* Wright. His raccoon eyes opened a fraction more. "It's been a rough day. I'm sure you took on bigger and badder opponents even in your prime. You're a boulder, man." I laughed quietly. "A few months ago, when I was cleaning your closet in the master bedroom, I found an old photo album. There was this one picture of you in a three-point stance, and there was this kid three times your size in your view. The next picture was the big kid stretched out on the ground with you over him." I laughed at the visual.

Jimmy's heavy eyes followed me, but I knew it was rest he needed. I dug beneath the mountains of beddings I kept on him and found his feet. They were cold, per usual, but after a few minutes of rubbing they began to warm. I stayed in there for countless minutes, attempting to neutralize the energy I brought on by my panicking earlier.

Pastor Carmichael had been teaching us more about energy. I streamed *RSfALC's* Bible study last night after Rut left and watched as he taught on changing the course of our destiny by controlling our tongues.

"Your mouth is the co-captain of your destiny," he rasped. *"Your heart has the other wheel."*

In my heart, I wanted Jimmy to be at peace at all times. I had to control the words I spoke to give life to my desire. At some point, I snapped out of my trance and realized Jimmy had dozed off. I was happy. Knowing he'd likely be out for a while, I decided to leave him to it. Nurse Jackie fed him before the end of her shift, so I knew I'd have quite some time before he needed anything else.

I left for upstairs to change out of my work clothes. It was Friday, the end of a work week, but my weeks had no relief. It was just a cycle of yesterday's fears turning into tomorrow's promises. As I pulled a clean tee over my head, a jolt of excitement bolted through me at the remembrance of having company downstairs. I hardly had guests that were not attached to Jimmy. It was either his nurses, old buddies, or on rare occasion, his children.

When I walked into the kitchen, I didn't look his way as I headed to the sink.

"This marks five days in a row. Your therapist pushing you to make it to six?"

Rut sighed, stretched his long legs out in front of him. If I wasn't careful, I could trip over him. "Nah. Haven't seen her since Wednesday. Won't go back until next week."

"Thanks for the groceries, by the way." Well after he'd left the night we had fancy pizza, I saw he brought over drinks, fruits, and a few pounds of halibut fish. "What made you choose halibut?"

I ripped off two pieces of paper towels to dry my hands before turning to him.

"It's my favorite," he yawned, looking puckered himself.

"Oh." I went back to the cabinets and pulled out plates. I saw Rut had warmed the food, so all I had to do was serve us. "Well, thanks again. I would have called or texted, but..."

"You don't have my number." He grunted, sitting up and now looking at me.

"No. I don't." My eyes fluttered in embarrassment. "And that's fine," I declared, not wanting him to think it was a subliminal request because it was not.

"'S'all good." I sat his plate in front of him. "I hope you enjoy it. Thought it wouldn't hurt to try and put you on seeing you go light on the pork and beef."

After praying, I forked the first of my food. "I'm trying to work myself up to becoming pescatarian. Maybe by the end of the year."

"That's what's up. As long as you don't put pig on my plate, it's all good."

"You eat beef?"

He finished chewing and swallowed. "Not in about three years."

"So you won't be hanging out at *B-Way Burger* with Trent, Jordan, and the rest of them your rookie year?"

"Not by choice." He chuckled with a full mouth.

It was pleasant, the view.

"Get ready. I heard they shut the place down for a few hours during training camp."

"I ain't hear that exactly, but I heard Trent represents his Jersey roots by supporting *B-Way Burger* up here."

"What does that place have to do with Jersey? They're nationwide."

"Yeah," he smacked, chewing while eating. Why did that horrible table manner appeal to me? *But not in a romantic way.* "But the first restaurant was in Jersey. A small, local hood joint in Paterson."

"Hmmm..." My brows met. "Why does that sound familiar?"

Rut shrugged, using his fork to congregate his food. "Prolly 'cause of Young Lord."

My face lit in recognition. "Oh, yeah!" I did recall hearing that. "Is that where Trent's from, too?"

"Nah. He's from down the Turnpike, past me but closer. Camden."

"And where are you from?"

"Trenton. State capital."

"And none of you live close to each other?"

He played in his plate where his regard was. "Definitely not Lord. He's all the way up in the New York tristate area. Trenton and Camden are their own worlds but not crazy far apart."

"Interesting." I nodded and chewed.

After a few minutes of silence, he spoke again.

"Ya family don't come see you? Check on you?"

His eyes were on me again.

My regard fell to my plate. "No."

"Why?"

"Why are you so nosy?"

He cracked an asshole smile that had begun to irritate me less. "It's my therapist's fault."

I rolled my eyes, cutting up my food on my plate with the fork. "My mom and I are..."

"Beefin'?"

"No. Just weird. We've been better lately, but it's hard keeping in touch when I know she doesn't approve of my decision to help Jimmy out." *She doesn't approve of any of my decisions, actually.* "I go visit her every now and then, but we mostly keep in touch via text and calls."

"And ya pops?"

"Is dead." My head came up. "Are you finished?" I gestured toward his empty plate.

"Yeah."

I grabbed our plates and took them over to the sink to clean.

"Everything all good with Wright?"

"What do you mean?" I tossed him a cursory glance over my shoulder.

"The nurse—at least I think she was in that uniform—you looked stressed next to her."

Oh...

"Nurse Jackie's one of his primary nurses. She's here the most out of the three we go between, depending on scheduling. I noticed bumps around the insertion of his trachea tube yesterday and I asked her this morning before I left out for work to take a look at it. When I got home, she said it concerned her, too." My shoulders tensed. "It kind of stressed me out. With ALS, it's always one complication after the next. It's almost like waiting for the other shoe to drop." I closed my eyes and shook my head, pausing over the sink. "I've never had real responsibilities. The most I recall being stressed was in college, trying to finish an impossible degree, all to spite my mother. This thing has aged me in just a few short years."

I thought then turned to him with narrowed but playful eyes.

"And no, I don't get any compensation, neither am I in a will that I'm aware of. And before you ask!" I was sure to speak louder for clarity. "I am neither interested or hoping to be paid for what I do!"

With a faint smirk, Rut shook his head.

"Then why do you do it?"

I shrugged. "My grandfather died alone. He was the sweetest man to me and provided handsomely for my mother. He was really old school beneath the doting PaPa." My face dropped toward my busied hands. "When my mother got pregnant with me her first year of college, he condemned her. He didn't push for an abortion but argued she needed a husband to help her care for her baby." I chuckled bitterly. "That was the wrong thing to say to that woman. She decided to have me and finished school. My grandfather paid for it, and even was good to me, but she never went back home.

"Their relationship never recovered. It didn't matter that he made sure he supported me every Christmas and birthday with gifts. She never forgave him. When he was diagnosed with prostate cancer, she let him battle it alone. She was his only child and hardly saw about him. She had him at the hospitals alone. I used to sneak up there after school and sit with his sedated body. It saddened me how she let him die alone."

"Is that why you do it?" he asked.

I nodded, now battling emotions sprouting from my core.

"I was never in love with Jimmy. As much as I wanted to be, we never had that time." I turned off the water and faced him, resting against the counter. "I'm sure you've heard about the assault. You've seen the pictures."

It was astounding to see Rut's eyes fall away, as he was unable to look at me.

"It's okay. I get it. They're a part of my history. And I'm also sure you're familiar with CTE. You're a player."

"Yeah, but..."

"But what?"

"You bought that as an excuse for why he beat you?"

I rolled my eyes, only partially offended. "Jimmy didn't beat me, Rut. About a year or so before I started seeing him, Jimmy began showing signs of what they believe is chronic traumatic encephalopathy."

"*Maaaaaan.*" He shifted in his chair, showing signs of dismissing my point. "That shit can't be proved until you die. They gotta autopsy your brain."

"I guess you're not aware of all the money being poured into research on the disease as of recent years with hundreds of cases displaying all the symptoms: most from the men with a history of repetitive brain trauma caused during football."

Rut didn't speak, his eyes bouncing all over except for on me.

"Well, before I met him, it was suggested Jimmy may have shown severe signs of it: mood changes, headaches, depression, memory loss..." I shook my head. "It was fragmented and hard to track because, until me, no one lived with or spent enough time with him to see the progression."

"How did you find out about it?"

"That first night he got violent with me. I told him I was leaving when he went off about me taking too long out at the grocery store. Well, first, he'd forgotten that's where I went. Then he accused me of taking too long. I'd told him three weeks before when he threatened to beat my ass after getting frustrated because he couldn't find his keys. Well, that night I'd had it. I tossed a few clothes in a bag and stormed down the stairs to leave." I switched stances, crossing my arms protectively and one leg over the other.

"He was on my heels, and before I could make it to the door, he grabbed me and threw me into it face first." I swallowed hard, crisply recalling the burst of heat to my face on impact.

"My nose was fractured and lip busted. Lucky for the both of us, Jimmy wasn't a naturally violent man because he could have finished me if he wanted. The man was two hundred and forty pounds, about a hundred more than me at the time. When he saw the blood, he had another mental lapse. Thankfully, this one was more compassionate and he called 911." I shrugged and caught Rut mumbling something with tight lips.

I continued, "That incident probably aided the case about his condition. And if all the stars weren't aligned then, he was diagnosed with ALS just months later. He was on the golf course and couldn't feel the club in his hand from time to time. Then one day, he was driving the cart and slammed into a tree. That's when he thought to seek help."

"You guys were together at that time?"

I nodded. "He hired high powered attorneys to file against the *League*. That cost money, money they got off the top when he was awarded."

"I'm sorry." Rut shook his head. "I'm still back at that night he put his hands on you. You ain't leave."

"I actually did," I corrected. "It wasn't for long, but I didn't come back here after leaving the hospital. I went to stay with Eli for two nights. He insisted I stay another... Didn't like that I left after that. He was so supportive and seemed completely honest and transparent about his friend's issues. I left there and stayed with a friend. When I finally took Jimmy's call, he came clean about his entire journey, starting from before we met. He asked that I help him through it, believing he had no true support. He even offered to give up his bedroom for me. He was offering me friendship at the time."

"And you thought of your grand-pops and couldn't refuse the offer," Rut observed.

"Do you know the life expectancy of someone diagnosed with ALS? Fifty percent of all people diagnosed live at least three years after diagnosis. Twenty percent survive five years. Within the first year and a half, Jimmy lost his ability to walk, dress, and write on his own. It's been a whirlwind." I shook my head realizing Rut was the first person in a long while whom I'd shared this with completely.

That reminded me to check the time.

"I need to check on him. He's had a rough day." I was dismissing him.

Even though I didn't want him to go, I also didn't understand why he was here...*for the fifth evening in a row.*

Rut checked his phone and sighed. "Yeah. It's time for me to pack it up myself. I got a long night ahead."

He stood to his feet. My breath hitched when I found him staring at me. His eyes dropped, causing me to feel extremely weird and foolish, so I pushed from the sink to leave. Rut grabbed me into a full-hold bear hug. It wasn't sensual or indifferent. It was friendly and gratifying. One big hand was at my shoulder and the other wide at the center of my back. His chin rested on the top of my head, and my face burrowed into his hard chest. And, god, he smelled like everything right in the world.

Slowly, my arms lifted and my hands pushed around his sides and I reciprocated that warm gesture.

"Thanks, Rut." He didn't respond. I pushed from his hard frame and peered up, eyes brushing over his full and sensually carved lips to meet his eyes. "I think your therapist would be proud of your consistency."

He snorted while rolling his eyes, and that caused me to bust out laughing. I could tell he abhorred the idea of therapy. I began our walk to the front door and could feel him following.

"You know, I have a therapist, too."

"You see a head doctor, too?"

I peered over my shoulder to find his shocked expression. "No. My person isn't a doctor, just a therapist."

"So what's the difference? No credentials?"

I made it to the door and turned to him, considering that. "I really don't know. I'm not sure of her credentials other than she's for sure no licensed professional. She was referred by Eli. In fact, he pays for everything. I don't see her as much as I used to. But I'll connect with her a couple of times a month when I need help sorting things out. So, there's nothing wrong with speaking to someone and having them help declutter your brain. They can help you get out of your head." I shrugged. "Or just listen. God, you can't pay for a listening, non-judgmental ear nowadays."

Rut didn't have a rebuttal, and for some reason, that felt strange to me. He didn't talk much tonight. He listened a lot. He even seemed subdued about the things I shared with him. Overall, I was grateful for the company and hoped it didn't show.

"Night, Rut."

"Lata, Parker." He strode out with a corner of his mouth propped.

chapter **seven**

"I just don't think we should keep this up."

"Sherry," James Junior lifted his palm in the air, silencing her. "We've been through this a million damn times! What's the better alternative?"

"Something more than this!" she continued to argue. "Can't we just hire somebody?" Her eyes lit with an idea. "What about Nancy?"

"His sister?" her brother posed, his face twisted with confusion.

"Yes. I spoke with ReRe a month ago. You remember her daughter? She told me Nancy is lonely. She's basically by herself most days a week and is always complaining of boredom. What if we move her in and let her take over?"

James Junior cupped his forehead with his hand. "Sherry, she's like seventy years old. Remember, they ain't spoke in years since Nancy said daddy made her pay an equal amount for their father's funeral?"

Sherry's arms shot up in the air. "That was fifteen years ago! Things change; people, too, Junior." James Junior shook his head.

The waiting room door swung open, taking my attention from Jimmy's kids—all of who were older than me—brainstorming on how to get me out of their father's life. Jerry, James Junior's twin brother, strode through with three cups of lidded drinks though there were four of us in the room.

"What people change?" Jerry asked, handing out cups to his siblings.

James Junior shook his head. "Sherry thinks dad's sister should move in and take over." His eyes cast out into the dark, rainy night at the window.

Jerry dropped himself into a seat next to me, his disposition was typically lighter than his brother and younger sister. His smiling eyes brushed against me before he removed the lid from his cup.

"Aunt Nancy? Ain't she ancient?"

James Junior scoffed. "That's what I'm saying."

"She could be old, but she's cautious. She'll guard him with her life and make sure he's safe at all times," Sherry cried.

"And I don't?" I finally spoke up.

We'd done this dance over the past few years. Each time Jimmy's disease progressed and we'd find ourselves in the hospital like tonight, they'd try to come up with new care plans. Of course, that included giving me the boot. And since the first time they did it to me, I'd been working on my plan B. I lived with never knowing when I'd be told to leave Jimmy's home.

"I'm just saying, she's family. You may not understand family bonds like that, but they do exist." She couldn't even face me when she spoke.

"You have no idea what I do or don't know. You don't know me," I reminded her.

Finally, she turned to face me. "Exactly. This is exactly our problem here. We don't know you. You're a damn kid—twenty-eight years old. You can't begin to understand the fear of having a child care for your dying father all because he couldn't keep his dick in his pants while going through a midlife crisis."

"Hey..." Jerry tried.

"It's too late for this bullshit," James Junior warned about fighting.

"I agree, James," my tone was leveled and controlled. "It's too late to go over the same facts over and over. Sherry, your father was not going through a midlife crisis. It's called brain trauma. It's been confirmed medically, even without an official CTE diagnosis. He has ALS, which is a degenerative disease. It means we have a long road ahead in terms of its progression. And lastly—which I know won't be the last time this comes up, knowing you—you cannot hire a human being to move in with him because you can't afford it."

"Maybe we could if you let us pawn the ring he gave you at the height of that *midlife* crisis!"

"Hey!" James Junior jolted to his feet from the windowsill and shot fire from his eyes at both Sherry and me. "Now ain't no need for all this tonight, I said!"

"But Junior," Sherry tried, turning to her big brother. "All I'm saying is..."

I didn't wait to hear her futile point. Grabbing my phone and purse, I stood to my feet and headed for the door. When I ambled down the hall, I had no idea Jerry was on my heels until I passed the nurses' station and one peered at me then behind me. I cringed before turning to confirm.

"Parker, don't be like that," Jerry attempted to sooth me. "We're just under stress from this."

I moved so we were out of the way from the station but still within sight. I didn't trust Jerry and his wandering eyes.

"And that's the problem. You, your brother, and sister think you're the only ones stressed here. I live with a man who's slowly slipping away. I'm keeping his spirits up and washing his bowel movements day after day. And each time something happens, I'm the one looking to be eliminated."

Just like today. I arranged for transportation to get Jimmy to the doctor about the bumps around his trachea. The doctor didn't like what he saw and had him sent here to the emergency room. Of course, when that call was made, I reached out to his children. I had always been transparent about his condition, although I knew it would lead to another night of questioning my care.

Jerry lifted one side of his mouth, basically conceding to my plight. "Look, I told you a long time ago, I got you at the end of the day." His eyes swept down my face, landing on my breasts.

"And I told you, it ain't that kind of party!" I spat through clenched teeth.

Out of the three of Jimmy's kids, Jerry was most threatening because he was creepy. Just a sleaze. Even before Jimmy fell into incapacitation, when Jerry would come around, he'd have an air of coquetry to his hellos, a deviant eye with his interactions, and a lingering touch to his goodbyes. I'd told Jimmy several times but the complaints fell on deaf ears. It wasn't the biggest of deals because Jerry hardly came around, living in New York City.

His sneaky eyes swept the left and right of us to see who'd heard me. "Damn, Parker," That sleek leer appeared. "you making this hard on a brother. All I'm trying to do is look out for you, but I see how you want it." He backed up.

"Look out for your father, Jerry. All would be right with the world if you made him your focus."

"Fine." He continued to back away, sneer in tow. "Have it your way."

As he turned to go back to the room, my phone vibrated in my hand.

Jade: *Look who's here...*

It was a picture of Rut with Emily Erceg under his arm. They were dressed in formal wear, looking Hollywood glammed. My mouth suddenly went dry and my pulse began to race.

Me: Where's this?

I hadn't seen Jade since the party at Eli Richardson's. Because I opted to go, I traded my Sunday care for Jimmy for that evening. But Jade was no fool. Word had gotten around that I'd left with Rut. Apparently, any woman leaving with Rut meant only one thing. Sex. She sent a text the next morning to check on me, but I wasn't exactly forthcoming with confirming I'd indeed had sex with him. I was too embarrassed.

Jade: *At a Mauve event in L.A.*

She sent a red-carpet picture of Rut's giant frame, smiling devilishly handsome. This was the Rut I recognized from seven days ago at the party. The one who sat at my kitchen table was physically the same guy, but energy-wise he'd been neutralized. Looking at the picture annoyed my already agitated mood.

Me: I thought you guys were leaving for vacation???

The last I'd spoken to Jade she shared their family was visiting France and Italy. She'd been so happy since Trent surprised her with it last month. *She swears her husband is cheap and doesn't splurge much.* It tickled me.

Jade: *We leave in the morning from here.*

Oh...

I didn't want to transition this conversation back to Rut. He was being him: a new player to a team in the *League* who'd just won the Super Bowl. I couldn't begin to make sense of who I was in his life. The one thing I was sure of was he owed me nothing.

But he could've said he'd be with his little friend....

Then again, he shouldn't have. It was my decision to share my life with him when I told him about my time with Jimmy. It was my idea to feed and entertain him each night he showed up on my doorstep this week, just like it was my stupid call to leave the party with him a week ago.

Me: Okay. Enjoy your family and time away! Bring me back something French!

I quoted a line from *Home Alone* I thought applied.

Jade: *Thanks Parker!*

I let out a breath, relieved she didn't mention Rut again. Now I had to decide what to do with myself until we heard back from Jimmy's doctor. I was for sure not going back in the waiting room. The nurse explained the doctor may release him tonight, depending on whether or not his condition declined. They were able to identify why the bumps appeared and treat it aggressively and topically with antibiotics. It was also made clear the error was on the practitioner who inserted the trachea tube and not me.

How long will you take this?

I had to question myself, but I knew Jimmy wanted me there. I could never forget the day he made me promise to not leave his side. He strongly believed his children would put him in a home, something he didn't want.

Love's Ineligible Receiver

Coffee...

The moment I decided to go and search for some, my phone vibrated again in my hand.

Terrance Grant: *Hey you.*

I'd forgotten all about Grant, one of the wide receivers from the *Kings*. He began texting me on Tuesday. We were going back and forth last night until I called it quits. I was tired, though I didn't sleep through the night anymore. Dating was something totally new to me. I hadn't been in the game in years. Since being with Jimmy, I'd aged twenty years it felt. Terrance didn't give off any indicators of "good chemistry" but had been consistent in pursuing me. Then again, I hadn't exactly been available to date. Look at my current situation: I was taking care of a man I hardly knew before he fell ill.

Me: Hey yourself...

By the time I made it to the elevator, he responded.

Terrance Grant: *I'm sitting here at the bar with a bunch of punks wondering why I'm not some place with you. When can we make that happen?*

Me: When do you have in mind?

Terrance Grant: *What about tomorrow?*

Tomorrow?

That stopped me in my tracks. I have no idea what I expected, but tomorrow seemed so...now. Tension ascended my shoulders and neck. This had to stop. The sermon Pastor Carmichael gave a couple of weeks ago about running the race and how we exhaust ourselves from overthinking things in life replayed in my mind. In so many instances, we should have a relax posture and let God move—or get out of His way. I'd been stressed over loneliness and the bleak path my life was on. I had to make a decision to take care of me. So what I didn't feel any sparks with Terrance? I had to start somewhere. Maybe he'd be a step in the right direction.

Me: How about drinks after work on Monday?

I was being brazen. What did I have to lose? Who did I owe a "no" to?

Jimmy? No.

Rut?

That last one was laughable.

RUT

"I think you should be the next *Mauve* man, not Trent Bailey. He's not as relevant." Her eyes sparkled just the way I liked to see in a chick: with mischief.

"Word?" I tried playing it cool, not laughing like I normally would.

"Yup." Her tone was firm as she stirred her cocktail glass by circling it on the bar top. "Who do I need to speak with to make it happen?"

My eyes combed over her head as she stood between me and the man who called the shots as far as *Mauve* went. Divine snorted, facing the screen behind the bar, even though I knew he'd been listening. I tossed my chin his way. "Mr. Azmir Divine Jacobs is conveniently right behind you."

"Oh, shit," Candice sang smoothly, though I knew she had no fucking clue Divine was there.

We were on a rooftop lounge at the annual *Night of Mauve* event where Trent was named the liquor line's ambassador of the year. It was a dope ass title for marketing purposes. *Mauve* kept relevant by choosing the right names to carry the line, and the chosen ambassador was recognized with an established brand known in the conservative and urban markets. I could only wish to be a brand ambassador, but had to earn my stripes.

But it was nice to know little Candice here thought so, too. It didn't matter I knew she was gaming me. I liked it. And I could like it all I wanted. I just couldn't bite.

"Hello, Miss Candice." Divine's eyes swept from her back to the screen across from him. "Glad you were able to come out tonight, young lady."

"And miss a night of networking and celebrating ebony skin like this? I swore after my seventeenth birthday I would never miss one!" Candice's words were convincing...*this time*.

"Glad to hear that," was his reply.

"And speaking of," Candice continued with her eyes back on me, glittering with a desire I was familiar with, but she was speaking to the man behind her. "The conference call you had last week, I facilitated it. When you said branding isn't just limited to business, but is essential for successful family legacy-creating as well... Whew!" Her smile was inspiring and, I could tell, sincere. "That changed something in me."

"Oh, yeah?" I was wrong, knew it, and didn't give a fuck. "Like what? And how deep?"

Her face relaxed, but her eyes stayed narrowed with lust. She was feeling the kid. Then her cheeks lifted again but just slightly.

"It reminds me that when my husband finally gets his shit together and tells me to give him babies, we have to think big." Her little hand pushed up my leg.

Her eyes locked onto mine. My eyes swept from her face to Divine behind her, still watching the basketball game in a tux, then down to her hand inching closer to my thickening cock.

I like this young chick...

If the circumstances were different, I'd fuck her hard until I reached her soul and make her question her purpose in life. As foul as that sounds, I'd done it before and could do it again. Candice was the perfect candidate: bold as shit, bad as hell, beautiful as fuck, and beasting for my dick. She had been since the first day I walked inside *Love is Action*, the sports agency I was signed to. The one her big brother owned.

This girl was connected in this industry. She may not have been that comfortable with Divine, who was straight up ignoring her at the moment, but he'd known her father before he died. Divine was crazy tight with her brother—personally and professionally. All these connections made her unfuckable in my book.

But damn... If I ever—

"Hey!" A sharp chirp had me jump a little on my stool. Candice's hand smoothly retracted from near my pelvis to my knee to her waist as she looked over my shoulder where I felt Emily leaning on. "Your brother doesn't drink, but I see who in the family makes up for it. Knock it the fuck off," she hissed.

Divine turned our way. Candice gave her a nasty look. Hard, bold, and challenging. Suddenly, the muscles in her face relaxed into a sleek "*fuck you*" grin.

See! The female Rut...

"Have you seen him naked *yet*?" Candice asked Emily and I peeped Divine's mouth fall.

"What's it to you?" Emily challenged.

"Just curious, but I see you haven't." Candice made the tsk sound with her tongue. "I wish this wasn't a formal affair and he didn't have on a tux. I'd roll up his sleeve and show you the symbol tattooed on his arm so you know how short your time with him is on the clock."

Shit...

"Oh, really?" Emily giggled, her hands pushing down onto my chest as she spoke over my head. "And who's going to replace me? You?"

"If he's lucky. But it'll at least be someone with real melanin in her skin."

My eyes closed as I watched Candice lift her cocktail glass to her face and sip with confidence.

"Candice, Trent and Jade are about to leave here for their vacation." My eyes opened to Candice's much older sister-in-law's glowering at her. "Don't you think now is a good time to be sure they have those tour dates for when he returns?"

"Sure thing, big sis." Candice's fiery eyes bounced between Emily and me before she swiped the tip of her tongue over the rim of her top lip.

Damn...

She winked then took off, and I peeped Divine snickering quietly as he scratched his brow.

"I'm so sorry for whatever I just walked up on," Elle, too, glanced between Emily and me. "I'm working on her...and, believe it or not, she's gotten so much better."

"Ain't nothing, Elle," I tried to play it cool.

Emily huffed over my ear, but I wasn't sure it was heard.

"I need to go find someone. I should see you before you leave." Elle rubbed Divine's shoulder as a means to acknowledge him then disappeared again.

It was late. The actual event took place downstairs in the ballroom. Divine and a few of us retreated to the rooftop for stogies and the game that he had the place DVR for him to watch after the party.

"I'm going to the ladies' room," Emily announced, squeezing my shoulder. "Try to stay out of trouble while I'm gone, why don't you."

She used a playful tone, but I knew she was dead ass serious. The problem was, Emily had no authority over me. She wasn't my lady. Divine's ass snickered at that, too, but his eyes never left the television. I shook it off and went back to my cigar.

"Rayna still down in the ballroom?" I asked Divine.

"Yeah." His eyes were locked to the screen. "She wanted to see the girls from her foundation off. We invited a few of them tonight." For a while he didn't say anything. We just watched the game. "So lil' Candice, though?" He took a pull from his stogie and blew it out. Then he winked at me, fucking with me.

"Yeah, you think that shit is cute till I fuck her lil' ass." Divine chuckled. "But I ain't, because I keep telling you I don't fuck everything that spreads its legs."

"I 'on't think you do."

"Well, how the fuck long is this gonna be with this Emily thing. Even *lil' Candice*"—I mocked him, using his voice. "know I'm a god and don't just fuck anything."

The first time I met Candice, she was a receptionist at the agency, and she mentioned she'd been following me since my junior year of college. That was probably how she knew I had the tattoo. It was another "thing" the coaches, scouts, and agents spoke about since I got it in college.

Divine sat up, blowing more smoke from his nostrils. "I really don't know about that part of it. Emily ain't who I would've chosen to do this with you. That was all Elle. You should've asked her while she was here."

He shrugged with his hands over the bar, a cigar standing between his fingers as he explained. "I was on board with you linking yourself with a celebrity to help get your name, face, and businesses out there. Unfortunately, in this game, if you want to make a name for yourself amongst the negative talk you've gotten so far, you have to align yourself with someone with a more popular name." He pointed past me where Emily once sat. "That definitely ain't my choosing. I remember when StentRo hooked up with her sister for similar reasons." He shook his head. "That clan ain't no good for the culture."

"Nah. Even lil' Candice knows we don't mix!"

Divine shrugged again, unusually passive on a topic I had strong feelings about. "I trust Elle. She's at the top of her game for a reason. Talk to her."

"Whew!" I heard behind me. Emily was sidling up next to me in her seat. "The bathroom up here is so cute. It has cute little gold fixtures in there. I love this place!"

"Oh, yeah?" I entertained her small talk.

"Yeah. It reminds me of what my designer tried to do in one of my powder rooms. I can't wait for you to see it." Her long nails pushed through my hair to my scalp.

It felt good. Don't get me wrong: I would fuck Emily without thought. The problem was I wouldn't wife her. And even though she knew what this was about between us, she demanded I played the role to a T. Playing the role meant I had to move with more stealth as far as chicks were concerned. Rut didn't sneak or hide shit. I was an undomesticated man. I fucked and flirted with who I wanted. I didn't like having to keep Emily in mind if I ran into a banger at the club.

"I know you don't have to be back in Connecticut until Tuesday," Divine spoke out of nowhere. "You staying in L.A. all weekend?"

My phone vibrated on the table. It was Mickey, a trainer for the *Kings*.

Mickey: *I'm here throwing a few back at the bar with your bff.*

I hated for a man to use the term BFF. *What grown as man did that?* Mickey with his white ass.

Me: *The fuck?*

I included the Obama shrug at the podium to emphasize how stupid his damn text was. Before it could go off, an incoming one popped on my screen.

Mickey: *Dumb ass Grant is here showing us texts of him asking the girl parker out. She said yes and now he thinks his dick has grown another inch.*

It took me a minute to realize he typed Parker and didn't have a typo about the park. *Why would Parker be going out with that whack ass nigga?* He was probably laying it on thick with her now that he knew I'd had her. I was no angel, but Grant was corny as fuck with whack ass game. Plus, it seemed by now everybody had heard about us leaving Eli's party together last weekend. Even Divine finally blasted my ass when it got back to him I'd fucked her.

She would get a bad name if she fucked him. And she claimed to not be that girl. *Shit.* She had me convinced she wasn't that girl, especially after our talk last night when she told me more about her situation with Wright. I didn't believe Parker was an angel. *No female's an angel...* But a small part of me did believe she was good peoples and didn't deserved to be thought of as a groupie.

And I couldn't believe I was copping to the emotion, but...

To be real...

Like... Really, really real...

Keeping it a buck...

I'd missed Parker. It was stupid as fuck. I didn't know the girl, but it seemed like since I stepped on the plane late last night to fly out here to Cali, she popped in my thoughts more than I was used to females doing. Before nodding off during the flight, a few things...nice gestures to make her smile came to mind. Of course, I dismissed them because I wasn't in the game to do romantic shit for a girl, but I couldn't shake my minutes of inclination to do them.

"Yurp!" snapped me out of my head. I looked over to Divine. His brows shot up and chin dipped letting me know he'd been waiting on a response from me. "Dasu'll go bananas if you pulled up on him. You staying the weekend?"

That's when I remembered the original question. I blinked hard. There were like twenty different thoughts running through my head, most of them with the same subject. Parker.

"*Na*—Nah. Nah." I cleared my throat. "It's gonna be a quick turnaround for me. I'm on the next redeye." When I brushed my hand down my head, my hand bumped against Emily's. I didn't realize her hand was still there.

"Shit, Rut!" she cried softly.

"My bad, sweetheart." I crowded her in my arms and pulled her into me because I knew what was coming.

"I thought you'd finally be spending time with me. You said the weekend," her baby voice was back. Were her feelings really hurt? "I had plans for us to spend the day in Santa Barbara. A friend of mine owns a winery out there." Emily pouted.

"I know, baby." I squeezed her, going hard because I did just spring this on her. Shit. That text sprung it on me. I hit her with my killer smile, bodying her with it. "But I promise to give you my best for these next few hours."

"This commercial shit only works on these odd-hour flights," I grumbled to Fats next to me.

I hated being up so early and being asked for a picture or autograph by airport staff. At the same time, I knew my stacks wasn't up for private flights. At times like this, while strapping in a commercial flight, I remembered my promise to myself to cop a jet like Divine. Expensive, I knew, but worth it. I didn't want to complain. Sitting back and taking a deep breath, I just hoped I could catch, at least, three hours of sleep.

My eyes closed and I hummed, thinking of the first thing I'd do when I landed. Jeremy wanted me to call him to prepare for a meeting we had with a vendor. Just as the attendant announced to turn off all devices, my damn phone rang. Recognizing the 609 area code, I answered without hesitation.

"Taking off. What?"

"Yo, Rut, man!" I heard the panic in his voice.

That cry.

My eyes shot the hell open. "The fuck?"

"B-Rocka, man!" C-god literally cried. "Rut! They got B-Rocka!"

My heart shot from my chest. B-Rocka was my first cousin. His pops and mine were brothers.

"Who?" I asked through hard, balled lips.

"Them Dolly Homes niggas. I told him to stop fuckin' wit' em!"

"Sir," a smaller voice called out not too far from me, but I couldn't focus on that.

"When?" I breathed into the phone, my body curled over.

"Like twenty minutes ago. Dinero and 'em just beat the cops from over there."

I could hear wailing in the background, making my stomach turn.

"Sir!"

"*FUCKIN' WAIT!*" I shouted at the lady in the shirt, blouse, and tie.

She jumped back.

"Easy," Fats raised his hand toward me then went back to the lady. "Sorry, ma'am. He's getting off now."

I felt winded, my eyes closed, and I swallowed hard. In the background of my left ear, I could hear the chatter of people going against Fats. In my right, I heard the painful cries of my peoples back home. A reel of images of B-Rocka and me began flashing in the back of my lids. When we were five, playing in the inflatable pool together. When we were twelve, in the alley, watching two crackheads fuck. When we were in the hospital at fifteen, being told his leg was broken after a football game, and he'd never play again. Then in my dorm room one weekend he pulled up, when the Spanish grad chick peed while fucking him. And draft night when my name wasn't being called after a while.

"*Brodie, these mufuckas gon' regret the day they passed ya name up,*" he whispered to me when my head was down and I prayed to "God" for the first time in my life.

My final memory was when he was up in Connecticut with me a couple of weeks ago, when I brought Chestnut Cherries and Brandee back to the crib. The next morning he woke up smiling from ear to ear, saying he'd had his ass eaten for the first time and was now addicted to it. It was crazy coming from two kids from the Five-Percent Nation. If our pops heard that shit, we'd be skinned. But it wouldn't have mattered as long as we were together when it happened. We'd always been together. Until now.

"I'll be there in a few hours. Easy on 'em." I powered down my phone.

love belvin

Parker

Just a few more hours...

I rubbed the lids of my eyes, careful not to disturb the eyeliner and mascara I put on this morning. I was too tired to apply much more than that. Tamping down another yawn, I opened my eyes and blinked a few times. I was able to focus them on my desktop and closed out of the spreadsheet I'd been cleaning all morning. Then I clicked on my *Kings* email tab to clear those out. There weren't as many waiting as I thought.

Hmmmmm...

However, there was one from *Eat Clean*. The subject line read: **Parker, Redeem Your Gift Certificate**. I clicked on it and found a gift card with a five-hundred-dollar value from a *Rutledge Amare*. What was this? I'd never heard of *Eat Clean*. I clicked again to go to their site and after some reading learned they were a new, black-owned, virtual grocer. They contracted with local farmers and delivered fresh, organic, and GMO-free foods.

Hmmmmm...

This was thoughtful...unexpected, too. But it was also a sweet gesture coming from Emily Erceg's boyfriend. Weird, but a fact.

What should I do?

I could have said thanks but didn't have his phone number. I was sure if I snooped around I could get it, but that didn't feel right. It was enough that so many in the company correctly presumed we'd slept together. Using the office to get any information wasn't the best approach.

Then how will I contact—

"Hey, Parker?"

I turned to find the Senior Vice President and Chief Financial Officer, Marshall Johnson, beaming down on me.

"Hi, Marshall." I tried with conspicuous efforts to close out of the email. "What can I help you with?"

"You're sitting in on the meeting this afternoon, am I correct?"

I blinked, waking my fuzzy brain. "*Ye*—yes. It's on my schedule." Today I'd been filling in for two admins. It had been a fast-paced but heavily labored day. "Two o'clock. Right?" I tried for a smile.

"Yes." She placed her hand on my shoulder. "As odd as it sounds, I'm so glad you're covering for my assistant. You're so thorough with your notes, and you think while relaying." That's when I realized she was excited...bubbly over this. "Should you change your mind and need permanent placement—" She winked. —"let me know."

I tried relaxing the muscles in my face. Her words and presence had taken me by surprise. "*Uh*—okay."

"Anyway. You have a minute to go over the report with me? I'd like to be prepared for them before they're presented to Eli this morning."

And there was that. Eli Richardson was in the office today, meeting with the larger departments. They were all updating him with numbers and reports, so mostly everyone was on pins and needles. I had to be a good sport about it.

"Sure." I nodded. "Give me a minute to get these documents over to finance and I'll meet you in your office?" I asked to be sure.

"How about in James' office?" Marshall proposed, reminding me I'd be with Jimmy's son today. Marshall here was his big boss and they were up for their time with the biggest boss. "I'd like him to be there, too."

After a hard swallow, I nodded again. "See you in a few."

She took off and I sulked.

Just a few more hours...

chapter
eight

"I'M GOING, TOO!" I STOOD UP, swaying.

Fuck! I hope nobody ain't see that...

"No!" everybody yelled at the same time.

A hand was at my shoulder, pushing me back into my seat.

"Rut, you know the rule. You don't fuckin' get involved!" My cousin, Trigger, yelled from across the room.

He was polishing his gat, just like my other cousins and roadies all around the room.

"And you get ghost before shit go the fuck down. Now, go!" Pop took the same tone.

"Nah, man. Fuck that! This my nigga." I slapped my chest, feeling nothing. "My mufuckin' brother. I'm serving that fuckin' bullet tonight."

"Rut, baby!" my mother cried. "You can't. They right. You ain't even 'posed to be here now. If you 'on't go, I'mma have Fats call Divine. We done came too damn far to lose you, too."

The pain in her warning cut through the numbness and anger wrapping around me, layer by layer, each hour since the plane took off in L.A. Fats and I drove from Connecticut where I landed yesterday morning, all the way down here to Trenton, New Jersey so I could be with my family. I'd been with my family since then. Had been drinking since then, too. The cops hadn't made an arrest, claiming not having enough information. That was strange as fuck, considering by the time I'd landed, my people knew who and where they were hiding.

My cousin, C-god, wanted to wait them out. He knew the streets were hot with cops waiting on our retaliation so the word was to wait. Tonight they were ready but I was being excluded from the fun and didn't like it one bit.

"Man, fuck that!" I stood again. "Fats gone take me back to moms' house. I'mma grab my heat and we gone ride on those Dolly niggas."

"Rut!" I was so far gone, I didn't know who'd called my name.

"Nah." I spoke even louder. "Hell no! B-Rocka was my fuckin' brother. My bullet."

"Rut!"

"C'mon, Rut!" someone else called as I moved toward the stairs.

For the first time, I felt a zing of excitement at the thought of revenge. B-Rocka's moms snuck pictures of his body in the morgue. I'd been sick ever since I saw them. Numb. Angry. Fucking empty.

As I got closer to the basement stairs, it had dawned on me. "I know both they baby's moms, too. I fucked the Myisha bitch in the back of the old Chinese store that got burned down a few years ago. And the other one..." I snapped my fingers, trying to remember her name. "Tinky...Teira? Something." I shook off the confusion in my head. "That bitch necked me like four times while he was in the house sleeping. We can go grab them if needed!"

Another rush of vindictive elation ran through me, and I realized they were too quiet on me. I hated that shit. Just because I was signed didn't mean I wasn't one of them anymore. We moved as a fucking unit, and this time, it was my duty to lead the pack. Fuck a celebrity. Fuck the *League*. Fuck my life. B-Rocka was gone. I turned to see who was following. It was only Fats and he was handing me a phone. Without thinking, I grabbed it.

"Who the fuck is this, yo?"

"It's that muthafuckin' G who could have a jet powered in less time than it'll take me to get to it. And if you 'on't get ya ass outta

Trenton, I swear on everything I love, I'm gonna get on it and fly to Jersey to whip yo' muthafuckin' ass," he growled. My eyes closed in recognition of the threat and the voice delivering it. Oh, I knew who the hell it was. It was the only man on earth who could take that tone with me. The one governing my world since my pops caught a heavy charge that got him sent up. "Not only am I gonna knock you the fuck out, I'mma beat the shit outta you for making me drop the dough it'll take for me to get to you. That ain't ya world. Get the fuck outta dodge and let C-god and them handle that weight." My nostrils flared and heart sped because it was now hard to breathe.

He may be able to talk to me that way but having him do it wasn't easy to sit through. This was fucking B-Rocka. My brother—fuck cousins! What would I expect him to do if my body was laying in a goddamn morgue?

"You got—" That rumble pushed through the phone again. "5, 4, 3, 2—"

I yanked by body around and saw Fats' big ass staring me down. Then with Divine's voice still in my head counting down, with everything I had, I hurled the phone to the nearest wall. I heard its pieces crashed into the floor as I trekked to the door.

A phone ringing had me up again. I didn't know how many times I heard it, but I couldn't move to do anything about it. Two days of straight drinking had finally caught up with me. The minute I slipped into the back seat of the truck I was out. It wasn't restful though. I kept waking up.

"Yeah," Fats mumbled. "We good. Nigga in the back, sleeping it off." My eyes couldn't stay open, but I tried ear hustling. "Yeah. I'm just glad you got him to calm down. You know how hotheaded he is from the jump. Then with him being sauced up, dude would've caught a body or a bullet tryna catch a body." He paused. "A'ight. We 'bout to hit the state line. I'll hit you when I get a new phone. Big ass mufucka smashed mine to pieces." Another pause. "One."

When I knew the call was over, I swallowed painfully; my mouth was so damn dry.

"Yo, take me to 60—" I had to wait for my head to stop spinning or for the wave of nausea to end. "609—"

"What?" Fats barked from the front seat.

I was too out of it to bark back, but I managed. "60609 Washington Street."

"What the fuck is that? Where Washington Street? You know what the hell time it—"

I faded to black again.

Parker

My eyes flashed open and chest pounded.

Was that the...

My head rolled for my phone. It was after three in the morning and felt like I'd just fallen asleep. It was my norm but being awakened at this hour was not. I swallowed hard. Then it happened again. The doorbell sounded.

At the pace of my pulse, I leaped from the bed and snatched my housecoat from the closet. Hanging onto the railing, I raced down the stairs. At the landing, my attention went straight to Jimmy's room. His atrophied frame was still, but I couldn't quite see his eyes. Instead, I headed straight to the door. From the side window two large frames could be seen. One seemed vertical and the other hanging onto one of the posts of the porch.

I stood frozen in fear. *Who could these imposing figures be at this hour?*

"Parker! Parker..." A masculine set of lungs sang my name. "I see you... Oh, shit—"

Then I heard what was indisputably a man vomiting in the garden bed. My eyes ballooned.

"Damn, Rut!" The other body turned an impressive one hundred and eighty degree angle to face who I now knew was Rut.

I went shakily for the alarm then the locks to open the door. Rut was wiping his mouth as he turned to face me. A devilish grin lifted from his face. It was clear he was drunk. But how in the hell could he still be dangerously handsome while shit-faced?

"What are you doing here?" I eyed him pointedly.

Less confidently, my regard brushed against his security I met the night of Eli Richardson's party. He was holding a carry-on luggage piece.

"I came to see you," Rut answered, bringing my attention back to him.

"At this insane hour?"

"Yup." He moved to crowd me in the doorway. "I needed to know why you going out with sucka-ass niggas."

I pushed him back outside. "What are you talking about, Rut?"

Rut stumbled backward but was caught by his security.

"I'm talking about bitch ass Grant. Why you going out with him? He only want you 'cause I tasted it."

Tasted—

"You show up here drunk just to ask me why I went out for a drink after work with someone?"

A drink I didn't finish because I was so tired after the weekend I'd had with Jimmy. And with someone I still found little chemistry with.

But he's nice...

And Terrance wasn't a womanizer like Rut. Even though he asked to come back to my place, he'd been a complete gentleman the entire time.

"I just wanna know if he bought you dinner and flowers." Rut neared me again. This time, I didn't push him off, no matter how much I wanted to. "I ain't no flowers type of nigga, but I do buy food."

I rolled my eyes. "Why are you here, Rut?"

He backed up, face morphing into what could appear to be a sober expression. "I wanna know why you ain't say thank you for the gift card I sent."

My lips parted and eyes grew wide when I understood the talk of food. Yesterday had been so crazy in the front office and today, being home all day with Jimmy, was beyond exhausting. I still hadn't recovered from the weekend.

My palm went to my forehead. "I'm sorry, Rut."

"Yeah..." he taunted. I glanced up to find his arrogant leer returned. "Sorry. I'm the nice nigga buying food, but he the nigga that gets ya time." He swayed. "That's fucked up, Gray."

Gray...

He'd called me Gray. It reached emotionally, and I began to feel bad.

"Rut, it's not like I have your number to call or send a text," I tried.

That was met with a bitter simper. "Oh, here you go with the bullshit. You ain't got my number, Gray?"

That annoyed me. Why would I lie?

"You know I don't! We just discussed it last week!"

"Nah. You said you didn't, and I made you think I believed it."

My forehead wrinkled. "What?"

"You got my fuckin' number, Parker!" he shouted, unkindly to the hour. The roguish grin was gone. "I texted you the night we met!"

My eyes ballooned again, remembering the text game he played that night. That memory caused my eyes to close and face to fall again.

"Look, man," his security spoke again. "What's you gone do?"

With the meanest glower to date, Rut eyed me. "I'm staying here. She takes care of everybody else... Parker gone take care of me tonight. We friends. Right?"

Before I could answer, Rut brushed past me into the house. His security gave me an apologetic smile as Rut muttered something about his cousin having a hole blown into his back.

My neck snapped up to his security.

"Sorry 'bout this, ma'am. If you want him to go, I'll get him out. But if you good with it, here's his phone," he whispered that part. "My name is Fats and my number's in there. I got two numbers in there. One is broken—"

Rut butted in seemingly so innocent. "Why ya phone broke, Fats?" His face was filled with concern.

"Because you threw it back in Jersey, Rut," Fats answered then turned to me. "I'll be at the store as soon as the doors open. But first I'mma run to the house and get my other phone in case you need me before then."

Was he saying he was leaving a drunk, six foot one, two hundred and three pound wide receiver here? With me?

"Rut!" he shouted rather loudly considering this was an ill man's house. "You be easy. I'll hit you in a few hours."

Rut didn't respond. He wobbled over to the foot of the steps and stood with his back to us. The door closed and I realized Fats had left us. Alone. With Rut being drunk.

"Where the hell ya room at?" I leaped around to find Rut swaying up the stairs.

Quickly, I grabbed his suitcase and followed him up the stairs, praying Jimmy was still resting. I didn't want him knowing another guy was in the house.

"To the left!" I whispered hard, directing him once he was at the top. Rut doddered down the hall. "The one on the end."

It dawned on me I hadn't cut on any lights when I went to answer the door. That ended when Rut flipped them on, brightening the hall, too. His head rotated around the room mutedly. I sauntered up next to his big frame to assist him to the chair in the corner because he didn't seem steady on his feet.

Instead, it seemed I startled him by the way his head snapped to face me. He peered down at me, eyes narrowing affectionately and cheeks widening with amusement. He lifted a hand to my face and sweetly swiped my cheek.

"I like ya room, Gray."

I swallowed, bizarrely nervous by his proximity. He smelled of weed, alcohol, and days old Rut.

"Thank you," I whispered, gazing up into his pinkish eyes.

They were still gleamingly beautiful. So wickedly dark with specs of redeeming corruption, mischief, and longing.

"You used to share it with Wright?"

I nodded, remembering this was his master bedroom not long ago.

His eyes danced in mine. "He 'boulder' you in here?"

My lids flew wide and Rut sputtered a hefty laughter, spraying me with his awful alcohol-stench breath.

"Ewwwwww!" My face tightened and I used my arm up to cover my nose. "Your mouth reeks, Rut!"

"It's talented, too. I bet two stacks it can make you do more than Wright's."

"Mmmmmhmmmm." I began to push him toward the bathroom. "We can debate that after you've washed and cleaned your mouth. When was the last time you've been inside a shower?"

"I 'on't know. I been out of it since Saturday night," he slurred. "Everything was going good..." He burped. I moved around to cut on the shower. "Everything was going good until I got a text about you going out with that sherm head ass nigga," his tone resembled realization as he stared into the distance.

"Up you go." I lifted his heavy arms, pushing them into the air.

"Yeah, and even after that, I wanted to do something nice for you. You know why?" His delivery was sardonic. "Because even though I only pulled up on you last week 'cause my damn head shrink told me I should, I for real for real think you're cool, Gray." That last part was muzzled from me pulling his shirt over his face.

Good grief!

The nigga was Hulked out with a thick and corded neck, hilly shoulders, and a carved chest and abs. Perhaps I wasn't paying much attention the night we met. I didn't recall all the fine details either, like the small patch of hair on his chest. It wasn't as full as I'd seen of men but definitely present.

"You're going to have to undo your pants," I informed.

Rut's eyes shifted down his torso then up to mine as he unleashed that no good smile again. *Gosh, he is a charmer!*

The humor disappeared from his face and he crossed his arms defiantly. "I don't want you seeing my no-no special place."

An unexpected guffaw shot from my belly and my palm slapped my mouth to catch it. He held his scowl for a long while before he smiled, confirming his drunken sense of humor.

"I'm going to find you a toothbrush then check on Jimmy." I snickered.

Before I could leave the bathroom, Rut was pulling down his sweats. I went to his suitcase, pulled it to the far end of the room to open, and spread it on the floor. It didn't take long to locate a *Louis Vuitton* toiletry bag. I found his electrical toothbrush and took it into the bathroom.

Through the glass shower wall, I could see Rut washing his arms when I placed the toothbrush near the sink.

"Here's your toothbrush. The toothpaste is in the top drawer. Okay?"

He sang Brielle's chorus to Young Lord's *"Sun Showers."*

"Rut?"

"I heard you," he made clear before continuing the slurs of the lyrics.

I left the door ajar and finally headed down to check in on Jimmy.

As I toed back up the stairs from Jimmy's room, I listened hard for sounds coming from the second floor. I'd been down with Jimmy for less than twenty minutes. He was still asleep but I didn't like the position he was in and tried rearranging his body, waking him. I noted how cool his feet felt so I added a blanket over him. After watching him drift off again, I stayed a few minutes longer to be sure he was resting.

Now Rut...

It was conspicuously quiet on the second floor but a beam of light came from one side of the house. As I approached from the hall, I saw the bathroom light was still on, and the door was wide open. I went straight into the bathroom and, right away, realized it was empty. Turning back for the bedroom, I immediately saw a long bare, hairy, striated leg suspended from the mattress. Above it was darker hued skin on top of globular muscles. His back was cut and swollen with graffiti inked on sheen smooth skin.

Closing my eyes, I took a cleansing breath. What in the world was I doing? Since when had it been okay to have men in Jimmy's home? Something about walking into my bedroom knowing a man was here felt wrong. But standing here, poring over his back and seeing him resting in my bed, felt so right. It was a draining confliction of emotions.

I walked to the other side of the bed, and with vicious force, yanked the bedding bunched underneath him. On the fourth tug, I was able to toss them over his lengthy frame. After pulling his leg up from the opposite side, I tucked Rut into bed just as I'd done Jimmy downstairs. I went into the bathroom to cut off the light and did the same in the bedroom. Then I found myself standing over my occupied bed, my body throbbing with fatigue. Sleeping with him was out of the question.

Decided on my next move, I grabbed one of the pillows from the bed and curled up on the sofa chair near the door.

My breath caught and belly leaped as I was pressed against a plank of muscle and encased by others. I smelled him and instinctively knew it was Rut. I could hardly open my eyes to confirm it but could tell he'd lifted me in the air. Wrestling from his hold could have been an option—should have been. But I was too desperately steeped in sleep to put up any fight.

Then I was straddled over him. His arm lay possessively over the small of my back. Again, instead of protesting, I willfully succumbed to a new round of siesta.

RUT

"Hey there, lil' buddy!" I spoke in my special voice exclusively for him. "You miss ol' Rut boy, ain't ya!"

Sharkie groaned like a man nutting in the best trap. His eyes were squeezed closed and tail wagged in a frenzy as I massaged his head.

"I been away a lot lately, huhn? They been taking care of you?"

I knew they were. *Kings Courts* had a pet sitter right here on the premises. Whenever Fats had to be away with me, we'd take him there and they'd tack his stay onto my rent. I, myself, had been away a lot lately, especially last week. I had to remember this place was new to Sharkie and me. We hadn't been here a full two months yet, and I'd been leaving him for most of the day.

I pulled him closer to me as I sat on the couch in my living room, giving him the attention he craved. Attention that calmed me, too.

"Well, ol' Rut missed you too, baby boy." I massaged his stomach, jealous as hell I had no one to do it to me.

I was tired as fuck. Being up two days straight, drinking, and mourning had caught up with me today while training. I performed my ass off, but it wasn't my best out there. I got to the field late this morning because I woke up from the heaviest sleep that didn't have shit to do with being drunk.

Now, I was ready to go. I knew it was crazy of me, but as I massaged Sharkie, I knew on the other side of this call I'd been waiting on was my therapy. And hopefully my comfort.

The house phone rang and for some reason scared me at first. Then excitement mushroomed in my damn belly and I reached for it.

"Yeah?"

I listened to the automated recording of FCI Oxford's prison system and waited for the prompt to accept the call. After sometime, I heard the voice that had brought about mixed feelings for me since elementary school.

"Peace to the god," his tone was the same.

Guarded.

"Peace, god." I rubbed my head from back to front, already feeling uneasy.

There was another pause, but his energy was thick. This call wouldn't be filled with silent stretches. It wasn't his way.

"Who is the devil?"

I rolled my eyes, already over this bullshit. But I had to answer.

It was his way.

"A devil is a grafted man, which is made weak and wicked. Any grafted, live germ from the original is a devil."

"And answer this: Would you hope to live to see god's taking the devil into hell in the very near future?"

My eyes closed and body tensed all over. I didn't know where this was going but felt like a sheep being led to slaughter. *This was his way.*

"Yeah." I had to answer. Had to answer and lie, "In the words of his Prophet, W.D. Fard, I fast and pray, Allah, in his own good time, takes the devil off our planet."

It was a joke. We didn't subscribe to the Islamic religion. He understood I was being an asshole with it. In the heavy moment, I could use any tactic to lighten the conversation.

"Then why the fuck is you wasting away in contradictory, walking around with a devil on ya arm like she your equal?"

Emily. Fucking. Erceg.

I took a deep breath.

"I don't believe she's my equal."

"But you posing and shit with her!" he shot right back. And I waited. "You know what her bloodline is?"

I tucked my chin and murmured. "Syrian."

"Yeah. That's what her daddy was. Her momma's Anglo-Saxon."

"I know, pops. This is all a PR front. Divine—"

"Divine did this? The dirty-blond, blue-eyed Jesus worshipping Azmir Divine Jacobs got you into this shit?" His temper heated up, tone peaked.

"Not exactly. I'm signed to a sports agency. A dope one that's working to get my name out there—cleaned from all the bullshit they tryna throw on it," I tried explaining. "They tryna position me to get a better deal next season."

"And Divine got you with these people?" I closed my eyes again, trying to remember how much longer we had on the call. "I bet they devils, too. They all working together to get my only seed to be the main clown in they fuckin' circus."

"They're black. From the top," I emphasized.

He got quiet.

I took a deep breath.

"You out there cooning for the fuckin' devil with the fuckin' devil and ya cousin in homeland losing his life."

"That ain't my fuckin' fault, man," I muttered, wanting to do more.

"That ain't the point!"

I sucked my teeth. "Then what's the point, my G?"

"The fuckin' point is you need to take advantage of this opportunity. I made sure—pushed goddamn hard to get you to the *League*—"

"And I'm here—"

"To continue with the legacy, not to parade around with a ass-eatin' devil in heels, Kadar!" He was there. The highest point of anger. Dude was now basing at me. Hard. "I know I left you to Azmir. Told him to carry out my plan—"

"And he ain't?"

"Oh, he did. He did," he shrieked, making it clear. "What he ain't is your father, Kadar! I am. You my fuckin' legacy. That lost, devil lovin' nigga can go throw his seed in the damn sideshow for the white man to be entertained by. But as far as mine, he only entertains on the field. Other than that, them devils can find a new clown to laugh at."

"That's kinda fucked up, don't you think?"

"Nah. It's called karma. I heard about the documentary. That man done sold his soul for fame. When he blew the hell up in Cali, I knew that nigga was gonna fall for the lights and cameras. One day I hear he quit the game. The next, he left the Nation of Islam and now a fuckin' Christian. What a joke, man." He scoffed. "You can't be an enlightened black man all ya life then claim you found Jesus. What the fuck type of Illuminati brainwashed shit is that? I been tellin' you for years now, that ain't the way of the righteous black man. The Asiatic man..."

Fifteen minutes...

I finally remembered and lifted the cordless to see how long it had been. Then I let out a long breath, counting down until dinner: the other side of this call.

"I'm so sorry!" Her little hand reached across the table, covering mine. Her faced folded as though in pain and her head leaned to the side. Parker's voice was soft yet strong. *Comforting.* "Why didn't you tell me?"

No matter how much I needed it, I wasn't comfortable with a female's sympathy. Not real sympathy anyway.

I pushed my plate away. "Dinner was good." I cleared my throat.

"Don't do that!"

My eyes snapped up to her. Parker shook her head again.

"If there's one thing I can't stand at my age, it's a man who can't express hurt and pain, believing it to be a sign of weakness. I'm a woman, yes. But my shoulders were strong enough to get you settled while drunk in my bedroom last night. They're strong enough to show compassion for your pain."

That shit shocked the hell out of me. I'd never seen her so snippy. Her cute lips pouted and eyebrows drew together. I wasn't a crying or complaining type of man, but that "comfort" she was offering was tempting.

"It's all good." I shook my head, sitting back in my seat at her table.

"No. It's not. You said it yourself: this B-Rocka was like a brother to you." This time Parker shook her head, her eyes falling to the table. "I should have known something was up. I know I don't know you well, but you being drunk like that last night... Your whole disposition." She lifted her head. "It all makes sense now. He's your father's nephew, you said?" I nodded. "How's he taking the news?"

My brows lifted, thinking about that. "The best way he can. Ain't shit he can do about it."

"Well..." She hesitated. "I mean... Of course, he's powerless like we all are, but I'm sure he's had a reaction to it."

This was getting uncomfortable. "My pops is locked up."

"Locked up?"

I nodded again. "Feds got him up in Wisconsin."

Her eyes dropped again. "Sorry, Rut."

I groaned, "Don't say sorry. Ain't your fault."

I hated pity. Didn't need that shit. I was Rut Amare. The fucking prince. I'd been good my whole life. My pops made sure from Wisconsin.

"How long has he been in there?"

"Since I was in elementary school."

"How much longer does he have to go?"

I shrugged. "Months."

"Months?" her voice perked up. "That's great!"

Stretching back in my seat, I let go of a long breath. "I guess so."

"You don't want him home?"

My neck jerked. "Sure, I do. They need to free him. But I can tell now he don't get I'mma man. I ain't got time to be 'fathered' by two dudes."

"What do you mean?"

I struggled. My reluctance wasn't because of what I was about to say but about who I was going to share it with. I never talked about my pops or Divine. Definitely not to a chick. Not even to my head doctor.

"When I was nine, my pops got fifteen years Fed time for trafficking and distributing heroine. He don't know I know what I'm about to tell you. My moms don't even know I know, but I do. He worked for one of the biggest drug lords at the time. Dude came up in Brooklyn and worked his way to Chicago then Cali. My pops was one of his soldiers for years. He started out with dude and worked his way up to top dog in Trenton. Pops was making low-level millions." I flicked my fingers over the table.

"He got knocked. The feds started down the chain in Trenton and worked their way up. When pop-dukes got his sentence, he made some kind of deal with the man at the top of the organization. Because they went way back, he asked the dude to look out for me. I wasn't there for the conversation, but between the two of them over the years, pouring this 'pact' down my throat, I get the 'General' was supposed to keep me outta trouble."

"Did he?" Parker asked with wide eyes.

I gave her one nod. "He did. He even did me one better: he got me into sports. When it was obvious I had a talent at football, my pops wanted me to stay with it." I dipped my chin. "The General put more money into that. Had me in camps and shit. My pops heard and was down with me pursuing it, so that's what we did."

"But how can the 'General' push you from another state…across the country? You mentioned Brooklyn, Chicago, and California," she explained her point.

"He had my moms as his enforcer. See, when my father got sent up, the General kept us fed. He made sure my moms had money, a house we owned, cars, and most of all, influence."

"What do you mean by influence?"

"I mean, I've been the prince of my hood since I was born. My pops was the fuckin' man in our hood. He ran the streets—literally. He owned blocks and blocks around my way. Did he have rivals?" I shrugged. "Yeah, but the organization he was down with had arms and legs all over the damn country. Pops had ammunition so local rivalries wasn't the biggest threat in his day. The Feds was. When they snatched him, the General took care of him by way of his family. Even after the Feds cleared my neighborhood, the ghost of the General and my pops was remembered. I was his only seed and nobody really fucked with us. His rep lived on."

"So you mean to tell me that's how cavalier 'Rut' came alive? That's where this big 'I'm the king of the world and don't worry about consequences' persona derived from?"

My head rocked back. "If that's what you wanna call it."

Her eyes rolled away and she mumbled, "I'd love to hear what your therapist calls it."

Something was with her. Parker had been different tonight. Since I showed unannounced again and even as she fixed my plate, her shoulder had been colder than usual. I didn't ask her about the little shade I'd been picking up. A small part of me thought it was because I showed up to her place last night drunk and then again tonight like last night never happened.

"Anyway..." I decided to finish. "Dude made good on his pact with my pops and here I am. But things between them ain't on the up and up."

"What do you mean?"

"Pops is a Five-Percent'er. It's how I got my teachings. The General was a member of the Nation of Islam but has converted to Christianity. My father's had a hard time with that."

"Why?"

"Because it's unheard of for a black man to go from all knowledge to following a so-called prophet from over two thousand years ago."

"Jesus wasn't a prophet. He was the Savior," she argued.

"I was actually being generous when I said he was a prophet. He wasn't shit to me." I looked her dead in the eyes to be clear of my position. "My point is you can't go from believing our former slave masters are obligated to provide a separate state or territory either on this continent or elsewhere to people whose parents or grandparents were descendants of slaves, to worshipping a prophet the slave masters told you was the savior. That shit's irrational."

"Let me guess: Your father's issues with your surrogate father has been influencing you."

I didn't like that.

"First, I only got one father. Plus, I'm my own man. Nobody

influences me. Either you're right with your opinion or you're wrong."

"So your father's correct?"

I shook my head. "I ain't saying that."

"So he's wrong. Your mentor, the General, has every right to evolve to a new belief system. He can adhere to the slave master's teachings and believe Jesus is the Messiah."

"Hell no!" I was offended. "I ain't say that shit either."

"Then what are you saying?"

"I'm saying shit ain't black and white all the damn time. His boy—" I had to be sure not to name Divine. He'd been going through enough with that fucking documentary. I wouldn't be the one corroborating shit. "—is a stand up dude. All wise. Ain't no way he should be looked at like a sucker. He still a real one."

"So he can be real and still believe in what the white slave masters taught him?"

"Why the hell are you trying to get me to validate shit the white man pushed down our throats?"

"Because I think it's easier since you're dating a white woman."

Rage hit. My face folded. "Man, I ain't dating no fuckin'—"

When Parker's face dipped and lips curled, I knew I'd been baited. She'd gotten my ass; hook, line, and sinker.

"So that's why you been so shady with me?"

"You show to my place after last night, *and* I serve you food. *Again*." Her chin dropped. "And I've been shady?"

"You have."

Then she cocked her head to the side. "Can I be honest for a moment?"

"By all means."

"Why didn't you tell me you were going to see her last weekend?"

"Because I didn't go see her last weekend."

"But you were on the red carpet with her."

Here we go...

"I was at a red-carpet event for my peoples. She was with me." I shrugged.

"Is she your girlfriend?"

"Is Grant ya man?"

That staggered her little ass.

Her head swung to the other side and her forehead wrinkled. "Why would you ask me something so asinine?"

"And you accusing me of having a girl ain't asinine?"

"No! You're photographed with her...rumored to be with her." Her eyes swung left to right on the table below. "And I'm quite sure you sleep with her!"

"I ain't never put my dick in no Emily Erceg—" Then I thought about the logistics of that. "—well, not in her pussy." Her mouth dropped. "Or her ass!"

"Rut." Her pitch was too calm.

"What? I'mma man, sweetheart. And why we talking about my dick? You don't see me asking you why you going out on dates and shit when Jimmy was in the hospital this weekend!"

While we were eating, she told me about Jimmy's emergency visit. That add on had me feeling a way I couldn't explain. I didn't give a shit about Jimmy Wright. I mean... May he live a long, peaceful life, but he wasn't a concern of mine. And I couldn't give a fuck about who Parker spent her time with. *Right?* I couldn't! I hardly knew her.

"You don't know me, Rut." Her voice was shaky but face stone hard. "Don't mistake me enjoying a break from an otherwise mundane and pre-aging life by having dinner company with me being a whore."

I flinched. *A whore?*

"I bring up one clown ass dude and that's calling you a whore?"

"So what is your problem? Jimmy's setback, me being friends with Terrance or sleeping with him?"

"You're the one jealous over me doing a PR stunt with a chick that don't matter—"

"Jealous?" Parker pushed away from the table. She stood and grabbed our plates. "I can't be jealous over a man, who thinks so little of women beyond the physical gratification they can bring him. I can't be jealous of a woman living in a universe where a cosmetic enhancement is as common as an educated black woman. I would never be jealous of a woman going down on a man who's crushing on me but is too weak to at least admit it." She walked over to the sink and roughly dropped the dishes inside. Then she started for the kitchen door. With her back to me, her voice was loud and clear. "I've got to tend to a grown-up's commitment down the hall. You've been here enough to be able to see your way out."

Parker was out. She didn't even give a final look. How had this gone south so damn fast? We were just kicking it about some shit I'd never shared with anyone outside of B-Rocka. *She was just expressing her condolences over him!* But now I was some asshole with a crush I couldn't cop to? And she was kicking me out.

Where the fuck they do that at?

"This bitch..." When I heard those words coming out my mouth, my whole body went stiff.

A phrase I'd used a gazillion times and with conviction had, for the first time, felt like fucking blasphemy.

My eyes circled the kitchen, beginning from the chair she just shot from, all the way to the sink where she left the dishes. It wasn't her usual style to leave them there. But why did I care to notice?

She kicked me out...

On a huff, I stood to my feet.

Parker

My body ached and heart sat heavily in my chest. Giving Jimmy a bed bath may not have been the most strenuous work, but it had become the most distressing task as of late. His body kept...shrinking. His skin, no matter how thick and nourishing the moisturizers I used or made, still resembled thin paper.

It was a painful task for both of us, because no matter how much Jimmy's body was degenerating, his mind was still present. He knew, likely more than I, the rate at which his body was decaying. But I braved through it. I even took my time massaging creams into his skin, hoping to relax him. Tonight I read to him, something I'd been doing a lot of lately. It would start with a passage from the Bible then move into a novel of sorts. Lately, I'd been reading *New York Times* best seller *It Ain't Over*, written by a two-time cancer survivor. He seemed to have liked it. We'd been at it since last week.

Now he was asleep and his room was cleaned. I could use a shower myself. It was close to eleven at night and I'd forgotten all about my dinner company until I crossed into the kitchen for a bottle of water. It was clean. The table had been washed down, stove scrubbed clean, and sink clear of dishes I was sure I'd left in there. I rolled my eyes then slammed my face into my palms. Rutledge Kadar Amare was a frustrating aberration.

He was immature, furiously sexy, clearly a womanizer, charming, spiritually deficient, amazingly talented according to my research on him last week, and...here almost every night for some unknown reason. After grabbing a bottle of water, I left the kitchen thinking to myself this could have possibly been the last I'd see him. I had no time for his spectrum of energy. Jimmy had been a task I'd committed to with an unknown end date.

I set the alarm and trekked up the stairs, chiding myself for not having the next phase of my life figured out. On my way to my bedroom, I ran down the same questions echoing in my heart for years now regarding a post-Jimmy life. Where would I go? What would happen to *Grayson's Skin Care*? Would I be too old to expect a family? Would I die alone? Had my mother been right all along?

By the time I made it into my room, I decided to march straight into the bathroom for a hot shower. I didn't sleep through the night but could hope to get a solid two hours in before the twisting and turning had me awakening for the first time.

The shower was nice and hot. The beads were weighty on my skin and the sound of droplets falling on my body and against the stall kept me in my head. I stepped out to dry myself off and wondered if I should begin looking for apartments just to learn the market. *Or should I go back to school for an advance degree—or possibly another bachelor's in business or something like it?*

I dried off, my body feeling heavier than it did before my shower. Heart feeling achier. I was tired. Frustrated. After slipping on a pajama shirt, I turned off the light and toed to my bed.

"Huh!" I squealed when my hand and knee landed on planks of muscle.

I jerked back, startled. Alarmed. That's when I smelled him. I leaped for the lamp. My eyes landed on an oversized muscular frame, too big for my mere queen mattress. My chest heaved and heart galloped. This. *This!* This was that exciting yet dangerous factor of Rut. He made his own rules, set his own pace—and I had a feeling not just with me. It was who he was to everyone he met. There were so many things I should have said in that very moment as I gazed down on his outstretched, carved body. There was that one thing I *should* have done, but I couldn't. I didn't want to.

I clicked off the light then ambled with a shaky frame to the other side of the bed. My hand trembled as I pulled back the comforter and crawled in. For the life of me, I couldn't stop trembling. Tears slipped from my closed eyes. Then a long, hard roped arm hooked around my waist and pulled me into a hot, unyielding body.

It was perfect and forbidden. Needed yet not welcomed. It felt like heaven. Like that element I craved all my life. This was that proverbial "strong arms to cry in" phenomenon. A strange squeal ripped from my chest and my body juddered.

"We can't do this, Rut." I heaved in a needed breath. "This is his house."

If it was possible, he pulled me even closer into his hot frame. Soft, moist lips kissed the back of my neck. My entire frame quivered.

When I was able to catch my breath and stop the tears, I was hoisted up on top of him to straddle. The moment my face met his bare chest, comfort and care enveloped me and I was drifting off to sleep.

chapter
nine

As I held the measuring cup and dropper in the air, adding vitamin E oil, I heard the doorbell sound. Lowering the dropper and cup, I turned and glanced into Jimmy's room. It was senseless. Jimmy wouldn't confirm the sound anyways. The bell rang again, prompting me to drop my instruments and remove my goggles.

I made my way to the door, wondering who could be here just before noon on a Thursday? I hadn't been expecting a delivery. My supplies arrived yesterday while I was at work and no nurses or doctors were due to visit.

When I pulled the door back, shock wouldn't accurately describe my reaction. And apparently, she had one, too. Her honey-brown irises appeared dilated. A few crow's feet etched the sides of her eyes, but other than that, she hardly looked her forty-seventh year around the sun.

From root to tip, her hair was its usual yellowish-blonde. For as long as I remembered, she kept it short in variations of a pixie cut. Today it could be no longer than an inch and a half with a natural wave. Her otherwise five-foot-nine frame seemed a few inches shorter than I recalled, but she was still slender-thick, hiding her mild curves behind the *London Fog* duster she had since I was a sophomore in high school. And those shoes. The *Stuart Weitzman* tassel flats I couldn't recall *not* seeing her in dated her. For a tenured professor, earning close to one hundred and fifty thousand dollars a year, she didn't use it to aid her wardrobe.

But when I glanced up, I found her eyes locked onto me in trance-like concentration. Her gawk was on my forehead then eyes, nose, lips...my apron and finally down to the black crocs I wore. It was the strangest forty seconds of my life in recent history. When her regard returned to my face, she blinked a few times, unable to speak. One thing was for sure: I'd never seen her so muted in my presence.

Should I invite her in?

Did I want to? I didn't know the protocol. This reminded me of how long it had been since I'd last seen her. I had to speak.

"This is surprising." My chin was low as was my voice.

"I had a dream."

My chin pushed further into my chest. "A dream?"

"Yes." Unsmiling, she continued. "I dreamt you had a baby—" Quickly, she sniffled and turned her head over her shoulder to swipe her pooling eyes.

My chest lifted as I sucked in a deep breath, surprised by this display of emotions from her.

With a racing heart, I tried to give her something. "I *swear* to you it's kind of hard to get pregnant by a man who is bedridden twenty-four hours a day and can't speak or swallow...can't even go to the bathroom on his own." Dry humor, but it was something.

"I know. And I hate it."

"Let's not go there."

"I won't." Her tone was firm. "I didn't come here to go there. I came here to say I got excited for the first time over the prospect of my daughter being pregnant. There's some form of retrogression going on in the solar system." She sniffled on a chuckle, wiping her leaking eye again. "Can you believe that?"

"Yeah," I returned wryly. "You, me, and a baby?" I transferred the weight of my legs. My sarcasm switched on without thought when inga was anywhere near. "Especially because I'd need a man or a product of the male species to make that happen."

"Yeah." She blew out a breath, eyes in the distance again as she returned in the same wry manner, "Let's just keep that between me and you."

"That still doesn't explain why you're here."

"Oh." She turned behind her, looking down. I followed her line of sight to an open box. She lifted it. "After the dream, I woke up and eventually went looking for this. It's a box your grandmother started of all your random things from a baby. When she passed away, your grandfather added to it. And when..." She tossed her head, shrugging. "Well, after him, I began tossing things in here. We've been so disconnected..." She couldn't look at me. "If by some odd—and convenient—perilous probability you are pregnant or will get there sooner or later, I thought you may want to share some of this with your own little girl."

Girl?

I grabbed my forehead with clenched eyes. "inga... All this crying and emotional babble of babies." I glanced up at her. "I'm sure you'll understand me wondering if you're a clone. The real inga grayson must be tucked in her basement office back on campus, drowning in books from wall to wall while hostilely grading a term paper. Surely, there is some poor student she feels has integrated too much demoiselle emotion in what should be a separatist, feminist narrative."

"Yup." She nodded, eyes cast away again. "That's actually where I'm going next and to do exactly that. I just wanted to bring you this."

She handed me the box. I didn't understand what was going on here. The last person I expected to see today and *here* was Dr. inga grayson. And with a box of memorabilia.

For a long while, we stood in silence. It was clear to me this had been just as awkward an experience for her as it was for me. For the second time in my life, my mother couldn't maintain consistent eye contact with me.

Then she nodded, nose red and eyes still low. I took it to mean she understood it was time for this strange exchange to come to a close.

Though she couldn't see me, I nodded, too. She turned away to leave but I stood there stock-still, holding remnants of my childhood.

My regard was blindly in the box when I heard, "Parker..." My eyes flew up but my brain didn't work fast enough to speak. "There's this new coffee shop a couple of blocks away from the campus. It'll be nice to meet there some day. Maybe share a latte?"

We hadn't shared a caffeinated drink since I was sixteen. What was going on?

I licked my lips and my brows narrowed, heavily confounded. "Maybe."

She nodded, rubbing her lips together with her eyes down cast. When she sauntered off, I closed the door.

She pulled the door open and her eyelashes batted.

"You're late."

I took a deep breath, aware and annoyed by that fact. "I know, man." I pushed my arms in the air, relaxation settled in already for the night just being near her. "I had a session with the head doctor today."

Her smile was shy as her eyes stayed low. "Hey," she muttered.

Her hair was up in a curly ponytail and a white tank top was tied behind her tiny waist. Parker always looked like a teenager when in house clothes. I couldn't decide if she was sexier like this or in those fitted skirts and sexy blouses she wore to work.

My cheeks stretched and belly tightened.

"Hey, Gray..." I sang playfully.

She tossed her head backward. "The table's set. I'm going to finish up with Jimmy and I'll join you."

So that meant she was expecting me? *Good.* I guessed she should have seeing I'd been coming every week night since the first time I visited.

I stepped in. "A'ight."

Then she was off. I watched the biker shorts she wore cling to her jiggly ass as she pranced down the hall. That made my damn mouth go dry and butterflies take off in my fucking belly. That shit hadn't happened since I was like eleven. I closed the door behind me and saw a box right next to it. The picture of a baby girl on top caught my attention. I kneeled to get a better view. The baby could be no more than a few months. The picture was framed in white wood with an inscribed plate. *Parker audre Grayson.*

She was beautiful. Even the typo on her name was cute. She was a gorgeous brown baby with a head full of hair, long curly lashes, a button nose, and drooling lips. There was other baby stuff underneath. I decided I'd done enough snooping and lay the picture back in the box.

My first stop in the kitchen was the sink to wash my hands. Then I went to the stove to peep what was inside the pots and pans. Looked like salmon with some kind of teriyaki sauce, brown rice, and snow peas. My phone started blowing up in my pocket so I decided to handle that as I waited. When I checked, all there was were texts from chicks, DMs from chicks, and missed calls from chicks. One was Chestnut Cherries from *Arch & Point*. I hadn't been through there since the night I bagged her. We did a little texting back and forth with promises to get up again. The problem was I hadn't had the time. Seeing her last text from earlier reminded me to read through it and reply.

CC: *U playn games I thot u was bout that lyfe*

She included the laughing emoji icon to soften her thirst.

Me: Nah. My bad been busy. I got you tho.

And no matter how much I meant that, I couldn't conceive the "when" part in my head. When would I pull up on *Arch & Point* again? Maybe this weekend? Nah. Couldn't. I was supposed to be getting the call any day now about B-Rocka's funeral arrangements. My moms told me they were working on it. One funeral home turned his mother down because of all the gun play still going on behind his death. Two dudes from Dolly got hit since I left Trenton Tuesday night. It wasn't safe at home at all. Before my peoples went in for retaliation, my moms, grandmoms, and a couple aunts left town for a hotel where they'd been laying low. It had been crazy.

CC: *Got me how*

I snickered at her.

Me: Didn't I make you shoot off last time?

I went into my *IG* app to clear a few of my DMs while I waited. I saw a few R.I.P. tags and messages. The word had begun to spread. Someone told me the other day my name was mentioned on the local news. People knew B-Rocka was my cousin.

A text came through.

CC: *U aint make me brandee did*

That gave me pause. It felt like an eternity since I'd fucked them broads. And after thinking for a few seconds, I did remember I used the girl, Brandee, to help with Chestnut Cherries' last nut.

Me: *But ya first one was all on me. The second was a bonus. I see it wasn't good enough for ya greedy ass.*

I shook my head, laughing to myself about sounding like I really gave a damn. There were some females I cared if they nutted when we fucked. Just because we weren't together didn't mean pleasure couldn't be a two-sided game.

Right?

I had to sit and think about my pleasure-giving ratio. Yeah, I had to think. Getting ass was easier for me than getting clean foods to eat in my line of work. When pussy is handed to you at a high volume, you could easily lose count of who you took care of or just used to get off. Not many were memorable.

In the last three years or so, I got into female orgasms. It was the biggest turn on being able to make one happen, which was why I could be generous that way. I knew dudes who got them off in ways it couldn't be returned by the female. Orgasms that weren't understood would be reciprocated. Divine told me that.

He told me, "*If your pleasure only comes from your arousal and your nut, you ain't fucking right. Go masturbate and leave a woman out of it.*"

Shiiiiiit...

Fuck no would I give and not get. I wasn't selfish but not stupid either.

"I spoke to my therapist today." When my head shot up, Parker was zipping by me, headed for the sink.

"Oh, word?"

She nodded, washing her hands.

"For what?" I asked, closing out of my apps.

I caught her little shoulders lift. "I told you. When I have a lot jumbled in my head, I'll hit her up for help sorting it."

I placed my phone on the table. "You can talk to me."

"About what?" That amused her.

I grinned. "About anything."

"And you're supposed to care?"

"I don't think ya therapist cares about your shit. She just helps you organize. Right?"

Parker turned the eyes to the stove on low to warm the food then reached for the plates.

That ass though...

A few weeks ago, Chestnut Cherries was my target. And now, looking at the contour of fat ass in front of me, the goal line had been moved. I needed something bigger and better to conquer because as men, that's what we did. We looked for bigger and better challenges in women. Thicker, more sexually skilled, better at discretion, less attached, prettier, sexier, doper in fashion... The list went on and on, and could vary depending on the man.

"Good point." Parker woke me from my thoughts. "But I don't think you care to hear about my mother showing up here unannounced with a box full of my childhood, hoping I was pregnant. That's one of a few things I wanted to talk about."

"That's what that big ass box by the door's about?"

"Mmhmm," she hummed, stirring the pot of snow peas. "I haven't even looked through it yet; I've been so busy around here."

"I peeped the big ass picture of you looking like Alf's baby." I laughed. Parker's head snatched around to look at me through narrowed eyes. "Yup. I saw the typo on the name plate, too. I hope ya moms got a few dollars off for that."

"What typo?"

"Your middle name. Your first and last were capitalized but the 'A' in Audre wasn't."

She was spooning food onto our plates when she explained, "That's not a typo. My mother's a noted feminist."

"A what?"

"A feminist. The type of woman that would eat chauvinistics like you alive." She carried my plate to me. "In fact, your coach is probably one. They can sniff limited minds in terms of sexuality out a mile away."

I lay my hand on my chest as I looked up to her while she organized my place setting. "That wounded me. I'm no chauvinist. I eat pussy, just not pork."

A howl let loose from Parker's belly. "What?" She laughed.

"The only meat I discriminate against is what goes into my mouth. I love ass, but pork gets no play from me." I grabbed my fork. "Neither do beef no more."

She cracked the hell up, going back for her plate. When she settled in across the table from me, I waited for her to say her grace.

She glanced up. "Do you always do that?"

"What?"

"Use humor to deflect confrontation."

I shrugged. "Who am I having confrontation with? A female?" I put the first forkful in my mouth and paused to let my tongue absorb the flavors. "I ain't conflicting with no chick, so maybe I use other means to diffuse the situation."

"With all women?"

I shrugged as I chewed. "I don't argue with females."

"Women, Rut. Yes, we are female in terms of human species but the more appropriate and dignified term for us is women."

I shook my head disagreeing. "All females ain't women."

"It's no different from calling a grown man a boy because he runs around sleeping with multiple women and breaking their hearts along the way. It's a respectful and dignified title that leaves the judgement out."

My phone lit and vibrated next to me on the table at the same time.

CC: *But wut that tong game like tho*

I busted out, laughing my fucking ass off with a full mouth. Because my head was back and eyes closed, I didn't see when Parker grabbed my phone.

"Sheesh! Is that how women request sex?"

"See!" I slowed my laughing. "Perfect example of her not being a woman. That shit ain't ladylike."

"Requesting sex instead of repressing your desires is very womanly, I'd have you to know. Society has progressed in terms of women's expression. If you can beat your chest and demand we come to please you, we can do the same."

But Parker wasn't Chestnut Cherries.

"Before Wright got sick, you used to send shit like that to him?"

"Like what?"

"Look at how she types."

"It's text. Nothing wrong with shorthand."

"Is that what *you* do, though?"

"No, but there's nothing wrong with how she—"

"Y'all ain't cut from the same cloth. Period."

"But we can sleep with the same kind of man." My eyes shot up to Parker scrolling through my text thread with Chestnut Cherries. "Apparently, we have." Her eyes were now on me as she gently slid my phone back over. "You can't judge women and not judge yourself. If she's trash because she doesn't type eloquently or because she allowed you to let another woman get her off because you couldn't, that means you're the dumpster who carries her. And if she slept with you casually and *I* slept with you casually, what does that make me in your eyes?" She scooped a piece of fish into her mouth and popped her fork back.

Her eyebrows were lifted; Parker was challenging me. Instantly, I hated the shit. She didn't get the point. She was nothing like Chestnut Cherries.

But I don't argue with fema—women, sooooo...

"Why don't you kick it with ya moms?" I asked with my eyes to my plate.

There was a pause before she answered.

"What makes you think I don't?"

"You told me last week you got the degree you have to spite her. And tonight you said she showed uninvited. Who don't keep in touch with their Earths if they're alive?"

Parker sat back and took a deep breath. "We're not programmed the same. It took years to get. I get it now and stay away."

"That's it?"

"Of course, not! It's just... She's everything I'm not. Undeniably confident, highly educated, driven with purpose, and...solitary." She shook her head. "She doesn't seem to mind living alone. My mother has always said she doesn't need a man, and if it wasn't for a silly mistake as a kid herself, she would have never had children. Proof of that is me being an only child. But on the other hand, she was strong and went through school from her Bachelor's, to Master's, all the way to her Doctorate's without complaining or breaking a sweat."

"What's wrong with that?"

"She wanted—*wants*—the same for me. She wants me to journey down the same path she has. She wanted me to take on women's studies in college, but I had no interest. Each time I dated a guy, she turned her nose up. She's the reason my whole goal game in life has changed. I mean, the list of things I wanted to accomplish by thirty was vastly different than they are now. And that's because I spent years trying to fight her reputation. Fighting her lofty and unoriginal expectations of me. I've been told more times than I can count I'm the typical cookie-cutter, American girl, believing having a man completes half of their purposes in life. Do you know how difficult it is growing up with that type of energy over you as a kid?"

I shook my head. Those things she described as her mother's life didn't sound at all like the Parker I'd been getting to know.

"It turns them into Mother Teresa. I'm caring for a man I accepted an engagement ring from knowing he didn't love me...I didn't love him. I just wanted to be chosen. It has me at twenty-eight years old with a degree in chemistry, working part time for a football team's corporate office just to keep my mind. But to make some type of living, I craft soaps, candles, and moisturizers. That is the closest I've come to using a degree I barely got because the classes were way over my learning curve."

I had no idea she did all that. When the hell did Parker find the time?

She shook her head and let go of a sigh as she went back to her food. "I told you there were a few things I called my therapist about. The other was...us."

"What about us?"

"Well, for starters, the fact we had sex."

"Told you I could handle this. You coulda called me for *that*. What made her more suitable?"

She took a sip of her tea, ignoring me. "That ties into my mother's visit."

"How so?"

"When I opened the door, she just...gaped at me. Like... From head to toe, she paid a scrutinizing eye to me. But it was different than what I've seen of her in the past; those times where she was clearly disgusted because I had a broken heart or when I struggled in my science courses, going for a degree I knew was far from the one she wanted me to pursue. This time she seemed...dazed. She paid a lot of attention to my face. Yeah, it was clean of makeup. I'm sure I looked a mess; I've been home with Jimmy. I didn't go out of the house today so I had no need to put any on..." Parker hesitated.

"Go on..."

She bit that bottom lip before she spoke again. "I know I'm not the young, spritely teenager or adolescent I used to be. And..." her voice morphed into a whisper. "I wonder did she see that. *Am I really pre-aging?*" Her eyes squinted.

Even then I saw the light in her eyes I noticed the first night we met. It didn't matter if Parker was expressing confusion, anger, happiness or sadness, there was the glow deep in her eyes. And when her face was naked from make-up and the natural tan circles showed like they did as I stared at her, I could still see that light I could get lost in. Those brown circles gave off that mature and wise vibe to her. It was like a promise of...unconditional commitment that turned me the fuck on.

I was willing to bet two stacks when her mother was staring at her as she described, she was remembering how beautiful this girl was. I probably should have shared that with her while she was in this vulnerable place. But of course, I wouldn't tell her right now. I wasn't on that corny shit. This was no romance story.

"Anyway," Parker spoke up. "No need for me lamenting over something I get and something I've been delivered from." She leaned into the table. "That's church folk talk." Parker giggled.

I didn't. I wanted her to get to her point.

"Whachu mean?"

"When Eli paired me with this therapist, one of the things we tackled first was my 'inside' and how I felt about myself. She recommended understanding me spiritually. Now I know what you're going to say. I know all people should not look to Christianity and, for sure, not the church as their first attempt at exploring spirituality. But she recommended *Redeeming Souls* in New York, and it's one of the best things I've done for myself in years."

"I thought Jade Bailey put you D with that church?"

Parker nodded her head. "Ironically, her too. We'd seen each other in the front office a few times and she invited me. The wives club hadn't been accepting of her, so she took another method to find friends in the organization. Anyway," She waved her hand, obviously and excitedly wanting to move on. "The second thing we took on was letting go of people who didn't appreciate being in my life. I got the memo too late with Jimmy, but he was one of those I could have applied that rule to. Jimmy didn't want a wife. He'd been sleeping with other women after I moved in." She leaned into the table again as though she was being secretive. "Rule numero uno: don't leave dirty trysts on your cell phone before you've been diagnosed with ALS." She found that funny.

Again, I didn't.

"It's funny now because I'm a different woman. I thought Jimmy wanted something serious. I didn't focus on the fact he was twenty-three years older than me and possibly past his prime. I saw he was fit, handsome, and charming. But he saw me as easily manipulative arm-candy. Then he got sick." She shrugged. "But my mother..." There was a pause. "She rode me hard about me being with him—as she should have, in retrospect. But what I couldn't take was her continuing to make me feel isolated when I decided to stay. She was an energy I could dismiss. She didn't accept me so she couldn't stay. So now, I'm able to let people who don't want to be here go."

"She wants you to have a kid. Sounds like she didn't want to go."

"Everything isn't black and white. I'm sure she loves me and has always. But if I was never able to make her proud being who I was, which was a kid simply trying to figure it out, she wasn't happy in my life. That made me unhappy, so I chose for her to go." Parker finished the last on her plate. "I'm done." She looked at my unfinished food. "You?"

I shook my head, sure it was cold by now but agreeing I was done would have meant saying goodnight. I wasn't ready to end the night with her.

Parker stood from the table and took her plate to the sink. She cleaned the stove of the pots and pans, loading them in the sink, too. I halfway watched as I nibbled on my cold food.

"Well, I'm going to make sure Jimmy's down for the night. Don't worry about the dishes tonight. I can take care of them," came out so softly—nervously but gentle. I knew the questions running through her mind. It was awkward wondering if I'd stay again tonight or if I'd leave like she was now inviting me to. But that was the thing: my gut told me Parker didn't want me to go. Welcoming to leave was the appropriate thing to do. "This was nice. Thanks." And she moved behind me to leave the kitchen.

"Park," I called after her, my back to her.

I could hear her footsteps stop right away. "Huhn?"

"I'm not going home tonight."

Then Parker backed up into my peripheral. "Hmmm!"

I shook my head to make clear. "Nah. I'm not going home tonight. I'm going to bed upstairs. In your bed." I wanted to make clear.

The whole room was so silent you could hear a pigeon shit on the roof.

She backed up more so we could easily see each other. "Can we unpack that?"

"I don't get a lot of sleep. And now with B-Roc—" It hurt to say his name. "With my mans gone..." I shook my head, not believing those words. "Being in this new state. New place...like my life now. I *swear*—" I remembered her crying in bed last night and wanted to make it clear. "You know this ain't about sex. It's just..." *Fuck it...* I groaned. "I feel at peace when you're on top of me sleeping." Parker's eyes fell to the floor and I panicked like a motherfucker. "If it's not cool, you can let me know. I won't be happy about it... I'm not the type of man used to being told no, but..." I rambled on.

"No," she whispered. "It's not that."

"Then what is it?"

"I suffer from insomnia. I have for the past few years." She paused again, fingers threading through one another. "I've dangerously gotten longer than four hours of sleep on your chest."

I let out the longest quiet breath, hoping she didn't hear it. *But...* That was all she said. Shit just went quiet.

"But what?" I knew there was one.

Her eyes finally rose to mine. "It's not my house."

"But it is your home. You've made it one. I know it, Wright knows it, and you do, too." I shrugged, wanting to convince her. "If I had it my way, I'd scoop you up, put you in your own place, and give you all the independency you need just so I can rest, but..." I swung my arm in the air. She knew where I was going with this.

"I may not be inga grayson, but I am very much independent and I would not go from one dependent situation with a man to another."

I nodded, not surprised at all at what she said. And *that* bothered me.

Parker left me alone in the kitchen with my conflicting thoughts I was sure my head doctor would get a damn kick out of.

Parker

Jimmy was tucked in and hopefully comfortable for the night and I was showered and in my bed with another man, one who was becoming less and less of a stranger. He stretched out over my small mattress like he owned it and been resting in it for years. In silence of the darkness, I began to think that was exactly how I met Rut. His first interaction with me was as though it was with experience.

"What about ya pops?" his thick chords vibrated.

"What about him?"

"He do anything to offset ya mom's feministic views?"

I wanted to laugh. "He never got a chance to."

The whole mattress vibrated when he hummed, "Huhn?"

I licked my lips, brows furrowed as I decided to go there. "I never knew my father. Never met him."

"Damn," he breathed.

"It's okay. I hope my bluntness didn't make you feel uncomfortable." I felt my shoulder lift as I lay on my side away from him. "That was a huge piece of my therapy, too. My mother was so rigid in her expectations, but she never allowed my father in my life. I asked about him a few times just to be told she didn't know where he was. My grandfather lived close by and we had a pretty good relationship so there weren't just women in my life. But it all caught up to my mother one day. My father's sister showed up to my grandfather's house saying my father had passed and I needed to be at his funeral. I was...maybe a junior in high school and could perceive her anger clearly.

"My grandfather fought with my mother and won that battle. I went to his funeral but the opportunity had been lost. He had other children—a family at that point. Being there was awkward for me, so I never kept in touch. What hurt worse was my mother. I was told in so many words at his funeral, by his mother and sister, how he wanted to keep in touch with me but my mother didn't allow it."

I giggled. "When I met Jade Bailey, it was probably our third conversation when we realized we shared the same experience of never having met our fathers, thanks to our mothers. Sad, but it made for great bonding with another woman."

Rut didn't speak, and that was okay. I understood how unusual that story could be for someone who had known their parents all their lives. Within seconds, I learned his response was better than anything I expected. He pulled me into him then lifted me like doll and arranged me to straddle him, just as he'd done before.

I hummed into his fragranced, lightly dusted chest. My arms found comfort astride his thick wings. Everything about this position screamed peaceful and...protective. Everything accept my sex laying against his raised abdomen. But Rut had proven himself to be a gentleman and never made this sexual.

"What're your new goals?" his chest rumbled as he muttered.

"New goals?"

"You said earlier ya moms going so hard made you change your original goals coming up."

Oh...

My eyes narrowed. "Well, I still desire to have a successful career, maybe using my craft. But I used to want those traditional girlie things like a husband, a house, and children."

"What do you want now?"

"Everything but the husband." He didn't ask why, but I felt comfortable sharing. "I think this thing with Jimmy tarnished my ideas of companionship, but I want a baby. Motherhood is the essence of a woman. It gives us our war scars in terms of the functionality of our bodies—those of us who can bear children. And as children grow, it sharpens our existence because we have all the tools needed to create and groom little people into big people. I'd love to have that job."

Then that big, hot hand was at the small of my back, soothingly rubbing. I didn't know if Rut was telling me to shut up or encouraging my day dreams, but in the end, once sleep fell upon me, it didn't matter.

chapter **ten**

JUST WHEN IT FELT LIKE I'D JUST come back to bed from checking in on Jimmy at my usual three am run, I felt my body being rolled over onto my back. Wonderfully scented heat instantly replaced cool air. This was the part of the deal I hated. When Rut left at the crack of dawn to prepare for his day, I eventually rose for mine. My restful sleep seemed to go out the door with him in the mornings. Then, between traces of his masculine aroma and my full bladder, my groin stirred viciously. It had been a torturous but worthwhile tradeoff, having his big body here as my mattress and pillow.

I moaned and stretched my arms over my head when I landed on my back. Hating having to open my eyes, I knew it was inevitable. I had to disarm the house for him to leave. That hot, heavy weight was on me. Soft, moist lips were on my neck. My pulse beat against my skin as my toes curled toward my backside. His mouth worked down my chest and over the thin slip. When his torso descended, I lowered my leg to not break his downward glide. My belly constricted when his hands lifted the material up my hips, gathering into his hands.

When his warm mouth touched the bare skin of my belly, my entire body shuttered. His teeth scraped across my jumpy belly, causing my hands to curl into tight fists. He licked downward, the tip of his tongue circling the rim of my naval. My head rolled left and right over the pillow, but I refused to utter a sound. It felt so good...so forbidden for some reason, and I didn't want to blow our cover.

My pulse roared in my ears as my arms pushed down on his shoulders. They flexed beneath my misted palms and moved lower. Hot air pushed from my lungs when his tongue rolled beneath my navel. His hands left a faint trace of heat down my inner thighs. That had my head and shoulders leaping from the mattress and my torso suspended in the air. He rolled his tongue down the same path his right hand had just left on my thigh.

I groaned, my back arching over the mattress.

His teeth bit into that tickly, sensitive place of my inner thigh. I swallowed the collecting saliva gathered in my mouth, so afraid to move at this point. My clit throbbed dangerously, feeling heavy and heated. His head shifted and lips dragged down the inside of my left thigh. His teeth scraped up, eliciting another helpless whimper from my belly. I couldn't take it anymore. I was feverish, body dampening all over.

"*Oh, shiiit*—" I cupped my mouth with both hands.

His teeth clamped on the skin joining my thigh and sex, his tongue slivered through that seam. Who was this? My hips shifted, body shimmying beneath him.

Then his mouth was there. He kissed me. *There*. Twice. Next his tongue swiped from my hind flesh all the way up to the opening of my sex. My spine spasmed.

"Rut..." croaked harshly from my throat.

"*Shhhhhhh...*" He blew over my wetness and my shoulders twitched.

His tongue swiped all over, swirling in places I didn't know were sensitive. He dipped inside my sex and I could feel it ripple. He slurped and stabbed, sucked and lashed all over. Rut was amazingly focused, thrilling, and noticeably practiced.

Suddenly, I felt wrong for arguing with him about the girl he was texting. Feeling my groin heat like this reminded me he did give me an orgasm—and first—the night we'd slept together. It was proof he didn't view me and the girl texting him the same. Should I now believe he thought of me as different?

Special?

I sure felt that way as his tongue rolled over and over my throbbing clit. When his big hands curled around my hips, pulling me into him, I felt supremely reverenced. He was capable of making a woman feel above his ego.

My hips vibrated in his hold, hands went to his head, and shoulders pushed into the mattress as my groin roiled and roiled until it imploded. He groaned, I shuddered boneless. The sensation rolled over and over, sending me awash to a new plateau. I couldn't move, couldn't catch my breath, and I certainly couldn't control the nonstop tremors.

His big hands were at the sides of my hips, rubbing reverentially. I shivered and sniffled, eyes shut tight, trying to gain myself.

What in the world just happened?

"Parker..."

At first, I couldn't speak. "*Ye—*" I swallowed. "Yeah?"

"You cool?"

My eyes shot open. How would I answer *that*?

"*I*—I... Uhhh. I don't know." I panted. "I think so."

He grumbled something more before shuffling between my legs. In the next movement, he had my back off the mattress. Then I was being tugged and flipped over. Hot air slew jaggedly from my lungs and I landed on my hands and knees. His soft and warm mouth was on me again. Full lips and aggressive tongue worked in tandem to caress the back of my thigh. I worked to stifle a moan. Initially, it was strange, holding on all fours while his mouth was near my ass.

But it was clear when his big palms slapped and cupped my cheeks, Rut was exactly where he intended to be. I couldn't believe what was happening. The level of sensitivity in the skin back there had been unknown to me until now. Pleasure seized my body, but my mind couldn't slow. This position made me think back to the interview I'd seen of him last week while on my break at the office. Ruby Vodoo of *Power 105.1 Morning Show* had her own podcast that was based on sex and sensuality. Apparently, Rut had done an episode with her and crew the week before I met him.

"Ahhhhh..." I swear I didn't mean to let that cry leave my lips.

But when his tongue laved the seam of my cheeks, abrupt pleasure toppled over. His face pushed deeper and tongue poked further, the tip circling around and around. That brought me back to Rut sharing on Ruby Vodoo's podcast his mixed feelings about using his mouth on more than half the women he slept with. He explained how there were so many over the years, he had to quickly develop a mental rule book about which ones he'd provide those intimate acts of tongues and perform cunnilingus on. He said he enjoyed it, but limited the number of women he shared that experience with based on chemist—

"Mmmmmmm..." another moan shot from my belly and my spine dipped, curving.

My face fell into the mattress and hips pushed into him. I could hear him attempt a breath back there or maybe it was a growl, I couldn't be sure. The first time I felt an intrusion of my rectum I stiffened, but Rut didn't stop. His tongue extended, thrashing my clit that had begun heating again. His tongue beat, pounded, and sucked until my hips began rocking again. Then his finger moved again, rimming me.

"Oh, gosh!" I cried, ready to lose my mind with this erotic stimulation.

And the sound... *Oh, my goo*— Hearing the erogenous sounds of him performing this forbidden act was foreign and invigorating. My nipples rubbed against the sheets as I rocked into him, creating a rhythm. Rut was the master multitasker, rendering me a salivating mess. I moved in sync with his laving and gentle swiping of a bundle of nerves new to me as well.

Then.

My entire frame quailed at what I knew was coming next. What *it* seemed to have known before my brain could quite prepare for. Tsunamic pleasure tumbled over me without warning. My hips lifted higher in the air and plopped up and down on its own accord. Hard mewls pushed through my tightened throat and my shoulders vibrated violently.

From shoulders to toes, my body shimmied until Rut's talented mouth left my slit. I fell on my face and rolled over onto the mattress, landing in a position unfit for seduction.

RUT

My ass dropped. On a strain, I lifted...lengthening my legs. Then I dropped again, keeping my balance as I squeezed my ass and thighs.

"Fifty!" my trainer, Mickey, shouted behind me while I hit my squats.

I hardly paid attention. With so much shooting through my mind, I tried to focus on my form. And not on *her*. Competing for my attention was the barrage of calls I got this morning from the time I stepped out of the shower at my condo. These last few days had felt unreal.

"Seventy-one!" Mickey yelled from behind me, but I didn't process the count.

Couldn't.

"Yo!" I did catch.

Someone shouted that with more urgency. I felt Mickey tap the side of my back, telling me to call it quits. I stepped forward, ducked my head, and transferred the weight bar on its rack. When I backed up, I turned around out of breath, trying to see what the commotion was all about. Young Lord rang throughout the gym as sounds of metal bars clanking and grown men grunting filled the area.

It was Coach Brooks.

"Nate wants you in his office, ASAP!" she shouted over the music.

I felt my face fold. *Why the hell would he call me from the gym?*

Figuring it was some shit I probably did wrong, like fuck with Brooks or the ticket I got on my way in when I was running late yesterday, I decided to go right away.

Grabbing my towel and jug of water, I headed out right away. The walk over to the front office from the gym wasn't that far or maybe it was. Maybe my busy mind didn't account for the distance because, before I knew it, I was inside the corporate doors of the *Connecticut Kings'* franchise.

I walked up to the receptionist's desk outside of his office. "Richardson called me up from the gym."

The young girl, who I'd seen around the practice field, scanned me from top to bottom. I believed she was an intern, at least that's what one of the trainers told me. She looked as though she couldn't speak at first. Then when her eyes made it back up to my face, her pupils flipped wickedly. She lifted the desk phone to her ear and on the second beep I heard a masculine voice say three words before hanging up.

"He's ready for you." She tossed her head toward his door.

I stepped off, ready to find out why he had me called from the middle of a workout. I was new here but had never seen anyone called from the gym or field into the front office.

Nate was on a call when I walked in.

"He's here," he informed the person on the other end while staring at me. "Hold on." He tapped a button on the box. "Azmir?"

Azmi—

"You got that Obama phone set up?"

My lips pushed out. "Huhn?"

"The Obama phone. The bootleg shit with inconsistent service?"

"Nah." My eyes went to Nate's, whose were locked on me as he leaned over his desk.

"You got a new private line?"

What? "Nah."

"Then why the fuck haven't I been able to reach you on ya phone?"

As realization hit me, my eyes closed and I shook my head. "My bad. It's dead—my phone." I was stumbling over my words, feeling so off. "It died this morning. Flat lined while I was kickin' it with mom dukes about the funeral."

But that was no reason for him to go drill sergeant on me.

I swung my arm. "Why you trippin'?"

Nate stood straight and walked over to the window like he knew what was coming.

"Why am I trippin'?" Divine repeated. "I'm trippin' because I don't need you going cowboy and hopping down the Turnpike to play street solider."

"Ain't no need." I gotta text late last night when Parker got up to check on Wright, saying the crew finally got the shooters...*in so many cryptic words*.

"What?"

"Nothing." I shook my head. "I'm good. Just gotta carry a charger, I guess."

"So you heard about the services?"

That's when Nate turned my way again. It was almost as though he was giving us privacy there for a minute.

I rubbed my chin, feeling that burn in my chest whenever I thought of B-Rocka.

Think of her... Think of her...

That was the only distraction I could use to retard the rage I felt when I allowed my mind to focus on his death. I hated that the tactic worked. Hated having to rely on a chick for anything. But I did in this case.

"Yeah. I heard," finally, I answered.

"And about that..." Nate shoved his hands in his suit's pants pockets as he strolled my way, sitting on the edge of the desk. "Given the nature of your cousin's death, we need to move smartly."

"What that mean?" I asked.

"It means we have to remember you're a *King* now, duke," Divine added. "You're a liability to the organization."

"Damn!"

"Let's try 'a pecuniary risk,'" Divine tried cleaning it up.

Nate snickered. I didn't find shit funny.

"What Azmir is saying, Rut, is we think it's best to add precautionary measures."

My face went tight. "Like the fuck what?"

"You'll have professional, strapped muscle with you that day. They'll scoop you in Connecticut and bring you back *that night*." There was emphasis on his last two words.

"I'm gonna be home, Divine. I'm good on security. And if I need heat, I got that, too."

"That's exactly the type of smoke we don't want," Nate explained. "Again, we need to be smart about the way we move around this shit."

I let out a deep breath, realizing my lungs had calmed from my workout.

"That all you called me up here for?" I groaned, rubbing my head with the towel around my neck.

When Nate nodded his answer, I turned for the door.

"You're not going to say goodbye to Azmir?"

Nate calling Divine "Azmir" reminded me how little he truly knew the dude. He may have known he was a real one but didn't know how real. He also didn't know how much of a pain in my fucking ass Divine could be. But because I knew him so well, and actually cared about the old fuck, I knew he had been stressed and crabby as fuck. Divine was still dealing with that documentary about his ties to the streets. He was a beast I couldn't take on right now. I would just ignore the heat from him and keep pushing forward.

With my back to him, I mumbled, "I'll holla."

The intern receptionist was all up in my grill when I closed the door behind me. I scrolled to the desk and hit her with a grin I knew would distract her.

"Hey, sweetheart." I rested my elbow on the shelf of the desk, leaning toward her.

"Heeeeeeeey, Rut!" she sang so sweetly.

"Oh. You know my name?"

"Stop playing, boy." She giggled. "I know more about you than you know."

My eyes flew wide, but I tried maintaining that smile.

"What's ya name?"

Her cheeks dropped but her eyes fucking danced. She was game for whatever.

"Richell Win—"

"Chelly, what's the name of shawtie that only works here a few days a week? Short chick, mocha skin, and wears her hair in a part down the middle? Long dark hair down her back—"

The spark of recognition hit her eyes.

"Oh!" She perked up. "You mean Parker?"

"Yeah." My forehead wrinkled and chin dipped to play like I wasn't confident. "Her, I think. She here today?"

She thought for a minute. "Yeah..."

There was a pause as she waited for more information on my inquiry.

My chin dipped lower. "You mind telling me where?"

I didn't have my phone or a watch on for the time.

Richell went for the phone. "I can call her down."

"Nah, I'm good. You could tell me where at." I didn't want to wait.

"Oh." She put the phone down on the receiver. Then she bit her lip, understanding this brief chat was about some other female. "She's covering in finance today. That's on the fourth floor."

I pointed. "Elevator that way?"

Richell nodded.

It only took walking around three corners for me to find her. She was sitting in a small office, typing away at a computer with a half-eaten peanut butter and jelly sandwich, sliced carrots and celery, and a bottle of water to her right. My dick swelled.

So engrossed in what she was doing, she didn't even notice me. Parker froze, considered something on the screen, cocked her head to the side, and bit her lip. Then she looked down at a mountain of a binder with tiny numbers before going back to the computer and tapping the keyboard at crazy speed.

I moved into the doorway and tapped on the glass I'd just watched her through. When her eyes rolled up, my damn heart pounded.

The fuck...

I was sure it was because of what happened this morning. It had been buried under the other crazy shit in my brain. I ate her pussy. And now, staring at her in the light of day, I could taste her musk in my mouth all over again. My eyes closed and I squeezed them tight, trying to shake off the memory of her ass in my face quivering.

Parker was on her feet, quickly shuffling over to me. Her darkly lined eyes shifted all over, I guessed to see who was around. She swung her chin to touch her shoulder then her eyes bounced around again. I didn't follow her actions. I couldn't give a fuck.

"Hi," she whispered.

"Aye."

"You okay?" She looked down at my tank, basketball shorts, jug of water, and sneakers.

"Yeah." I tossed my thumb over my shoulder. "Was working out and Richardson called me to his office."

Her eyes blew the hell up. "Which one?" she kept her voice low, but I caught the concern.

I snorted. "Nate. He's my—"

"*Director of Players' Success*, I know."

"Oh. You do?" She nodded, eyes still combing around us. "Seems like everybody in here knows something about ol' Rut, I see."

"What do you mean?"

"Nothing. I jetted up here to ask you something real quick."

Parker bit her lip and pulled it back. "Okay..."

"I got the call about B-Rocka's funeral and shit." I brushed the back of my head with my hand, feeling uneasy. I didn't think the shit through. "I want you to go with me." The silence was what made my eyes roll down to hers.

My chest pounded like a motherfucker.

Parker's lashes blinked and eyes rolled down to the floor, swinging left and right. "You kissed me," she whispered.

Huhn?

"When?" I asked like it was an accusation.

Parker looked left then right before stepping closer to me. "The first night we met. You kissed me...in the mouth." She rushed out, "With your tongue."

I fought the smile on my face with a frown. "Okay..."

Her head lifted again. "I heard the Ruby Voodoo podcast," she whispered again. "I heard what you said about how often you don't use your mouth."

"Okay?" I chuckled.

Parker shrugged. "I guess... Thank you for trusting me with that."

I didn't know what to say. I never had a girl say thanks for oral or a real kiss. Where do you go from that?

"Yes," she whispered.

"Huhn?"

"I'll go with you to the funeral. Yes."

I sucked in so much air, my eyes went wild and I grabbed my chest. Trying to play it off, I began to back away.

"Cool. I gotta bounce." Then I stopped. "Oh, I gotta meeting tonight." My arms swung in the air as I thought to explain more. "My partner's in town... Some shit he needs to go over with me."

"Oh!" Her shoulders lifted as she responded, eyes back down below somewhere. "Well, there are those leftovers in there. Thanks for telling me." Her tone was too polite. Too professional. "Now that I know, I'll only warm up half."

"Nah, I'm still gonna be there. It'll be too late to eat, but I'll call before I pull up." I found myself backing away again, feeling too raw this close to her. This shit was weird. "Just don't fall asleep without me."

For the first time, as distance grew between us, Parker looked mad shy and lonely. It was like she had so much to say, but as two people who were talking walked between us, scary ass Parker ain't say shit.

"So, to sum this up," I sat up in my chair, tired as hell. We were downtown, at a restaurant I was underdressed for but didn't give a shit. I was ready to go and hoped Parker hadn't fallen asleep. "We're gonna go with the two grand openings but on different weekends."

"Yes." Jeremy nodded. "The one in Center City...Philadelphia will happen first. Then we'll hit the Trenton location."

"Okay. And that one, in Trenton, is going to be like the one in Princeton?"

Princeton was the first sneaker boutique we opened three years ago. It was killing in profits, and since our inventory had just opened more, we decided to open two new boutiques.

"Yes. It'll be a block party opening like you suggested," Jeremy answered.

"But the Philly location will be limited to inside the store?" He nodded. "And the place ain't ready?"

"Correct."

"And they're saying it won't be ready until the week before?"

"Correct." He nodded again.

"Bullshit. You know the game. That shit won't be ready till like the day before, *if* we lucky!"

"It's what he assured me, Rut."

"Assure these nuts, man," I groaned, sitting back in my chair. "I 'on't want no bootleg shit like we had in Princeton. We got them white boys in there and they took their precious time, not giving a fuck about our schedule. I told you we shoulda used my cousins and them."

Jeremy rubbed his face with his hands, pushing his thick, black plastic frames up as he grumbled. It was usual for me to unload a lot on him, but he typically kept his cool about it. It was just tonight I'd been in a foul mood for many reasons and had no tolerance for getting fucked over.

And we probably looked like a pair. Where I was over six feet tall, Jeremy was hardly five feet seven. I weighed over a hundred pounds more than him, was a shimmering, fine ass toffee hued brother while Jeremey was a vanilla bean crème frapp—at least, that's what I would say when clowning his ass. My dawg was a straight up geek in appearance:

dark thick, unruly curls, glasses, dingy ass Steve Urkel cardigan sweater, and scuffed up ass saddle shoes. For a sneaker head, he only wore two pair of those oxfords. These he wore tonight were purchased six years ago. Jeremy was your classic cheap ass Jew, but he was my G; one of few I could depend on. Even if he came with the bitter and sweet tonight.

"Rut, you know we had to go with contractors from Pennsylvania. They're locally licensed." He groaned again.

"Fuck that. We could've snuck my cousins and them in."

"For how long? Day two when someone heard the construction and decided to call the city?" He shook his head. "This isn't the *Rut Show*. We can't do everything your way—legal or illegal."

I took a sip of my brandy. "And those *Jordan 11 Concords* been delayed?" I didn't wait for an answer. "Dawg! You know those are a staple. We can't have a fucking sneaker boutique without that design; fuck a grand opening. We're gonna get clowned."

Jeremy's arms swung in the air. "I'll leave you to deal with Eugene from over there about that matter. He never takes my calls no ways."

"Oh, he'll take my fuckin' calls or I'm going to that warehouse and fuckin' shit up."

"Totally unnecessary." He rubbed his eyes behind his frames. "We're legit now, Rut. Our ammunition is the contracts we have in place. No need to go *The Town* on any of these vendors. We'll get the shipment."

I took a moment to stare at him. Jeremy was tired. He rarely slept. All he did was mind the business of *Rubber Soles* and play video games. He was my brain, and I was the muscle of the company. Don't get me wrong, the brand was built on my vision and strategic moves, but Jeremy made shit happen on paper. He was instrumental in legitimizing the company. Because of the NFL draft he'd been pulling most of the load all year, especially for these two boutique openings. I remembered the hoops we had to jump through for the first, so I understood the stress of it all. All that aside, I still needed him to go hard on our affiliates.

"We've come a long way, man," I sighed, feeling accomplished for something I did with my first and only real passion.

"Sure have, dude!" Jeremy took a long sip of his beer. He turned to look at something on the other side of the restaurant. A smile topped his face out of nowhere. "Remember how we started?"

I thought for a minute. "Yeah. Witcha scary ass!" I laughed.

"Dude! I didn't want *Foot Locker* coming after me for fraud."

"Ain't no fraud if you ain't doing nothing wrong!"

"Taking advantage of their employee discount isn't fraud?" I thought for a second then smiled. Jeremy rolled his eyes, not knowing where my mind was going. Remember Neeka?" With a big ass smirk, I nodded as Jeremy rolled his eyes even harder this time.

Back in tenth grade, when Jeremy and I had discovered the only thing we had in common outside of the school we went to, he told me he had a friend that worked at the sneaker store in the mall. Her name was Neeka. I asked him if he could get her to let us use her employee discount. Jeremy choked, saying he'd never have the balls to ask her for it and he didn't want to get her in trouble. I said, 'fuck it' and approached her the best way I knew how. Neeka was older than me but the skinniest girl I'd ever put my dick inside of. It took three long ass weeks, but I finally got her after three movie dates, four dozens of roses, and sitting with her every day in the cafeteria. Painful, but worth it.

We were in business and *Foot Locker* was the plug back then. When a sneaker didn't perform well, in terms of profit, the retailer would put them on sale. We'd then buy as many as we could through her and sell them. For two years, we bought shoes from that sneaker store then sold them from our book bags and even crates on the weekend.

When Neeka left town after her parents' divorce, she secured a relationship with a coworker of hers. Not only was I grateful for the hook up, I was happy as hell Neeka didn't try to hit me up after she left. She'd actually stopped a few months before she left and I understood why. Neeka needed me for clout around the school like I needed her discount for my budding business. I understood the game. All females had it.

"Yip." Jeremy nodded. "And after *Foot Locker* was *eBay*."

"And we slaughtered the sneaker game on there!" I whistled, recalling making sometimes five thousand a week.

"After *eBay* was *StockX*," he reminded me.

I stretched my arm across the table. "And that's when we couldn't hide the money no more."

Jeremy gave me some dap as he sat up in his seat. "Yeah, man. You were right. We've pulled it off—are pulling it off." He shook his head, looking a bit dazed. "You were right all this time."

I found myself nodding. He spoke truth. One of the many things Divine taught me over the years was to develop multiple streams of income. When he saw I was focused on the sneaker game, he gave me a few stacks to boost our wholesale inventory. He sat with Jeremy and me on a few occasions when in town and gave us mad jewels. But this baby was mine. It wasn't like football; something my pops dreamt up for me and had Divine enforce.

"So, what's next?"

Jeremy looked my way. "What?"

"After these two grand openings. I told you I wanted a few sneaker stores. We got that." I shrugged. "What's next for you? *Or* for us?"

With his index finger, Jeremy rubbed the area between his nose and top lip. His eyes circled around the way it did when he was thinking or plotting.

"A family," he didn't exactly speak clearly.

My face dropped. "A what?"

"Family." His eyes dribbled again.

"For who?"

Jeremy slapped his hands on his lap, making a loud whack of it. "Me." I could feel the muscles in my face go tight and my forehead lift. "Gracie and I want to—" His eyelashes began to flutter. "Ummmm... Trying. We're trying for a baby."

"Fuck you mean, a baby?"

Jeremy wouldn't look at me, but I caught those black eyes rolling toward the other side of the restaurant. "It's not a big deal, bro."

"The fuck it ain't. Jeremy, we talking about a fuckin' kid. A lock down maneuver!"

Finally, he looked me dead in the eyes. "Who's locking down who, Rut?"

"At first, I thought you was locking her down for her disability check." He sucked his teeth and looked away from me again. "Then I realized the girl was already locked down, seeing she's in a wheelchair and all."

He groaned, stretching his neck before his head whipped over to me. "Would you stop your shit for once!"

"What?" My palms turned up at my sides.

"She's not confined to the wheelchair, Rut. She only uses it outside of her apartment, and you know it!"

"I don't! I don't go to Gracie's place, man."

"Because you don't accept her invitations to."

"I haven't gotten an invite in a minute, man."

He leaped toward me in his chair and grated, "Because she stopped inviting your misogynistic, ableist ass to her events."

"Able what?" I shook my head, not even caring what that meant. "I'm good with not being invited. What I don't want is her trying to trap you with no baby because you on the come up!"

His laugh was bitter as he looked away from me. "On the come up..." was all he said for a while. "You think I give a shit about money, Rutledge? I can understand you came up with all the fly gear, money in your pocket, and could afford private schools. I get your popularity was based on what you wore and the legacy of your father. But that's not my story. You think I care she has a minor disability—"

"Missing half a leg ain't minor, bruh."

"And what does that have to do with starting a family?"

"She gotta spinal injury, dawg. And she's a cancer survivor. You gone put all that on that girl's poor body?"

"Fuck you, Rut!"

I lifted my hands in the air. "I'm just looking out for you, J."

"Like hell you are." He shook off the argument. "Let's just drop it. We've discussed everything concerning *Rubber Soles* and even my personal life. I think that's about enough for one night." He pulled out his wallet.

I had no argument on that.

As I checked my phone, I asked, "So where you staying in town?"

"Your place." He stood from his seat.

"Cheap ass." Of course, he would. "You sleeping in Sharkie's room. I 'on't care if I ain't gone be there. My bed is off limits, my G." Jeremy sighed, shaking his head again. "Where ya things? I can drop you off there."

"This is all I brought." He pointed to the small tote on the empty chair. "I have a flight out first thing in the morning."

"Why so early?"

"Gracie's—" He placed his fist over his mouth, guarding his words. Then he dropped it and took a deep breath. "Gracie's ovulating. You may not know, but there's a small window of opportunity involved in that. I need to be back there."

I pretended to gag.

"Fuck you," he spat before walking off.

I didn't take it personal. Lately, he'd been more sensitive about Gracie. I didn't get it but didn't get mad either. I caught up to him to make sure he was good.

"Yo, man—" From the side of my eye, I caught two chicks behind the bar, beaming my way. I smiled at them and waved. Without hesitation, they waved back. One even winked her eye. *If I only had time, sweetheart...* Maybe a different night when I wasn't rushing off to something I didn't understand. "Slow down." I finally caught up to Jeremy. "You know I spit the truth and my truth is you my peoples. I just want what's good for you."

We made it outside to the valet when Jeremy turned to me.

"But you don't want what's best for me. And that's the problem, Amare."

"Fuck that mean?"

"It means you project your bullshit about women onto me. You know, deep down inside I think you know there are good women out here."

"I know there's some decent females—"

"No. Women. We're almost in our mid-twenties now. We're well-earning men. Don't you think it's time we act like it? You're not in college anymore. I'm not in my parents' basement, playing video games, eating pizza, and scratching my nuts anymore—"

"Well..." I pushed my hand in the air. "You just moved out of your moms' crib a few months ago. And I'm quite sure you still do video gambling and scratch your paper bag colored sac." That made me laugh even if it didn't Jeremy.

It was the truth!

"Are you done?" he asked as I howled, handing the valet guy my ticket.

"Hold up!" I croaked out, hooting. "One last second!"

When I was able to slow down, he stepped closer. "I used to want to be just like you. Yeah, the awkward Jewish kid from Ewing wanted to be like the swaggered out prince of Trenton. From the first day you tried to clown me in front of your 'cool guy' friends sophomore year in high school and I had to tell you, you weren't wearing the latest *Air Max* and how they were two seasons old, I said I wanted to be just like you. It didn't matter that you were big, black, athletic, with street cred, and already with money. I wanted to be you." He stabbed my chest with his finger. "Now, I find myself almost neck and neck with you in money and with so many of the same connects, and you know what? I'd be sick if I woke up one day being Rut Amare."

My head shot back.

What the fuck?

"You're a lonely motherfucker. And so was I. But you..." He sucked in a breath. "You don't fully trust anyone."

"I did, and now he's dead!" I shouted in his face, fist balled at my side.

Jeremy flinched, swallowed, and inched his chin higher to meet my glare. "That's bullshit. You hardly brought him on your college campus. You don't cross social lanes, Rut, and you know it. A few years ago, I realized you compartmentalize all your relationships, believing that laughable 'skill' makes you the master of people." He scoffed, "Well, that's where I got off the train. I may be a natural introvert, but unlike you, I can open my mind and heart to love a woman. I can marry her and blend our worlds. I can make babies with her and give her fidelity. And you know what, Rut? That's when I didn't feel lonely anymore."

I cocked my head to the side, not believing he put feeling lonely on me. When I met this dude, he didn't have one physical friend. They were all virtual; online, all over the globe. But I made him lonely? I always had friends...family!

"I feel..." He turned his head as he thought. "Free! Free to breathe and to trust. And to lay down at night and speak freely to a warm body, who I know has my best interest at heart. Someone I know would give me sound advice. Someone who believes if I lose, she loses. Someone who doesn't scheme on my vulnerability but values it." He backed away. "Same body, one heart, the set of legs from yesterday, the day before, and the day before that." He was out of breath at his last words.

My whip pulled up and I turned to acknowledge it with my eyes only. Then my attention went back to Jeremy.

"Three quarters of a set."

His face went tight, glasses lifting as his nose raised. "Pardon?"

"Gracie. She got three quarters of a set. You know... With the bottom half of the right one being gone." I moved to the car. "And don't forget her back that goes out. You can't fuck her hard enough to put a baby in there. Good luck with that." I went on and on busting his chops. Jeremy's whole face turned red as he hopped into my ride, slamming the door behind him.

chapter
eleven

"I don't blame him, you know?"

"About what?"

Rut showed up close to thirty minutes ago, went straight into the bathroom, stripped down to his boxers, and climbed into bed with me. He told me about his day and how he'd just left a meeting with his business partner. It was also when I learned about his side business—or primary, according to him—as a sneaker retailer. I was sorry to hear that meeting ended in a fight between the two.

"About changing his stance on his future as it concerns a family. I told you I wanted a husband and a family since I began to understand soap operas, but now I'd be perfectly fine with half that. People change. It's a fact of life," I susurrated under the sound of the creaking ceiling fan.

"Yeah," he snorted softly. "Your plan don't make much sense either. How you gonna have a baby without the father?"

I shrugged with one shoulder, though I doubted he could see it. "It happens all the time. I'm sure you know." I sighed, not wanting to travel into that topic. "Anyway... It's cool that you have a legit business outside of football. I'm constantly hearing the finance people in the front office snicker and sometimes complain about the way players lack financial intelligence no matter how much the *Kings* put into educating them."

"Yeah," he yawned, the tantalizing scent of mint mixed with a nutty brandy puckered my nipples. "We've been killing the game. The company hit four million this year and we're looking at seven next year." Rut rubbed his nose. "I had to learn way before the *League*. My pops been down since I was in grammar school. He may have left us sitting on something, but he made it clear that was more for my moms than me. Said real men are made from hardworking, hustling boys."

"How were you supposed to earn money that young?"

"By figuring it out. He said he'd give me a few years, but I was on the clock."

"Did he expect you to follow his footsteps and sell drugs?" That prospect angered me.

I grew up with guys who only had that as an option to survive, but many of them didn't have fathers to provide. Their fathers were either dead, imprisoned, or strung out on something.

I could feel the mattress tremble from laughter spurring from his belly. "Nah. Flippin' chickens wasn't an option for me. I hated it at first."

"Why?"

"Because all my niggas was trappin'. It was all we knew. The difference was I didn't do it. Couldn't do it. It kinda interfered with our social time. They'd be on the block and sometimes when it was hot, I had to sit in the damn house by myself until their shift was up."

A fluttery laugh shot from my lips. "Shift?"

"Yeah. For the projects, they took shifts. There were other crews competing for sells. If you wanted that money to stay in your click, you had to hustle. So I'd sneak and sit through shifts with them."

"But you didn't sell it yourself?"

"Nah." He chuckled sexily. God, help me; he smelled like a masculine flower garden. "I wanted to bad as hell. I even tried to threaten them to put me D, but that ain't work. The O.G.s were everywhere and they reported every fuckin' thing back to my father. That had my crew shook."

I cracked up at that.

"But…" He wiggled onto his side on the small mattress. "we eventually got over it. I chilled on trying to be something my pops and the General was fuckin' hell bent on keeping me from."

My cackle quieted and mind raced with this new information. Rut turned out to be full of wonder, a true anomaly. He had a full fledging business for Christ's sakes. That isn't mentioned with other stories about him of the scandalous type.

"Hey," I called out softer than I intended.

But Rut hummed he was listening.

"I started my business around eight years ago, too—well," I needed to clarify. "I began making products."

"Oh, yeah?"

"Mmmhmm…" I nodded, knowing he couldn't see me. "It was before I met Jimmy, of course. I did it for fun. Something to exercise my brain between…growing up, you know?" Rut lay muted, but I knew he was listening. "When I moved in with Jimmy, I told him I'd like a room for my 'hobby.' He wasn't too crazy about me having a mess room. To entice him, I requested the smallest one in the house, which is the washroom outside of the family room. It just so happened that we'd transform the family room into his bedroom once he couldn't get around anymore."

That fact saddened me. Jimmy was less than half the man I met. He was lively and well-known. Since he'd fallen ill, the only person consistent with visiting and checking in was Eli Richardson, and not even he came around weekly. He was a busy man, I understood more now working in the front office.

"Hey," he croaked just when I thought he'd fallen asleep.

"Yeah?"

"What's ableist?"

"As in ableism?"

"I guess."

"Where did you hear it from?"

"Jeremy. That's one of the things he called me."

I swallowed hard, eyes swinging in the dark. His partner and childhood friend called him an ableist.

Gosh, Rut…

"That bad?"

I mewled, "Probably."

Then I felt him rustling in the sheets. He groaned as he reached for me. "Fuck him."

Rut pulled me on top of his big body to straddle, and with natural ease, I did. This meant only one thing: it was time for bed.

My groin toiled, orgasm eminent as his tongue kneaded my clit. His mouth roved over the lips of my sex furiously. Heat dispersed from my core, reaching from my arms and fingers to my legs and curled toes.

"No!" I panted, grasping for his hard, broad shoulders underneath the backs of my thighs. "Rut..." I swallowed. "Not another one. Not like this." My pants were audible.

All those words and I couldn't say I wanted him inside me. I wanted to be chest to chest with him. Mouth to mouth. But I wasn't given a choice. Like yesterday, I was rolled over this morning, hours after I checked on Jimmy, and his face was busy between my thighs.

Was this his thing? Did Rut enjoy morning cunnilingus?

And he was generous—my god, he was unselfish with this act of pleasure. Rut had already given me a spine-shattering orgasm while lying on my side. And now with me on my back and his big hands on my cheeks, pulling me into his face—

I exploded.

Arms swinging in the air, shoulders leaping fitfully, and thighs flapping around his head as my hips rolled. And I took his lingering licks on my sensitive nub until my entire frame collapsed from exhaustion. I couldn't catch my breath and endured the zings racing across my body.

"What were you tryna say?" his thick, graveled morning tenor susurrated.

I couldn't speak at first, utterly shattered at this point.

After a few moments, I was able to whisper between wheezes, "I wanted you to..."

"To what?"

"To come...up."

His face folded. "To stop?"

I managed to lick my dry lips. "To..."

"To what, Parker?" His tone was edgy.

"To...do *it*."

His eyes flashed wild. "To fuck?" he breathed.

"Well..." I panted. That word irritated me, but it was what he was used to. "I guess."

Rut immediately shook his head, resolute. "Nah. Nope!"

My heart fell in my chest. "Why not?"

"Because that gets you in trouble!"

"Who? Me?"

He shrugged. "I 'on't know. You. Me. Us, maybe. Just no."

"But we already..." I felt lightheaded and not just from the orgasm. "So, is this all we do?"

Rut didn't answer. Neither did he look at me in the gray lighting of the early morning sun rising.

I rolled my eyes, my tongue swiped my lips. "What if I just..."

"What?" His head whipped to face me.

"What if I wanted to kiss you?"

"I 'on't know. Like... How?"

My eyes went wild with disbelief. "Like this!" My arm managed to lift from the bed and I pointed to his glistening mouth. "With you wearing me like lip gloss." He didn't answer at first. "I don't understand. Why did you go down on me this morning?"

Half his face went up in the cutest smirk. "I liked the taste of your lip gloss from yesterday."

"Well, can I taste it, too?" I hated how whiney my words fell.

But Rut was on me. He leaned down, taking me at the sides of my face and kissed me. At first, it was a yank of my bottom lip then his tongue pushed through. And oh, my skittles... His morning breath and my personal musk mixed with his cologne and heat had my head lifting just to get closer to him. I wrapped my legs around his thighs and tried to pull him into me. With more patience than my own, he dropped lower and I inched up until I could feel his erection at my core.

Rut lips brushed against me, sharing my gloss, and he curled his tongue around mine. As ridiculous as it sounds, he felt loss to the kiss. He angled his head and his breathing grew choppy. I lifted my sex, communicating my willingness. My need. I rolled against him then moaned.

Rut's head flew up, eyes wild. "No!" he growled.

Wha—

Out of breath again, I asked, "Why did you go down on me yesterday if you didn't want sex? You didn't know how I tasted then."

Rut's eyes rolled down and closed. "I really don't know," he murmured.

"Okay, so you asked her to attend the funeral with you? That's a milestone for you. Wouldn't you agree?" The therapist lady cocked her head to the side.

Her eyes went squinty and I knew she was beasting for me to say something corny as hell.

"I 'on't know about all that. But I can't front, it's like some of those weird things I told you I've been noticing."

"Your thinking about her." Her head rocked slowly back and forth. "Post-thoughts and questions from previous conversations flood your mind when you're not with her."

"I ain't say it like that, but... Yeah, I guess."

"Has she asked anything of you yet?"

"What do you mean?"

"Like for money..." She shrugged. "Tickets to a game? New shoes? A bag? To get her nails done?" she began to sing. "Gas money? A bundle of Brazilian hair?"

She asked me to fuck her...

And I had crazy mixed feelings about that. Asking for sex was a tool of manipulation from chicks, too. They thought if they fucked you good they could get the bag that way.

"Nah. None of that."

"Okay." She glanced down at her wrist for the time.

"That's it?"

Her head shot up and lips parted. "Did I miss something?"

I sat up on the chaise. "You ain't got nothing to say after a question like that?"

"About her not asking you for anything?"

"Yeah."

"No."

"Why?"

"Because it's been almost an hour, and that was my agreement with you."

"What?"

She sat back in her fancy ass judgement chair across from me. "I agreed when you began talking in these sessions last week to a challenge. I said you not dismissing her could be an opportunity to learn something different. You're still in the race. We'll just have to allow time to run its course at this point."

But that's really it, though?

I shook that out of my head, needing to move on to another matter.

"I... Uhhh..." I hesitated for a minute, something I wasn't used to doing. "About that one rule."

"You slept with her?" Her brows rose to her hairline.

Damn, she was quick with it!

"No!" I shook my head. "Not at all." Then I sat still, hesitating again. "I ate her pussy, though." Then I thought to make clear. "And I ain't gone stop."

Unless Parker tells me to...

She swung her chin toward her right shoulder, probably stumped. Then she scratched her forehead.

"I can't police your bedroom—"

"*Shiiiiit...* Damn right, you can't!"

"And I don't want to. My only hope is sex doesn't damage something with the potential of being groundbreaking for you, Amare. Your perception and history with women is extremely fragile and jaded. I understood the possibility of you not being able to carry it through, but—"

"I have! I swear to you, I ain't put my dick in her since that first night we met."

"Oh, and I believe you!" she perked up in pitch. "I completely do. It's just that sex is gravely complicated and irreversible."

"Doc," I chuckled. "Women are complicated, but their asses can definitely be reversed in *Rut's World*."

"Hi!" Her green eyes were big as fucking saucers when she swung the door open. I almost forgot where I was. "We haven't met." Her open hand flew to me like a jab. "I'm Mandee! I live across the street from Mr. Wright and Parker."

I looked down at her pale white hand trembling in the air.

"What up." I switched stances and pulled out my wallet. "Rut." I peeled off a few bills and put them into her hand. "Parker ready?"

I saw when her smile fell. Honestly, I didn't give a shit. I wasn't in the mood for Parker running late either as I looked over ol' girl's shoulder.

"Oh!" She turned to look behind her before turning to face me again with her eyes toward the ground. "She's wrapping up the last of the food. I'll go get her." She shuffled away from the door clumsily.

Then she looked at me over her shoulder and raised the money. "Thanks for this!" I noticed she didn't make eye contact with me this time either.

I stepped in, hearing voices in the kitchen. But the whishing sounds to my right yanked my attention. It was Wright's room. The two doors were wide open and more obvious than the digital sounds of the room were a set of eyes directly on me. At first, I froze. The man was on his death bed. I didn't know much about ALS before Parker but since her, I learned it's a downhill disease. Wright would die; it was just a matter of when.

There was something *for real* alive in his eyes. Something that wasn't helpless at all. Call me crazy, but he stared at me like he wanted me to see him. Like he wanted to see me. Being the type of man who never bowed my head for nobody, I wouldn't start today.

As I walked into the room, I remembered where my foul mood began. Right there, as I crossed the threshold of his room. Two nights ago, I came down to see about Parker when she took too long with her usual check in on Wright. I stood at the doorway and saw her lay over his bed, singing to him. Her voice wasn't loud, neither was it strong, but it was soothing as hell. That made me listen in when she began to talk to him.

"Do you feel better?"
I didn't hear anything, of course, because Wright couldn't speak.
"Jimmy, if you don't blink, we can't communicate."
More silence.
She took a deep breath. "I couldn't tell if that was one blink or you said no with two blinks, and I think you know this. Please don't do that," she cried.

Not with tears but with her heart in her throat. She really cared about this dude and it became so clear in the few minutes of ear-hustling.

"Okay. Have it your way. It's not like I've lied to you. Yes, I've waited all week to tell you he's been staying here. You say you don't like it, but you also said you remember freeing me. You said you remember telling me before you lost your voice to go and date other people. That was two and a half years ago, Jimmy. I haven't even *given my number out to a guy since meeting you, let alone spent time with one."*

Things went silent again.

"Do you want me to tell him to leave?"

My heart thundered in my fucking chest at that offer. I would only leave if Parker wanted me to. Fuck Wright! He owed her more than just letting company come over after putting his hands on her.

Parker let go of a breath. "Here you go, not answering again. You know that upsets me, Jimmy." *Her voice broke. Parker was close to crying.* "I need you to communicate to know you're not in pain."

Nothing from Wright.

Parker took a long breath then stood to walk over to the chair near his hospital bed. "Okay. Then I'll sit here until you answer."

Parker never came back to bed. When I left out that morning, I peeped her curled in that chair asleep with her mouth wide open. And because I was so mad, I didn't stay here last night. When I shot her a text to tell her, she didn't seem so disappointed.

My eyes combed the room. It was my first time this deep inside. I turned to look over my shoulder to be sure Parker wasn't there. Then I moved closer and saw he was frowning, mean mugging me with his eyebrows bunched together. Wright had one shoulder higher than the other and one leg curled, but both clearly atrophied in his paralyzed state. Still, dude was throwing me rocks.

"This ain't no black or white situation. I respect it's ya place and all, but I believe her when she says y'all ain't together and ain't been together basically since you put your hands on her." I shifted in my stance. "I swear if I could spend time with her outside of here I would, but I'm sure you know you monopolize all her time. If she ain't here taking care of you, she at her lil' gig at the front office."

His mouth didn't move. I knew this, but for some reason, I was ready for it to. I was expecting something from him because I knew it was foul spending nights at his crib, knowing damn well I fucked his girl—ex girl. But I couldn't stop. I wouldn't. Parker wasn't the type of chick you could stand down from.

"I ain't never meet a fema—" That didn't feel right. "A gir—" *Fuck!* I couldn't talk. "A woman like her before. I'm not gonna stop being friends with her unless she tells me to. Until we can figure out a better situation, I'll just..." I took a breath and brushed my palms down my face.

Compromising or explaining myself to anybody but Divine or a coach wasn't a usual occurrence for me. This shit was hard.

But I can't walk away from her. Not right now, at least...

"I'll make myself invisible until the situation changes." I turned to leave.

Then something hit me. I went back to Wright's bed, but this time close enough to touch him. I leaned into him to be sure he heard me.

"I know you can answer questions. One blink for yes...two for no." Wright's frown he rocked straightened for three seconds, making it clear as ever he was still in that fragile shell.

"Parker. She a real one?" I shifted closer to his face. "She playing you?" I swallowed hard. "Me?"

Wright's lids didn't fucking move, and that made my heart pound in my chest the same way it had been doing when it came to fucking Parker. Then my breathing got heavy, but I tried to play it cool. I didn't want Wright to know how vulnerable I felt. Why was I asking this man this shit? What did he owe me? Shit... He was dying. I was fucked up for this.

Besides... He probably answering by not answering...

I pushed off the side railing of the bed to finally leave.

Blink.

I froze. A blink! *But...* Just one? I felt the first of sweat push from my damn pores. He was answering. Wright was giving me the answer that would put all this shit to bed. The answer that'll prove me right to that goddamn head doctor.

Blink.

Were those blinks together? They were seconds apart.

"That a yes or a no, Wright?" I didn't mean to growl in his face.

Or did I?

I needed to know. This girl was driving me fucking crazy. My cousin was dead. *My fucking ace!* And all week, all I craved was her. I understood the timing was fucked up. Hell, we were about to drive down to Jersey for the funeral. But if Wright told me she was playing me, I'd walk away right then and there.

"Parker 'bout that game life?"

Blink. Blink.

All the fucking air left my lungs as I held onto the side rail of his bed. Quickly, I stood to straighten myself. No way was I going to fall the hell out, rolling on the floor for no *fema*—Parker!

Wright's eyes were still on me. This time they glistened. Was he about to cry? For what?

"She's still here with you day and night, bruh. She's committed to you." I ain't like it but thought I'd give him something for answering me.

When I heard a female's voice from outside of the room, I tossed Wright a nod and turned to leave. Just as I made it by the front door, the white girl who let me in was carrying a tray of food. A big ass aluminum pan.

"You mind getting the door for me?"

I jumped into action, still feeling tight, but now hopeful about not being played. Right after she left out the door, Parker's little frame strutted out of the kitchen, holding a pan as big. She zipped passed me with the meanest switch. With my eyes glued to her ass in a black dress, I followed her out. That's when I saw Fats had hopped out of the truck and was accepting the tray from Mandee. Next, Parker handed him hers. Both girls passed me on their way back in the house.

"Where you going?" I asked Parker as she sashayed past me with a smile.

"To get the rest. There are four more."

That's when it hit me. This was food for the funeral. I found myself jumping into action again, and I followed them back into the house. In the kitchen, I had Parker stack the last three trays and I carried them out behind Mandee, who had the other one.

A few minutes later, I was in the truck as Parker carried a bag and purse with her. Fats held the door open for her and she thanked him as she hopped in the truck. I didn't like the distance. Parker sat all the way on the other side. It made the interior feel bigger than what it was. My irritation kicked in again as we pulled off.

The conversation—or communication—with Wright began to play in my mind all over again. *Did I overstep?* I may be a hard ass, but I did have a conscience. The man was sick. He was still a man, though. He proved it two nights ago when he caught feelings with Parker over me being there. Wright may have lost his body for the most part, but his brain was still intact.

"Did you say hello to Mandee?" Parker's voice broke my thoughts. "She said you seemed upset."

I was fucking upset. Didn't matter I'd just finished pissing all over her man. He was no real competition from a hospital bed. What I really wanted to conquer was sitting next to me, texting the house she just left. I peeped Mandee's name as she typed, and I was sure it was about Wright.

When she was done, she checked her make up in the little compact mirror she carried in her bag.

"Next time be nice. Mandee canceled plans to do this for me. I'm sure knowing I'd be with you made the deal sweeter. She followed your college numbers." She looked around, out of the back window after seeing the other black SUV pull up behind us. "And who is that? Are they with us?"

I forgot to mention the security the *Kings* hired for the day. They showed at my condo first thing this morning. That was a topic I didn't feel like getting into. Mandee was another. I wanted to tell her I didn't care about her following my college career, but that wouldn't have been completely true. I decided to go another route.

"What made you do all this?"

"The other night—you know…the last one you stayed with me—when your mother called with your aunt on a three way and said they needed help with the food."

"I told them I'd handle it."

"Okay. Did you? This can be extra food. You know black folk will take food as long as there's foil. You don't even need plates." She laughed at her own damn joke.

"How you even pay for all this?"

"Remember that generous *Eat Clean* gift card?" Her smile was fucking smug.

I turned my head to fight against the butterflies in my fucking stomach from her prettiness. I hated she was so fucking pretty.

"That's how you say thanks, by re-gifting?"

"I thought you giving it to me in the first place was a gesture of thanks. I can choose how to spend what's mine."

I turned to her. "No. You can use this as a way of flashing that feminist card in my face."

She cocked her head to the side and her eyebrows touched. "Would it make you feel better if I told you I paid for the To-Go containers myself?" Shit got quiet. I wasn't answering that. "I can understand this is a difficult time for you. I can even accept if you're going to be a little distant today. But you don't get to be cold. You invited me here. I'm prepared to comfort you as best I can, but I don't work well under 'punching bag' conditions. Got it?"

I turned away from her again. She was sonnin' me and I ain't like that shit either. She knew better than accusing me of mistreating her. That may have been Wright's steeze, but it wasn't mine. I never stayed around a chick long enough to get moody.

I guessed she got the hint when I kept on my side of the truck with my mouth closed. I heard her shuffling over there before she relaxed in her seat. So many things ran through my mind. How was I going to get through today? What if B-Rocka had kids? What would be needed to hold them down? Would my moms hold it together, at least until the repass? She was off the hook with hers lately. If she couldn't keep her shit together, and pops was locked the fuck down, who would be there for me? This lost was painful as hell.

You invited me here. I'm prepared to comfort you as best I can.

My head swung over to her. Parker was staring out of the window, probably not even paying attention to the cars zipping past us on the highway. In that moment, I didn't feel vulnerable. I felt safe. I didn't think twice when I reached over and pulled her little ass next to me. I wanted her closer. Wished I could bury my face in the soft skin of her neck. I didn't want to scare her off, so I settled on just holding her.

chapter twelve

"THIS BITCH KILLIN' THE GAME!" Paula slapped the table with one hand while holding a bottle of *Corona* in the other.

The folding table shook and the *Connect Four* chips rattled. It was my seventh game in a row and my sixth win. My only loss was game two with another one of Rut's cousins because I got distracted when Rut walked away, appearing weary. I decided to give him his time and kicked the butts of everyone wanting smoke out here.

"You fittin' in very well, Miss Lady." Paula nodded so hard I thought her little body would tilt over.

But she stayed on her feet, even as she wobbled away to the picnic table next to me. Rut never mentioned his mother had a high tolerance for alcohol. In fact, since I was introduced to her a few hours earlier at the funeral, I tried to recall all things he'd said about her. I turned to find the next person taking to the table.

"And what's your name?" I asked the lanky brown skinned gentlemen with old box braids sitting across from me.

He snickered, shyly with yellow eyes. "Bootsie," he croaked.

"Hi, Bootsie. I'm Parker, Rut's friend. How're you related to him?" *Because everyone claims to be.* I'd been trying to keep up with names and relationships.

"Cousins. My Daddy and his' cousins." He gathered the red chips that seemed favored by all the relatives I'd played when I offered them to pick a color.

No one picked black, so I stopped asking.

"Okay. Let's go." I sat up, offering him to go first.

We were in Rut's childhood home where B-Rocka's, also known as Brian Barton, repass was hosted. Jeff Redd's "You Called and Told Me" sprouted from the speakers in the spaciously green backyard. It was here where I, too, learned Rut had moved to, away from the streets of Trenton. Apparently, the "General" he told me about had purchased Paula and Rut a home to get him out of Trenton and in a safer environment so he could focus on football. But B-Rocka and the rest of the family lived back in Trenton where the funeral was held. And what a sad funeral it was.

B-Rocka's mother, Tameeka, was completely distraught at the church. She wailed to painful volumes and even laid out over the body. His imprisoned father was able to view his body minutes before the service began. The sight of a black man shackled from wrist to waist to ankles as he quietly sobbed over his son's dead body had me swallowing back tears. It was an intense service to say the least. The entire time, Rut sat tall and thick in one position next to me. His long arm rested on the back of the pew behind me and one leg lay over the opposite thigh. He only brought the one leg down twice the whole service.

The food I made was here when we arrived after the service. Apparently, Fats had someone run it over during the funeral. Rut only introduced me to his mother, grandmother, and B-Rocka's mother. That was an awkward introduction, but Tameeka made it bearable by shaking my hand and speaking sweetly. I knew that was out of respect for Rut. Apparently, everyone respected him. It had been made clear since we showed to the church, Rut was a leader amongst this group of people. There were few men older than him around.

And his mother...

I didn't know what I had in mind before meeting Paula. Maybe a mother who didn't have the countenance of a sister? I couldn't decide. But who I met was a slender, rather short woman, who doted heavily on her son and was a veteran drinker. When we were officially introduced here in her home, Paula was polite and offered me a shot of vodka. It was the last thing I would've guessed Rut's mother would do, but I understood the family was grieving, so I accepted it when I saw Rut reluctantly agree to one himself. Since then, she hadn't been without a drink in her hands.

Paula worked her grounds, greeting everyone in her yard. She occasionally circled back to my little table to check in. This Bootsie here was more skilled than any of the other players I'd battled today. As our game commenced, Paula's loud voice could be heard throughout the yard. I had to focus to be sure to stay ahead of my new opponent. It took a few strategic moves, but Bootsie became a victim of my tactical mastery. If only I could be that deliberate in real life. I did my shoulder shuffle to express my seventh victory, and Boostsie offered a hand-slap before standing to leave the table. I had to crack up at his moping promenade over to the coolers where drinks were.

"Who he paid to make all that food?" That startled the crap out of me.

I glanced up over my shoulder and saw Paula standing there. One hand rested on the back of my chair and one leg crossed over the other. She was inarguably comfortable around me. Familiar.

I blinked her way. "Paid? You mean..."

"Who made all that?"

"I did."

She stomped her foot as she laughed, offering a hi-five with her bottleless hand. "Girl, you know how to work 'em. That's fuckin' right, bitch!"

Stunned and confused, I raised my palm for Paula to slap.

"It wasn't that big of a deal. It was my pleasure. Honestly," I tried.

"Them niggas tore that shit up the first hour we got here. They said that mac-n-cheese was bangin'." She gulped down a bit of her *Corona*. "They ain't leave me none of that, but I had everything else: macaroni salad, potato salad, string beans, baked chicken, and uhhhh..." She tapped her head, thinking.

I cracked a smile. "You taste the rice and beans?"

"Yeah!" she blasted like a water hose. "That shit was bangin'!" She offered another hi-five. "You make sure he line ya pockets for that hook up, girl!"

"It's all good," I assured. "He actually paid for it, so we're even."

Paula's neck popped back. "No, y'all ain't! Bitch, you better get a few dollars for that shit. All these muthafuckas feasted today. It gotta be close to a hundred people out here!"

I wanted to remind her there was other food here. There was no opportunity when a young girl appeared at Paula's side. They exchanged a few words before Paula acknowledged me.

"This here Rut's lady," she told the girl, who had to be around sixteen years old. Then Paula peered over to me. "This Rut's god-sister, Aisha."

"Hi, Aisha!" I went for her hand, a move that clearly made her uncomfortable, but she reciprocated with a limp wrist. "I'm Parker, Rut's friend." I attempted to correct his mother.

Aisha, Rut's god-sister, with a thick coat of shimmery silver lipstick and counterfeit *Gucci* bag, didn't have much to say with her mouth after that introduction, but she did communicate to Paula by way of her eyes. The message, however, was unclear to me.

"Where he at anyway?"

"Who?" Paula's frail frame bounced when she croaked out that one syllable.

"Rut."

"Oh, he in the house. Probably in his space in the basement," Paula seemed to sulk. "It's been hard on him."

"Aye, Paula P..." Another woman, a much older one cut in. Aisha took off, leaving the two women. My attention went to cleaning up the *Connect Four* chips, seeing no one else came over to play. I was over it anyway. "You got that for me?"

"Got what?" I peered up in just enough time to see Paula's face go taut with contempt.

"That money you owe me from bingo last week," the woman with big framed black sunglasses made clear.

"Oh! Dammit!" Paula slapped her forehead. "Shit, I forgot, Gina."

Her eyes brushed around the yard. "Rut! Rut here. I'mma get it from him! How much I owe you? Fifty?"

"Yeah. And I'm about to go. Junie waiting for me in front of the house. I'mma catch a ride back to Trenton with him, but Georgie staying. Give it to him."

"Oh. Okay! I'll give it to Georgie." Paula glanced around.

"I mean it, Paula," Gina whispered. "I need it to pay on my *Rent-A-Center*!"

"Okay, bitch," Paula droned. "I'mma get you yo' shit."

"Alright, now," Gina warned before walking off.

Feeling uncomfortable from having privy to that exchange, I grabbed my bag from the back of my folding chair.

I stood. "You said Rut's downstairs?"

"Yeah," Paula answered before taking a last gulp of her beer. "Let me get another one of these and I'll show you." I began to follow her. "You want another shot?"

My eyes swelled. "Oh, no." I rubbed my empty belly. "That one from earlier is still in my system." I tried laughing it off.

Truth was I was hungry and wanted Rut. I hoped he was okay. On our way there, she was stopped by a school-aged boy.

"Hey, Aunt P!"

"Hey, Rocky!" Paula's arms shot up in the air before wrapping around the young boy. "You seen Rut?"

"Yeah. He flipped me on my head!" His big smile exposed his missing tooth. "You ain't seen that?"

"Naw, baby! He give you a few dollars?"

"No." The boy shook his head.

"Why the hell you ain't ask him for some? He coulda gave you five or twenty."

The boy could only laugh, not being that developed mentally when an adult is encouraging him to ask another for money. Then his eyes shifted to me.

"Oh!" Paula turned toward me. "This Rut's new lady." She glanced my way. "This Rut's god-brother."

Another god-something?

I swear, that had to be the fifth one she introduced me to in the past hour and a half. First it was a god-aunt then cousin. I guessed they made up titles in this family.

All to be connected to Rut...

When we made it inside the house, Rut's grandmother, Annalise, was at the table, playing cards with two other women. She was a beautiful caramel coated woman in her sixties, maybe. She kept a low natural cut that resembled a high-top fade, just not as extreme as I'd seen. It actually worked for her.

"Ma, Rut-Rut downstairs?"

Annalise nodded and hummed her answer. She returned my smile as I fussed with my purse and tote on my one shoulder.

"Ma, you know this girl made all the food by herself?"

"Oh, nice!" Annalise noted. "I woulda done it myself, but he ain't give me the money so..." She flicked her wrists over the table. "You told him about my front door?"

Paula scratched her head, visibly overwhelmed with the details of her son's wallet.

"I got so much shit to tell him already. You may be on your own with that one, ma. How much is it?"

"The guy said two seventy-five." Annalise shrugged and went for her red Solo cup. "I'll make him some grits in the morning." She winked, taking a sip from the plastic cup.

"He ain't staying!" Paula informed. Then she peered over to me. "Y'all leaving tonight. Right?"

My palm went to my chest. "I'm going home."

Suddenly, I was unsure about Rut. Had he planned on staying down here?

"Shit. I gotta pee," Paula groaned. "There go the basement door right there." She pointed to a small hallway just off the kitchen. "I'll be down in a minute."

Without a moment of uncertainty, I crossed the room and found my way down the stairs of the door. The steps were carpeted and I could smell a little water damage the further down I went. I jumped in my heels when I turned the corner and saw a half a dozen male figures dispersed throughout the open area. The smell of alcohol and marijuana mixed with "boy" had my nostrils flaring immediately.

Then I recognized two of the men standing erect with their hands crossed over their pelvises. They were the security Rut brought down with us. One gestured with his forehead to the opposite end of the expansive space. My eyes traveled to a king-sized bed with a thick, lanky body stretched across it. I knew it was Rut. I managed to tread around the other guys down there sitting in silence, likely stoned out. One smoked a blunt and the others were not without double Styrofoam cups.

"Hey," I offered softly as I sat on the bed next to him.

Gently, I touched his back. Rut still had his suit jacket on. I heard him sniffle first. Then his head pulled up and his squinted eyes appeared. They were red and the skin of his face wrinkled from the folds of his jacket.

"You okay?" I spoke close to him.

Rut didn't respond at first. He seemed dazed. But this close to him, I didn't smell alcohol or weed.

"What time is it?" he grumbled.

I pulled out my phone. "Five thirty-five."

His heavy eyes hit me, sudden recognition flashing through them. That sinful scent of his cologne and natural odor flooding my olfactory had me straightening my neck. Rut sat up on the bed and wiped his face roughly with the heels of his palms. He glanced around before his regard landed on me. His orbs brushed against my upper torso, landing on my face before he turned away. Then he sniffled again. His body turned a few ways before he found the culprit. Weed.

"Aye, yo," he called across the way. "Y'all mind giving me some privacy?"

Quietly, and on command, the guys began filing out.

"You didn't want me being the only female in your crew?" I joked.

Humorlessly, Rut grumbled, "I didn't even know they were down here." He looked me over again. "You good?"

I nodded. Then I glanced behind me and saw the security was still there. That was strange. No longer able to delay it, I went for my bag and pulled out my lunch.

"What the hell is that?" Rut asked with a dark grimace.

I bit into my sandwich half then garbled. "Almond butter and jelly sandwich. I'm starving."

"All that food upstairs," his heavy, sleepy vocals produced. "Why you ain't eat?"

"That food's gone. Plus, I hardly eat the stuff I cooked." I shrugged with one shoulder before deciding on the truth. "I can't eat at everybody's house. I didn't know if it would be clean here so I packed a lunch in case. Good thing I did. They cleaned those trays as soon as the foil was ripped from them."

Rut cracked a half a smile. "Sorry for leaving you out there. You were killing my cousin, Alfreda, and I ain't feel like being around a bunch of people."

"I know the feeling. I lost my best friend since high school right after I graduated college." I swallowed, clearing my mouth before going for another bite. "I couldn't make it to the repass. I cut out after the funeral, and it took a long while to recover. I stayed in the house for a whole month." I nodded, recalling the ordeal. "I only left when my mother forced me to go see a doctor friend of hers."

After a few muted moments, Rut grabbed the other half of my sandwich and took a ginormous bite, which was half of it. "How'd you get over it?"

"I haven't." My brows lifted in revelation. "I don't think you ever do. You just manage through it. You understand she'll never see you get married. She won't be the godmother of your children. She won't be there to rub your back when you get shitfaced drunk the night of your thirtieth birthday party."

Rut stopped chewing and his head reared, but it came back up with that grin of his that now warmed me. "You're supposed to be making me feel better."

"You ate half my sandwich. I don't have enough sustenance in me for that." Then I remembered. "Hang on." I pulled out a bag of organic salt and vinegar chips.

A goofy grin splayed on my lips.

"Oooooh... You got the hook up," he declared throatily and snatched the bag.

"I got these, too." I pulled out a sandwich bag of sliced carrots and pulled one out.

Rut grabbed that, too, then took out three and stuffed them into his mouth. He flashed a sarcastic smile that disappeared as quickly as it raised on his sleepy face.

"Munchies from that blow?" I bit into a carrot, peering him directly in his eyes.

Rut's forehead wrinkled. "I ain't smoke in years." My mouth dropped. "Actually, I did blow one with B-Rocka two summers ago when we found out a bird he fucked was pregnant by another dude."

"You weren't just down here smoking with them?"

Rut shook his head, ripping open the bag of chips. "On everything; I came down here with just my cousin, Red. I woke up to you and all them other niggas, including security." He shrugged with his lips. "But we roll like that. If I wasn't ballin', I'd be right in Trenton with them niggas. That's my family. We all in pain right now. Plus, when I'm in town, they stick around me for protection." Then he gave me a long stare. Out of nowhere, Rut chuckled. "They don't even pass me the blunt no more. Just like they used to trap back in the day, ignoring me when their transactions happened. They never pass to me."

I wanted to laugh at the exclusion, too, but decided not to. Instead, I scoped out the place. Rut's place. It reminded me I'd never explored his condo in Connecticut. Here, in his real home, was a monstrous sized television mounted on the wall across from the bed. Sneakers, paired according to models and colors inhabited a corner. A wall of trophies took up lots of space a few yards from where I sat. And then there was the lounge area where his crew sat before they left. In there was a living room set and another mounted television. Rut seemed to have his own living quarters right here in the basement.

How many girls has he had down here?

"It was gang-related and then it wasn't."

My head whipped to face him. "Huhn?"

Rut's regard was straight ahead on a poster-sized picture of him as a teen and another kid I hadn't noticed until now.

"B-Rocka..." he breathed out while gazing at the image. "He was fuckin' a girl who claimed she was done with a dude from the Northerners, a gang in North Trenton. We haven't had problems with them in years. And even then, it was over a girl. They were at a party last Saturday and dude from the Northerners had a few pills and shots of Henny in him. The *bitc*—chick was there with her girls and got mad when she saw her nigga all up in somebody else's face. She decided to start twerking in front of B-Rocka. He was drunk off his ass and with it."

Rut hung his head and took a deep breath.

"Is that him...B-Rocka?" I gestured for the wall.

"Yeah."

My hand found his thigh and squeezed. "I'm sorry."

"For what?"

"For not having the superpower to take the pain away."

"You'd do that for me?"

I scoffed. "In a heartbeat."

After a pregnant pause, he uttered, "Why?"

I shrugged, gazing at the poster picture of the pair. "Because I'm a sucker for assholes, they say."

Slowly, I turned to face him. His dark eyes made my heart flutter.

I yanked my head away. "Stop it."

"Stop what?"

"Stop looking at me like that. Today's about comfort, not that other stuff." I trained my eyes to the cups left behind on the coffee table.

"What other stuff? How you got my fuckin' nose wide open?"

My hair flew in the air from the speed of my neck turning to face him.

I snorted. "I do not!"

Rut scoffed, his eyes rolling from me as he shook his head. "Then why, while my heart is bleeding, all I wanna do is taste your lips?"

I skipped a breath, swallowing hard. The cutesy smirk planted on my face earlier had been washed away by that remark. Then we locked eyes. Rut's swung down to my mouth, making me throb below the waistline.

"Why were you so mean to me earlier?" I whispered, hearing the echoes of my mouth movements bounce off the walls. "Why didn't you come over last night?"

"Because I was mad at you," he returned in the softest, most frank tenor...almost childlike.

"Why?"

"Because I'm a stingy muthafucka, Gray. Because I hate to see you devoted to another man. 'Cause I've only known you for two weeks and feel like you belong to me. 'Cause I'm a crazy ass fucker."

My throat tightened to the point I couldn't breathe. Until a heap of air broke through producing a croak. Rut leaned down, his head angling as his eyes focused on his target. I found my spine gravitating to mirror his movements.

"*Ut...*" There was a thump at the far end of the room. "*Shit!*" Then a thud.

I was on my feet, startled out of my mind. Rut's big body rounded mine swiftly.

"C'mon, man!" he barked. "You know better, ma!"

I shifted until I could see Paula's little frame on her knees, holding her head. "Fuck, Rut!" she whined. "One of the damn steps disappeared!"

"No, it didn't! You OD'd today. I told you since that first shot to pace ya'self; people over!"

"Rut, I'm good!" she shouted as he reached down to stand her on her feet. Paula yanked away from him and wobbled until she found her balance. "I just came down here to see ya friend. I wanna know if she gone help me with your party."

"What party?" I couldn't help myself.

Paula tripped over her feet to get to me. "His college graduation and draft party. We throwin' him one before the season start. You gone help me?"

My eyes shot over to Rut's big body flexing behind her like the Hulk.

"I'd love to." I beamed, knowing it irritated him.

Also, it was then I realized Rut had gotten his degree last month. That warmed me.

"Good! Now I'm just waiting for him to give me the money to do it." Paula was next to me now, leaning on my arm. "You know them white men with him from the *Kings*?"

"Ma!"

"No." My eyes blinked successively. "I didn't."

"Yeah. They think them fuckin' Northerners gone try my son. Let them bitches roll up!" Paula kissed the tips of her fingers then dotted her chest and two narrow shoulders. "I got something for all them mufuckas, they mommas, and babies. I swear on everything. Rut a good man. My only!"

I nodded, my eyes locked on a brewing Rutledge.

"You real wit him, ain't you?" My eyes shot down to Paula. "You ain't like them other thot bitches, is you?"

"You mean like his girlfriend, Emily?"

"C'mon, Gray!" Rut growled. "Don't play like that!"

A giggle shot from my belly. "Paula, you give her the same set of questions?"

"Don't listen to her, ma!" he barked.

Paula's little head swung back and forth from Rut to me.

"You told me you ain't fuck with her like that! You said that was all publicity, nigga! That's why ya father flippin' the hell out in his cell!"

My mouth formed an "O" while my eyes went wild. This was fun. A wonderful distraction to the grieving, I hoped.

"I ain't got time for this," Rut mumbled and grabbed my bag and snacks from his bed. "C'mon. I gotta get you back to Connecticut at a decent hour."

"You ain't staying?" Paula trilled alarmed.

"Nah, I got mandatory minicamp tomorrow, Wednesday, and Thursday." Rut grabbed my hand.

Paula was behind us as we headed for the stairs.

"Wait, Rut! I need a few dollars," Paula slurred. "I owe Gina a hun'ned dollars from bingo last week, Lil' Rocky need thirty dollars for camp this week, and Mommy's door needs fixing. The guy quoted her three seventy-five."

My eyes blinked fast, hard, and repetitively at those inflated numbers. And I didn't recall that little boy, Rocky, even asking for money.

Rut stopped just at the base of the steps and turned to her. He sighed and his shoulders hung with exhaustion. "I just saw the hotel bill from the past week. You ran it up with the mini bar. What the hell were you doing in town to play bingo when you was supposed to be laying low from all the drama?" Before Paula could defend herself, he continued. "Rocky ain't in camp this week, school ain't even out yet for them. And I'll holla at my mans about Grandma's door." He started up the stairs.

"Rut!" Paula shouted.

"What?"

She didn't say another word. She popped back on one leg, propping her fist on her hip expectantly. For a few seconds, we all stood frozen. Then Rut let go of my hand and dug into his pocket. He pulled out his wallet and peeled off a few bills.

"This better last you a couple of weeks. I keep telling you, we ain't rich yet."

"Okay. But what about the party?"

"I don't need a party. I ain't even making money yet. We celebrate when the money starts flowing."

"And when that 'posed to be?"

"Maybe next season, ma. I don't know. But right now, we gotta chill on all this spending shit." The undertone of his words was a pleading one.

This was hard to listen in on. Paula was draining her son, financially and emotionally. However, it was clear to me he loved her in spite of it.

Rut resumed his lead up the stairs.

"But what about your father?" Paula asked close behind. "He come home in a couple of months. You 'on't want a joint party?"

"No, baby girl. No party for me. We'll talk about what we'll do for him closer to the time," he droned.

We weren't fully on the main floor when a commotion sounded. I saw one of the suited security was headed our way full force. Rut pulled me behind him.

"Where the fuck he at, though?" a woman's voice struggled to maintain a calm façade. "I just wanna talk to him!"

Behind me, I could hear Paula clonking up the stairs. "Shit! That's Kim?" She was in the hall in no time, pushing me to get around Rut.

Her little frame disappeared among the big bodies in front of me.

"Now wait a fuckin' minute, Kim!" Paula yelled without a slur. "Don't come all the way out here to my house with that shit. This ain't Trenton!"

"No, Ms. Paula! You said he was gonna call me!"

"He said he did, but even if he didn't, you ain't got no right coming up in my house like this. Fuck outta here with that bullshit!"

I could even hear Annalise, Rut's grandmother, trying to diffuse the situation.

"Yo, get me the fuck outta here," Rut demanded of the suited security in front of him.

"Sir," he answered. "The trucks are being pulled around now. We're gonna make a path to the front door."

"Then let's go!" Rut demanded.

"I just got a call from my partner outside about several men arriving with this irate woman. We have to be sure they aren't armed."

"Man, fuck them Hawkins'! They know what time it is." Then he got louder. "Kim, man, you need go the fuck on with this bullshit!"

"Yeah," Annalise cried. "You gone hurt that baby!"

Baby?

I couldn't see anything. Rut's big back was in my face and when I craned my neck, there was another long suit. And that's when I saw a gun. The security—the one the *Kings* hired—was armed! My mouth went dry.

"I ain't even come over here on no bullshit. I just want you to be a man and tell me why you started actin' funny style? Why you ain't even call me about B-Rocka? Why I had to hear it from the whole fuckin' Trenton but not from you? And now it's '*Fuck the Hawkins?*'" The girl sounded to be on the verge of tears.

I tugged the hem of Rut's suit jacket. "Who is that?"

"No fuckin' body!" he yelled, likely not able to come down from his anger. "Get her the fuck outta here, Rich!"

So many people were yelling at one time: men and women. Threats were being hurled and furniture being moved.

The armed security spoke into his wrist. "Okay. Let's go," he commanded Rut.

Rut pulled me in front of him and practically caped my shoulders and back with his big frame.

"Sorry about this," he murmured in my ear as we shuffled into the kitchen, en route to the door.

I didn't know what to say as my heart thundered. Who was she? What was going on?

"You fuckin' coward!" the girl screamed. "You said we was gonna stay cool!"

"Kim, don't make me get my niece to beat ya ass!" Paula yelled from somewhere in the house. I still couldn't see much with all the big bodies surrounding me. "Where Sheema at? You better be lucky they holding me back!"

"Fuck you and Sheema, P! You said we was cool, too. Now you stuntin' on me just like him!"

"Kim!" Annalise cried out again. "You gone hurt that baby. You too close to your due date!"

Is that Rut's baby they're talking about?

My body began to tremble from familiar symptoms of betrayal. We moved and swiftly. Before I knew it, we were outside on the porch of the house.

"Take her to the truck," Rut order. "I gotta go back and straighten this shit out."

"Amare," one security spoke up. "You can't go back in there with that melee, sir."

"It ain't what you think. She my high school girl. She pregnant—" His eyes flew to me in the doorway of the truck. "Not by me! She a lil' off but not dangerous. I just gotta make sure my moms and grams is okay."

"Richardson and I will have to go with you."

As soon as Rut nodded in agreement, Paula appeared on the porch of the middle-class neighborhood home. "Rut, y'all go 'head.

We all right. Bobby came with her. He in there calming her down now!"

"Grandma okay?" Rut asked.

"Yeah. She gone fix her some water. She just trippin' the fuck out. That's why I told you to call her!"

Rut grumbled something underneath his breath. Then he looked back at me, as I was halfway in the truck.

"I'll call you in a few," he shouted to Paula.

"Okay, baby." Paula waved. "Love you, Rut-Butt!"

Rut didn't answer when he moved to enter the truck. I hopped inside and scooted over. He brought my bag in and the door was closed behind him. I shuffled on my knees to peer out of the back window when I asked, "What was that?"

"Bullshit," he groaned, leaning back in his seat and closing his eyes.

"You sure the baby ain't yours?" I teased, sitting back down. I never got a look at her.

"No. Kim's just crazy as hell. I was tryna tell people that so long ago. They thought it was her just wildin' out over her first 'love.'" He used air quotations. "But I knew it was more. She liked to fight any and everybody and for no reason. The girl never drank but would be on the dancefloor for hours like a molly-head. She wouldn't sleep for days and would pop up at my crib at four in the morning to try to bust me with a chick."

"Did she?" I lifted a brow.

But Rut's eyes were closed.

"Only once," he cracked a smile anyway. "But that wasn't it. It was something more. When she pulled out on that girl back in high school, everybody woke the hell up then."

"Pulled out?" I yanked my head back. "As in a gun?"

He nodded. "She got arrested and everything. They did a mental evaluation on her and turns out she got some form of depression."

"What made her 'pull out' on a girl? Did she catch you with her?"

"I never even touched the girl...didn't even know her. She came to our prom with another girl from our school. Kim said I was sneaking conversations with her that night. I barely remembered her. She waited over a month later when I left for football camp to fuck with her. She stalked the girl, found out where she and her friends lived, and went to her house one night that summer with a gun."

"Oh, my god!"

"The gun wasn't loaded, but she planned to use it. The girl pressed charges on Kim. Her parents fought crazy hard for jail time. But without the bullets, Kim's lucky ass got off easy. She had to go to therapy and was on parole."

"Why would your mother want you to keep in touch with her? You're clearly a trigger for her."

"A few years went by and I started school. Kim went to MCCC—community college—and had been laying low. My mom keeps up with her aunt and heard Kim's therapist was saying she was doing better and needed to try to make good with the people she fucked up with." He shrugged.

"Is that why you're so adverse to therapy?"

At first, Rut didn't answer. "She crazy as fuck. I ain't. The one other person I ever heard going to see a head-fucker is you. And I know you ain't..." He hesitated.

With full-on demure and a smiling heart, I asked, "Crazy?"

Rut rolled his eyes, not wanting to answer directly.

"I told you therapy isn't just for the mentally insane. I think they require a little more. Therapy is just regular conversations with a mental housekeeper. Therapists, how I see it, are available to help you stay ahead of you. People like you and me can get ahead of ourselves with our actions, egos, and self-esteem even."

"My self-esteem good," he scoffed, eyes out of the window. "Real good."

"Yeah. Too good for your britches at times." I rolled my eyes. "My point is, it's good the woman Kim received the diagnosis. She could have hurt someone without it." I snorted, "Looks like she still may. And I find it awesome that you're talking your thoughts out with a professional, too. It's better than with your boys."

"All I'm talking to her about is not fuckin' you again," Rut grated.

"What?"

"Yeah. I told you she the one who said to try to get to know you."

"Yeah, you did."

"But she keeps saying to do it without my dick."

Fats, in the driver's seat, shifted up there while clearing his throat. That caught Rut's and my attention.

I laughed.

"What?" Rut asked.

"My therapist suggested the same thing when I called her a few days ago about you again."

His forehead wrinkled. "Why you call her again? I thought you don't see her no more."

"I don't as much as I used to, but she gave me an open invite to keep in touch, even if it's through telephone or text." I shrugged. "I'm just not clear about you." My eyes went out to the highway we were now traveling.

"What do you mean?"

"I don't know. It's like you said earlier: I met you exactly sixteen days ago. You're the first guy I've slept with in years and it was a one-night stand!"

"And what's wrong with that?"

I turned back to him. "I don't do one-night stands, Rut! I'm almost thirty years old. I should be more settled than that."

"I 'on't get it," he mumbled, seemingly irritated by the conversation.

"And that's sad. You're what?" I jumped in my seat, my back no longer on the chair. "How old are you?"

Rut looked at me as though I'd lost my mind. "Twenty-four."

"Oh, god!" I had lost my mind.

"What's the deal?"

"I've been wanting to jump your bones all week and you're only twenty-four? This is awful!"

"Aren't you from Waterbury? You flippin' out like a Milford girl." He chuckled. "You got a degree in chemistry and ain't do the math on my age?"

Without looking at him, I shook my head, feeling pathetic. How stupid of me not to think of how young he was. Most rookies drafted were younger than twenty-four. Then it dawned on me. "How are you twenty-four and just graduating college?"

A lazy smirk lifted from his face. "I got left back in second grade."

"How does a kid get left back in second grade?"

"When their mother doesn't send him to school every day."

"So that put you behind?"

"That and getting redshirted in college."

I sucked in a breath. "Why were you redshirted?"

"I was a wild boy going in. I had some maturing to do. My ass almost got kicked out my freshmen year." He wouldn't look at me as he admitted that.

"Because of the threesome tape?" I recalled reading about that after we met. The story rang familiar. Like I'd heard it before.

Rut nodded. "They wanted to clip me. The only reason they didn't was because it wasn't me who recorded it or shared it. I was actually the victim. One of the girls' boyfriends sent it out. He got expelled. My…mentor got his lawyer on it right away to be sure the black kid didn't get disposed of even though I had nothing to do with it being recorded." He paused for a moment. "The decision was to sit me for the next year."

I scooted closer and curled my body underneath him, resting my head on his shoulder. "I'm sorry, Rut."

He chuckled. "For what? I was lucky. I had the resources to protect my ass. If I was any other poor boy from Trenton, I would've been expelled. Good shit…second-chance opportunities don't happen to cats like me. Not no regular Trenton nigga."

My eyes swept up his neck until I reached his eyes that were cast out the window.

"Not even B-Rocka?" I whispered.

Wordlessly, Rut reached for my hand, pulled it over his leg, and squeezed.

chapter
thirteen

MY PHONE RANG LOUD IN MY HAND.
Shit...
I tapped to answer quickly while Parker wriggled on my lap.
"Yeah?" I tried whispering.
"Yo, Rut Rut!" Mickey screamed into the phone. There was loud music and people shouting in the background. "Where yo pussy ass at, boy?" He laughed.
"On my way back to Connecticut. What's up?"
"Ohhhhhh!" I cringed from the shrieking of his voice. "My bad! I forgot you had a funeral. God bless the dead, homie."
"Whatcu want?" That annoyed me coming from Mickey's vanilla, greasy hair ass.
"We rounding up to head over to *Townhouse Hall*. Young Lord's performing there. I was trying to see if you wanted to hang out."
I hesitated for a minute. Tomorrow was the start of minicamp. I didn't think it was wise to be out all night, drinking and shit. But after the day I had, I could blow off some steam. More squirming underneath me snatched my attention.
Wright...
"I'mma have to pass on it, Mick. I'm not by myself."
"Why? You said you're on your way back. We got a few extra

Love's Ineligible Receiver

tickets if you have a few people from home coming back up with you."

Parker sat up. Mickey's ass was so loud, he woke her up. Parker pulled out her phone and tapped a few times. Seconds later, it was clear she was FaceTiming someone.

"You there, Rut?" he shouted.

My head pushed back at how loud he was. "Yeah, man, I'm here. I 'on't know, man. Let me wake up. I'll hit you back in a few."

"Okay. Peace!" he shouted before disconnecting.

Then the girl, Mandee's, face lit up on Parker's phone.

"Hey, Parker!"

"Hey!" Parker yawned. "How is he?"

"He's good." She rubbed her eyes.

"Did you remember to stretch his legs?" That question bothered me and I hated it.

"Yup. I let him beat me in a few sumo rounds, he's had dinner, and is now sleeping. I'm here getting much quiet study time. Damn, I can't get this done at my house with my niece and nephew being off from school. Everything's okay?"

Parker laughed at the joke and maybe if I wasn't sour about her checking in again today I would've let go of a chuckle or two myself.

"Yeah. I'm close to home, and Rut just got a call about some friends in Connecticut getting together."

"Oh! Totally! Go. Hang out. It's going to be an all-nighter for me."

Parker bit her lip and my cock twitched with excitement at her wanting to chill some more.

Nooooo...

I had to tell my strongman to be easy. The head doctor said no sex, and I would keep with it.

"You sure?"

"Of course!" Mandee waved her off. "This is honestly helping me."

I'd pay her. *Shit.* I would double the three hundred I paid her for the day.

Parker turned to me with a hesitant stare. I didn't move. No matter how bad I wanted her to go for it just to feel she chose me over Wright for once, this was a call she'd have to make on her own. A sour taste covered my tongue. Was I nervous?

"Okay. Just for a few hours. Call or text the moment you're ready to go. I'll be home by one, the latest."

It was almost nine thirty.

"Okay, girlie. Have fun. Too much fun." She winked, causing Parker to giggle.

When they disconnected, I warned her. "We don't have time to change."

She put her phone back in her bag and sat back, circling her arm around my abs. "We're going to have to go as we are. I can take this jacket off and look a little more casual. You'll just have to look like a Milford geek, who wears tighty-whities."

Where she at?

I kept looking toward the door for her instead of the stage where Young Lord was tearing down the building. *Townhouse Hall* was packed. It wasn't the biggest venue, which is why I was surprised Young was performing here. Bodies were pinned against one another with little moving space on the main floor the venue lined chairs with. *Kings'* nation managed to reserve the balcony where Fats escorted us up to. At least fifty heads were up here. A few veterans with their peoples and just a couple of rookies. There was even a private bar out in the hall.

Parker was finally coming back into the stands, holding two drinks up in the air as she threaded through people. And what a mean walk she had. With her arms in the air, her already tiny waist pronounced her hips more. I was still surprised at how just taking off the little jacket she wore with the dress and tucking its straps inside the top changed the whole look. She looked seductive, mature, and totally fuckable.

"They didn't have *Mauve*, so I got you this."

"What is it?" I spoke directly into her ear.

"A Gray Park special." She smiled before taking a sip of her drink.

I was lost. "A *wha*—" Then it dawned on me. Her name. "Cute."

Parker stood in front of me and swayed as Young went into another track. It was my shit. I bobbed to the bass, sipping the cocktail Parker had given me. It wasn't bad at all. Maybe I'd have it again after tonight. It put me into a nice zone as I rocked out with him. I loved this track. It was actually a cut he recorded alone on the *Korrupt Hearts* album, a group Young came out with. "*I'll Never Love Another*" was a song I could identify with. It told the truth about females and how they all were about the bullshit.

I did my shoulder dance as he made it to my favorite verse and sang the last few bars with him.

"*Bitches be the set up...get wet up...*
Let you nut up...then burn you the fuck up.
They seduce you with that shit...
Stroke ya dick...then have they hands all up in ya pocket.
Shit, I know we all got our hustle and I ain't tryna knock it.
But to the crack bitch, groupie bitch—and corny bitches, y'all be the same...
Stay the fuck out my hustle because, man, all y'all be fuckin' lame."

Parker spun around with alarmed speed. She carried a playful smile, even though I had a feeling she wasn't happy with my celebration of those particular lyrics.

Shit! Not you, though!

I busted out laughing, grabbing her at the shoulders then kissed her on the forehead. I may still have been struggling with my feelings about Parker, but one thing was for sure, she was my boo-boo. I kissed her again saying so. She wasn't like them. Maybe it was the vibes of the drink settling in that fast because I hadn't really eaten much all day, but on my unborn seed, I was good on Ms. Parker G. She was my hitta today.

Sipping on my drink with an arm draped around her chest, I swayed without singing along with Lord anymore for this track. We rocked out with Young through the next song. Mickey brought over a round of shots for us. He carried a big ass tray and walked it through the balcony.

Parker necked the shot and double cupped it with the cocktail she was still working on. I did the same and pulled her back into me.

She looked up, signaling wanting my attention so I leaned down into her.

"I can't remember the last time I've seen a live performance," she spoke loud so I could hear her over the blasting music.

"You too busy making soap and shit. Gotta get out more," I teased.

Parker laughed as her attention went back to the stage.

"What the fuck up, Connecticut!" Young Lord shouted when the music dropped.

The crowd went wild.

"Shit!" He whistled. "Y'all showing the kid crazy love up in this muthafucka!" He tented his hand to see out into the crowd. His head tilted up toward the balcony. That's when people up here began hooting and whistling. "I heard the *Kings* up in this bitch!" Another spray of applause ripped through the air.

He smiled and gave a salute. "I 'on't do much football, but my lil' king is a big fan. So, because of him, I got love for the throne." The guys all around went nuts. Whites, blacks, Hispanics...everybody loved good hip hop. And Young's wordplay couldn't be missed. He used his hand as a tent against the blinding stage lights again. "I fucks with Jordan Johnson. I 'on't know if he in the building, but salute to my Jersey brethren, T. Bailey and the wild boy rookie, Amare!"

The crowd turned up again. I was shocked as hell. Lord knew me. That was a dumb realization. *I'm fucking Rut the Receiver! Of course, he knows me.* As I raised my drink in the air, Parker turned in my arm and a few guys slapped my shoulders in congratulations.

"Speaking of saluting kings from my home state," Young announced in the mic. "Fuck with me on this..."

The beat dropped and a familiar bass and drum sounded. It didn't take long to realize it was "Supreme Being," another cut from *Korrupt Hearts*' album. Young sang the hook and his verse. It was crazy how his group mates weren't around to perform it with him. One was locked up and the other a vegetable with brain damage, but the song hit something deep down inside. They dedicated the track to their street mentor, their "General," Supreme Being. Dude was locked up, serving FED time and ended up dying in there.

It was one of those cases of paying someone their respect while they were alive because you don't know when their last day would be. I heard dude was mad young and died suddenly in there. That was secretly one of my fears for my pops. He was serving federal time, too. Had been since I was a pup, barely able to piss without dripping out of the bowl. Every year, I thanked something, somebody...somewhere for sparring dude's life. No matter how hard he went on me, I loved my pops. Hard.

So Young's lyrics hit home. I sang those with him, too.

"*And to Supreme...*
You couldn't live out ya dreams.
Father to a mass of soldiers...
We stand on ya shoulders.
Life don't end 'cause you down in the pen.
Every day I breathe a free man, I'm soaring on the wings of ya sins."

Though it seemed weird as fuck, when Parker squeezed my arm draped across her chest, it felt like she understood.

Then she rubbed the side of her face on my shoulder.

This fucking girl...

She was doing shit to me. We stayed that way until the end of the cut. When Young introduced one of his artists who was about to perform, Parker lifted her head to get my attention.

I kneeled and she shouted, "I gotta pee." Her tone no more than a child's.

"Okay. C'mon."

"No! I can go by myself."

"Hell no!"

"Fats is right there!" she yelled even louder.

I looked up and saw Fats was staring our way. Parker saw him, too, and waved. He nodded, letting us know we had his attention.

"Three minutes or I'm coming in there."

She nodded then handed me her double empty cups and took off. I watched until she made it to Fats. He dipped his chin to me before following her out. I didn't miss the heads that turned, checking out her plump ass in that tight ass dress I didn't realize was so fitted earlier.

I tried keeping up with the show, but it was hard with her out of my eyesight and not leaning against me. I swear, each time I felt those bitch ass feelings for her I hated myself for feeling so weak. Parker was only a woman. She shouldn't have made me feel different from any other one.

Tim Bleaks, a tight end, came over and gave me some dap. We exchanged a few words about minicamp in the morning and kept it moving. I checked the time. She wasn't back, but I told myself to chill; Fats had gone with her. Then I checked my text messages that had been ignored all damn day. Two were from Emily Erceg, saying something about hearing about the funeral from somebody. I wasn't beat to even read the full messages.

Raised voices here, on the balcony, snatched my attention. A few more bodies came through the door. It took a few seconds to recognize Terrance Grant, the last motherfucker I wanted to see. I'd just started feeling numb from my loss. He swept the front walkway, giving dap to everybody. When he made it to me, I automatically fell in line.

I returned his dap, giving him a dry, "Whaddup, god."

"Coming from church?" He looked me up and down, joking on my gear.

I cocked my head to the side and looked him dead in the eyes. "Yeah. Ya grandma's funeral. I killed her pussy."

With swiftness, I released and let him go. Then my mood shifted. I didn't fuck with Grant since the first time I met him at an event last year. When I got drafted and started working out on the *Kings'* property, my opinion of him didn't change. I only learned my feelings for him were popular. Hardly nobody fucked with Grant. He was an arrogant fuckboy. What annoyed me the most was him being such a risk to me. I played it cool but didn't have much patience like the other players. I knew my temper. I'd crack his shit without thought of getting fined or cut. He was an energy I couldn't afford having around.

And he wanted Parker. Usually, I wouldn't care. Until recently, I honestly didn't. Matter of fact, one of my main motivations of taking her home that first night was to snip his clown ass. Now, I didn't want him nowhere around her. How crazy was it that he was here tonight, the night I had her out?

What if she plays me?

Parker was a sweet girl. She seemed like the type to make everybody feel special, just as she had me feel all damn day. I couldn't handle her giving him no kind of attention, but I had to eat it. I had to tell myself now they'd have a conversation—it would be a short one—then she'd walk away because she was with me.

For the next few minutes, I couldn't relax to get back into the show, worried about *the next few minutes* when she'd return. Switching the mood swiftly, Young came back to the stage, going into a new track by another one of his artists, Wally, featuring Young and Hov. The room went up when the females knew what was coming. It seemed like all the ones around me threw their arms up in a dance. This one was newer and had a trap feel with heavy and fast drums. This joint was fire. It was one of the regular plays at *Arch & Point*. The dancers in there dipped low to this shit, especially Young's verse, which was the second. It reminded me how much I missed that damn place.

Movement at the other end of the balcony caught my attention. Finally, Parker was coming back, and I started feeling tight all over again. Grant made his way down toward the door. They'd definitely see each other. I watched from the corner of my eye as Parker strutted back down the walkway and was hooked by a hand on her arm. I squeezed the empty plastic cups in my hand. She looked up, saw it was Grant, and smiled. He went down to hug her. Then I turned my head to fully look at them.

Parker didn't hug him back. As a matter of fact, she grabbed his hand from her arm and gave it a squeeze instead of returning the hug. Her smile seemed genuine, but what was also real was she wasn't trying to stay in his face long. He said something to her. She laughed—quickly—nodded and took off, almost in a rush.

The closer she got to me, the more her pace picked up until she was in a full-on sprint in her heels. Her arms shot up in the air when she was a couple of yards away. Then Parker landed right in front of me on beat, bent over, stuck her ass out, and wiggled. She was twerking...and I mean artfully. She clapped her hands together then grabbed her hair from her shoulder so she could look back at me. My fucking word, she held her head as she twerked her ass right in my crotch. She must have caught the shock in my eyes because she hit me with a seductive grin and rolled her eyes as her spine controlled the lifts and drops of her ass.

She was definitely with the vibe. Her ass bounced so rhythmically, I couldn't help but grab it. *Shit...* Parker could dance! Who the fuck knew? She turned around, laughing but still dancing. Then she took my hand, lifted it in the air, and twisted until she fell into another twerk. My damn mind was blown. I forgot Parker was a cheerleader. That had to give her moves alone. I found myself biting the inside of my lip, watching her.

Young transitioned into the ladies' favorite, "*Sunset Showers.*" It was a freaky song they went crazy for. Mickey's ass came back with another round of shots. When I thought she'd had enough, Parker grabbed one so I followed suit. Then she turned to me and raised her plastic cup.

"To life with lots of '*Sunset Showers!*'" she shouted with the biggest and prettiest smile.

Her eyes were low from being tipsy and she looked...younger than I'd ever seen her. Twenty-eight wasn't all that old to me, but Parker had the life of a sixty-eight year old. She seemed so responsible and like a homebody. These chinked eyes made her appear youthful and...

Sexy as shit...

I clinked cups with her and she downed hers right away. After a deep swallow, she laughed. At what, I didn't know. Then she pushed her little arms around my waist and stepped into me. Because I stood one step above her, Parker's tits pushed into my dick. I'd be damned if it didn't swell against her. When she sucked in a breath and dropped the goofy grin, I knew she felt my response to this new woman standing before me.

And I wanted her. Bad. I knew I had a deal with the head doctor lady, and I planned to keep it. But in this moment, I wanted her alone. I wanted to smell her pussy. Needed to feel her juices all over my face and hands. I *had* to feel her vibrate beneath my face from my head game. And I fucking loved eating her pussy. I couldn't get enough of her heavy breathing or her cries she tried to swallow in the middle of her bed.

My hand went down to her hair. With my fingers, I combed her bangs from her face and ear. Then I leaned down and whispered, "I got something for you. Time to go."

Out of nowhere, I felt her hand claw my lower back. Parker was fucking game. That's when I grabbed my phone and shot a text to Fats.

Parker

I was so revved up, so shamefully hot for him. I couldn't remember the last time I was this horny. As my hand was clasped in Rut's, allowing him to lead me out of the venue, my pulse pounded and my clit throbbed a heated rhythm faster than my feet paced. My head hung with my dedicated focus on his trail. I wanted him so bad.

We were close to the door when I felt a cold touch on my bare shoulders. My head flew up and I saw Terrance standing with a drink in his hand. There was a knowing gleam in his eyes. A message of *"I know what you're doing with him."* Ordinarily, it would affect me, shame me. But tonight—just for tonight—I belonged to him. My attention, focus, and body belonged to Rutledge Kadar Amare.

My god, I didn't know this man and the thought of seeing his dick animated me near delirium.

I didn't break my stride, though my gaze lingered on Terrance until we cut the corner for the door. As Fats led the way, once again, Rut's big body caped me like a shawl. He wrapped me in a protective cocoon, something I don't believe I'd ever had. He made me feel precious, a type of care I used to crave until I gave up on the possibility of equal reciprocity with a man.

My arm swung back and hand clutched his hard thigh. Keeping up with Fats' pace in front of me while a few people greeted Rut, I pushed up to his groin, feeling him jump slightly in surprise. The arm he draped around my chest and shoulder tightened in response. My greedy hand found his thick, raging cock and stroked it as much as I could without making it obvious. I struggled to keep my eyes open and on the back of Fats' shoes.

When we were out in the cool night of early June, my lungs filled with air and back arched into his body as he rounded me and pulled me behind him. My heels click-clacked against the concrete of the sidewalk. It was nearly two blocks before Fats was tapping the remote to unlock the truck. That's when I wondered how long would it be to get back to my bed—or his place? What time was it? Did I have time?

Rut hopped in the truck and I was being lifted and pulled inside right after him. He reached around me and slammed the door shut. Then he was on me. Rut leaned his big body into me, reclining me into the corner. I moaned when his tongue slipped into my mouth. My hands grabbed the back of his head, pulling him closer. Music sounded and was turned up to blasting levels. I was cocooned yet again in his scent and heat. I tasted the vodka from his drink and his need for me all from his tongue.

He managed to spread my legs eagle for him, immediately releasing my natural aroma and shooting my arousal levels through the roof. His hand was at the bed of my panties, the back of his fingers rubbing teasingly, his mouth overwhelming me with pleasure. I was lost in him, for so long unable to think past what I felt. My hands fumbled to his waist, hitting his chest along the way before I snatched his belt from the loop. I pulled my other to unhook it and open his pants. Feverishly, my hand searched for him until I felt a throbbing rope of steel. Rut adjusted, almost desperately, to allow me to pull him out. The first blatant sign of vulnerability I'd seen of him.

A sigh of excitement pushed from my lungs as I fisted him. My panties drew tightly into my skin. The gradual feeling of the near painful pinch had me realizing they were being ripped from me. He pushed the tube of my dress down along with my bra, exposing my breasts to the coolness of the truck. My eyes flared open to total darkness. Rut's wide back shielded me from Fats' view and the tinted windows ensured our privacy.

His lips roved down to my right breast. The tip of his tongue sloppily lashed across my distended nipple. The movements were swift and the weight of his tongue heavy. I moaned louder than I should have, fisted his swollenness faster. My body strained under his rushed touch; I wanted him so bad. The moment his thumb pressed into my engorged clit, I pushed back on Rut. He reclined and lowered to his back where I was able to straddle him.

The slamming of the door startled me. My head reared and I searched the truck. Fats was gone but the music still boomed inside. Rut lifted to meet my face.

He pulled my head to his and spoke in my ear, "Chill. He's giving us privacy."

Then his tongue distracted me again. Those big hands of his went to the back of my thighs and lifted my dress over my butt. My back arched, breasts reaching his mouth as he suckled. My head collapsed backward and I moaned. The head of his erection brushed against my thigh and I lowered onto him. Before I landed, Rut was pushing me up his body while scooting himself down some. Before long, I understood his plan. He wanted me on his face. I had little choice in the confined space of the back seat.

The irony wasn't lost upon me how Young Lord's *"Sunset Showers"* began to flow from the speakers.

His tongue brushed along my sex and I rocked into the bliss. My hips rolled over his head and neck swung as pleasure stirred in my groin. The things his tongue could do. I grabbed the top of his head, trying to control his movements. The buildup concerned me. It was too fast, felt too intense for public. My eyes shot open again, halting my stride and I broke my fall with my arm behind me. When I turned to see where I would land my arm, I caught the most arousing sight ever. Rut's big palm was down to his pelvis, fisting his thick, veiny shaft. The engorged crown made my tongue twitch. Rut's tongue stabbed beneath me at the same pace and rhythm as his hand stroked his cock. *The sight of it...* It aroused and angered me. Frustrated and challenged me. Quickly, I shifted, standing to my one knee and swung the other over his head until I was on the floor of the cab, going for him.

I could feel Rut's torso rise in alarm from my movements, but I ignored it. Oral had never been high on my list of masteries, but tonight, confidence came from the combination of being tipsy, unbelievably horny, and bizarrely comfortable with this guy's body. My mouth rushed for his mushroomed head and my hands followed, pushing his aside. He throbbed inside my busy hands and the ridges of him felt like steel against my tightened lips. I marveled at the smoothness of his soft skin. When I thought my movements were too fast and un-paced, his hand was on the back of my head, encouraging me...guiding me.

"Fuck!" ripped into the air as his pelvis jerked.

Quickly, I was grabbed and awkwardly arranged until my body was on top of his again. His dick in my face and his mouth on my sex. Rut sucked my lips then my clit. I could feel him pull it between his tongue. Instantly, I was deluded again. This was all going so fast, my body wound tight again. His hand pushed the back of my head, forcing my face on his standing erection. He wanted me to suck him again. With gusto, my mouth and hands were on him. I moved with manic speed. Jerking him, inhaling him.

My hips rocked, butt rode in the air until I met that plateau and my groin exploded. I screamed against his throbbing dick sliding up and down my tongue. My spine flopped and I struggled to balance myself against the wave of bliss inundating my weakened frame. Then the hardness of his body beneath me shuttered and I almost didn't catch the first spurt hitting the spot between my mouth and throat. I almost choked, but luckily, my throat closed and I was able to catch it. And there was more. Warm, thick, creamy liquid jutted into my throat as his entire erection pulsated in my mouth.

Maybe doing this after drinking wasn't the best idea.

But damn, was it worth it when I felt his big body seize underneath me. His heavy arm lay across my back and hand clutched my shoulder to keep me in place. When I thought he was done, I plopped him out of my mouth and began to swallow the puddle, not knowing what else to do with it. Slowly, I began to peel my depleted body from his. I slid to the floor, sitting on the back of my knees with my sex still throbbing.

Rut shuffled in a sitting position, straightening his pants. He then reached for me, pulling my boneless body between his legs to lower my dress over my butt and placed my heavy breasts inside the dress before banging on the window hard. Seconds later the door opened and Fats slid behind the wheel. Rut rustled with his zipper and belt. The windows were rolled down as we pulled off and I was situated into his chest, my eyes struggling to stay open.

"Let's hit up the *B-Way Burger* on MLK Boulevard," Rut's thick vocals ordered before I succumbed to slumber.

"I'm here, Nurse Jackie!" I called out the moment I closed the door behind me.

I was finally home. My feet throbbed and head ached from exhaustion. I pushed off my heels and kicked them underneath the small table in the corner near the door. Then I took a deep breath and let it out as an act of mental recharge.

It was two days after B-Rocka's funeral and so much had seemed to happen since Rut and I crawled in the house Monday night and sprawled across my bed for sleep. He had an early start the next day for minicamp, and I had a long day with Jimmy...and social media. My phone wouldn't stop ringing from people I hadn't heard from in years...and Rut.

Today was the end of my first day back to work since Friday, and all I wanted to do was go straight to bed and rest. But such was the life of a normal, childless twenty-eight year old. Not mine. I had to take over with Jimmy, give him a bath, and pack up soap and body cream orders that were filled Friday but never sent out. The only silver lining to my night was I didn't have to cook. I had enough leftovers from last night.

I heard the toilet flush from the small powder room near the front door and my eyes blinked open. Nurse Jackie stepped out, drying her hands with a paper towel.

"Oh, hey." She smiled mildly.

"Hey." I stood straight on my feet. "How was he today?"

"Good. Temp's been slightly high since this morning, but he's been fighting."

I recoiled and lifted the paperback in my hand. "The doctor sent over a script for an antibiotic, just in case an infection is brewing from the trach adjustment. I'm going to start him on it this evening and give him a bath. Hopefully he'll feel more comfortable by tonight."

She moved toward his room. "Yeah, that should do it. Oh!" She turned my way. "His friend is over."

My nose went into the air. "Who?"

A goofy grin opened on Nurse Jackie's face. "The big time one: Eli Richardson." My heart dropped from my bottom. "He's been here for about thirty minutes."

He didn't park in the garage and I didn't recall a new car out on the street. Eli visited Jimmy every now and then, but he'd call ahead of time first. What was with the pop up today?

I didn't have to wait long to find out. As Nurse Jackie ambled into Jimmy's room, Eli sauntered out. His salt and pepper dusted face suited him well. The absence of friendliness and warmth in his eyes he usually shared with me didn't. I took a few steps to meet him in the center of the foyer.

"Parker." He offered a neck bow and a soft smile.

"Eli... Hi." My eyes danced in his, not knowing what to say.

Love's Ineligible Receiver

"I know you just got in from work. You mind if we talk for a minute?"

My eyes widened as my shoulders lifted. "Sure." I pointed toward the small living room.

He followed me inside the seldom used room. It reminded me I needed to dust in here. I sat in the sofa chair across from him. Eli rested on the edge of the love sofa, increasing my anxiety of his presence.

"How are you, Parker?"

"Tired, but good." My answer was honest.

"Do you need anything? Anything I could help with?"

I shook my head, eyes wide and cheeks spreading. "I don't think so." This felt bizarre. "You've been more than generous. The only source of help throughout this craziness."

Eli nodded. "I can imagine the toll this has taken on someone like you. You're young, smart. I understand how difficult this could all be."

"It is what it is. I told Jimmy I'd do this with him." I shrugged. "I'm doing it."

"Parker, it's not my practice to involve myself in your personal life —anyone's personal life. But I think I'd be remiss if I didn't warn you against Amare—"

"Rut?" My eyes exploded.

So *that* was the reason for this visit.

"Yes. I can understand the appeal. Amare is young, talented, and has begun an amazing journey, using pop culture to make a name for himself. But there's more that comes with those attractive...attributes."

"Like what?"

"Like what the world doesn't know. What not everyone sees. Rut has a history. He comes from unusual circumstances."

"Trenton isn't that unusual from Waterbury."

"It's more than an urban city. It's his breeding, dear. His ties to the street...decisions he's made." He lifted his hand, gesturing to me. "You're probably well aware of attention he attracts and the energy he keeps around him. You, yourself have been a victim of privacy invasion."

"Eli, is this about the pictures on the blogs?" I knew it! "Rut didn't ask people at his cousin's funeral and mother's home to secretly take pictures and record videos of him during a private and peaceful event."

"That pandemonium at his mother's home was anything but peaceful, sweetheart."

"I understand the security you guys hired to babysit him reported back, but no one was hurt. Rut left right away. What could he do? Sit home from his cousin and best friend's funeral *in case* his truck got shot up leaving Connecticut, or a meteor fell from the sky as he walked into the church, or his high school friend showed up uninvited at his mother's house having a meltdown? It was his cousin. He had to go pay his final respects and grieve with his family."

Eli shot me a long look. He didn't like my sarcasm.

"Did he also have to go to a concert right after? Because he didn't have to do his 'grieving' there."

My head swung to the side at that shot, but I could see it from an outsider's perspective. As luck would have it, my *former* favorite blog, *Spilling That Hot Tea*, was able to get their hands on grainy but distinct enough pictures of Rut and me rendezvousing in the shadows of *Townhouse Hall*'s balcony.

Why was Rut a hot item for a popular blog like *Spilling That Hot Tea*? Two words: Emily Erceg. That family was no longer made of human beings; they were simply cash grab fodder for the media. And Emily was purportedly dating new *Connecticut Kings'* recruit, Rut Amare. Rut had gotten the call just as he plodded out the door yesterday morning for his first day at minicamp. His PR person Face-Time'd him—a gorgeous woman with smooth pecan skin and blonde curly hair—animated about pictures on a blog.

I had no idea what pictures or what blog and didn't have time to ask as Rut walked out to a waiting Fats. But less than thirty minutes later, my phone exploded with calls and texts. The first came from Jade Bailey, who was more frantic than Rut's PR person. I had a script for each person who reached out, a calming one. Even to Rut, I had to assure I was fine when he snuck off the field to call late that morning making sure I was okay. I explained I was powerless to those pictures getting out. There was no reason for me to be up in arms about them. I'd leave that to his public relations team.

And there was enough work for them to do. The images from *Townhouse Hall* were damning. The embrace Rut held me in virtually the entire time we were there read "couple" big time. There were several with me twerking and his eyes fixed on my hips below him. And the two images of us leaving were shady. Rut liked to drape his body around my body like a chinchilla coat to protect me, but it could be debated if he was hiding me. Hiding as in him not wanting it to get back to Emily.

So Eli's jibe about Rut not looking as though he'd been mourning at all that night was certainly plausible.

I took a deep breath, too exhausted for this battle, and honestly pissed I had to take it on.

"Look, Parker. I just wanted to be sure you're okay. This is nothing personal against Rut."

"Are you sure?" One eye narrowed as I gaped at him with suspicion. "Because you've named several negative 'attributes'"—I used his term—"yet you failed to balance them. You didn't mention how hard he's working off-season, how he's adhering to the team's contingency in his contract of therapy. You didn't mention his business acumen and how he's had an impressive run of success before he became a *King*."

Eli shrugged with his head. "I didn't mention how he has incredible charitable ties to his community either. I can tell you about the book bag giveaway he's been doing since his last year of high school." The walls of my heart quaked. "We can even discuss the food truck program he does in the poorest areas of the city." Then Eli's expression fell. "So, I guess you didn't know? He has small food trucks deliver healthy foods to kids in the neighborhood. Fruits, vegetables, and all natural snacks." He nodded. "Yeah, Parker, I know in detail because I just read his file on my way here to provide that balance you mentioned.

"And even with all those good mentions, Rut still has a convoluted past. No. I will not sit here and lie about the faith I have of him turning over a new leaf. I've been in this business long enough to have seen countless examples of kids who couldn't shake the block. And my name Eli Richardson. I can write books on how disposable young, lonely, heavy burden women are to successful athletes."

My lips were parted and eyes danced on the floor. This was news to me. Rut shared a lot with me over the past two and a half weeks, but he rarely spoke of the good other than his skills on the field. He had something to prove to the *Kings*, his mentor, and father. Shoot, he rarely spoke of his sneaker business to me. Maybe he wasn't the pompous asshole even he thought himself to be.

"Look, Parker," Eli's voice had my head snapping north. "This isn't about Wright. It's certainly not about Amare. My concern is for you. You're a good young woman, Parker. What are you? Thirty years old?" *No.* "I'm sorry to intrude, but you're old enough to be my daughter. You know I have a daughter your age?"

"But we know I'm not your daughter or nowhere near it. Because if I were, you would have never allowed Jimmy to approach me. You would've protected me against his charm and lies. If you cared about me so, you would've told me the first time he brought me to your home for dinner that he was bringing different women even after I'd moved in. You were there the night I met him. If I were your daughter, would you have told me he'd been showing signs of CTE and even had fears of having it? Because you knew, Eli. He told me."

For the first time, I'd seen a look of reproof and conviction on his face. "Parker—"

"You've been generous, Eli. But how much of it has been from guilt? I don't know. I don't even focus on it. You saw my bloodied face. You saw what he did to me. You knew the risk I signed on to when he begged me to stay here with him although we were broken up. If his children don't know the ugly facts, you do." I stood. "So, if you want to start questioning my judgement as far as the men I choose, I'd say now is too late considering the shitload of facts you withheld when your friend was concerned. You should have done that six years ago to the twenty-two-year-old fool."

He hung his head in the opposite direction. My body trembled with nervous energy. Never did I think I'd take this tone with Eli Richardson. He was not only my boss, but a billionaire—an astoundingly powerful man. But that's all he was. Just as I was human and had to figure out my own way, even in the valley of my circumstances, so did he. Rut had been a distraction from the shadows of loneliness and regret. No. He wasn't a sure thing, but he damn sure was my now thing.

Eli stood, width returning to the wings of his back. "A man of my tenure isn't used to doing this, but I'm going to step back. However, Parker, if Amare is as reckless with you as we've seen him with other facets of his world, I'll be as relentless as I should have been years ago when I first laid eyes on your innocence."

A tear slipped.

chapter fourteen

"You killed it this week, Amare!" Coach Brooks, of all people, shouted over to me as I jogged off the field.

It was the closing of the last day of mini-camp and my body was beat the hell up, but I didn't mind. I performed way better than I did in rookie camp. I could tell the coaches were impressed when they didn't say shit after plays, just grunted and nodded. Tuesday, which was day one, was a little rough because of all the shit hitting the blog. Having that happen just before I needed to focus was just bad timing, but I got through it.

"Sorry to hear that, man," Jordan Johnson softly replied to Jameson as I made it to the water table.

I wanted to roll my eyes as I stopped in front to get a bottle of *Gatorade*. After untwisting the bottle, I turned my back to them and gulped down as much as I could take. Jameson was still bitching about his finances. Dude was going broke and wanted every damn body to feel sorry for him. He overdid it with his spending, got in over his head, and was now going down like a damn sucker.

He was from Albany and had a house there his family stayed most of the time. Foolishly, he had a crib built out here in Connecticut for "options" for his family. Jameson had sixteen cars at the top of the year. Now he was down four and needed to chuck more. Instead of flying through our drills this week, we were distracted by his constant talk of losing money.

"Yeah. My wife's fucking flipping on me, bro. Jess thinks I've been blowing money on a mistress." Jameson spit out a hard laugh. "Man, I'm too focused for that cheating shit. I'm a family man. I guess I just moved too slow."

"Oh, damn," Jordan's tone was less than excited.

I guess dude didn't know what to say.

"And you know that second house here in Connecticut? I bought it for one-point-nine, and that was when it was a buyer's market a few years ago. Now the property is underwater. The fucker's valued at nine hundred thousand!"

"Shit!" Jordan whistled more convincingly.

I wondered if he knew he was being finessed.

"Yeah. And check this out: I only owe four seventy-five on it, but my accountant said I should consider selling it for a little more. I don't know. My wife and her mother are fucking distraught over it now, bro."

"That's fucked up," Jordan went back to muttering.

He was a good dude. I, on the other hand, tossed my bottle in the trash and took off for the locker room.

"Yo, Rut?" Jordan called behind me. I turned and saw him excusing himself from the whack ass conversation with Jameson's broke ass.

He jogged a little to catch up.

"Peace, god." I snickered. "You finally sick of that whining shit, I see."

Jordan laughed quietly. "Nah. The homey Jameson's a good guy. Just made some bad calls recently."

"Yeah. Don't we all." It wasn't an introspective response, just a response.

"I heard about your dilemma."

"Who hasn't?"

"You got a point there." Jordan found that amusing. "You got good people at *Love is Action,* some of the best in the business. Just follow the script."

"Bruh, I'm so sick of fuckin' scripts. I just wanna do me. I'm fuckin' Rutledge Amare; I don't follow shit to the T."

He laughed again. "Well, now that you're in the big league, young homie, you gotta learn how to walk the line. I'm sure there's a pot of gold at the end of the tunnel for you. You got the skills out here, my G. Just walk the line."

That pot of gold he referred to was endorsement deals. They *were* on the table as we spoke. The shit Elle Hunter and her team had cooking up for me made my contract with the *Kings* look like a fucking eleven year old's weekly allowance.

It actually is…

We were walking into the locker room when I muttered, "I'm trying, king. I swear on everything, I'm trying."

We past Trent Bailey, going through his duffle bag when Jordan joked, "And if you need help walking that line, we'll have the Reverend, Bishop, Elder, Apostle *Shoot 'Em Up!* lay hands on you in prayer."

We busted out laughing.

Bailey stood straight and cracked up himself. "That boy's a fool."

I knew he had to be fucking burned out. Bailey flew in from Europe just for these mandatory minicamp days.

"How's Europe?" I asked, going for my bag to get to my phone.

"Expensive, bruh!" he groaned.

"Word?"

"Word!" He shook his head.

"But *you got it*!" I sang, teasing him.

"I know, right?" Jordan laughed. "Cheap ass."

"What's ya lady saying?" I genuinely wanted to know, prolonging the shit storm waiting for me when I powered up my phone.

"Oh, Jade?" Trent asked. "She's in heaven. Her and the kids are having a ball. We all are. They're leaving France now, on their way to Italy. I'm hopping back on a plane at five in the morning to meet them out there to finish up the vacation."

"Nice!" Jordan commented.

And my mind went black, rewinding back to a time I never had but could see vivid as fuck.

I was holding a small and hella soft hand as I walked on a glossy cobblestone road. I couldn't focus on our destination because I was too concerned about her five-inch heels.

"Stop."

I dropped to one knee before she caught my command. Then I pulled her back to me, eyes locked on her feet.

I heard her breathy giggle over my head. "What are you doing?"

I didn't answer, just went about the job of fixing the buckle of one of her high heeled boots. And by fixing, I mean making sure they were tight enough. Maybe that would make sure she didn't fall.

Then I stood, took her hand, and continued down the road.

"This is beautiful, isn't it?"

I didn't answer, but she knew what I'd felt. This was more than beautiful, and it wasn't because of where we were for me. It was because of the peace I felt having her with me. For real.

"First London, now St. Tropez. I can't believe we're in France—"

"Aye, Rut!"

My neck snapped from my black faced phone to Trent.

"You heard what I said?"

"Nah." I blinked. "I must've missed that."

"Jade wanted me to ask you how Parker doing with the *Spilling That Hot Tea* mess. She don't believe she's okay, even though Parker said she's good."

I took a deep breath, feeling the tension in my shoulders at the mention of that. Parker had been a damn trooper these last few days. I hadn't seen her since Tuesday morning when I left her crib. Even though I sacrificed sleep, I'd been staying at my place to catch a call with my pops, spend some time with Sharkie, and get my damn laundry situated. Parker didn't complain and I'd taken that as a sign of her needing a break after my temper tantrum over her commitment to Wright, going down to the funeral, that fucking Kim Hawkins drama, and then the pictures posted by the blog.

And I hoped she'd enjoyed it because her break was over. I would

Love Belvin

be falling asleep with Parker on my chest tonight. Fuck that. I needed some sleep after the work I put in here this week.

"She seems good." I powered on my phone. "I'll be over there tonight."

I heard someone clear their throat and looked up. Trent's eyes were on me and Jordan's had just rolled over.

"What?" I asked rougher than I meant.

For a while, Trent said nothing. Jordan went back to pulling shit out of his bag to shower, and I was looking stupid as fuck.

My phone began ringing in my hand, but my attention was too locked on him to address it. I low key wanted to know what he had to say. The other side—the more familiar side—didn't give a shit. I knew I had to get to the phone before I could shower but couldn't move my eyes yet though.

Trent shrugged. "Parker just seems like cool peoples. The kind you want good things to happen for." He closed the locker and walked off for the showers.

A heap of air left my lungs. I had no idea why I'd been feeling uneasy about these pictures with Parker—shit, everything about her. I knew her situation with Wright made shit sticky, but that was her life to live. It was her decision to make day after day. I knew I had this *League* shit and it somehow roped this Emily chick into my world, but I could handle that. No matter how I rationalized it in my mind, thinking about my situation with Parker made my belly feel like it was floating. It was nervous excitement, and that wasn't necessarily a good thing.

I tapped the green circle on the phone, not even looking at it.

"Yo."

"Are you done?"

"I ain't shower yet, but..."

"Okay. So you're done." She wasn't letting off me. "We've spoken to Emily and her people. This one's going to cost us a little bit, but it can be salvaged."

"Cost?"

"Yeah. An apology gift that will be posted—"

"Elle! I don't owe that broad shit! I did nothing wrong!"

"Rut, this may have been proposed to you, but you agreed! You said you'd publicly date her for a short period to help spread your name. Technically, you need Emily more than she needs you. We can end this today and she'll be—quote, unquote—dating the next unheard of NBA rookie."

I scoffed. "And 'I'm supposed to give a fuck' is written where?"

She groaned, frustrated into the phone. "Rut," was delivered in a way I knew would be followed by a sharp tongue. "The last line on the unprecedented endorsement deal with *Asé Garb* is almost typed. They're giving you your own line without a non-compete clause that would interfere with your *Rubber Soles* brand. A *major* line of their premium status never does deals with rookies like you. And that's not to mention the other ones we're working on like *EA's Madden* and *Opti-Free*. Now is not the time to trip over a short term acting gig, dawg."

As much as I wanted to scream, "I don't want shit to do with this girl!" I knew it would be a waste of time. It was nothing I hadn't said before, and I had agreed to it. There were two reasons I was obedient in football. The first was to make my pops happy. It was his dream. The second was to secure my family. And even though *Rubber Soles* was doing well and currently my top earner, it didn't have the trajectory signing to the *League* had. This was one of those moments I was teaching myself to swallow my pride and eat shit because it was actually good for me.

"Whatchu want me to do, Elle?"

"Okay." She took a deep breath. "First we're going to start with an indirect apology gift. Maybe jewelry—"

"Try flowers!"

"Flowers die."

"And so does this bullshit. Real soon!" I pulled out fresh clothes from my locker.

"I'll consider that. But on to more connective and tangible actions, hope you don't have plans this weekend…"

The door swung open and Mandee's smiling face appeared. She was just as bubbly as she was on Monday. Tonight I decided to be nice. She did me a solid by staying longer with Wright so I could have more alone time with Parker.

"How you doin'?" I smiled at her.

"Hey, Rut! Come on in!" She moved aside to give me room. "Parker's— *Ut!*" She turned to look behind her. "She's right here!" Mandee giggled.

Parker was dragging a big, heavy looking ass trash bag from Wright's room. She stopped to take a break. Then she turned to close the doors behind her, reminding me of her commitment to someone else. Another man.

"Hey." Her greeting was low...tired, but that light in her eye told me I was welcomed.

"Hey, Gray." My eyes rubbed against her full body.

Parker was wearing gray biker shorts again with a matching tank and black ankle socks. Of course, I searched for her camel toe. When my eyes pushed up to her face, what I knew for sure was a blush raised her cheeks.

"Can I help you with anything before I go?" Mandee asked.

"I thought I would be able to take this out back to throw in the trash bin out there, but sheesh! It's heavy. I doubt you can do it."

"You mind taking it back there, *King*?"

When the foyer got quiet, I realized someone said something to me. I looked over to Mandee who was waiting.

"Oh!" *Me!* "Yeah, I got you." I made it over to Parker in two steps. "How do I get back there?"

"Through the kitchen." She pointed.

Grabbing the bag, I headed that way. The kitchen was cleaned, no food left out for me. I called her earlier to tell her I'd be later than I planned because something came up.

Something fucked up came up...

Love's Ineligible Receiver

Taking a deep breath, I mentally shook it off. I'd made it to my destination. I'd be sleeping with her tonight. That's what I'd been craving for days. It's what I needed.

Outside, a sensor light lit brightly and I peeped the bin right away. I lifted the lid and tossed the heavy bag inside. Then I walked out farther, wondering how big the yard was. It wasn't the biggest, a modest size with high wooden fences for privacy. The space couldn't be no more than forty feet by forty and was unkempt. Weeds growing all around...vines and shit. An old table and chair set was knocked over off to the side. I guessed Parker couldn't do it all by herself. It was fucked up how Wright's sons didn't come cut the grass or pay somebody to do it, at least.

I shook my head and went back inside, making sure to lock the door again. Parker and Mandee were still in the foyer.

"Rut, would you convince this woman to hang out with me and Nurse Jackie?" Mandee asked, animated with it.

"Who's Nurse Jackie?"

Parker rolled her eyes. "One of Jimmy's visiting nurses. You've seen her."

"What's wrong with hanging out with them?"

Parker's eyes went wild. "Nothing. They've been jewels for me. My sanity and lifelines."

"But she won't let us plan something for her birthday," Mandee argued. "She can schedule a nurse here for a few hours that night."

My eyes were glued to Parker. "When's ya birthday?"

"The twenty-seventh," Mandee answered first. "She's a sensitive ass Cancer!" She teased.

"No. I am *not*, and you know it, Mandee!"

"Could you talk to her?" Mandee cried, dramatically.

I had no idea what to say. I was still stuck on her having a birthday coming.

"I'll see what I can do."

Mandee's arms shot into the air and dropped. "Thank you!"

"Whatever!" Parker waved her off.

Mandee picked up a bag near her feet. "Well, I'm going to get out of here," she yawned. "I'm sure you two have a packed agenda that doesn't include the neighbor from across the street."

I snorted. "An agenda like what?"

Parker covered her face with her hands and shook her head.

"You know, like bump and grind." I almost died when ol' girl rolled her hips.

"Mandee!" Parker shouted, but not too loud. She laughed when Mandee's shoulders and hands lifted in the air. "Trust me, as appealing as it sounds, it's not that type of party."

An expression of confusion was etched on her face. "I know I'm young, but you can keep it real with me. I won't be running to *Spilling That Hot Tea*." She winked. So damn corny this white girl—or maybe she was Asian.

I wasn't sure; she looked both.

"Mandee!" Parker warned her again.

Mandee turned for the door. "Okay. I'm out. Thanks for the extra cash Monday night, Rut. It went a long way on *Porn Hut*."

"Mandee!" This time Parker yelled louder than she usually liked it around here due to Wright.

Mandee hurried out, obviously knowing she went too far. Parker closed and locked the door behind her and put her back to it, taking a deep breath.

"I'm sorry. She's a gabby twenty-one-year-old." Parker smiled.

"She white?"

"Mixed. Mom's white and her father is Vietnamese." I nodded, seeing I wasn't too far off. "She came to clean out my old stock. I'm making room for new formulas for my lotions. Oh!" She stood straight. "That reminds me. I have something for you."

"That's what's up."

"You sure you aren't hungry? I can warm you up something."

I stared at her. Parker was so damn pretty. Even with tired eyes and no makeup on when she rocked that high ponytail.

"I'm good. I grabbed something on my way home from camp."

"Okay," she sang, teasing me. "You can go ahead upstairs. I'm going to make sure he's good then I'll be up for a much needed shower."

She took off for Wright's room, leaving me to it.

Parker

"I missed you," was the masculine rumble I heard as I sat on the bed, positioned at his side.

My hands that were about to move the blanket down to his lower back, hovered in the air. Those three words danced in my chest, they hugged my lungs.

Shrouded in the darkness of my room, I quietly emitted, "You did, huhn?"

"Mmhmm..." he hummed.

I reached over to where I lay the bottle of oil near my feet and squirted the liquid into my hand.

"I've been thinking about you in your absence, too." I had to admit. "A little," I joked.

Then I found his back. When I left the bathroom from my shower, the light in there illuminated into the bedroom and I saw him lying on his stomach shirtless. As soon as I gauged his position underneath me, I began to rub it in.

Oh, his back...

Jimmy was fit for his age, but he was average height and weight. I'd been getting used to appreciating broad muscle mass areas of the male anatomy. The cut and grooves in Rut's back, shoulders, arms, abs—heck, all over his body were beautiful. They were the hallmarks of a lifelong athlete. My days as a cheerleader were long gone, but I remembered being in prime shape and working out regularly to maintain and strengthen, so my respect for his dedication was immense.

"What's this?" his thick, lazy chords rang out.

"Something I made just for you yesterday," my delivery was slow, hopefully soothing. "It's an oil mix I thought would work well with your natural body odors." After being in his lap Monday night, I couldn't get his scent out of my head. Mixing aromas had been a craft of mine, and I was inspired to create something for him. "I mixed a base note of sandalwood with jojoba oil, jasmine, musk, and a few more goodies. All of those, and came up with my new fragrance."

"What's it called?" His mouth was slack, it sounded.

"Kadar," I whispered, turned on by the lumps on his sides, separating his hip from his waist.

"Kadar," he mumbled. "I like that."

"I do, too. I like Kadar a lot." My hands froze.

That didn't come out right. I didn't mean—

"Don't stop," he almost pleaded clearly when he lifted his head. "It's been a week of posturin' and frontin'. Let's dead that for the night."

"Okay," creaked from my tight throat.

Seconds later, my hands began to move again.

"Speaking of this week, Bailey asked about you."

Bailey?

"Oh!" I remembered. "Trent?"

"Yeah. He left the family in Europe for a few days while he flew in for minicamp. Supposed to be flying back out to them in the morning."

"So you both have morning flights?" I noted.

When Rut texted me earlier saying he'd be coming later tonight, he mentioned it was because he had to prepare for a last minute flight in the morning.

"Yup. And I hate it," he mumbled against the pillow again. Things quieted and I got lost in his right shoulder. I had no experience at massages but hoped I was giving a good rub down.

"You never answered my question?"

"Huhn?" That snapped me out of my thoughts. "What?"

"How've you been?"

"We've spoken every day this week."

"But I haven't seen you. Ain't been in your bed to know for sure."

"So you have to be in my bed to gauge my mood?"

He snorted. "Pretty much."

"I've been tired. Not a lot of sleep for me—at least, not restful. Jimmy's been running a fever on and off. We have him on a script now to hopefully address that. I worry about his comfort levels all the time. Couple that with hearing from James Junior, who hardly calls me or come by, about these pictures on the Internet of me and the rookie from team... Yadda, yadda." I rolled my eyes, though no one could see.

"Sorry."

"No need to be. I'm a big girl."

"And what did he say?"

"Nothing really. We went back and forth with me telling him I'm none of his business and he should be more concerned about his father. Then he threatened to kick me out—"

The muscles in Rut's back went rigid.

"Kick you out?"

My face folded. "Yeah. It's been a while, but that's nothing new with Jimmy's kids. They're always talking about alternative living arrangements for him."

"And you stand for that?" his tone was coarse. "They know how much you slave around here after him?"

"Ummmm..." My head slowly turned to my shoulder as my lips pouted. "That's a good question. They know all of his major care changes because they have to consent to them, but they're honestly hardly around to see them implemented."

Rut's body swiveled around with athletic speed and I was tossed in the air and swung on the other side of him, landing on my back. Then he rolled me on to my side to face him.

I couldn't abandon my hysteric laughter. His quickness and strength always blew me away.

"What was that about?" I asked, my hands raised.

"I don't want you talking about them anymore. You're tired."

"I still have oil on my hands."

"Then here." When Rut pushed them into his hard chest, my smile was gone in an instant. "Put it here," he murmured.

I rubbed against his pecs and shoulders then up to his thick neck. When I went back down to his dusted chest, I thumbed his peaked nipples. Swallowing hard, I wondered how they'd feel on my tongue. Rut's heavy and uneven breathing built a throb between my thighs. My greedy hands slid low, rubbing the last of the oil into his taut skin. When I felt the beginning of his pubic trail, my heart thundered. My grip was uneasy from the shakes that had begun, but I went lower. I wanted to. Rut had been a gentleman the past couple of weeks, but I now wanted the hellion from Trenton with the big ego.

And big...

Against my thumping pulse, my hand pushed down in to the heat of his boxer brief's elastic waist. The moment the tips of my finger made it to the thick root of his erection, my arm was pulled away.

"No."

Then my body was turned over so my back was to him.

"Go to sleep, Gray."

And that was it.

My hands clawed the sheet, spine arched over the mattress, and toes curled.

"Rut!" I panted.

His long arms pushed from my hips and palmed my breasts. I knew I wouldn't hold out much longer. His thumbs strummed my nipples, tongue pelted my engorged clit. My groin tightened, hips rolled to meet the rhythm of his lashes.

Until I imploded.

"Oh!" My head whipped from side to side. "Oh!" My sex rode his face as my shoulders danced over the mattress.

Rut stopped when my butt slammed against the mattress in fatigue. His big hand stroked my hip with adoration as he leaned his head against my thigh. After long seconds of my ragged breath cutting the dark air of the early morning, he shuffled from between my thighs and took off for the bathroom.

Instantly, I felt bereft. My eyes watered and face contorted, but I fought back the tears. He'd done it again. Once I was fast asleep from my last check in on Jimmy, Rut awakened me with tongue kisses below. And once again, he delivered spine-bending orgasms, leaving me feeling vulnerable and confused.

I heard the shower run and I rolled over, cupping my face from the barrage of emotions encroaching upon me. What were we doing? Tomorrow would make three weeks since I've met this guy and I felt like I've known him all my life. I craved his presence, adored his mind, and ached for his touch. Why did I not feel as close to him as I'd liked?

This is insane!

I wouldn't be that girl who wanted more from a guy than he wanted from her anymore. *Absolutely not!* Rut was young, too young. And he had no business being backed into a corner for a relationship with me. Hell, I was knocking on thirty's door. He wasn't even twenty-five. *But still...* I couldn't deny the emotional connection we'd found ourselves into in no time at all.

Even if he wanted something with me, it could never work. I couldn't be in a relationship with a high profile athlete. Monday was a patent example of what life would be like with someone like Rut. And could I expect him to be faithful? I honestly didn't know the answer to that. At his age, his sex drive was to heaven's height. But I couldn't corroborate that, considering he'd been holding to 'no sex with Parker' with his therapist. I'd long since wanted to abandon the same heeding from my own.

Ughhhh...

This was frustrating. I needed to focus on my priority. Unfortunately, it wasn't to me. It was to Jimmy. His health continued to decline, and I needed to make things as comfortable as I could for him. Each day in this battle with him, I was astounded at his spot-on prediction of his children's support. I was all he had. Until I completed my commitment to Jimmy, I'd just take what Rut offered in terms of companionship. Maybe this obscure relationship thing worked for him, too.

Ughhhhh...

"You ever been to France?" his voice was thick and hoarse, and such a turn on.

I rolled over and saw him standing over the bed through the streak of the light from the bathroom. Letting off a little sniffle, I turned over completely to face him.

"Uhhhh..." I swallowed, grateful I hadn't cried. "No. Can't say I have."

"It'll be cool to go."

"Have you been?"

"Nah."

Oh.

"You good?" His eyes darkened as they swept down my exposed body.

No!

"*Ye*-yeah, I guess." I snickered nervously.

"I gotta hit the road. Fats waiting for me at the crib so we can hit up this flight."

"Okay."

He reached down and offered a pound with his fist. Shakily, my arm raised and I reciprocated.

Rut moved for the door. He opened it and turned to me.

"Park?" his voice was lowered, humbled.

"Yeah?"

"This L.A. trip for business..."

"Yeah?" I hung on to his every word, something not unfounded considering the orgasms and *need* of him.

"It's with Emily. Just want you to know before some other shit pop off."

I swallowed hard. "Oh. Okay."

What else was I supposed to say? Do? Should I have asked for details? Was I allowed to? Of course, not. Instead, I left the bed to disarm the alarm system so he could go.

chapter
fifteen

I MISSED HER. DAMN, I MISSED THE fuck out of her. It had only been a day, and I couldn't stop thinking about her.

"Rut, dear..." I looked up to see Emily's moms, Ellis, combing her fingers through her short, jet black hair. Her eyes were red from all the champagne she had tonight. "Are you okay?"

"I'm good, Ms. E. Just out here to make a call," I lied about being on the balcony.

I came out here to take a damn breath. There were so many people in their Simi Valley, California mansion to celebrate her sixty-fifth birthday. Too many people in my damn face, asking when I was going to propose to Emily, a fucking stranger to me. One lady from the *Bravo Network* asked when we were going to have a baby. She said she'd love to get us a reality show. *The fuck?* That's when I had to get out of there.

"Okay. We'll be taking a family picture soon, so don't stay out here too long." She giggled before taking off in her long gown and high heels she could barely walk in now.

I was ready to fucking go. I'd been bored as hell since I landed yesterday. Divine wasn't in town. Apparently, Rayna took him out of the country from all the hype coming out over the damn documentary. That fucking blog, *Spilling That Hot Tea*, was in the lead with releasing pictures and anonymous DMs from people confirming connections they had to drug dealers loosely connected to Divine back in the day. So far, my name had been kept out of it, even though each day I wondered if the relationship between my pops and D would surface.

So, I was here. Alone. Emily wanted to go out last night and I lied about being tired from leaving minicamp and hopping on the plane to be here at her moms' celebration tonight. She didn't ride me much on it but she did show to my hotel late this morning, wanting to go out to brunch. We did. And guess what? Those fucking pictures were floating around in cyberspace.

I think today was the first day the beast of the media finally came full circle for me. This is what Elle and her team wanted: my face out there. A handsome kid, and talented athlete from urban, USA at the start of a successful career. Those pictures from a restaurant in L.A. had earned me an expedited endorsement deal from *Asé Garb*. Already, they were offering me twenty-seven million for a shoe design. And Elle was right: it was unprecedented. I'd heard of the deal they did with StentRo, Bailey, and Tori McNabb last year—all of who were signed to *Love Is Action* sports agency like me. That was pennies compared to this.

I should be jumping for joy and trying to fuck Emily for her part in this, but I didn't want to. I wanted to get back to Connecticut. I wanted sleep. Wanted soul food that nourished more than my belly. I wondered what Parker was doing now. It was late on the East Coast, but she didn't sleep through the night. She hadn't called me since I'd been out here. I hadn't called either and couldn't justify why.

I pulled out my phone and scrolled through Instagram. It was more popping than this party. My moms was hosting bingo in her yard. I laughed at her and her old ass friends posing for pictures with beer, *Henny*, and *Mauve* bottles she made sure Divine kept her stocked with. She stayed lit with that bingo shit. Jordan was with his lady, Cole, in the water where he said they opened the pool for the summer. Terrance Grant's whack ass was in my feed. It reminded me to delete him. His shits stayed corny. What black man mountain climbed?

"Fuckin' dweeb," I whispered to myself.

But Grant had a picture of a big ass bouquet of roses. His caption said something about he was about to hand deliver them to that special lady. *See!* Soft ass motherfucker. I kept scrolling and saw *Kings* running back, Ramsey Bishop and his wife, Wil Cunningham, giving their little boy a bath. Kids were corny to me, but this pic was kind of cute. Bishop was a good guy. He was probably a good dad, too.

Then there was a video of StentRo in his big ass backyard filled with lights, a bouncy house, a merry-go-round carousel, and other festive looking shit. He held his little girl in the air, making her believe she was flying. I didn't know whose smile was bigger: his or hers. StentRo had the smile that made his damn eyes disappear. His laughter in the video with hers made me chuckle.

I saw pictures from my peoples in college. A few from my peoples on the block came up, too. They were still mourning B-Rocka, something I could've been doing if I didn't have this career to chase. Then there came pictures Erika Erceg had begun posting from the party. I saw a few of me in the background, and she caught one of that conversation with the *Bravo* lady. That's when I decided to get off.

There was no privacy anymore. Every fucking thing was on a social media app. The only quiet time I had was with Parker. That reminded me of her birthday coming up. It would be cool to do something for her, especially with how she held me down at B-Rocka's funeral. My mind started going with how I could do something with a chick who couldn't leave her front door step.

I tapped the phone and dialed my assigned assistant at *Love Is Action*. Elle made sure I had someone who could help me with booking shit like flights and car rides. She said anything I needed.

"Hello?" she whispered.

"I know you're sleep. My bad," I hope I sounded convincing.

"No. No!" she spoke even louder. "Totally cool, Rut! What can I help you with?"

I let go of a deep breath, not used to this beck and call shit.

"I need a gardener."

"Like a landscaper?"

"Yeah. Them. Just some basic shit, nothing fancy. I'll text you the address for them to go and cut and clean out weeds and maybe trim a tree or two."

"Okay."

"And I need rentals for a movie set up—but first!" Something else hit me.

"I need flowers delivered to my coach."

"Coach?"

"Yeah, Coach Brooks. They can go to her office."

"Any particular kind?"

I had no clue.

"I'll let you decide. Just make them pretty."

"What should the note in them say?"

I hadn't thought of that either. Brooks complimented me at the close of minicamp. That hadn't escaped my mind. She was trying. She was a *fema*—woman. Women deserved sweet gestures.

"Just thank you." I shrugged.

"Okay. Got it."

"Then I need chocolates delivered to somebody else."

"What kind of chocolates?"

"I 'on't know. Good ones." I looked around me and only saw a guy walk down the hall the balcony was off. It was Rick, Ellis' ex-boyfriend. He looked behind himself, real suspicious like. I turned to face that way, leaning on the railing. "What do cute girls like?"

She laughed. "I'll figure something out."

"Okay. Send her that and a pair of shoes."

"Shoes? What shoes?"

"*YSL*s. I got a pic in my phone I can send you."

"Okay. What size?"

"I think a six and a half."

"Okay." Emily zipped down the hall in the same direction as Rick just seconds ago. And like him, she was so busy looking over her shoulder she didn't even recognize my big ass outside, a few yards away. "Anything else?"

I hesitated, feeling that familiar gut instinct. "That's all for tonight. I fly out tomorrow. If I think of anything else, I'll hit you before I board."

"Okay. Cool."

"A'ight."

"By—" I dropped the phone and tapped out of the call before she could get out the last syllable.

I made my way into the hall. My head swung left where the door to the room of the party was, and Erik, Emily's brother, stuck his head out.

"Yo." He raised his *Corona* bottle. "Mom said the photographer's ready. You and Em need to come on."

I tossed my chin. "A'ight."

Erik went back into the room and I went right where I saw Emily take off just two minutes ago. This was a formal dinner party where the dudes had to wear fucking tuxedos and hard bottom shoes so I made sure I treaded lightly. That gut feeling told me to be easy. I went all the way to the end of the hall where there was nowhere left to go but left. Trekking down another long hall, I checked a few doors along the way that were locked. I walked all the way down to turn another left, which meant I was on the other side of the house from where I started.

After a few steps, I heard smacking, a familiar version of it. That made my steps even more stealth. I stopped at the first short hall and what I saw made my fucking face open.

Emily peeled her face then body from around Rick before screaming. Rick went to comfort her and she pushed him away.

"Holy shit. Rut!" She started my way.

The smile on my face was from the weight being lifted from my back.

Parker

The moment I saw the lights of a car pull into the driveway, I took to the front door. After stepping outside on bare feet, I closed the door behind me. This was a surprise I was still processing. I waited until he stepped out of the car, jogged over to the passenger seat, and pulled out a huge bouquet of flowers.

When he made it to the steps, I smiled. "You didn't have to do this."

"I did. Especially after seeing those pictures of him out in L.A."

I shook my head and rolled my eyes. "Rut is a single man. He has every right to behave like one."

"But he wasn't behaving like one when he pulled you out of *Townhouse Hall* before Young Lord finished his set."

I took the bouquet that reached wider than my frame, planted in a square metal vase and sniffed.

"Mmmmmmm..." I sniffled again. "These look and smell amazing. Thanks, Terrance."

"Ain't no thing." He swiped my cheek. "I'm just glad you let a brother drop them off. I know you're busy with your hands full in there." He nodded toward the house.

Jimmy had a rough time last night and had been sleeping all day. It was close to nine at night and I wondered if I'd be sleeping in his room to keep an eye on him because he'd be wide awake tonight.

"Yeah. It's been a time," was all I offered, not wanting to share the details of Jimmy's health with strangers. "Not our best day."

Terrance stepped closer. "That's why I'm grateful for you letting me stop by."

Grateful? It's not like I was inviting him in.

"Well, thanks for these. I can't remember the last time I was given flowers."

"That's because I'm a man. Women should only give their time to men, not boys, who chase fame out in Hollywood."

I knew that was a jab at Rut, and after seeing those pictures with him, Emily, and her brother, Erik, eating at that restaurant earlier, I didn't think it was wise to defend him. Rut told me in so many words he was going to L.A. for business with her, but seeing the "business" tore at something in me. I'd been telling myself for hours to not take it personally. Rut was young, rich, and free. He shouldn't be chained to someone who has the lifestyle of a seventy-year-old married woman.

"Thanks for these, Terrance. I should be getting back inside now."

"Hang on." He stepped closer. "When can I take you out again?"

"I don't know. It's kind of rough to do much after five."

"We did it before."

I sighed. "I know. That was an unusual circumstance. I told you."

"And what about the concert this week? You were out late."

That's because Rut paid double for the whole day, something I didn't want to get used to him doing.

"Another rare circumstance. But maybe lunch. There are a couple of new restaurants around the office. I can take a few extra minutes more at lunch."

"Okay. I'll take whatever I can get from you, beautiful."

That sounded so cheesy coming from him, but I grinned and bore it. I even held my breath as he bent down and kissed my forehead. Not being able to take much more, I stepped back.

"Thanks again, Terrance." I opened the door and stepped in. "I'll see you around."

He gave a neck bow as I closed and locked the door.

My phone vibrating caused my eyes to fly open. I turned to the nightstand and tapped for it. The bright light glared in my eyes.

Rut: *You sleep?*

My heart galloped at his name.

Me: Yes.
Now leave me alone...
I swallowed hard over that lie as I turned over, kicking my leg in the sheets.
Rut: *I'm 2 blocks away. Open the door.*
My eyes flew open at that. *Here?* He was coming here? It was almost two in the morning. I didn't even know he was back on the East Coast. And at this hour? Was he crazy?
Is my heart really beating like a mad woman?
Why was I appalled and excited at the same time? I leaped out of bed for my purse. *Lip gloss.* I needed sprucing.

The cut of his engine could be heard from inside the house. I watched from the window near the door as he jogged up the driveway to the door. Before he could ring or knock, I pulled it open.

He wasn't out of breath and his expression was cloaked of emotion, but his eyes glimmered with vibrancy. And it was there. Hidden beneath the repression of desire was a teeming volcanic energy fomenting. He wanted me but showed restraint. That act went against constitutional Rut.

And I hated it.

I rolled my eyes, rounding him to lock the door.

"I'm going back to bed," I muttered on my way to the stairs.

Beyond beautiful.
He couldn't help it. His foot covered in a black ankle sock was just at the edge of the mattress. The opposite knee was folded, nearly reaching the other end of the bed. How was I able to fit on there with

him was beyond me. Then I remembered my place was on his chest. My head against his chest was where I found the most peaceful cadence providing siesta. His arm folded over his head bulged with wrecking balls. His entire upper body sparsely littered with colorful graffiti. His full lips were parted and his lashes made infinitesimal flutters. That's how I knew he was awakening.

Rut patted his chest. I knew he was in search of me. When his eyes flapped open, I turned my head to the side cheekily.

"I made breakfast." I lifted my brows before walking away.

I made sure to do it slowly and make a show out of my attire. Bra, panties, thigh-high hosiery, and black patent leather *YSL Opyum* sandals that were delivered yesterday.

"You're up already? I wanted to sleep in."

That stopped me in my tracks.

I turned to peer at him from over my shoulder. "I couldn't sleep after I checked in on Jimmy a few hours ago," I fibbed.

I slept so well on his chest, I'd actually overslept and didn't get to Jimmy until about an hour ago. I stayed away so Rut couldn't wake me in his usual fashion. Each moment since, I wondered if I made the right call. I'd love any form of intimacy with him. Craved it.

"I wanna go away," those morning chords churned out.

"Excuse me?"

He rubbed his eyes. "I wanna go away." His hand dropped, and Rut looked me in my eyes. "With you."

"I can't, and you know it."

"Do I?"

I didn't answer.

"You can ask one of Wright's kids to pick up for a couple of weeks—"

"Breakfast is getting cold." I continued into the bathroom and closed the door.

I'd just put the orange juice away and closed the door when I was pressed into the refrigerator, groped at the waist up to my breasts, and my chin was yanked up until my mouth met soft, moist lips.

"Mmmmmm!" I released something between a startling cry and a moan.

I couldn't decide before his tongue pierced my lips and swiped against my teeth. A delicious yet familiar fragrance danced in my nostrils. My mouth opened to him with ease and our tongues caressed each other with slow speed, rendering me tingly and stinging at the nipples. I stood on the tips of my toes to get closer to him and could feel the excitement of his efforts against my cheeks behind. He wanted me.

Good.

I pulled my mouth away. He breathed down heavily on me, nostrils angrily wide.

"Why've I been picking up crazy cold vibes from you?"

"Making you a hot breakfast is cold?"

"I don't like not waking you up before I go."

A delicious sigh coursed my lungs and anger flashed just as swiftly. I bumped him to move.

"I have to work today. And so do you," I murmured, going to the table.

"Nah. I'm off today." He turned toward the table. "I plan to chill, maybe get a damn massag—"

His abrupt silence had me looking up from my plate. Rut's eyes were on the bouquet of flowers on the table. I watched how the muscles in his face went south.

"Where those come from?"

My throat closed, eyeing the roses as though they were foreign to me.

"Terrance," slipped my lips softly.

"He was here?"

"Briefly."

Then his eyes landed on me. "Why?"

"He called and ask if he could drop something off."

"When?"

Love's Ineligible Receiver

"Saturday." Victory swelled in my chest. "Why?"

"Why?"

"Yes. Why?"

"Because he got no business coming by Wright's place."

"But you do?"

"C'mon, man," he breathed. Rut rolled his eyes and switched stances. "Because I'm your friend."

I angled my head and pushed out my lips, considering that claim. "Friends like Terrance and me or friends like you and Emily? I'm asking for a friend."

"Oh, that's what this's about? Fucking Emily!"

"Yeah. Are you fucking Emily? Because that would then be a different friendship than what you have with me and I have with Terrance."

Rut's eyes widened. "*That's* what this's about! Us not fucking?"

When I gave him a pointed stare, he got his answer.

"Shouldn't you be happy I'm not trying to fuck? Don't that make girls like you happy?"

"No. Because I'm not a girl, Rut. I'm a woman. And more than the sex we don't have, I have every right to be concerned about the sex you do have with other women."

"I don't have sex with nobody! My dick been drier than a desert since—"

My finger shot in the air. "Don't lie! You told me she went down on you two weeks ago."

Rut recoiled, almost in disgust. That reaction decreased my faith in male species just slightly. How can you be repulsed by a woman but let her put her mouth on you?

"But I eat your pussy and ass almost every day! Shouldn't that mean something?"

"It's just weird."

"Weird?"

"Yes! I could understand if oral was your fetish, but you've made it clear to the world you're particular about where you put your mouth on a woman."

"Because I fuckin' am!"

"But you put it on me—a lot! You come here at night and spill your heart and mind out, wake in the morning and make my body quake like a Taser, and go about your day. Meanwhile, back here on the ranch, I'm left deluded from orgasms and confused as to why a young, spritely man your age won't go any further!"

"*I WANT TO!*" thundered from his belly.

I jumped in my seat, pulse pounding in my neck as I tried catching my breath.

"Then why don't you?" I whispered. "I know I'm being selfish here. I know I can't give you more than that." I ducked my head and swallowed back upending tears. "I get that I've pre-aged myself with this commitment I've taken on. I really do. But since you've come around, I realized how lonely I've been. How starved I've been of companionship. If you don't want to—" I sucked in a breath, not knowing what to say.

Rut didn't seem to either.

"I'm lost in this. As fast of a time as it's been, I don't know the protocol." I lifted my head to face him. "I like you, Rut. A lot. I don't pretend to agree with half of your views, but I trust your heart. Almost every day, I learn something new about it. Like..." My eyes danced across the table. "Your charity work in Trenton. You didn't even share it with me, but it was no surprise you could extend yourself to people that way."

"I'm...scared to..." He made a gesture with his hands. "take it there with you because it's been working for...us." Rut closed his eyes, dropped his head, and pinched the bridge of his nose. This seemed so hard for him. To speak about *us*. "Me keeping my dick out of you is giving me a view of a woman—women, including Coach Brooks—I've never seen. It puts you on the safe side of the cold...negative and manipulative ways of females in my eyes.

"This damn therapist challenged me to some shit I ain't take seriously at first. I just wanted to prove I wasn't thirsty for ass, and could be selective and disciplined. I just didn't expect to get to know a beautiful side of you and a trusting side to Coach Brooks. You, her, and this fuckin' head doctor don't ask for shit outside of honesty from me. No money, no hookups, no sex."

Love's Ineligible Receiver

I winced, closing my eyes in shame. "I think I just did."

"Yeah, but I don't feel you're trying to do it to manipulate me. I just feel—" He heaved in a quick breath. "I feel like the ineligible receiver you said Wright was. I just want to be the right kind, but I know I'm gonna fuck this up."

"Why do you say that? How do you know?"

"Because I ain't had a girl since high school and I damn sure don't know what to do with a woman."

"What were you supposed to do with Emily?" My eyes fell.

Those words felt shameful.

"Just chill with her. C'mon, Parker. You know that's industry shit. It's for gain."

"Can I take a few seconds to be liberal with jealousy?" I bit my lip.

"Whatever the hell that means. Yeah."

"It's what you felt when you saw those flowers and learned they were from Terrance."

Rut shook his head. "Let's get back to your 'jealous.' I can stomach that better."

I rolled my eyes.

"It looked like more than business in those pictures."

"What pictures?"

"All of them. The ones with her brother at the restaurant. The ones of you dancing with her at her mother's shindig. They all looked..." I rocked my head, girdling my true feelings. "More intimate than what I feel we have as friends. The laughing, the—"

"The laughing at the restaurant was probably me clowning her brother's corny ass for ordering up the whole damn menu. The smiling while dancing with Emily was right after I learned she's fucking her moms' ex. Now I got leverage for when I'm photographed taking you out of the fuckin' country, something I don't know when or how will happen."

My mouth dropped.

"Wait a minute. Emily sleeping with her mother's ex delights you?"

"That and the twenty-seven million-dollar deal I'm about to sign with *Asé Garb* this afternoon. I'm happy out my ass, Miss."

My regard was fastened to his lips when a routine knock on the front door sounded and I heard my name being called.

"That's the nurse. Eat your breakfast. I'm going to say good morning." I took off.

"Gray..." I turned in the doorway to face him. "I know my situation's fucked up, but work with the kid. Be my friend until I get through these next few months of political bullshit."

My brows met in confusion. "What does that mean?"

His eyes rolled over to the bouquet on the table. "No more of that. It can get ugly. Real quick."

I caught the threat in his undertone.

"But you get to keep your friends?"

"I get to keep my peace of mind. You."

I didn't like that. I may not have been a feminist lion like my mother, inga, but I believed in the simplicity of intimate relationships. I turned to leave again.

"Aye," he called out. I turned to find him switching weight on his hips, once again appearing incredibly uncomfortable. "I do want your ass." My eyes fell to the floor, embarrassed. "I'm gonna talk to the head doctor."

I nodded without my eyes and left for Jimmy's room.

chapter sixteen

"WELL," SHE LET OUT A DEEP BREATH. "That's your hour, Amare."

Already?

It sure as hell didn't feel like it. As I lay on my back on the chaise, I pulled my phone out and saw it was five minutes before my hour was done.

I sat up. "That was painless."

The head doctor smiled. "It usually is when you open up."

"Ain't nobody do all that." I scoffed. "I guess I'm getting used to your questions." Standing to my feet, I stretched with my arms toward the ceiling. I was tired as fuck. "Oh, and thanks for the good report. My DPS, Nate, told me he got a copy of a satisfactory update on these sessions."

"We did make a deal."

"That's what's up. Thanks for the early dismissal."

"You've had an eventful week with the press and all." She typed into her iPad. "No need to belabor you."

"It damn sure has been," I breathed.

And it wasn't over. For a week and a half, a camera crew from a sports network, *WAWG*, would be following my prep for the season as a rookie to the *League*. This was another opportunity *Love In Action* was able to make happen for me to get my name and face out there. It was bullshit considering they did it at the end of June instead of July when I'd actually be prepping for the season. The upside of it was being interviewed by fine ass Wil Cunningham—now—Bishop. She married a fellow *King*, Ramsey Bishop, recently. It was cool talking to an athlete and not just a journalist or spectator about sports. Coach Brooks was teaching me to appreciate that.

But the past two weeks had been long and brutal. I stayed more nights at my place than I preferred because they shot footage from there. I even had my moms come up for a few days for a feature. That was too much damn energy for me. And on top of the circus following me with cameras, today was Parker's birthday.

It fucked with me how I couldn't take her away or out for the day to celebrate. That meant I had to find other ways to celebrate her. Along with the shit I started planning when in L.A. a couple of weeks ago, I bought her a few things all week and had them shipped to her place. It was the least I could do with the camera crew around.

Now it was time to get to her. I'd be staying the night there and getting much needed sleep on her tit.

"A'ight, doc," I yawned on my way to the door. "I'm out."

"Rut…"

My head flew back to peep what she was on. Her tone was different. Concerned. And she'd never called me "Rut."

"I read somewhere earlier about your father's release in August."

I tossed my chin, telling her to go on. It was crazy she brought it up at the end, but that was probably because it was one of the many things I wasn't open to discussing.

For a while, she didn't speak. Her eyes fell to my sneakers somewhere and she leaned over her crossed knees in her chair.

"Fifteen years is a long time for a nine-year-old boy to be separated from his father."

Okay…

I snickered. "Yeah. Kinda."

She took a deep breath. "My point is, you're an adult male. There were some points of growth—quite a few—your father missed and was unable to assist you with. Those opportunities are loss."

"No shit."

Where the fuck is she going with this?

"But still, there are social-emotional developments he'll be helpless on."

I stepped back into the office. "What do you mean?"

"In several ways, you're still developing emotionally. It's a topic I'd love to explore with you but understand your limited desire of therapy. However, there may be conflict between your life views and your father's. His world perspective has been blocked off by towers and barbwire. Your world view has been a tad broader than the average black man your age. If you're looking for him to fully understand your viewpoints and decisions, he may not."

"Why you say that?"

"Because he cannot. Long term prisonization as in his case creates norms of how one receives, responds, and processes. His emotional development has been stunted by institutionalization. He's been programmed to regulation. The bounds of his world shrank fifteen years ago. Yours broadened several years after. That exceptional endorsement deal you signed last week is a remarkable example of it."

"I get what're saying, but I don't get where you're going with it."

"I'm saying you're a good man. No matter what your flaws are, we all have our vices and crosses to bear. You've made a commitment to success and have been sticking to it; these sessions are proof. Keep going. Maintain your self-esteem and don't allow a narrowed-perspective mind to advise your boundless universe."

I could feel my face holding tight, my damn tongue, too. Like I said, I understood what she said, just not the reason. Too damn tired, I decided to not go any further. I nodded and walked out.

Instead of ringing the doorbell, I thought it was best for me to walk around back. That's where her little "party" should have taken place. I could hear the theatrical sounds pouring from speakers the closer I got to the yard. The grass was sparse, naked dirt spots all around, but in the middle was a huge blanket of artificial grass with bean bag chairs across it. At the back fence was a big ass projection screen where "Happy Birthday, Parker" was in yellow. That wasn't my genius. Ol' girl from the agency threw that in there like she did so many other small but cute details as I glanced around the yard. It looked completely different from the miniature forest I saw a couple of weeks ago.

"Look who's here!" Mandee screamed. "Woooo-hoooo!"

"Yeah!" the nurse, who's name I couldn't remember shouted and pumped her fist in the air. "Go, Rutty Rut!"

"This was so cute!" somebody in their cipher cried.

There were three other feminine bodies at the base of the short set of steps leading into the back of the house. They all waved and giggled. I waved back but didn't join them. Yeah, I was a selfish motherfucker, wanting their birthday celebration to end so I could have her alone to make her a pillow for sleep. I wanted to talk to her about these crazy ass two weeks, share with her my pops' thoughts on my endorsement deal, and apologize for giving my moms her number about this party I wish would never happen. So, yeah, I waved and waited for them to go into the house before I stepped onto the fake grass.

"I'll be right back!" Parker yelled, wearing a big ass smile. That lifted my spirits more than it should have. "I'm going to check on Jimmy after I walk them out."

I nodded and walked over to one of the tepee tents. They were small with black and white stripes. I didn't get the purpose of them to watch a movie, but it was another one of ol' girl's ideas. I recognized Parker's phone and crawled inside with the boxes I'd been carrying. I put them to the side then I stretched out on a big ass pillow and looked around. There was a clear view of the screen outside. Two red plastic cups were against the canvas. I sniffed inside and detected wine. Striped popcorn boxes were there, too. I stuffed a handful in my mouth as I pulled out my phone.

Out of the gazillion DMs waiting on me on *IG*, the one from Chestnut Cherries caught my attention.

dancing_cherries: *Ur phone must be broke*

I snickered to myself.

Me: I was gonna say the same about yours.

It was game. Game I was familiar with and could spit back. Chestnut Cherries had been blowing up my phone since *Love In Action* sent out the press release about the *Asé Garb* deal last week. I wasn't stupid. I went into another safe DM. This one was from my cousin, asking for jerseys for her kids and their father. I told her to hit up my other cousin who had the plug for them through my agency. By that time, Chestnut Cherries hit me back.

dancing_cherries: mine wrk fine hit a bitch up you still owe me

I spit out a hard laugh. This chick still on that? Picture me owing her shit; I ain't even know the girl. What's crazy is I thought I would have by now. I hadn't been back to *Arch & Point* in over a month. I O.D.'d on it the first couple weeks I was up here. Then I got caught up at Wright's and hadn't been back.

At first, I jumped when I felt a touch on my legs. She moved up my body like a snake. At first, all I saw was lashes, cleavage, and arms.

"What's so funny?" She giggled in my face, biting her lip.

"Somebody reminded me of you." I tucked my phone away.

She kissed my lips and my chest warmed. "How?"

"It's more like what."

Parker's thighs parted and she straddled me. It was natural at first. This was the position we slept in at night, after all. She snuggled into my chest, her little arms cupping my sides.

"Nah. Where's the movie? I wanna see what the 'glamping' hype's all about."

Parker giggled. "The remotes're over there." She pointed to the right of me.

I reached until I found two remotes. Parker's mouth was at my neck, distracting me from figuring the system out.

"Baby..."

"Hmmmm?" Her soft lips were on my cheek.

"I don't know how to work this."

Parker sat up and took the remotes. She twisted around to

communicate with the machines and a few seconds later, a movie was starting.

"What's this?" I asked as she laid back down on me.

"A jazz documentary."

I laughed hollowly from her weight on my stomach. "Who the fuck gonna watch a jazz documentary?"

"Us." She kissed my lips again then looked into my eyes. "It's my birthday," she reminded me so innocently.

And even though I smelled the wine on her breath, I felt safe with Parker and her birthday behaving ass. I combed back pieces of her hair falling into her face. She was so pretty. Dark brown eyes, long lashes, and kissable lips.

"How was ya birthday?"

"It's been glorious all week, beginning with the first gifts on Monday from this young wide receiver I'm trying to bag." She smiled.

"You mean 'tryna bag'?"

"I guess. I'm from Waterbury; I know the lingo, my G."

"You're a long way from Waterbury, queen. A long fuckin' way."

She smiled. Horns from the documentary sounded.

"You have a good time with ya girls?"

"When Mandee called me yesterday and told me to dress for my back yard, I didn't know what think."

Mandee was the plug for this. I put her in touch with my agency assistant and they got shit popping.

"Oh, yeah?"

"Yeah. She told me earlier this week to invite my friends from school and back home but wouldn't say what we'd be doing. I didn't want people roaming with Jimmy..." She hesitated. "You know what I mean." Parker shrugged. "So I didn't invite anyone. Mandee and Nurse Jackie brought friends of theirs I've seen and heard of from them to fill the space."

"How was the food?"

"Good. And the drinks, even better." She dropped her head and kissed me, showing me how good the drinks were being to her.

Her tongue pushed inside my mouth and rolled around and around. Parker always tasted good. Pure. Even in the mornings, she was the best flavor. When she pulled my tongue into her mouth and started sucking, my dick bucked and I pulled it back.

"Whoa!" I laughed and wiped my mouth. "How much you have to drink, shawtie?"

"A girl never tells, Rutledge." She giggled. "I ever tell you how much I love your name?"

"Nah."

"It's a mature one. Over the past month I've found that in you. I've found Rutledge and not just Rut. I'm glad Paula won that battle."

Oh, wow...

It dawned on me I really told this girl too much.

"Thanks, Gray." I smiled with gums.

She nodded and kissed me again. This time sucking on my lips. My whole damn body heated.

"Thank *you* for all of this." She pecked my lips. "And for the materials for my lab." *Another kiss.* "And for the lingerie." *Kiss.* "And for the gift card for a new and bigger mattress." *A juicy kiss.* "And for the white silk sheet bedding set for when I get it." *Kiss.* "And for the set up out here." *Peck.* "And for the chocolates two weeks ago when you were in L.A." *Another one.*

I laughed. "Oh. You remember that?"

"I remember everything, Rutledge." She pushed her tongue in my mouth again and rolled her hips over my lap. I moaned, holding her at her small back. If I went any lower, I'd be in the red zone. "And after all those wonderful gifts, I'd like to request another."

My eyes were closed, I was so dazed. Horny.

I licked my lips. "What's that?"

"I want you to cum in my mouth again."

My eyes shot the hell open so fast they hurt.

"Park—"

"It's my birthday!" she whined, pouting those lips that made me crazy.

My shit was rock hard. Still, I didn't feel good about this. Having Parker rocking my mic was something I thought about before she did it a few weeks ago. Since then, it had been an obsession but...

"Out here?"

She nodded, biting that damn lip again.

"But ya neighbors can see us." I tried to fight it off: Parker's sexy ass and my cock's need for her mouth right now. Her whole body. "Look how my legs're hanging out of this lil ass tent."

She sat up and widened her thighs. "You can scoot up." She pushed me into action. "Just your feet'll be out."

"Park—"

"Please, Rut!" she sang. "Let's at least try."

"At least try? Like once you put your mouth on me I'm gonna say sto—"

She yanked down the top of her dress, her tits spilling out over the fabric. Then she pulled her arms from the straps. Parker shuffled closer until her hard nipples touched my lips. *Fuck it...* We had a little bit of privacy, music, and I could smell Parker's pussy from underneath the little summery dress she rocked.

I swiped a nipple and heard her suck in air between her teeth over my head. I licked again and again then sucked while rolling the right one between my fingers. Parker rolled her hips over me again, making this so dangerous for me. More than a blow job, I wanted to be buried inside her.

She whimpered, grabbing the back of my head. That shit even turned me on. Her head over mine and elbows on my shoulders, grinded over me. My mouth was wet, slipping over her boobs. I pulled them together and ran my tongue back and forth.

"Mmmmm..." she moaned and I felt her body shiver. "I'm ready," she whispered in my ear.

I wasn't. I could've sucked on her perky tits all night but I stopped, pushing back against the pillows to let her handle her business. It didn't take her long to undo my belt and shorts. She moved down my legs and pulled my throbbing dick out. I looked at her, peeped the lust in her eyes, and heard the heaviness in her breathing over the music.

She fisted me first. Her eyes were stapled to mine as she caressed me in her soft hands. I cocked my head to the side, mesmerized by her touch and the sight of her. When she reached over and put her mouth on me, my eyes closed like I was free falling on a rollercoaster. I sucked in a heap of air at the first stroke of her tongue. She worked until my whole cock was coated with her and my head rolled. This was more than being waxed. This was Parker being bold, sexy, and aggressive. I could handle this. I could give her what she wanted and not go gorilla on her. But, damn, I wanted to be ass naked with her, running my tongue over every inch of her body. The same way she curled her tongue around me when she pushed down and widened it coming up. My hips started to move with her. I grabbed the back of her head, gripping her at the roots.

That's when she slowed. Her head lifted and I wanted to ask if I did something wrong. But I couldn't have.

Parker crawled up my body and kissed me. Hard. She moaned into my mouth when I grabbed her head, pulling her to me.

"Rut..." I opened my eyes to her. "You haven't said happy birthday."

I felt her shift over me, coming closer.

Silly ass...

My grin was big as hell. "Happy *bi*—"

Then we connected. The hairs of her pussy moved against the head of my cock, and I knew what time it was.

"Parker," I grunted, my eyes closed and hands shot in the air as though it was a stick up.

"Happy..." she grunted, pulling the head of my cock to her opening and squatting down. "Birth—" She sucked in a breath through her teeth again. "day, Ms. Grayson."

She struggled at first. I grabbed her at the waist to keep her still. "Don't."

"Huhn? You got a few in you."

I didn't want her hurting herself.

"I put a few in me to kill my nerves for this. To buffer me for your rejection. Don't make me go and get more."

Our breathing was loud as we stared at each other like warriors. My fear was all this good shit falling apart.

"I 'on't wanna fuck this up, Gray," I begged her like a bitch, wanting her at the same damn time.

"You won't." She inched closer. "I won't let you."

Her lips met mine and the decision was made. I wrapped my arms around her small back, bit into her chin, and helped her navigate her hips until she fit me all the way in.

My fuckin' life...

My spine seemed to have disappeared for a minute. She felt so damn good. Her thighs moving against my waist, her pussy quaking around my raging dick. I felt shit I never had. In the moment, while feeling everything, I realized I didn't usually *think* when fucking. I just handled my biz. With Parker, my mind was sensitive to everything, like the first time we did this. Just like now, I could hear her soft wheezing as she clutched my shoulders.

She giggled. "I don't think I remembered how big you are," she breathed.

This was sweet, slow, fucking romantic—some shit I ain't do. But it was cool to do with her. It was something I'd been wanting for so long but was in no rush to risk. But shit, we were here. Her smell drove me crazy. The taste of her nipples made me wild. And the feel of the muscles in her back moving in sync with the ones in her shoulders and stomach told me how determined she was to put in work.

"Oooh..." she moaned over my head while I sucked on her tits. Her soaking pussy rocked faster around me, throbbed around me. "Ohhhh!"

The tips of her fingers pressed into my neck and her back curled backwards. Licking and sucking, biting, and teasing had her folded legs tightening around me. I felt every-fucking-thing.

Feel. Every. Fuck—

Oh, shit!

I wasn't wearing a cape. *How the fuck did I forget to strap the hell up?*

Then she started plopping up and down in my lap, her rhythm unsteady. *Shit.* My girl was coming.

Her breathing was harsh, head flung back, and hips still rolling over me.

"*So good...*" she heaved. "*Rut.*" I started plowing into her, excited as hell to see this new, free, and incredibly fucking sexy vixen dancing on my lap. "The best!" she groaned. "Oh, the best!"

That's when I lost it. My balls drew up out of nowhere and I blasted into her, losing my goddamn mind.

And a chunk of my soul...

RUT

"*Oh, baby!*" I cried, rubbing the underline of my breasts with the palms of my hands and pinching my taut nipples between my thumbs and index fingers.

Rut's face was buried at the apex of my thighs. His tongue kissed my engorged nub, his two fingers winding in my tremoring sex.

"Come, Park," he lifted briefly to demand. "I need to hear it again."

Then he reached underneath me with both hands, cupping my butt and lifting it to his mouth as he stood on his knees. I lay in the air, balanced on my shoulders. He was an intimating vista from this angle. He was broad, muscular, and teeming with unbridled stamina. We'd been at this for two rounds already, and he'd made my body quake as many times. He, himself, had detonated inside me just minutes ago. And here he was, determined to have me skip galaxies once again.

And I did. My hips bucked, head rolled back on its crown, and legs locked over his shoulders. Not only did I explode in his mouth, my petal opened to him as it had been for weeks now.

My eyelids were weakened, body boneless. Rut's tongue teased my tender clitoris.

"Stop!" I laughed as I jerked at his shoulders.

His cheeks rose in mirth as he performed his last stroke. Then he lowered my legs, laying my full body on the mattress. I noticed his excessive blinking as he backed off the bed. Rut rubbed his eye with the back of his hand. I turned over in the bed and hummed with contented exhaustion as I watched him.

"I'mma shower and get some menus to order for dinner," his delivery was throaty.

Rut was tired. And as he peeled off the used condom and turned for the bathroom in his bedroom, I was reminded how fit he was by the view of his wide back and tapered waist. Rut's ass was amazing, too. The man was perfection to me. And I was addicted to having him around.

Two weeks ago we kicked off our sexual affair with real intercourse, and each day since, we'd been together. We'd spoken, slept together, celebrated together, and sexed each other with liberty I never thought I'd have in my circumstances. We've learned he enjoys my soaps as much as he did my oils. I was there when he got the call from his agent about another endorsement deal. We lay in bed at night, counting our childhood scars and sharing the stories behind them. He crept into the front office just to steal kisses in the janitor's room. I endured the heavy arousal it caused as well as his musky frame from working out and running plays.

He'd let me drive his *Ferrari*—insisted that I borrow it to be exact —when my old *Benz* from my grandfather conked out on me before church a couple of weeks ago. Because it was an older model, it had been a task finding someone to repair it at a reasonable price for days. Until that happened, Rut practically pushed me into his sexy convertible *California*, making it available at my disposal. I'd been in a "Rut Zone" and enjoying it. Nurse Jackie mentioned me finally experiencing the life of a woman my age, even if just a little. Maybe she was right. Either way, I'd been filled with a piece of joy new to me. But it hadn't been stress free.

Jordan Johnson, the *Kings'* franchise wide receiver, married Cole Richardson, who so happened to be the owner's daughter and an executive in the front office. It was a *Kings'* celebration Rut attended...with Emily Erceg. That was the longest day of my life, it seemed. Hours of checking all social media handles for pictures. Googling Rut and Emily's name for updates on the day. Each image I saw of them was scrutinized for the slightest bit of genuine happiness. Or chemistry. Or attraction. Or flirtation.

Ughhh!

The memory of that day still burned me. Although I understood the business aspect of it, I hated seeing him with another woman. I didn't care if anyone knew he slept in my bed every night; I didn't want them believing he had the slightest attachment to someone else. The only upshot of that day was him sending me silly selfies and knowing Emily had to be on a plane that night.

Probably back to her lover...

It didn't matter. That evening, while Mr. and Mrs. Jordan Johnson were consummating their new union, Rut and I were mimicking them in the shower after I washed the scent and fingerprints of Emily from his robust frame.

Things had been happening fast and unexpectedly. Sometimes too fast for me. I'd been here to his place three times within the past two weeks. The first two were just for an hour or two on the days I worked at the front office, and I had to forego my lunch to makeup the time for it. We filled that limited time with the craziest, most explorative sex I'd known.

Rut being the aggressor he could be, made a big fuss of me never having stayed the night. He was so fixated on the idea, he sparked a conversation with Nurse Jackie one day last week and texted Mandee to arrange tag-team care so I could stay with him tonight. The determined man did half the plotting behind my back but I'd acquiesced, knowing I could FaceTime whenever I needed, and Jimmy could hear my voice as well as see my face. I knew he wasn't happy, yet also knew he was safe.

I sighed, rolling over to reach for my phone. After sending a short check-in text to Mandee, who was now with Jimmy, I did the mindless social media troll. Over the past month or so, Eli Richardson's friend, Azmir Jacobs, had been in blogs' headlines. I hadn't seen any major coverage of it, but apparently, a documentary that had been floating around since the spring had been gaining notoriety. I faintly recalled that topic popping up in their conversation back in…March, which was coincidentally, the last time I'd seen Azmir Jacobs.

The repeated headlines littered down my 'Explore' page on *Instagram* was how the documentary that was once being consider getting picked up by *HBO*, *Netflix*, and *Starz* had been shut down. Apparently, the director recanted a few details in the piece. No matter how many times I tapped on an image, I couldn't find why. Which details were shaky? Did it include Azmir Jacobs' mentions?

Rut opening the door to the steamy bathroom broke my attention. An envy-worthy towel clung to his carved hips. And he wore… glasses. Thick plastic frame glasses. Coke bottle glasses.

He barely glanced my way when he muttered, "I'm going to get the menus. There're a few good restaurants over here."

And he was out of the room, closing the door behind him. Behind it, I could hear the galloping clanks of Sharkie's paws. It had been comical to see how much of a child Rut turned into when with his gigantic Tosa. My phone vibrated in my hand.

Mandee: *We're heavily engaged in a tap dancing lesson. Leave us alone.*

I laughed at that and typed back I'd be FaceTiming for verification soon. As much as I trusted Mandee, there was still a palpable anxiousness and unmoving guilt from being away from Jimmy like this.

"What the hell's so funny?" Rut was plopping down on the bed before I registered his presence.

"Mandee. She's a riot." I tapped my phone to get back to *Instagram* and finish the last article I was skimming through about Azmir Jacobs.

"Yup," he agreed. "My girl."

"Oh! She's your girl now? Last month you barely returned her greetings."

"That's 'cause I ain't know how real she was. Plus, she's about her paper."

"She's about her paper because she accepted your proposal to stay with Jimmy tonight?"

"Yup. And next Friday so I can sleep in late with you on my chest."

My mouth dropped. "Rut!"

"What?" he reached behind the plastic frames and pinched his nose.

"You wear glasses?"

"I'm blind," his voice bland.

"What's the difference?"

"The difference is I hardly wear my glasses, which is why my damn eyes are so dry now." He rubbed his eyes.

"How is it that I've been sleeping with you every night all this time and I didn't know you were visually impaired?"

He turned to face me, and for the first time, I saw just how bad it was. Rut's lenses were so thick, his eyes looked distorted through them. I would have laughed if I didn't find him so freaking adorable right now.

Rut Amare, king of assholes and jokers, is blind as a bat!

"How you think I got the *Alcon/Opti Free* endorsement? Go 'head. You can crack ya best joke, and it won't be nothing I ain't never heard. I tell that to every nigga who try to clown me over it. And after that, I tell 'em I don't need these shits to see enough to fuck 'em up."

I laughed. "And what do you tell women?"

He shrugged, going back to rubbing his eyes. "I 'on't have chicks in my room. I 'on't have them hanging around my crib."

"You're so tough. What do you have to say to me?"

"That I 'on't need these shits to make you scream my name."

A pulse of pleasure lit across my belly at that. I didn't doubt him at all.

"*Uhn-huhn*," he hummed cockily. My Rut. "Look at you, biting ya lip."

"But how did I not know all this time?"

"Because I been sleeping in my contacts, some shit I ain't supposed to be doing. It's catching up to me now."

"Then you should bring your glasses when you come over. We can use them to role play," my voice turned dark, sultry.

I could see a tent rising underneath his towel. When he saw me gaping, Rut handed me a small stack of menus while snatching the phone from my hand. "What you got going on over here?" he playfully growled. "*Hmmm!*" he hummed again, reading. "Oh, damn. He back in town?"

My brows narrowed. "Who?"

Rut peered over to me and blinked, clearly caught between thoughts. "Nobody. You see what you want? I'm hungry."

My regard went to the menus in my hands and I began going through them. Indian, Japanese, Soul Food... Thai looked tempting. I opened that one and browsed the columns.

"You know..." his deep vocals called my attention. "I've been thinking—"

"Oh, brother..." I droned playfully.

"Nah. For real. What you've been doing with your cosmetic line is dope. You actually got some quality shit. My moms, who swears everything breaks out her sensitive skin, hit me up yesterday wanting more soap and lotion. She want some for her girls, too. She said her neck marks from tweezing has been clearing up."

When Paula was here a few weeks ago for Rut's *WAWG* coverage, I sent her a few of my products as a warm gesture. I'd forgotten all about it.

"That's amazing." My eyes were back on the Thai menu, deciding.

"What I'm tryna say is you should go legit with it."

"How?" I handed him back the Thai menu. "The veggie Penang." I pointed to it.

"Like broaden your exposure. Increase sales."

"How?" I stuck out my tongue, being silly.

"Trademark...file a patent. How 'bout proper labeling and business insurance? Go to stores who sell the same products and would retail it to their audience. There's mad shit to do to grow ya brand, Gray. You're too young to sit on ya talent, shawtie. You gotta chase the bag. You know how many people don't even know what hustle they have in them? How many people waste away, working for the white man instead of making good of the natural intelligence we've been born with? You know we, black people, were the original people on Earth? Education should be fashioned to enable us to be self-sufficient as a people. You just need the tools, Gray."

I nodded, considering his advice. So soon, I became overwhelmed by the prospect and collapsed dramatically on the bed.

Rut chuckled. "The hell's that about?"

"You have no idea how many times I've thought about what's that next level for me. I earn a few dollars from it but mostly enjoy the process of creating. I'm inspired by setting and enhancing moods through scent and texture of the skin; have been since I started toying around with it in college when I thought I'd flunk out. But I've been stuck on the business end of it since."

Rut stood, holding his towel that covered a valued possession by me. "I'mma see what I can dig up for you. We gone get you off the ground, Gray." He moved for the door, murmuring, "I'm gonna see what Fats want then put in the order."

Needing to pee, I moved to leave the bed. But I wasn't left unmoved. Rut's words of entrepreneurship rang like belief...in me. That was something I hadn't had in almost forever. It almost made me forget about his four eyes.

chapter seventeen

HE PICKED UP AFTER THE THIRD RING.

"Peace. Peace."

"What it do, king?"

"Getting this paper, man. How you?"

"Everything's everything."

"Indeed. Congrats are in order, I see," Divine's voice seemed to perk up.

"Yup. Tried to hit you a few weeks ago. Heard you skipped town."

"More like was put in timeout by my bone."

"Oh, word? Ray-Choppa snatched you up like that?" I laughed.

"Aye!" he growled. "Easy. The hell you know about that alias anyway?"

"That's her name on *IG*, dawg!" I cracked the hell up.

"Say word?" He sounded genuinely shocked, making it funnier.

"Yo, you showing ya age by not being on social media, D."

"I'm proud of my age. Fuck a social media when you control the media."

"A'ight, playa." I couldn't stop laughing at his cool ass. I knew Divine had people running social media for his companies, so he didn't feel like he skipped beats. "Nah. But you good, big homie?"

"Always. Just had to blow some time. Wait for shit to settle. I see it has. Dude done apologized and all for the documentary."

"Yeah, that nigga copped to putting fake shit in there." It had been all over social media.

"As he should. Anyway... Enough of that." He took a deep breath. "You ready for next month?"

I thought about it for a minute. He was referring to my pops' release. Lots of people had been talking about it, including my therapist and moms.

"Yeah, I guess." I didn't know what else to say. "Been a long time coming."

"Indeed."

That was a topic I didn't want to take on. "The reason I'm hitting you up is because I gotta friend of mine who has a fragrance business."

"What kind?"

I thought for a moment. "Candles and body, I guess. She makes candles, soaps, lotions, hair conditioners, and some other shit. Real smart girl...chemistry degree. I wanna put her on but don't exactly know how. Then I remembered I knew the ultimate hustler," I tried to finesse. "You got somewhere to plug her product?"

For a while, Divine didn't say anything, but I knew that was his way of processing.

"What kind of friend is she to you?"

"The best kind you can think of."

Again, he went silent on me. I knew I'd just hit him with some shit, but I had to do what was necessary to answer his question. Divine wouldn't put much thought into a random chick I was busting down, but he should have also known I wouldn't have expected him to.

"At best, I can do the rec and clubs back home and all *DiFillippo's*. If her paperwork is legit, I can buy up liquid soap, candles, and lotion wholesale."

"Oh, word?" I didn't think about that. Then another thought struck. "What about your casino?"

"That's still in development. We won't be at that phase for a minute. But if she can produce in mass like that, I can put her in contact with the Drakes. They're always down for small black businesses—she *is* black, ain't she?" Before I could flip, he busted out laughing. "I'm just fuckin' with you, Rut."

"Yeah. Yeah." I shook my head with the phone against my ear.

I caught Jameson walking into the weight room with Grant, and I could tell right away he was yapping about his money.

"Look, duke," Azmir spoke up, and I could tell he was still chuckling. "I got a meeting to hit up. Hit me with her product write up and I'll get it to the right people at *ADJ Enterprise*. I'm gonna send a text to Lincoln Drake on my way to the meeting."

"'Preciate that, king."

"Indeed."

When I pulled the phone from my ear, I'd be damned if I wasn't right about Jameson.

"Man, the place is sixty-five hundred square feet. The kitchen was just upgraded a year ago. It even has a pool in the back. The place is almost fully furnished and my realtor's saying I'm going to have to take a hit." Jameson ran a hand through his dark brown silk strands of hair, heated by the subject. "Can you believe that shit? I paid one-point-nine *M*s for that shit, bro! It's some bullshit..." he kept bitching.

And as he spoke, Grant tossed me a nasty ass look with half his face lifted. And he wanted me to see it, not giving a shit who was around. I knew the purpose of it. Parker friend-zoned his ass. She fucking better had. There was no goddamn way I was going to be easy on him thinking she was free game. We were on the same team; I could lose respect in the locker room before I gained it on the field this season.

So, I hit him with a blank stare nod. I didn't even include one of my hallmark cocky grins. He needed to know wasn't shit funny when it came to Parker being off limits.

My chest felt light.

That was the first thing pulling me from my sleep. I struggled, wanting to stay in it, being wrapped in her scent. It was citrus mixed with her natural body odor. Damn, I loved that blend. It made my dick hard. But my chest was still light and...cool. My eyes fluttered open and I saw the morning sun pushing through the drapes.

Shit!

I sat up, looking for my phone. It read six thirty-eight. I'd slept almost an hour later. Sounds of the shower running caught my attention.

So she could get up and ready, but leave me sleeping?

I tossed the sheet from my waist and stood from the bed. My arms reached out wide into the air and spine arched as I stretched. I saw her silhouette from the shower the moment I stepped into the bathroom. When I opened the door, she lifted her arms, one by one to rinse the soap off as I stepped in. She turned toward the back of the shower and her eyes grew then softened when they processed me. Her smile surfaced, too. The one that was so sincere and the purest I'd ever seen on a woman. My dick jutted, but I didn't let that rouse my mind. I had to go.

I grabbed the soap and scrub naturally, realizing how comfortable I'd become in another man's home. I didn't know which thought was more wild: the fact she was good with it because of her obligation to another man or that I wished Parker could be convinced to stay nights at my place more often. I never wanted a woman in my personal space. Shit. Back at home, we eventually bought a house in a nearby suburb of Trenton—*compliments of an Azmir Divine Jacobs*—where I had the basement all to myself. I didn't even want to share much of the same space with my Earth. Having her upstairs was too close those times I wanted to wild out.

"Grilled tilapia and sweet potatoes with sautéed string beans' for dinner." So lost in my head, I didn't realize Parker was on her toes, inches away until she rubbed her nose against mine.

Before I could register or respond, she was rounding me, leaving the shower.

"I 'on't know about that tilapia. The team's nutritionist ain't big on that type of fish. You should try trout or bass."

As I rubbed my body down with the soapy scrub, she didn't respond right away, but I knew she was considering what I said. I could see her going for her toothbrush and the toothpaste at the sink.

"*Hmmmmm...* Okay," she garbled around her toothpaste. "There's a fish market not too far from the office. I'll stop by after work and see what they have and what I can afford."

I rolled my eyes but wouldn't dare speak a word about money. It was enough I had been trying to figure out what this thing was between Parker and me. I wasn't in the mood to be arguing about a few bucks to pay for food. It was an argument I wouldn't win with her no way.

Quickly, I decided to switch my thoughts to the day ahead and what it would bring. Training camp was right around the corner and I had to mentally prepare to be isolated with a new set of guys. That, *and* I'd have to work out with Jameson's whining ass today. Dude wouldn't stop complaining about losing his assets. Jordan mentioned Jameson had a bad gambling habit that was catching up to—

My head whipped around while under the shower-head to Parker. She stood alarmed with her frosted tooth brush inches from her mouth as she stared in the mirror. Then her head jerked behind her and my pulse raced as I moved to open the shower door.

"What are you doing here?"

There was a woman in the doorway, her wild eyes going between Parker wrapped in a towel and my naked body. She was stunned, couldn't seem to utter a word at first.

"Sherry, what are you doing in my bathroom?" Parker repeated.

Sherry's eyes blinked a few times and I could see her swallow as I moved to grab the towel.

I ain't never put my hands on a woman, but I'll beat the shit outta this broad if she in here on some crazy shit.

"*I*—I..." she screeched. "I was calling you—"

"You could have waited until I answered!" Parker spit at her.

Her eyes went tight as she focused on Parker. "This is my father's house! I can damn well come in here if I suspect something fishy happening!"

Love's Ineligible Receiver

"What is fishy besides you snooping in my personal space, Sherry?"

"I'm not snooping!"

"But you're in my bathroom and didn't knock. I didn't hear you knock."

"I was knocking on the bedroom door for some time now."

"But you could hear the shower going in here and you just come in? Sounds kind of perv'ish to me, Sherry!"

"Let me tell you something, Miss Parker! This is *my* father's home. He's incapacitated. I can come into any room if I want. The home nurse came early and was outside waiting for someone to answer the door!"

"And that requires this FBI-level house search? Get out!" Parker moved toward her.

The Sherry chick started to back out. "I see I need to come more often, seeing you have random men in my father's house!"

"First of all, he's not random. He's my damn boyfriend—" *Boyfriend?* My heart began to pound even more. "and he's indecent. Secondly, I check in on Jimmy every morning before washing my damn face. You'd know this if you visited more often..."

I couldn't hear much more after that because they were out in the bedroom. But two things did come to mind. The first was I had to get Parker out of Wright's house ASAP. The way that broad walked up on us was some ol' 'getting caught with a girl in your moms' house high school' shit. The second thing screaming in my head was less important, but comical.

That's the broad tryna to holla at me at Eli's party back in May...

RUT

"Everything okay, Parker?"

Startled, my body leaped in my chair. "Hmmm?"

Nyree stepped to the front of my desk, her chin lowered toward her neck. "You okay?"

My eyes were wild with disorientation. "Yeah. Why? What's up?"

"You've been zoned out all day...finished assignments before blinking." She snorted. "I'm grateful for the boost in productivity, but you've always been proficient. I'd rather have my usual engaging Parker Grayson back." Her head angled and she offered a genteel beam, trying to encourage mine.

Taking a deep breath, my eyes fell and I dropped the pencil I just realized I'd been drumming when she walked up on me.

"Nyree, are you familiar with the condo property the *Kings* own?"

"*Kings Courts*. Well, of course." She switched stances to open her body language.

"I know they rent them out to players—employees—and affiliates according to their salary." She nodded in confirmation, though I knew this from work I did with payroll, filling in for the admins from time to time. "You think I, as a floater in the front office, would be allowed the same privilege?" Her eyes widened and mine did, too, in reaction as I dipped my chin. "According to my salary?"

Nyree stood still for moments long, eyes squinting as she processed her thoughts. Taking a deep breath, she moved toward my desk and leaned against it. My pulse banged in my neck. Though I didn't exactly confide in Nyree, she knew my employment arrangement. She knew my being here was nepotism grandstanding.

"I've worked for Eli Richardson for a number of years now, and I've seen his generosity in action more times than I can count. He doesn't boast about what he does, he simply tries to keep a family-like atmosphere around here for loyal people. I've seen what he's done for you, and I've seen how you've made good on accepting his generosity. If you need assistance with..." Her chin and voice lowered and she swallowed. "housing, I would ask. The worst he could say is no and that would be because of policy and nothing personal."

There was a sincerity in her eyes though her tone was formal. We were walking a tight rope. Nyree was an older woman, so I was sure she'd heard things about Jimmy and his womanizing ways—experienced it with her own eyes, possibly. I didn't want to know. Neither did I want to divulge the details of our relationship.

My cheeks spread in a warm yet contained smile. "Thanks, Nyree. I'll reach out to him."

She stood straight and gave a neck bow and wink before walking off.

I turned to my desktop. My plan was to begin an email to Eli. With him being an investor in his primary work, he wasn't always in the *Kings'* front office. But as soon as I opened a message box, my phone rang.

"Hello?"

"Yo..."

My pulse hammered in my neck again at the rash introduction of his call.

I licked my lips and swallowed hard as I turned to curl toward my monitor for privacy.

"Yes?" I carried the *s* pathetically.

"You good?" He was referring to this morning when Sherry walked in on his hanging dick in the shower.

I could have clocked her for that. I felt protective and violent in a way never dreamed of in those long moments. I couldn't care less about my invasion of privacy; it was protecting Rut that had me floored and angry.

And I called him my boyfriend...

How laughable! As much as I'd like that to be true, Rut and I were in an unusual place at this point of whatever it was we had. I thought for sure he'd correct me when I managed to get Sherry out of my bedroom. Then I thought it would come when he stepped out of the bathroom and dressed to leave. We didn't exchange a lone word.

Yet a single gesture of him kissing my cheek said so much. It left me inexplicably emotional.

"Yeah. Why wouldn't I be?"

"You picked up that fish?"

I stifled a giggle. "I'm still at work. I haven't left the office yet, so of course not."

I didn't know if it was okay to plan to cook for two. Sherry threatened to tell her brothers if she saw Rut at the house again.

"A'ight. Can you swim?"

"Yeah…"

"You know how to garden?"

I scratched my neck. "I could figure it out."

"Oh."

Oh?

"What do you think about contemporary kitchens?"

One brow lifted. "I like new…"

"Well," his tone was humorless. "Just wanted to make sure you good."

He was worried.

My face fell. "O—okay." My mind drew a blank. I didn't know how to respond.

I would normally ask about his day, something more important to me than Sherry's intrusion. I wanted to put it behind me and not focus on Rut never coming over again.

"A'ight. Hit you later."

And that was it. The line was dead.

That was weird because my bladder cried. I had to pee. I slipped my phone in the drawer of my desk and took off for the bathroom. My mind running with wording for my email to Eli as I passed a few friendly faces in the hall. My last conversations with the man wasn't with much gratitude on my part. What if he'd cut off the faucet of generosity? Would I go back to Waterbury? To my mother's?

I made it to the bathroom and relieved myself. After washing my hands and checking my face in the mirror, I'd decided on my message to him and started back to my cubicle. Just a few feet into the journey, I ran into James Junior.

I was prepared to simply acknowledge him with a nod, something he'd done to me since I began working in the front office, but he stopped and fixed his attention to me.

"Ms. Grayson."

Oooh! He kicked off the exchange with a browbeating tone. I didn't return his mention verbally. I sauntered his way and offered a mild grin instead. This was my professional face.

"I got a call from Sherry this morning. It wasn't a long conversation but it wasn't friendly either, and I can guess you know why." I fought from rolling my eyes. "She wouldn't tell me what she saw but said she stopped by the house this morning. Whatever she walked in on, pissed her off."

"Considering where she walked into, I can see how she was at risk of that."

His eyes narrowed. "What did she see?"

"That's none of your business, James."

"Anything concerning my father and his home is my business, girl." His mouth balled as he glared upon me.

Nyree strolled passed with her eyes fastened to us. As she did, James Junior switched his posture as he cleared his throat.

He waited until she was gone to continue. "Listen, I don't have time for this. I didn't come to work to see your face or lecture you on how to keep your thotting, as my kids say, away from my father's home. Sherry's making calls today. My advice to you is to start looking for a place to stay. And I hope for your sake it's not with that Rut Amare you've been in the blogs with. That kid has seen more pretty girls with tight bodies than you realize exists."

He went too far!

"Let me tell you somethi—"

"Shut the hell up." He waved me off with his hand. "I used to think maybe you were in this for my father. Maybe I was wrong when he decided he wanted a damn girl six years younger than my brother and me taking care of him after he'd been diagnosed with a degenerative disease. I thought my dad was right and I was wrong. But I guess it's like they say, 'how you get 'em is how you keep 'em.' You were an opportunist then and you're just the same now. You fooled me for a few years there. I guess you tried." He turned and walked off.

I choked on air, my eyes blinked successively to keep the tears away.

"Hey, Parker," Nurse Joan, the other home care nurse who alternated with Nurse Jackie, was wiping her hands dry as I stepped into Jimmy's room.

I forced a happy face. "How was he today?"

"Pretty good. No fever at all today and the drooling has slowed. That switch to Atropine was a good call by you. And the physical therapist scheduled for this morning says she's seeing effects of your stretching him out during the week." Nurse Joan stopped and paid Jimmy, who was awake, a long gaze. "Today was a good day, wouldn't you say, bud?"

That made me smile from the heart. I was happy to get good reports of his care. God knew Jimmy had been through a lot. We'd been trying to perfect his pain management lately. I was able to pick up his eye strain from muscle spasms in his legs.

"I'm happy for you, Jimmy." I smiled his way.

"I'm going to get going," Joan announced, collecting her things around the room. "My nephew has a recital early this evening, and I promised him I'd be in the front row." She rolled her eyes. "Why did I promise that?" I chuckled, watching her move about the room. She stopped at one point, just gazing around. "I think that's everything. Jimmy, I'll see you in a few days. Okay?" Nurse Joan started for the front door. "I'll lock it behind me," she shouted over her shoulder.

When I heard the door slam closed, I took a deep breath. My shoulders were heavy and heart weary as I ambled over to his bed and pulled up a chair. I sat down and faced him as I'd do from time to time when I wasn't working on him. Jimmy's body may have been cachectic, but his eyes were very much alive and he actually appeared well-rested. I stroked his hand that was as soft and paper thin as an ultra-elderly person. His frail legs were hiked over pillows and cushioned in warmers. The tube lodged in his throat seemed no more than an ornament like a gold chain at this point to me.

James "The Boulder" Wright was in this shell of an invalid. There was a heart, soul, and a human being in there.

My emotions came slamming to the surface by way of a cry unexpected.

I stood to stretch my arms around him. "*Jimmeeeeeeeee!*" I blurted a sob so hard it scared me.

I don't know how long I stayed there, but the moment I recalled his feeding tube, I let up. But the sobs didn't stop. I sat in the chair, facing him as I tried to calm myself.

"I've tried. I've tried so hard." I attempted a deep breath. "This has been such a hardship on me. And I just realized about a month ago how lonely I've been. My mother's words are coming back with truth in spades. I've been in over my head but I swore I could do it. No matter how hard it's been, I'd keep my word."

My eyes closed and I shook my head. "But I can't do this *and* fight your kids. I can't keep floundering in loneliness, having my life on pause, and battle with James Junior, Jerry, and Sherry every other month. I can't keep having my housing threatened. I can't keep trying to walk a fine line with your friend, Eli, to keep a job: a job I have no potential of growth at."

I let a few tears fall without a fight.

"Jimmy, you're not the only one wasting away before your time. I am, too." I cupped my mouth.

That revelation I'd been refusing to dwell on, refusing to speak, was painful to finally put into the atmosphere. When I thought to face him, I found Jimmy's eyes glossed, about to spill tears.

"I'm sorry," I sobbed mutedly, feeling even worse. "I really am. But Jimmy, the next time they tell me to go, I won't fight. I've got a pride about me. You know this. You've seen it in me. I can't stay where I'm being harmed."

Indisputable tears tipped from his eyes, rendering me weak. I lay my arm across his bony legs and begin to pray. I prayed for Jimmy: his body, heart, and soul. I prayed for me: my mind, will, and strength. I lay there, adrift in petition so long I lost track of time and possibly slipped into sleep. I didn't come to until I heard an intrusive knock on the door.

My head shot into the air. The first thing I thought of was beneath me. Jimmy's eyes were closed, lost into sleep. Slowly and disoriented, I stood. Another aggressive knock had me headed out of his room. I rubbed my eyes on the way, trying to wake myself up.

I pulled the door back, but hid behind it. My heavy, and I was sure, swollen eyes cowardly speaking for me. Stupidly. He'd shown later than usual. I honestly wasn't expecting him at this point.

Rut stood there in basketball shorts, a *Kings* T-shirt, black ankle socks, and shower shoes holding a paper shopping bag. His thick brows pushed together, head angled slightly in questioning. I knew he could pick up on my unease.

"What's in the bag?" I didn't move to invite him in.

At first, he didn't respond. He spent countless seconds inspecting me from head to toe. I knew I looked a sight. God, did a feel like a wreck on the inside.

He lifted it in his arm. "Trout and bass. Couldn't decide which one, so I got both because I knew ya punk ass wouldn't."

I wanted to talk tough and say I had gotten it and more to prove I wasn't a punk. But instead, I grabbed the *B-Way Burger* milkshake cup from where I left it on the table when I got in this afternoon and raised to in the air.

"I decided to eat out. Had a mean craving."

He snorted, eyes rolled adorably angry. "Listen, Parker—"

"She's right, Rut. This is Jimmy's house. It's not right for me to have male company here. No matter how unsettled things were between us before he deteriorated, we were engaged—at some point," I had to amend.

Our engagement was so brief it was a joke.

"This morning I was your boyfriend. Tonight I'm male company?"

I scoffed. "You know I didn't mean it that way—"

"Yeah. I do. And you know what, Ms. Parker? I know either I'm coming inside for dinner and to sleep or you're packing a big ass bag and coming to my place." He turned toward the street. "Which house do my girl, Mandee, live in over there? 6071?" I sucked in a heap of air as he turned back to me. "Me personally... I prefer that latter." He readjusted his stance, widening his long thick legs B-boy style and cocked his head to the side. His brows shot up with full on Rut-arrogance. "But I'mma let you pick."

I wanted to cry. All afternoon, I struggled with what to do since hanging up with him. Then my run in with James Junior magnified my circumstances to the point I knew I had to prepare Jimmy. My thoughts were so vacuumed into this decision of letting this thing with Rut go I'd forgotten to eat lunch. Then the coward in me bought fast food to create an excuse as to why I wouldn't cook dinner tonight. I hated it, the indecision in my heart. Rut was my friend—even if he didn't admit it, he was. He'd been a rock and a beautiful distraction all in one.

"Don't fuckin' play with me, Par—"

On a quick jolt backward, I moved to widen the door. Rut's monstrous frame promenaded inside like he was at home. That was exactly how I'd come to feel around him.

Domesticated.
Familiar.

I crawled into bed after tucking Jimmy in and taking a much needed shower. It was pitch dark and peacefully noiseless in the room. The minute my back hit the mattress, a sinewy arm hooked me at the waist and pulled me into a hot plank of muscle.

His mouth was to my ear. "You ready to tell me why you were crying before I got here or am I gone have to tickle it out of you?"

That annoyingly pushed my lips into a half a grin. I rolled my eyes and sighed.

"I don't want to be that girl."

"What girl?"

"The type looking for a savior. As you were made aware of—to my dismay—this morning, I have issues I need to work through. Just like I need to figure out how to legitimize my company, I have to figure out how to reconcile my living arrangement with my commitment to Jimmy. And by the grace of God, I'm going to do it."

I had to believe this. I'd been praying about it and saving for it. It was the implementation and fear I hadn't settled.

"Don't be that girl," his vocals were hoarse yet snippy.

"What girl?"

"The tough one, who thinks getting help from a man is weak."

"My mom is actually that *woman*," I corrected. "But that doesn't sound like the worst type of independence to me. Plus," I took another painful breath, over it all.

"Plus, what?"

"Plus, Rut," I whined. "I don't know how long this thing's going to last between us. I'm fully aware of our age difference, your lifestyle, your wealth, and attention span. I get the reality before me. What I don't know is what's that next step. What's going to happen next and if I'm going to be prepared for it." I wasn't rambling, but I wasn't articulating well either.

Rut turned onto his back and breathed, "I feel you."

My brows and eyes narrowed. "You do?" my voice down an octave with disbelief.

"Yeah," his went up. "I do."

"Pray tell." I turned on my side to face him, though I couldn't make much out in the darkness.

"All this shit. The season, Coach Brooks, the money, you...my pops coming home...training camp. All that shit been—I hate to say this word, but—stressing me the hell out."

I bit my lip, uneasy. "I've been wondering about your father's release."

"You, too?" Rut exhaled, clearly exasperated.

"You were upset with how he responded to your endorsement with *Asé Garb*—"

"I wasn't mad. It was just..."

"You don't have to lie to me, remember? There's no judgement here, Rut. You're going tough guy now." I moved closer, laying my hand on his chest and inched closer to his face. "You'd never seem weak in my eyes for admitting your fears."

He chuckled, sarcasm excluded for once. "Funny... That's what he thinks."

"Who? Your father?"

He didn't answer right away. "It seems like everything I do, it's always something imperfect in it. Even with the draft. He blamed me for not being the first pick. Yeah, I know I fucked up a lil' in school, but because of that I couldn't control what happened that night. Then the low-ball contract they gave me. He had shit to say about that. You know I had a nice bank nest before the endorsements started a few weeks ago?" It was an unrhetorical question.

"No," I whispered anyway.

"I've been sitting on something since I was like eighteen/nineteen years old. I never told my moms, pops, niggas from home. I only told B-Rocka and deflated how much. My moms live on an allowance from the General and I give her money every month on top of that. I've been independent since high school. I ain't have no daddy to run and ask for money for kicks or to take a girl out to the movies. *Shit.* Some of my football expenses came from my pocket. When it was something I could handle, I just took care of it. But when he comes at me with complaints, it just..."

"It hurts," I murmured.

It wasn't a question in my mind. Rut confirmed it with his silence.

"Rut, as much as I thought you were an asshole when I met you, I've come to learn you're one of the smartest, business savvy, and generous souls on the planet. I was able to gather this only three weeks of knowing you. If your father isn't aware of those qualities after twenty-four years, you, my friend, clearly aren't the problem." I swallowed hard. "Don't let his title in your life shrink you. You're proven already. You're already a success, bud." I kissed his cheek, feeling how tense his body had turned.

That's when I decided to change the subject.

"Training camp? That's a part of your commitment. You've been to camps before—loads of times, I'm sure. This one should be the best."

"They're going out further this year. Last year they had it at a university, not too far from here. This year, it's way out in no-fuckin'-where land. Some school in the forest. A whole three weeks with these niggas I 'on't even know if I like."

"You don't know, though. You have to give it a chance, Rut."

"How? Sitting with a bunch of nasty ass niggas all day every day for three fuckin' weeks? I can't even..."

"What?" I laughed. "Get some booty?"

"No!" his tone turned nasty. "I was gonna say make sure you're good with Wright's kids."

My face folded and heart dropped from my chest. In no time, I was overcome with guilt. I straddled him, shifting my weight to get comfortable on top of his taut body.

"Rutledge Kadar Amare, I will be fine."

"How do I know that?"

"We'll be in touch. You can still call, text. FaceTime." I giggled naughtily. "We can make it fun."

Rut didn't bite. "But what if some shit goes down? What if they try to do some crazy shit to make you leave?"

"Then I'll leave."

"How? With what?"

"With my resources. You're not the only one who knows how to stow money. I've been able to save a few bucks myself."

"How you save? Buying budget meals?"

"By doing exactly that. I may have opposing views from inga grayson, but I've learned a few tricks from her along the way."

That reminded me to call my mother. I had to make the next move.

"You can go to my crib."

"I don't think I like the idea of rooming with Sharkie," I joked.

"It would just be until we can figure out your next move."

I pushed my hand behind me, finding his crotch, and whispered, "Oh, I already know my next move, Rut."

chapter
eighteen

"OH, YOU LOOK CUTE!" MANDEE complimented before chomping down on the tip of her pizza when I entered the kitchen.

Parker

Nurse Jackie turned from pulling her own slice from the pie and her eyes lit up. "Oh, wow, Parker! You make me want to find a stallion to take me out."

It was a bit unusual to have them both here at the same time. Jimmy was one of Nurse Jackie's assigned patients by her employer. Mandee, a nursing student, used Jimmy's care as hands on experience —and now extra cash since Rut had been paying her to keep him while we go out. They both got something out of the deal. Like tonight, Mandee agreed to sit with Jimmy while we went to see a movie. She agreed exuberantly, as she had been for close to a month now.

I smiled, shaking my head at the joke. Then I sashayed in my *Saint Laurent* sandals with cropped boyfriend jeans and a *"I'll Never Love Another"* tank I was handed when Rut and I went to see Young Lord perform last month. I thought it would be a nice ode to Rut, seeing it was his "joint."

"Thanks, ladies." I moved closer to the table. "That smells friggin' amazing." I groaned. "Makes me wanna ask Rut to stop at a *B-Way Burger* on our way to the theater and sneak in food."

"Have a slice," Nurse Jackie urged. "When I was in the dating game, I'd eat a little something before so the guy wouldn't know how well I could pack it in."

"I would, but don't want any parts of those sausages or pepperoni."

"Yeah," Mandee spoke with a mouthful. "Parker's pescatarian."

"Pescatarian?" Nurse Jackie shrilled. Her head bounced, sending her orange bangs into the air. "Then what're you eating at *B-Way Burger*?"

I closed my eyes and licked my lips as I smiled. "Their fish with cheese, and oh my god, those loaded fries, minus the bacon! Whew!" I rubbed my belly. "I've been running to the one by the office for the past two weeks, shamefully." I recoiled.

"Uhn-huhn..." Mandee's eyes widened.

"My niece used to work at that one. You know..." She nodded toward me. "the one who had the bypass surgery when she reached six hundred pounds a couple of years ago. She used to tell me stories of closing down the place late night for some of the players. She and her co-workers would dance for hours with that Trent Bailey. This was before he went to prison." Nurse Jackie fell into a gut-filled laughter, turning her face scarlet. "She used to crush so hard on 'The Flash!'" she guffawed.

"Jordan Johnson?" Mandee asked.

"Yes." Nurse Jackie leaned over barely breathing, she was laughing so hard. "She said she would dance so hard with Bailey to get Johnson's attention, one night she had to go to the emergency room! Could you imagine this white girl, who can't dance to feed birds, dancing to seduce one of the most popular wide receivers in the world?"

Her hard laughing made us all cackle. I found myself cracking up.

"But let's get back to the *B-Way Burger* runs," Mandee bit into her pizza.

I cringed. "Yeah, that. I think it's this summer cold I've caught.

My nose has been stuffy and I've been sniffling on and off for a couple of weeks."

"On and off?" Nurse Jackie echoed. "That's pretty unusual, kiddo."

"Unusual?" I shook my head. "You wanna hear unusual? Waking up in the middle of the night from cold sweats."

"Cold sweats?" Mandee shrieked with balls of food in her cheeks. "That's crazy shit."

"You've been stressed, Parker." Nurse Jackie's solemn tone concerned me. She shrugged, regard to her folded pizza. "You're not fooling anyone around here."

"Yeah," Mandee agreed. "Why do you think we've been sticking around her so much lately?"

My mouth dropped as I fought back a smile. "*You've* been around for extra cash!"

"This is true," she mumbled, rolling her eyes. "But for real. You ever think about taking a pregnancy test?"

I sputtered a laugh, "Whatever for?"

"For what they're meant for. To see if you're pregnant. Duh!"

Nurse Jackie laughed.

"What if that's not possible?" I challenged.

"Pregnancy's always possible when you getting that *Vitamin D!*" she projected loudly across the kitchen.

"Mandee!" I cried.

"Sorry. Since I heard Beyoncé say that in that song with Jay Z, it's been stuck in my head."

That set off another round of laughter for Nurse Jackie. "She's a crack up, this one!" She bit into her pizza.

I took off for Jimmy's room, leaving them to their dinner. Rut would be here any minute to pick me up. We were going to the movie theater on the *Kings Courts* property. I'd come to learn all the amenities available there. The movie theater, like the restaurants, was open to the public. It was just the housing that was closed off to non-residents. Rut likely chose that one instead of the one closest to here because he wanted a romp before coming back here and going to bed.

I didn't want him to walk in on a conversation as insane as pregnancy. The guy would die on the spot. Not to mention, other than on my birthday, Rut and I had been having safe sex. He was pretty militant about condoms. We'd been quite a pair, him and me. I'd still been sleeping on his chest every night and peeling back layers of his being. He'd been sweet, determined to make me act my age by doing things like we were doing tonight: going out on a date. It all started with the glamping movie theater he had set up in the backyard for a whole week before the rental company picked up everything. And apparently, it was going to continue into next week when he was taking me to the Brielle concert.

Yup...

Mandee would be here with Jimmy for that, too.

Shoot!

I placed the three sticks on the counter next to the sink to quickly wipe myself.

Who in the world takes three at a time?

Me. That's who. I stood to flush the toilet then washed my hands. My darkly lined eyes caught my attention in the mirror and after drying off, I began to fuss with my hair. Too much was happening at once. I was getting ready for a for real date—a double date, actually—with Rut and his friends. I couldn't remember the last time I'd been on a date before Rut. Maybe in the earlier days of knowing Jimmy? We'd go out a lot. But did I have the anxiety I felt bubbling in my gut tonight?

I smoothed back the slick pull of my ponytail, going back to an afro puff I bought yesterday from the beauty supply store. Taking a breath, I decided my look actually came together. *Gosh!* When was the last time I stressed over what to wear, wanting to look good for a guy?

But as I adjusted the straps on my dress, I approved my look and hoped Rut would, too.

Rut...

My shoulders sank from a flash of grief as I lifted the pregnancy test sticks, trying to decipher what one meant from another. They were three different brands: *Clearblue*, *First Response*, and some generic brand I plucked for good measure. It had been just two weeks since the Sherry episode, and just as before it, Rut had been over nearly every night. The man refused to allow more than two nights away from me.

And the sex...

It had been just as consistent and spell-bounding as it started. He went home to visit last week and was supposed to stay two nights but ended up at my door, knocking at three in the morning, claiming he tried hanging out at one of his regular strip clubs down there but needed sleep more. Sleep was synonymous with "*Parker*" according to Rut. I believed that was a bunch of bologna. Rut liked spending time with me as much as I did him. I, too, tossed and turned when he wasn't underneath me, but I stifled my grievances well.

But we made the most of the time we spent together. If we weren't laughing at his arrogance, we were sharing about our days. If we weren't fighting over my business model I'd been putting together, we were making love—although Rut referred to all sex, using the 'F' word to my extreme dismay. Either way, we'd pretty much been responsible with protection the whole month since we'd kicked off this part of our relationship. However, Mandee's cautioning that evening, more than a week ago hadn't escaped my conscience. And it led me here, out of all days. I was sure it was senseless, I'd been feeling like myself lately.

The knocking at my bedroom door startled me.

"Parker!" Mandee yelled out to me. "Rut's here!"

I leaped in my heels and placed the sticks down before clucking out of the bathroom. After grabbing my purse, I made my way down to the living room where Rut was on the phone, his back to me. Almost as though he sensed me, he turned with a tight brow line. His expression was hard as his dark eyes perused my body, beginning from my open toe sandals to my sleek pullback crown. When his regard returned to meet my eyes, he didn't speak. He switched hands with the phone and extended his arm, inviting me to join fingers. I couldn't help my smile when I bolted, my feet taking off for him.

"And my heart...
My heart's no longer your toy.
Time's up for the fuckboys!"

I was hoarse but highly emotional as I sang along with Brielle. My thrumming body swayed left to right with my arm in the air as I sang. *Man!* I loved that song. It was new from her latest album, but I knew each word to that track—most of her tracks.

The anxiousness felt back in Connecticut was still with me but in a new way. Jordan Johnson and my boss' daughter, Cole Richardson, were our double date. That, I was expecting. Rut told me last night how instead of a triple date, as originally planned, it would only be four of us. It was cool hanging out with the newlyweds. I may not have been able to bear witness to their nuptials, but it felt good experiencing their wonderful energy as man and wife.

I couldn't believe we drove down to New York City to see Brielle's show at *Madison Square Garden*! When I asked why didn't we catch her last week when she played the *Hotep Black Financial Bank Stadium*, Rut said he wanted to make me feel like we were on a real date. Going to "work" for play seemed rather bootleg to him. I appreciated the thoughtful gesture.

And it had been a romantic night, beginning with dinner at *DiFillippo's* where I had Rut's favorite pizza again. I'd never been before tonight and had only been familiar with it because of Eli's friend, Azmir Jacobs. He owned the restaurants.

Cole sat next to me and had been surprisingly different all night than I was used to seeing of her. Around the office complex, she was all business with little pleasantries and zero small talk. Here, with her new husband and *Kings'* franchise wide receiver, she was...a girlie girl.

Tonight I learned Cole was...funny, smart, and very much cultured. I hadn't met many women my age who could speak to the display of cultural gender bias black American cellist, Ameerah, received when a video of her performing oral sex on rapper, Young Lord, "leaked" in one breath, and the evolution of twerking in the next. My Rut didn't like the topic involving his latest favorite rapper although we argued great points on how Young did nothing to stand by her side when the video broke and fans were calling her all types of come-up whores known in the urban dictionary. Cole agreed it was also disgusting how basketball player, Alton Alston, had Young Lord perform at his birthday party last year to poster against them having beef for both having slept with Ameerah. I mean... I liked Young Lord, he was a skilled rapper, but what if Ameerah used them both instead of the popular belief of her having been dominated by them?

When Brielle closed the show, my heart was filled yet disappointed. Very few could command a stage like this woman. I would forever be a fan of hers. She was strong, fearless, cutting edge, and unapologetically *wo*man.

"C'mon, Park." Rut's warm hand rested on my lower back, cuing me to follow Cole.

She'd begun trailing after Jordan to leave the arena. My pulse was still racing from the endless reservoir of stamina Brielle had delivered for over two hours. We managed out of the massive seating area where people—mostly women—shouted for Jordan, and surprisingly, Rut's attention. I kept my face low, following the backs of Cole's red sole heels as Rut clutched me protectively. I couldn't believe it when we stopped at what was clearly backstage where there was a small crowd gathered in front of a backdrop and cloth flooring. I stood to the tips of my toes to peer ahead of the sea of bodies and spotted Brielle smiling for the camera as she posed with a fan.

My neck shot over and up to Rut, who coolly nodded, answering my unspoken question. We were back there to meet Brielle. And it didn't take long. Jordan's bodyguard was barking for us to come to the front of the line where Jordan greeted Brielle first. She was tiny in person yet flawlessly gorgeous as she appeared on camera. Her eyes lit with familiar discovery when Jordan approached.

I could hear Cole croak, "Hi," shyer than I thought she was capable of when Jordan immediately hooked her by the waist and invited her into their greeting.

Right away, the three took pictures together. Jordan's security was sure to capture it with their phones. Then Jordan whispered something to Brielle just before waving us over.

"Go, Gray," Rut's thick vocals commanded. "I'mma take the pic for you."

My eyes swelled nervously. Really? I was about to take a picture with *the* Brielle and my Rut was going to facilitate it?

"Come on, Parker," Jordan's deep vocals called as Rut swiped my phone from my misted palm.

I quickly ambled over to them, under the bright spotlights. Jordan and Cole backed up and small toned arms of the entertainment goddess, whose frame was not much different from my own, encased me. Of course, Brielle was more fit and stunning. She smelled divinely to have just stepped off the stage after hours of dancing in heels.

"Hi," she beamed. "Parker?"

My eye ballooned. "*Ye*—yeah. Yes!" I couldn't believe she knew my name. "Oh, my god, Brielle, I can't believe I'm here with you!" My body began to tremble.

"Well, I'm here. I see your rookie boo brought you to see me." She tossed her chin ahead.

When I followed, I heard, "Yo, Gray!"

It was a familiar bark before lights began to go off. My eyes blinked for the first seconds then settled and I forged a smile I was sure was goofy.

"It was nice meeting you. Maybe I'll see you around at one of Jordan and Trent's crazy ass parties."

My eyes flew wide again. She was looking forward to seeing *me* again?

"Gray!" Rut shouted with impatience.

It worked. I was reminded I was on someone else's time and got with the program.

With a gentle nod of appreciation, I replied, "Looking forward to it. Thanks, Brielle."

"See ya!" She waved with the brightest smile.

Before I knew it, an Asian woman with fire bright red hair was stepping between Brielle and me. I turned to look for my party and found Cole and Jordan laughing way too hard while staring at me. Then my regard shifted to Rut, who shook his head as his hand extended my way, urging me to him. On a small leap, I skipped his way, causing Cole and Jordan to sputter in laughter even louder.

"Yo, why TB and them ain't come tonight?"

I knew TB was Trent Bailey, but Rut's question made me curious.

Jordan snorted and Cole rolled her eyes while she chuckled as though embarrassed.

"Man, you know TB and Brielle got some history."

"Oh, word?" Rut gasped. "That shit true?"

Cole answered, "Depending on which part of it."

"Like..." Rut hesitated. "They fucked?"

"Ugh!" Cole covered her face and curled over playfully.

"What?" Rut laughed, confused.

I was, too.

Jordan took Cole at her shoulder, pulling her into him. "My lady likes to think of Brielle as some damn saint." His dimples deepened as he glanced down at Cole, eyes filled with mischief.

"No. I don't!" Cole protested, still in humor. "Brielle is a woman of the time. She's a girl millennial boss—"

"See!" Jordan joked, speaking over her. "Told you. Stanning!"

"No!" Cole argued. "My point is, she's a woman. Why wouldn't she have a sex life? Just because something she wants to keep to herself goes public doesn't make it a scandal."

Jordan rolled his eyes teasingly.

"Yeah. That was crazy," Rut added. "But I 'on't even think the blogs picked up on it. I was surprised as hell."

I was, too. When that story broke a couple of years ago, the whole front office was buzzing with shock. Brielle and Trent Bailey?

"But TB was cool on it," Rut continued. "I 'on't see him trippin' on Brielle."

"Oh, he ain't," Jordan made clear.

"But my girl, Jade..." Cole added before she and Jordan's regards met knowingly and they both fell out laughing at the same time.

The alcohol had definitely been flowing all night. Even I was ready for a private after party with Mr. Amare.

"What about Jade?" Rut tossed his chin down to me. "That's Parker's peoples."

"Let's just put it this way. When it comes to that nigga, everybody's defeated when Jade steps in the ring." Jordan couldn't stop laughing.

"Let's put it *this* way." Cole's hand shot in the air. "Jade would have shot up *The Garden* before Brielle sang her first note tonight."

Another round of laughter shot through the limo. This time by all four of us. Jade had spoken of jealousy issues when it came to her husband, but I'd dismissed it as new bride tough talk. Besides, Jade married a celebrity. Trent was a franchise player for the *Kings*. But Jordan and Cole's reaction here in the limo told me my dear Jade was a pint-sized pit bull.

"That's crazy," Rut hummed, stretching his long legs as he sat back, arm gripping me tighter to him. "I didn't believe everything I heard in the media before I got signed. And now that I am a *King*, I definitely don't believe shit they say. Especially them bootleg ass blogs."

"Don't sleep on all of them, though," Cole warned, tucking her feet beneath her on the bench as she leaned into Jordan.

"Which ones?" I asked, wondering what she meant.

"There are a couple of them with a seventy percent or more accuracy ratings," Cole assured.

"Like who?" Rut trilled.

Love's Ineligible Receiver

"For sure, *Arnez and Arizona*." Jordan counted from his hand. "Definitely, *Spilling That Hot Tea*. Them bitches—"

"Jordan!" Cole scolded.

"What?" he shrieked. "Nobody know who they are. And if it's some dudes involved in gossiping, they're hardcore bitches, too!"

I busted out laughing, head tossed back.

"I'm just saying." Cole rolled her eyes, snuggling more into him.

"What the hell you saying?" Jordan scoffed. "You saw that string of posts they did on Jameson's finances. They posted his foreclosure threat notices from his fuckin' bank, Nicki!"

I felt Rut's big frame tense around me.

Shit...

We needed to change the subject and quick.

"All I'm saying is we, the *Kings'* franchise, are passionate and active about teaching financial sustainability and social responsibility." Cole paused to yawn. "We give resources to you players to warn you of the dangers of mismanaging money and overspending. We also have resources for personal crisis such as addiction. If players don't take advantage and leave themselves at risk for the media to use their crisis as fodder to sell tabloids or get likes on a status, what more can we do?"

"But he good," Jordan kept with the back and forth. His hand even swung in my direction. "He working the shit out."

Parker's eyes climbed up to me.

My brain spit out something I ain't even know was anywhere near it. "So y'all believe what they're saying about ya boy, Ragee?"

Jordan and Cole's heads whipped to face me at the same time as they both spoke. "What?"

What?

I had no fucking clue why I even mentioned dude until I realized one of his songs was playing in the limo.

I unscrewed the water bottle and pulled it up to my mouth. "You know."

"About him being gay?" Cole scoffed then laughed.

"Fake marriage?"

"He goes to my church," Parker chimed in. I almost pissed in my pants, so relieved that had her attention. "I'm still new and don't see him a lot. But I've seen him a time or two and that man is crazy spiritual—not that it can't mean he's gay. But I don't know... I just don't get those vibes from him at all. Maybe weird, but not queer."

"Long as you know I ain't queer, you good," I growled at her, pulling her on my lap. Parker's cry was sharp in the limo, but I didn't give a damn. I leaned over and sucked on her neck, loving the taste/smell combination. *Damn. This girl is driving me fucking insane.* "What's queer about what my dick make you do?"

"*Daaaaaaaaaaaaaaamn!*" Cole shouted.

"*Kadaaaaaaar!*" Parker screamed then giggled over my lap.

"Oh, she know that *full* government!" Jordan laughed.

I felt the limo slow to a stop.

"Yo, that's you two," Jordan yawned.

My head drew up and through the dim lights of the limo I saw a row of lawns and houses.

Shit...

I lifted Parker from my lap and grabbed her clutch. "Peace to the god and earth," I was swift with my words. "I gotta pee like a muthafucka."

I reached over and gave Jordan some love then crouched to land a kiss on Cole's cheek.

"C'mon, Gray," I rushed as Parker repeated my actions, giggling with Cole at my flash movements.

We were out of the door and I pushed Parker on at the waist, leaning over her. She laughed all the way up the driveway.

"Rut!" she whispered hard, not being able to stop laughing. "You better not make me fall!"

"Hurry up and get the key out, dawg!"

She fumbled to open her purse, hand wiggling inside for the keys. I breathed a sigh of relief when I heard them coming out. She let us in without a minute to spare, and I bolted straight to the stairs for her room. When I walked in, the bathroom light was still on, opening a path there. I went straight for my belt buckle before hitting the doorway. I came to a sloppy stop at the toilet and groaned when the first of it spurted inside. My eyes closed and head rolled back.

Now I could finally plan how I was going to blow her damn back out tonight. I struggled keeping my hands off her since the moment she stepped into the living room when I picked her up. My moan had me craving her cries of pleasure. That damn Parker was driving me crazy with the way she stayed on my mind. I never felt this way about a broad. Never had a chick made me want to do the crazy shit I had and the rest I'd been thinking to make happen.

I wiggled to make sure the last was released before wiping myself and flushing the toilet. I hit the faucet to turn on the water and my attention went straight to my face. My eyes were pink. *Shit...* I was tired. *League* life was different from college ball—or maybe I'd been working harder because I had so much to prove? Either way, Parker had been a good distraction for me. Being under her this past month or so kept me out of the streets and clubs. I wasn't sure how long this would keep my attention, but I damn sure knew I wasn't trying to let her go.

I sighed, happy as hell to be getting ready to cuddle up with my favorite blanket. But first I'd make her legs shake and spine wobble... maybe mine, too.

I snickered to myself. My eyes fell to turn off the faucet when all the soap had been rinsed off. Three sticks caught my attention instead. But it wasn't until I saw two lines in all three that I froze, leaning over the fucking sink.

"The fuck?" I thought out loud, picking up two then the last and holding them in the air.

Were these Mandee's? Why would she be up here in Parker's room? I kept personal shit over here I didn't want stranger's having access to. They had to be hers.

Or is Parker gonna try it?

My heart started jumping on my lungs. I couldn't breathe for a minute and I started to feel wet all over. I was sweating everywhere, including my fucking eyes! Dropping the sticks where I stood, I went for my phone in my pocket and shot a quick text to Fats.

Me: Come scoop me fuckin' now!!!!

I felt sick and the room spun. Knowing I didn't drink that much, I panicked and my hand grabbed the wall to keep my balance. My eyes closed to a tight ass squeeze and I tried controlling my breathing like I did when working out.

What the fuck is she doing?

"Rut," I heard her behind me, and at first, I was scared to open my eyes. I didn't want to see anyone other than the Parker I knew. Or thought I knew. "You okay?"

Slowly, I did open my eyes. I didn't feel dizzy anymore but could still feel my stomach spinning. Two of the sticks were near my foot and I leaned to pick them up. Holding them in the air, I finally turned to face her.

Parker's lashes batted. I could tell by her neck movements she swallowed.

"These yours?"

It took her a minute to respond. "I'm so sorry about this. I took them just before you came to pick me up."

"Why?"

She jumped a little, but I ain't give a flying shit. I felt...betrayed.

"For a few reasons. Those hot flashes—"

"C'mon, Parker! Who the fuck takes pregnancy tests for hot flashes?" I cocked my head to the side. "You set me up?"

Her eyes flashed wide and a tear fell. Then another.

Her lips shivered and that fucked with me. "Why would I do that, Rut? Why would I set you up in any kind of way?" she whispered.

"You tell me! I've been strapping up. Only one time I slipped. Ya birthday wasn't even a month ago and you expect me to believe you're pregnant?"

She licked her lips, taking a deep breath. "That was my frame of thought at first until I remembered—"

"Remembered what? I was there every fuckin' time!"

"Remember the first time? The night of Eli's part—"

"Maaaaaan," My face went tight. I wasn't trying to hear that bullshit. I remembered that night well. "I strapped up all that ni—"

My eyes went down to my sneakers.

"Before we had sex, when you...masturbated over me..." she whispered, the tears thick in her voice kept her from finishing, but I knew.

I remembered being so caught up, I wanted to show her what I was working with and make it memorable by stroking my cock in front of her. Problem was, she was so fucking into it, looking innocent and sexy, I got turned on too much and busted on her.

"Shit." I threw the sticks in the sink, feeling sick all over again.

I'd just signed two endorsement deals, had been struggling with the coaching staff on my team, and on top of that, stressing about leaving her for three weeks, knowing Wright's kids had been fucking with her. I couldn't do this *and* a fucking baby!

"How the fuck somebody ya age get pregnant?" I yelled from the bottom of my damn gut.

Parker blinked more tears, but her shoulders squared up and her face went tight. "How the fuck somebody in your position at the top get somebody pregnant?"

For the first time, I heard the Waterbury in her.

Was this a game for her? It sure as hell wasn't for me. I felt betrayed. Fucking pain like never before. This was it. This was that trust shit going all wrong. This was what I had been avoiding with bitches all my life. Takers. They were all fucking takers. Including Parker.

I swung around her, leaving the bathroom. If I stayed a minute longer, looking in her face, the confusion I now struggled with would be just as loud as the pain.

The pain in his eyes would haunt me for the rest of my life. I could read eyes, could communicate using them only. It started with my grandfather. It was how he disciplined me without hands. Then it sharpened years later with Jimmy. Optical articulation was how he'd been surviving for the past few years. And with Rut, right now, his pain was palpable in his eyes and body. He looked sickened and betrayed. That lashed at me fiercely as he rounded me to leave the bathroom.

I watched his thick, lanky frame built like a grown man hold the child in him as he tromped toward the door of my bedroom.

"I won't chase you..." that last word barely escaping the cry breaking through my lungs.

Rut turned to me, seething with dripping disdain. I needed him to know. He may have been having a tantrum now, but I was the girl that never forgot. The one who bore the lashings enough to know to remember the offenses of my adversaries. I didn't fall back in harmony as easy as others.

"I wouldn't advise you to waste your fuckin' time." He didn't turn back as he spoke.

chapter nineteen

"Good," the physical therapist's voice sounded genuinely encouraging. "You're doing well, James."

I sat in a chair near the doors of the room and watched with tense limbs. Physical therapy was arduous for those with limited mobility, it could be similar for someone with less than that, too. I was happy but not content. No amount of exercises would improve mobility for a degenerative disease like ALS. However, these techniques, out of his bed, hopefully helped to lessen the rate and intensity of muscle cramping. It also possibly kept nerves plugged into muscles and protected them from further deterioration. Anything to decrease his pain made me happy.

I watched with rapt interest each movement the therapist made, hoping to emulate it in his absence. The doorbell ringing stole my attention. I ambled quickly to the door, wanting to get back to Jimmy and his therapist right away.

I don't know why Fats' towering stout frame caught me off guard when I opened the door. He texted me last night, asking when could he come by and pick up Rut's glasses. He apparently needed them up at training. It had been three days since Rut stormed out of here like a man on fire. I hadn't heard from him and neither did I expect to.

Even if I was that kind of girl, I wouldn't have had the time—didn't have the time—considering the past few days with Jimmy. Two days ago, when another fever plagued his body, I had the mind to go to the emergency room where he was admitted. And that set off the usual presence of his children in the hospital where they fought amongst themselves—mostly James Junior and Sherry—about better care for Jimmy. The doctor ordered him to stay overnight where they aggressively fought the fever until it broke. Again, they could find no reason for it.

So I'd been by his side, keenly watching him and his expressions to see if I could find some correlation. I almost canceled this physical therapy session until his doctor insisted on it, wanting to be sure it wasn't related to muscle cramping. I'd even called out of work today to be here while his session was happening. I told Nurse Jackie to take the day for herself. She could stop in to take his vitals and go on about her day. Because I'd been obsessively monitoring Jimmy, I'd honestly forgotten Fats and I agreed on him stopping by this morning to pick the glasses up.

"Oh." I blinked a few times before my brain kicked into gear. "The bag's in the kitchen, give me a minute." I waved him in, not expecting many words from him.

Fats didn't speak much other than to Rut, but he never bothered me or had been particularly rude. He stepped in and stood off to the side as I left for the kitchen. My phone rang in my hand on the way. With one glance, I saw it was Jade calling.

"Hey," I answered.

"Hey, girl. Everything okay on that end? I didn't see you in church last night."

"Oh." I rolled my eyes, realizing I never told her I wouldn't be making it. Earlier on in the week, I arranged for Mandee to be with Jimmy last night, as I did on occasion, for Bible study on Thursdays. The problem was, I'd canceled with Mandee and didn't tell Jade. "I'm sorry. I've had the week from hell. I forgot to let you know I wouldn't be there."

I made it to the kitchen grabbed the bag I packed with more than Rut's glasses and turned for the foyer again.

"I'm sorry to hear about that. I was looking forward to it."

"Yeah, my car broke down on me again." I hadn't decided to share the rest of my nightmare with her.

I wanted to get back to Jimmy.

"Again? What's the problem now?"

As I made it back to Fats, the front door was opening. Sherry stepped in and glanced around, quickly taken by Fats' burly frame.

"Jade, I have to go. I'll call you later to fill you in."

"Okay—"

I lowered the phone before tapping to disconnect. Sherry's eyes located me as I made it to the door.

"Oh!" was all she said at first.

"Everything okay?" I borrowed Jade's words, not knowing how else to break the ice.

Sherry tossed a glance to Fats as a nervous grin spread on her face. "No."

"Okay?" I was standing in front of her.

Sherry handed me an envelope. "This is for you."

"What is it?"

She turned again to Fats, who I'd completely forgotten until she did. "You can read it."

Although I accepted the envelope, I pushed. "You can save me the time so I can get back in there with Jimmy before his therapy session is over."

Again she turned to Fats, clearly uncomfortable with his presence or saying whatever she had to say in front of him.

"Parker, those are papers I'm serving you about your eviction."

My neck jerked back. "What?"

"This is why I told you to read it. You have to go. We have a new medical team that will be transferring Daddy to a facility where he'll receive round the clock professional care."

And here it was.

"Is this about those pictures?"

"It's about that and more. This should have never been. We let our father make his own call and respected his wishes. Now things are getting out of control. You're all over social media with a rookie. That just doesn't look good, Parker. He's been over here, spending the night and doing god only knows what here while my father's health is constantly failing. It isn't ironic to you how two days after you were frolicking around with Amare and leaving him with the neighbor, he was hospitalized? *Again?*"

Just as it happened after the Young Lord concert, pictures were released on the blogs of Rut, Jordan, Cole, and me at the Brielle concert. The original story ran by *Spilling That Hot Tea* was about Jordan and how he and his wife were dating so soon after getting married. It was a sweet spin. The B side was the fodder of the rookie, Rut Amare, being spotted again with the unknown woman.

And in true *Spilling That Hot Tea* fashion, they'd found my name, age, and connection to the *Kings*. Considering I was the thot fiancée of the sick *King* alum, who apparently had a thing for football players, Jordan's syrupy tale of wedded bliss was doused with hot sauce. Add to that the "fact" of Rut and Emily dating and he'd obviously cheated on her again *with me*. It was ridiculous and was the main point of contention in the hospital amongst Jimmy's children.

Between finding out I was pregnant, being betrayed by an intimate friend, having my personal life exposed and edited for entertainment, and Jimmy's failing health, I had no strength in me for this routine battle with the Wright children. I couldn't do it anymore. I'd have to fail Jimmy, too. Expelling a breath of defeat, I shook my head with closed eyes.

"When does this take effect?"

"August first," Sherry's voice was strong. "you have to go."

"That's next Wednesday! When's this transfer supposed to happen?"

"Monday morning." She gave a firm nod.

I took a deep breath. The physical therapist sauntering from Jimmy's room caught my attention. That's when I remembered Fats. Shaking my head again, I handed him the bag and opened the door for him to leave. Fats moved according to my lead.

When he was outside, he turned to me. "You good, Parker?"

I snorted. "Just dandy."

Then I closed the door to deal with my new reality.

RUT

I rubbed my dry eyes, feeling miserable. I was hungry, tired, and stressed the fuck out.

"Now, by a show of hands, tell me who always seems to get into it with their wife or girl before we have to go away to these training camps!" Deacon, a tight end, stood from his seat and shouted around the Hibachi table they had set up in the lunch room. "Show of hands..." he pushed for people to answer.

I looked around the room to see mostly everybody was paying attention, surprised they could actually hear with so many people in the joint.

"And no single dudes with just jump-offs," Mitchell, an offensive lineman, added, laughing. "Them bitches don't count!"

Everybody started laughing and even I snickered at that.

"Yeah. None of y'all wild ass cowboys, who fuck a different one every night," Deacon laughed. "Yeah, like Amare! No threesome *Kings!*" His face turned red as shit.

Jordan slapped my shoulder, cracking the hell up.

Lazily, I smiled. "Fuck you talking 'bout, bruh?"

That made them laugh even louder.

"You know. You played college ball with my girl's cousin. He stayed with those wild stories! The one when you made two cum at the same goddamn ti—"

"Aye!" I shouted over him. "Easy!" I laughed but wasn't good on talking about my dick in groups.

"C'mon." Deacon brought our attention back to him as the chefs chopped, squirted, and sautéed in front of us. "Raise of hands!"

I was shocked to see so many go up. Jordan and Trent's were a few of the last.

"Told you!" Deacon pointed to Mitchell, who nodded as he laughed. "It's like some weird cosmic alignment that happens so you don't get fucked before you're locked away with nothing but men for three damn weeks!"

A few shouts and laughs confirmed his theory.

"I swear," Mitchell spoke up. "I cleaned out the damn garage, made sure the pool was in good condition, and even fixed my mother-in-law's goddamn kitchen sink leak. And I'll be damn if she didn't start bitching about the closet being too messy the night before I left!"

The group laughed again. I shook my head, so disconnected from these complaints.

"What's the newly wed arguing about?" Deacon nodded over to Johnson.

"Yeah?" Mitchell looked shocked. "Pussy should be overflowing for you."

"Hey, I ain't say it wasn't. My answer was the stupidest ass fights occur right before any camp. This one was about cutting the birth control. I'm ready to fuckin' multiply."

"Ahhhhhh!" a few of the guys sang like they've been there before.

"Yo, you kidding me?" Trent seemed shocked as he looked at Jordan.

"I wish the hell I was." Jordan laughed.

"Yo, Jade put me on knock two days before I left, *calling me insensitive and barbaric*," he put on a whiney voice. "All because I said we should start trying again."

The table was in sync with their response to that, too.

My eyes went crazy wide, something I didn't think was possible considering how tight they were. This topic was blowing my mind. Who the fuck wanted babies when there was so many Ms to get?

"C'mon, man." Jordan chuckled. "You know yo' ass better chill with that and be grateful for my lil' Ava Nese. Calm your raging soldiers in there. Jade ain't 'bout that baby machine life, bruh."

"She my wife now. She better be about our family," Trent argued playfully.

"You know if Jade Bailey ain't about shit, she about the business of keeping TB straight," Jordan made clear.

The conversation went on and I mentally stepped out, not believing what I was hearing. They were yapping about wanting to get pregnant. And here I was, hoping the one I knocked up hadn't smashed my glasses into small pieces. It would be, at best, a week before I could get a new pair. And I didn't have an eye doctor in Connecticut yet so the distance shit would be inconvenient.

Leaving Parker's place the night before camp the way I did had me forget my glasses. I'd been needing them but had been too damn stubborn to do anything about it until yesterday. My eyes needed to breathe.

"You and your lady got issues?" Something about the greasiness in that tone called me back to the table. I looked up and down the row of bodies across from me. "You, Rut." Grant's smile was slick.

My phone on the table rang. I looked down and saw Fats' name.

Then my attention went back to Grant's corny ass. "Her gratitude for choosing my cock over yours. She can't stop praising His name."

I grabbed my phone, knowing I was wrong...knowing anybody who knew Parker went to church would catch the jab.

I made sure I walked far enough away from them before I answered. The way my stomach turned while I answered reminded me of the way it flipped each time I thought about Parker since the night of the concert.

"Yeah?"

"Some crazy shit," Fats' voice was calm, but his word play had me feeling some kind of way. "Wright's daughter came through while I was there…"

Parker

They were still there.

As I hauled my fourth garbage bag of clothes down the stairs, James Junior was at the bottom of the step speaking on his phone and Jerry was a few feet away tapping away at his. No one spoke. Not even the sheriff's officer, who arrived at seven o'clock, saying he had to be sure I left without issue.

I struggled with the bag all the way out to my car. The car that was almost full when I still had lots to load from my bedroom. It amazed me the amount of stuff that could accumulate over just a few short years.

With a few pushes, I was able to gauge I had room for one more. My eyes filled with tears again when I thought it was impossible. I'd been crying since an ambulance came on Monday to get Jimmy. He cried as I kissed him goodbye while they carried him out. The house had seemed so quiet without the rhythmic pulsating of his medical equipment, without his soul. He may have been a helpless maim, but Jimmy's spirit was very much alive in his home.

I made it back up to my soundless room, crying and began yanking at my chest. It was big, heavy, and antique, making it solid. I should have started with it but put it off because of its impossible weight. By the time I pushed it to the top of the stairs, my shoulders and arms throbbed. Low commotion caught my attention.

"And who are you?" I recognized as James Junior's voice.

"Her peoples," a male tenor answered with ire.

Slowly, I took down the stairs, wiping my eyes. I sucked in a breath when I saw Fats glaring down at James Junior. His brother, Jerry, was behind him but with an unusual sobered expression.

Fats turned to me on my way down. "All that's going is what's in the car?" he asked with full on authority.

I shook my head and sniffled then pointed over my shoulder. "I have more up in my room."

Fats turned toward the door and whistled. "Aye, Jake! Got more in her room."

I didn't understand what he was doing, though I could imagine why he was here. Fats bore witness to me being served with eviction paperwork.

Two guys marched with lightning speed into the house.

"Wait!" James Junior chirped. "Who're these people?" he asked Fats.

"My help," Fats swiftly answered then addressed me. "Parker, show them where the rest of your stuff is."

"Hell no!" James Junior, yelled. "They're not allowed in here. You ain't either!"

"The fuck you care? You putting her out. The quicker we move the quicker we can make it happen."

"No!" James shouted.

"Oh, hell nah," Jerry backed him.

The officer was already moving between James Junior and Fats before I could think about how this could end.

"She's allowed assistance so long as they are not destroying property," he informed James Junior and Jerry. Then he spoke to Fats. "Let's not be all day about this."

After a long nasty glare between the officer and the Wright brothers, Fats gave a nod, prompting the guys to go upstairs. I pointed to the chest and quickly, they hiked up there and carried it down and out of the house.

"C'mon, Parker. Let's get the rest of your shit," Fats ordered, moving toward the stairs himself.

I led the way up to my room. And before I knew it, the guys were there, grabbing bags and boxes. Where they were taking them I didn't know, until I grabbed my sit under hair dryer and carried it out of the house. That's when I saw a twenty-six feet long *U-Haul* truck parked horizontal to the driveway. The guys were loading my things in there. I gazed between my car and the truck, so confused.

Is this Rut?

It had to be. Fats had to have told him. Fats was here, moving me out. The tears began to fall again.

"C'mon, Parker." Fats was rounding me, carrying several shoe boxes. "Let's get the rest of this shit before I get in some heat out here."

Through clouded eyes I moved, going back into the house for more things. Less than thirty minutes later, all my things were out of the house.

"You can follow me," Fats ordered as we walked onto the driveway near my car.

"Follow you where?" I had a hotel reservation until I decided my next move.

"To the crib. It's about a forty-minute drive," he spoke over his shoulder while on the move.

I shook my head. "I'm not going to *Kings Courts*." I'd told Rut that long ago.

Nothing had changed, especially now.

"We ain't going there. Follow me, sweetheart." There was that authority in his voice.

I checked the time on my phone. I couldn't cancel my hotel now. It was mid-morning but less than the required twenty-four hour period.

What could be forty minutes away?

I wasn't in the mood to ask, but they had most of my things, leaving me with limited options. I was behind the wheel of my car, trying to start it. It wouldn't budge. My head fell to the wheel.

Come on...

I tried again and she roared to life. Taking a deep breath, I whispered a thanks to God. Then I peered into my rearview mirror and saw the *U-Haul* had moved up and at the end of the driveway was the Yukon truck I'd become conversant with. Fats was waving me on before taking off himself. I backed out of the driveway, refusing to pay the house I'd called a home for six years a final glance. I couldn't cry and drive, especially not forty minutes to an unknown place. When I backed into the street, Fats was down the block, at the corner with his left blinker going.

The top three-fifths of the black, steel French doors to the house was made of thick, diamond shaped bevel glass panes, but as Fats keyed into one, I could see to the back windows. He opened one door and stepped inside. With trepidation, I followed. The place was huge, three times the size of the one I'd just left. The walls were lofty and painted a cozy grey with their frames a stark white. The hardwood floors were chestnut. A few yards directly in front of us was a curved staircase with black wooden railing and stairs.

"The alarm people 'posed to be here tomorrow. If you see any shit that don't look like it belong here, hit me up. I'll move it."

To my left was a four-inch step up dining room, I assumed. It was lined with eight feet sliding windows with a dome shaped transom above. To the right looked to be a living room. The windows were the same vast shape with a few actual doors exposing the late morning sun, but leading into a much larger space.

The guys were behind me, swiftly carrying familiar bags into the house.

"Y'all carry everything upstairs to the room on the right," Fats ordered. "And don't block the damn door with it," he amended.

I shook my head, understanding that command. "Whose house is this?"

"Oh." Fats handed me a keyring. "Yours."

I looked at the large ring hanging from his stubby fingers. Then I peered into his eyes, shaking my head.

"This isn't my house," I muttered.

"It ain't my place to say what's what other than this is where you can get comfortable. Rut said some paperwork should be delivered tomorrow, too." Fats yawned, unfazed by my shaken disposition. "He said something about you not working on Thursdays. That right?"

I didn't answer. Instead, my attention went ahead to what had to be the kitchen at the back of the house. It was separated from the foyer by a mazy hallway. Moving out of the "movers" way had me amble closer to the hall, and I kept going until I crossed over into the biggest kitchen I'd ever stepped foot in. Spacious wouldn't begin to describe its vastness. It was an open design and to the right was a step-down, gated den. Windows all over dazzled the home, but it made the white outfitted decor sparkle.

"Aye, yo, Parker," Fats called from behind me. "I gotta help them finish unpacking the truck and ya car. I need ya keys."

I turned and Fats was placing the big keyring he tried handing me seconds ago on the white marble island countertop.

He didn't understand.

"Fats, I can't stay—"

"Oh, yeah." He stepped into my person, taking my car key from my hand. "A bed 'posed to be here between twelve and four."

"Bed?"

Fats strode out of the kitchen, headed for the front door.

She came bustling into the doors of the coffee shop dislodging her sopping umbrella. inga's boy short bleach blonde tapered hair style was still in perfect place. Her eyes brightened when she located me near the wall, and in her approach, her *London Fog* duster dripped and *Stuart Weitzman* tassel flats pattered quickly toward me.

She slowed just a few feet away. The awkwardness of the haul forced my obligatory smile. Then my mother took to the seat across from me.

"Wow," she breathed with a beautiful smile. A warming throwback to better days. "A latte."

"Yeah. The kid looked at me like I was crazy when I asked him to split it into two cups." A wry smile formed on my face. "This place is nice. You come often?" My regard swept the room.

"Not that often. I've been in an affair with a *Kureg* since last fall. They erected this place in January."

I nodded as a couple walked inside, heading straight to the counter.

"So," I turned to face my mother again. "I'm glad you called."

My brows furrowed and a soft grin lifted on my face from mixed feelings. "So am I."

She took a sip from her mug. "You're gorgeous, Parker. You know that?"

Whoa! I didn't think she'd ever called me anything but challenging since middle school. As powerful as those words would have been since then, today they were simply a nice gesture.

I took a deep breath, sitting back. "Thanks. I haven't been feeling that way lately."

She placed the mug down and neared me with an expression of deep concern. "What's been going on?"

"A little bit of counseling. You know… That tool needed for misguided kids, who grow into chaotic adults."

"Counseling?"

I should have shared how my therapist pushed me to seek out my Pastor's counsel, but that would have been pushing it.

I waved the concept off, bringing my elbows to the table. "I'm being melodramatic…auto-sarcasm that switches on when I'm in your presence."

Her eyes fell into her lap. "I'm sorry."

"You should be. I developed it to survive your missiles of critiques." I sucked in a deep breath and my regard fell, too. "I'm sorry," I whispered.

"It's okay. Really." Her hand reached across the table, but she didn't touch me. "It's okay."

I shook my head, chin still to my chest. "It's not. It really isn't." It took a few seconds to gather myself. I lifted my head. "I've had three long sessions of counseling with my Pastor over the past two weeks. And when I say long…" I rolled my eyes. "The money the man could have made from me for each three-plus hours of my issues…"

"I didn't know you went to church."

"It hasn't been that long, but it's been one of my best self-investments. Nothing like grandma's religious obligations. More like a spiritual awakening for me."

"I'm glad you're finding it useful. I'm a strong proponent for therapy, you know?"

"Even if it's a man?"

"Well..." She shrugged. "The end result is what counts. Right?" her tone wasn't convincing, but something else was.

"You're really committed to convincing me you've been cloned, aren't you?"

"Parker, it's been years since we've been connected. Even adults have room to grow up."

I nodded, agreeing with that notion. "I'm no longer at Jimmy's."

Her face lit with surprise. "You left him?"

Mine folded. "It depends on which sense you're referring to. We hadn't been 'together' in years. And no. It wasn't my decision to leave exactly. His kids evicted me."

"Who's there taking care of him now?"

"He's not there. He's been transferred to a hospice facility."

"When was this? Has it been better for him there?"

"He left over two weeks ago, and I don't know how he's been. I only know where he is because my boss told me last week when I finally asked him. He didn't know Jimmy had been put in a facility. He contacted Jimmy's family and was given the information. I haven't seen him since he left the house." And that had been the most painful part of this transition in my life.

"Where have you been staying?"

I took a deep breath and rolled my eyes. "In a house."

"A boarding house?" she trilled.

"No." I shook my head, not knowing which words to choose to explain. "It's my home on paper—well..." I massaged my temples.

The day after Fats moved me into the house, a courier delivered legal papers. The documents contained a proposal that my name would be on the deed of the house but the mortgage had been settled by Rutledge Kadar Amare. The paperwork dated as early as July, weeks before I'd seen the place. I'd still been confused about this. And since training season wouldn't be over until next week, I hadn't talked to Rut about it. In fact, my communication with Rut had been sparse. He had a security system installed and a bed, washer, and dryer delivered. And he sent Fats back with cash for me to get settled in the place with. But no answers and very little communication, letting me know he'd still been upset.

"I don't get it," that authoritative tone I'd always known reared.

Taking a deep breath, I sat up and gripped my coffee mug. My eyes were to my joined thumbs.

"You remember how grandma used to have the wackiest dreams and would declare things behind them?"

inga scoffed. "Yeah. Like the one time she dreamt that racist ass pizzeria burned down? In all of her Jesus crazy, she marched down there and told Paulie unless they changed their ways, the days of the shop would be numbered?" I sputtered a laugh, vividly remembering that day. I was with her and told my mother how she dragged me by my little fist to that place. "Yeah." inga snickered a bit, too.

"She did that a lot, didn't she?"

"You have no idea. I spent more time with her than you. Way more moons."

"But the pizza shop didn't burn down." My focus went back to the mug in my hands.

"No. The building was condemned about two years later."

I nodded, peering up at her. "Some would argue her dream was true."

inga bit her lips together. "In retrospect, she was right on a lot of her craziness. Those dreams of hers could be as accurate as they were crazy."

"So was yours." My words were quick and piercing, I could tell by the flip in her eyes.

inga didn't speak. I reached down into my bag near my feet and pulled out a picture frame. As I rotated it her way, my lungs leaped and I rebuked myself for nearly breaking.

"I'll be in my second trimester on Saturday." An errant tear slipped and, quickly, I swiped it away, unable to look at her. This was harder than I thought it would be. "I'm sure you've seen the blog posts; you're on social media. Thanks for not making it a point of criticism. And before you ask; no. He's not my knight in shining armor. We were friends." A betraying tear of mucous shot from my nostril and I swiped that, too. "Good friends, who expressed our feelings for each other in a reckless manner. I'm not foolish. I have no expectations of him. You'd be happy to know I have a fair amount of inga grayson in my blood."

"Does this mean he's not going to be involved?" I heard the tears in her voice and peered up to see them pooling in her eyes, too.

My mother had an emotional connection to me. *Holy crap!* This was hard to get used to.

I forged a smile of strength. "It means I'll—*we'll* be okay. It means you were not the worst kind of mother for teaching me independence and despising the naïve storybook-guided psyche I carried as a little girl. It means I understand you disciplined me the way you understood the world to be. One of my breakthroughs over the past two weeks in counseling is how I may be my own woman, but so much of me is your good intentions and not your poor delivery."

Her face was glossed with tears, and for the first time in my life, inga grayson was speechless.

"I'm in the deepest pain I've experienced in years, but I know I'll survive it. I have so much to look forward to. My time is up. I'll be having a child who I'll have to shape and mold, too. I'll have to give the best of me, too, to ensure their development and survival in this ugly world. One of the biggest demons I have to tackle right now is—"

"Forgiveness," her delivery was low, throaty as her eyes were fixed onto me.

I nodded, ghosted by her accuracy. "I have to let go of all the bitterness. All of the years I felt misunderstood by my only parent. All of the years I hoped my father would knock on the door and help you understand me. I have to let go of all the times you were mean to my grandfather and treated him like an adversary instead of your flesh and blood. I have to revisit the day I decided I'd cross over to a non-kin place, too, believing it would numb the pain. Cutting you off was wrong of me." I had to look her in the eyes for this part.

It was something Pastor Carmichael made so clear to me.

"You didn't ask me to leave your life. I did it cowardly. *I* couldn't take my own disappointment from not being as purposed as you'd always been. You had a crisp idea of what you wanted to do in life. You knew who you were. *I* didn't, and rejected your guidance. *I* decided to go into chemistry instead of women's study, knowing I didn't have the capacity for it. *I* decided to forego a career in that field or going back to school for another degree, and went into cheerleading instead. *I* decided to get a crappy, dead end job instead of living up to the potential you made clear to me. And it was *my* choice to move in with a man older than you as a shortcut to fulfilling that potential."

I took a deep breath and swallowed back the impending, roaring cry. My God, admitting to your crap was painful. When a soft, shaking hand reached for mine, I let go of the air holding in my lungs and cried.

Shaking my head, I blubbered, "I swear, I didn't mean to do this here."

"It's okay. It's been a long time coming. And so has my list of apologies. There are too many to itemize in public. But, sweetheart, I'm sorry for projecting my pain and implementing them into parenting you. I dragged you into my pain and anger toward my father and that wasn't right. I kept you from your own father and I could never forgive myself for it. Ever."

I was able to peer up at her.

"It was wrong of me, Parker—all of the patriarchy I hated, I ended up shoving down my baby girl's throat. It took that time out you put me into for me to sit with myself, in my shit. And then one day, I looked up from all the books and papers in my tiny ass basement office and realized how damn lonely I'd been. My father was gone and my baby girl left me to myself." Her head shook softly, nose burned red as she tried fighting more tears. "I'm so damn lucky to have a piece of this." She grabbed the framed photo of a sonogram I had done last week and hugged it to her chest. "I hope you'll let me be a part of this. Every step of the way, Parker. I hope he doesn't mind an overbearing and overly-doting grandmother," her voice but a squeak.

I chuckled, eyes rolling to the ceiling at that. "I doubt if he cares either way. Like I said, I'm not foolish. I have no expectations of him."

Her hand squeezed over mine. "You're not foolish because you're not me. Make it work for your child. Even if it takes him longer than what's mature: if he wants in, don't deny him. It's a pain I'll take to my grave, honey."

After long seconds of energy exchange, the tears followed. I had no idea she'd be so receptive. My plan was to do as Pastor Carmichael prescribed: "*Go, declare the demons of your bloodline vanished. Clear your heart of hurt and plant the seeds of healthy development for your unborn child.*"

At best, I thought I'd say my piece, leave, and feel like a fool on my drive back. But something more was set up here before I arrived. There was a spirit of reconciliation at work for my mother and me. And I realized I needed it more than I wanted to admit.

chapter twenty

I TRAILED BEHIND COACH BROOKS AS she led me out of the common area where everyone was kicking back at the end of another long, grueling day in the sun. We turned down too many halls and passed through too many doorways to know where the hell I was. If I was back at home or maybe if this was just a couple of months ago when I first met her, I'd think this could be a set up. But Brooks had been cool with me. She'd been a necessary pain in my ass and that had been proven on the field.

Plus, checking her out from behind, it was clear something was off about her. I peeped it a little early on in training camp but tonight she seemed...feminine. Usually, she wore a bun or some type of braids and sometimes covered her head with a *Kings* baseball cap. Tonight her hair was long—*and real*—down her back and over her shoulder as her head tilted to the side. But Brooks was militant about her appearance. She wasn't...girlie like she looked now. *Shit*. I wasn't mad; we were all tired with just two more days of camp to go.

Finally, she stopped at a door and swung it open. I stood in the doorway and saw Nate standing to his feet. Panic ran through me at first, and I stepped inside. This couldn't be good. Why the hell was

Richardson here? I hadn't called him. My eyes went to Coach Brooks, who was closing the door with her eyes hung low.

"Hey, man." He smiled with a confused expression.

"How you?" my tone was dry and I was more confused than he was.

"I'm good." He lowered himself to the chair I'd found him in. "Have a seat." When I did, and looked at him like he was crazy, Nate asked, "Everything okay up here?"

I dropped my face. "You heard different?"

Nate chuckled, scratching his chin with his thumbnail. He looked tired, too. It was after eight at night, on a campus in the woods. He probably was exhausted as fuck, coming all the way up here for what?

"You tell me. How's it been out there?"

I shrugged. "I put in work. It's what I do." My hand swung back to the door. "Only thing's different is that broad. My mother-coach ain't been herself," I joked with honesty. "I 'on't think I like that shit." I shook my head. "But, the fuck I know what to do with a female coach who got the blues? I can't take her to a tits and ass bar to get her right."

Nate laughed. He knew the politics between Brooks and me. He knew just about everything concerning me and this team.

"That's funny 'cause she says the same thing about you. Y'all out here syncing moods like when roommates sync menstrual cycles?"

I chuckled at that, swiping my nose. Nate knew the journey it had been, me and Brooks getting on the same page these past couple of months. Like I said, he knew everything.

Slowing his laughter, Nate pushed, "What's up, man? I heard your focus has been the sharpest they've seen; numbers are impressive, plays have improved compared to minicamp."

I flicked my wrists, palms toward the ceiling. "Then why is my DPS all the way out here in dirt county?"

"Because I got word your performance has been on autopilot."

"The hell that mean?"

He sat up, putting his elbows on his knees. "It means your light has been out, bruh."

I spit a laugh. "Those good reports don't sound like a vacant house."

"But they sound like a dark, sunken place."

Shit just got real...

My eyes rolled away and found interest at tip of the armrest of my chair. For a while, I scratched into the material there, not knowing what to say. Talking shit came easy to me. Sharing pain wasn't.

"Rut..." he almost sang, trying to loosen me up.

I shook my head, not wanting to get into this.

I could hear him take a deep breath. "You're here. You made it. Camp'll be over in a couple of days and your performance has secured your seat on the roster. All the bullshit with Brooks and the other doubting coaches has been put to bed. You did it."

My eyes finally swung over to him and I nodded. He was right. I got my shit together. Even Grant was feeling uneasy next to me out there practicing. I'd been killing his numbers.

"*I*—I..." I cleared my throat. "I fuckin' did."

"Then what the fuck can possibly be the problem?" his tone was more dramatic than I'd ever seen of Nate.

He wanted me to be real. I knew this was just business. I was just one of many of his clients on the team. And even though he came with the bad along with the good since I met him, Nate seemed like a real one. *Shit*. He was a man—older than me—and had seen a lot. Had been through a lot, probably, too.

"How old were you the first time you nutted in some pussy?"

I could tell that caught him off guard. Nate sat back, pulled his ankle over his knee, put his hand over his mouth, and looked at me.

He tossed his wrist. "Seventeen."

"You caught feelings for her?"

"Not at all."

"How 'bout the first time you went raw and bust in a girl? You caught feelings then?"

"College. And *hell* yes!" He laughed.

"You know I ain't never catch feelings behind no ass? The closest I got was my high school girl—*shit*, my first and last girlfriend—Kim Hawkins. She was crazy as shit, but she was all about me. Loyal.

Straight the fuck up, without no games." I nodded, twisting my lips. "But you know when I did catch feelings in some ass?"

He frowned with suspicion. Even my DPS didn't believe I was capable. "When?"

"When I got into the *League*." His face went even tighter. "You know when I made my first baby?"

"When?"

"After I signed my first multi-million-dollar endorsement deal... pre-season." I felt weak, copping to that bullshit.

Nate sat up in his seat and twisted his neck. "Come again?"

I took a deep breath, rubbing my forehead. I couldn't believe the words leaving my mouth were about me. This shit didn't seem real. Parker did. But a fucking baby?

I looked at Nate again and nodded.

"Emily Erceg?" one brow went into the air.

"Nigga, I'mma *Five Percent*er. I may have agreed to the propaganda to get this paper, but I ain't never running up in that pussy. And if I did, it wouldn't have been raw."

"Then who?"

We spoke at the same time, "Parker."

"Parker Grayson?" Nate referred to her whole government.

I guess that was how he knew her from temping in the front office.

"Shit," he whispered, looking toward the floor.

"Try 'fuck.'" That's the one I'd been going with. "Fuckin' stupid. A fuckin' shame. Fuckin' got me here—well, not exactly." Like a fucking idiot, I knock her up without intercourse. "But you get the picture."

Nate straightened his spine in his seat and scratched his brow. "And that's had you stressed all camp," he spoke mostly to himself. "When did you find out?"

"The night before I reported in."

He nodded.

"And Parker...?"

"Ain't got shit to lose in this. In fact, I gave her one. She's been wanting a baby."

"Parker? I didn't take her for a gamer. I've known her for like six years. My father and *The Boulder* are—"

"I know!" I groaned, not wanting to hear Wright's fucking name. I could choke that nigga. Wished he was well so he could "see" me. The fuck was he thinking? His kids put her out. Parker didn't deserve that shit. "And nah. Even though I thought she was gaming me for the first few minutes after finding out, I remembered shawtie don't even want a man. She just want a kid."

And I was the dumb fucker who supplied it.

"Everybody got what they wanted from me, but I never received shit in return. And what made this situation more hurtful is that I lost a friend." My body jerked in the air, arms stretched and head bobbed. "I 'on't even do female friends, Richardson. How the fuck did the game fold on me like this?"

"Because you 'did' a friend, I'm guessing."

"Not exactly how it went down, but it's still fucked up. I mean..." I rubbed the tip of my nose with the back of my index finger as I thought. "I want kids, but maybe after I retire. You remember that article StentRo did for *Sports Illustrated* after he had lil' Jordan? He said he thought he'd be the type of father rolling into his kids' high school graduation in a damn wheelchair." I slapped the arm of my chair. "Man, that was my fuckin' hashtag. Wheelchair goals!"

I couldn't even laugh at my stupid ass. Nate didn't either. He just pouted his lips as he nodded. It was a thing he did that made me believe he was "with" me and not against me like everybody else.

"I know it sounds fucked up, I'm keeping it a brick here..."

"I get it."

Huhn?

"Get what?"

"I get the kid thing. That isn't everyone's...hashtag goals. I've never wanted kids and still don't. It's never been appealing to me." He scoffed. "I've lost a few, holding tight to that conviction. My father won't be made a grandparent from these loins." He shrugged. "Maybe he'll be lucky to get a step-grandchild from me, but that's the best I can do for him."

"Damn!" I breathed, chuckling.

Nate raised his shoulders and hands. "You ain't the only one capable of keeping it trill. It's my truth, so I get a man wanting to be reserved about planting seeds in a world of reckless shooters. But I also get adapting to the shit life doles out. A man in your position can't just fuck up on the field: You can do it off the field, too. And I don't mean just having a baby unexpectedly. I've seen decent women turn into vengeful, scorned nightmares all because of the first two...three decisions the man made after finding out about conception. Be careful. Your actions and words over the next two years will set the tone. Your response could bring you good or do you harm."

I nodded, lost in his mouthful. I couldn't stunt on Parker. No matter how fucked up this situation was, I couldn't make myself believe she was on some bullshit. Her character was built different. She was the most selfless person I met in my life. My grandmother wasn't as generous as that girl.

"Anything I can do to help with this?" I shook my head. "I don't think anyone knows about it. She's been in the office every day lately. I thought that was strange." My eyes rolled up to Nate. "Wonder what's this going to mean for *The Boulder*'s care."

I could give a shit about Wright's care but was too damn exhausted to go there. Plus, it was obvious Nate didn't know they put her out on her ass. That shit still fucked with me.

"You cool with his son?"

Nate's eyes shot over to me. "Which one?"

"Either one of them?"

"I can't stand James. Jerry moved away, so I don't see him often. He's an asshole. Sherry...gets around." He snickered. "She likes to hide behind that idyllic lifestyle of going to school, marrying her college sweetheart, and having three point five kids, but locker room gossip is worse than a fucking beauty shop. She done scratched too many of my players to count. She got a thing for rookies, especially."

I snorted. "Yeah. So I've heard."

I stood from my seat. "I'm out, god." I stretched my arms and throbbing ass legs. "Gotta early start tomorrow."

Nate was out of his seat to give me dap. "Rut, if you keep shit like this to yourself again, I'm gonna have to recommend your ass stay in therapy a little while longer."

"Fuck you," I whined like a kid as I walked to the door.

I rang the doorbell and waited. It was after eight at night and mostly dark out. From the bevel glass on the set of doors, I could see the place was just as empty as the last time I'd been here. It was dark inside, the only light I could see was from the kitchen in the back of the house. I didn't even see her coming until she was damn near in my face. I stood straight as she opened the door.

She pulled it back and I stepped in.

"Hey." Why was I so damn nervous all of a sudden?

"Hey," she whispered with tight eyes.

"You were sleep?"

Parker rubbed her eyes. "I guess I was. I told myself it was close to time to expect you... I guess sleep crept up on me." She giggled quietly.

I could smell the citrusy scent from her hair and body. She looked like the same old Parker to me. She wore tight biker shorts that were hiked up her toned thighs and a baby doll shirt. She didn't look pregnant at all. This seemed to be the girl I trusted and could laugh with. But I knew. I knew behind that loose T-shirt was an unwanted truth.

I trained my eyes away from her, looking around the tall naked walls. "You like it?"

"It's beautiful." She took a deep breath, looking up and around, too. "Still confused about the place, but it's gorgeous nonetheless."

I chuckled at her formal tone. "Let's start off with it's a house."

Parker made an expression of shock, her hands going to her face. "Shocker!" she whispered.

I shook my head. "Somebody I know couldn't maintain the mortgage on it and needed extra cash, so I took it off his hands."

"And so timely..." She was reaching.

"I made the offer that morning Wright's daughter showed to the house. I even threw in an extra hun'ned K to expedite the deal. I didn't think it would happen as fast as I needed it to, but..." I looked behind me at the living room I remembered leading to a sunroom and family room.

"You needed it?" her chirp brought my attention back to her.

"I did." I nodded, eyes up on the balcony. "For a friend."

"So you bought this house for me?"

I shrugged, lifting my lips. "It felt like the right thing to do."

"And storming out the night we learned I'm pregnant felt the same?" her tone was deceptively sweet.

I closed my eyes, not ready to take that on. I knew we had to at some point, but I didn't know how.

"That wasn't my finest hour. I was caught off guard and angry."

"And yet you allowed me to stay here for a little while?"

"Nah." I shook my head, still looking around. "This is yours. That's what the paperwork was about. I hear you haven't signed it, though."

"I haven't spoken to you to know what your plans were. You've been like God, making things happen without your physical form."

"Because I've been working."

"And so has your phone." She put her fist over her mouth and shifted away. "I don't want to fight."

Shit. I didn't either. It was late, I was tired. After leaving camp, I drove straight down to *Love Is Action* in New York City and sat through a long ass image spin meeting with my PR people. Elle cut into my ass something fierce all afternoon about the Brielle concert pictures and how me cheating on Emily was now a 'thing' that wouldn't go away unless Emily and I broke up or I cut Parker off. After I told her why Parker wouldn't disappear, shit hit the fan. It was fucking draining.

I scratched my head. "Me either. I came up here to check up on you." I swung my hand toward the living room. "See if we can get you some furniture and shit."

"I don't need your little endorsement money. You've spent enough of it on this house I'm not sure how long I'll be in."

My head swung back. "What's so fuckin' lil' about my endorsement checks? Something I *didn't* use to buy this shit. And where the hell you going if you don't stay here?"

Parker cut me the first nasty eye since I walked through the door. "I have options, Rut. They may not be as lavish as the sixty-five hundred square feet custom designed house, but no matter where I go, I'll be fine."

"The fuck you mean, 'where you go'? Why you saying it like that?"

"Like what?"

"Like I'm not fuckin' trying here!" I didn't mean to yell.

But she was pissing me the fuck off. Why was she being mean?

"Trying?" She switched weight from one hip to the other. "You don't get to throw tantrums and expect for people be okay with it until you've calmed down. And you shouldn't expect for me to be okay with that."

"It caught me off guard! *Gooood*damn. I'm not perfect, Parker!"

"And you're not a child either. You shouldn't act like one. In the real world, Rut, adults don't get the opportunity to have emotional meltdowns when life turns shitty for them!" My eyes went wild. "They don't get to fall to the floor, cry, and lay blame elsewhere. In the real world, you just have to brave through the bad shit and hold out for a new fucking day!" She screamed to the point of her neck bulging. I never heard her use so many cuss words.

"You have to stick your chin up and maybe even stand still in the pain by your-damn-self. But you don't get to run from things!" She shoved her hand to the floor. "You stand firm through it, and if you're lucky—as in your case—you have someone next to you to figure it out with. Not like in my case where all the pain, the betrayal, and fucking loss is all on my shoulders alone!"

My face opened up when it hit me.

"Everything's good with Wright?"

Her eyes squeezed closed and tears raced down her tight face. "He died today, Rut."

I jumped to grab her into my arms.

Parker

"Congratulations, Parker!" my mother trilled with the widest smile. She grabbed me in her arms and squeezed. "That's amazing, *and* I'm glad to know my money on that chemistry degree was not in vain."

I shrugged with my brows, giving the sentiment of touché. "This is true."

"How did you even get in contact with *The Drake Casino and Hotel*?"

"Rut. He made some calls back in July then he helped me with getting labels, insurance, and things like that." I shrugged not knowing what else to say.

With inga grayson, you couldn't dote on a man too much.

Her smile was still in place. "Well, I'm happy for you, Parker. I really am." She stepped back and glanced around the room. "So you think this will be the baby's room?"

Today was my mother's first day over. I'd been showing her the house when I shared the news that came in yesterday about me getting product placement in the casino. There was a strange comfort showing her around the home I hadn't decided I'd even stay in.

My regard swept from wall to wall. "I haven't thought that far yet. My focus has been down in the wash room where I've set up shop for my lab. That, and looking for warehouses to use my formula to make my products in mass or a commercial kitchen to make larger quantities than I can here."

She followed me out of the second largest bedroom of the house into the hall.

"I heard the news about Jimmy's funeral happening next week," she shared behind me. "His memorial will be near the stadium. Are you going?"

"I am. I haven't exactly been invited, but it is open to the public. His neighbor and former home nurse plans to sit with me."

She stopped in the middle of the carpeted hall. "I'm sorry about all of this, Parker. I really am. For all the negative things I've said about your relationship, your dedication to him was one of champions."

My throat burned. "Thanks, inga."

The front door opened below. There, from the loft, I could see a towering frame crane his neck inside.

"Park!" he shouted.

In a less alarmed tone, I answered, "Up here."

Rut's regard met us. "Oh." He stepped inside. "Just wanted to let you know I was here, dropping the boxes off."

I smiled kindly—formally—wanting to see more of him under the *Asé Garb* baseball cap. "I left one of the garage doors open for you."

He'd called last night, something he'd done every day since I learned of Jimmy's passing, and mentioned needing to drop a box of *Asé Garb* samples off that he didn't have the space for at his condo. I reminded him of this being his home and he was more than welcome to do what he needed to do.

"Oh." Rut seemed stuck.

"Hi," my mother waved. "I'm inga, Parker's mom."

"Oh!" Rut emitted with more energy. He took for the rounding staircase and charged them like lightning. As he drew closer to us, his scent announced him and my nipples stung. "My bad." He extended his hand to inga. "I'm Rutledge. Nice to meet you."

"The pleasure is all mine. I hear congratulations are in order." She beamed that non-inga beam I still couldn't get used to.

Rut's eyes hit me then softened as they dropped down my frame. He couldn't see proof of my expectancy. I hadn't gained an excessive amount of weight and so far, had been all belly but a small belly.

"Yeah," he spoke to her, but his unsmiling eyes were on me. Then he faced her. "Thanks. Glad you're over. You like Parker's new place?"

My head shifted back and brows lifted. *My place?*

"It's gorgeous. Very spacious."

Both their eyes were on me now. What could I say that wouldn't make this "meeting" awkward.

"I know you have to leave for Cleveland. I can lock up the garage when you're done." He told me about his game there tomorrow. "Just shoot me a text."

Rut nodded, his eyes still on me. I couldn't stare at him for too long. It wouldn't be good for me.

"Nice to meet you, Dr. grayson."

"Same here, Rutledge. I look forward to being over more often. I'm very excited about this next chapter in my life." There was a bit of formality in that claim.

That inga could intimidate the most confident.

Rut took off for the stairs. Before I could turn to confirm, he was out of the door.

"That was interesting," she let out a deep breath, but was smiling from ear to ear.

"What's that?"

"In the split second when he arrived up here, I saw a glimpse of my tender Parker. The one who believed the world to be good and that men are gods."

I shook my head. "I seriously doubt that."

"*Oh*. I'll never forget the bright spirit of that girl." She took me at the shoulders, leaning her head into mine. "Let inga be the bitch. You be the loving, caring Parker Grayson you were born to be. I like what your pastor said about the demons of our bloodline vanishing. Start with unpacking and settling into your new home here."

I stopped. "My new home? I don't know about that."

Unperturbed, she urged me ahead, down the hall as she laughed hard at my expense. "Honey, if you weren't planning on staying, you would've been out of this lovely home by now. So cut the shit."

chapter twenty-one

Sept. 2018

I heard the *oohs* and *ahhhs* as I let us into the house.

"This place is gorgeous, Parker!" Nurse Jackie marveled.

"Holy shit, it's big," Mandee screeched.

My eyes went to the tables and chairs planted sparsely around the empty rooms. A long table was in the dining room decorated with elegance and packed with colorful foods. Overly stimulated, my eyes scoured the place I'd just left hours earlier. *Where did all this stuff come from?*

Then I connected eyes with him. Rut was in the kitchen, sitting at a table watching. He stood and sauntered across the house for me. I watched him take long lunges in a *Kings* T-shirt, basketball shorts, black ankle socks, and shower shoes.

"What's this?"

He towered over me with concerned eyes. "I got a few things and people together for a repass here."

"Here?"

"Yeah. I was able to get a catering company and buy a few pieces of furniture to fill the empty space."

"You did all that during preseason?"

Rut shrugged as he chewed his lip. I hoped he didn't think I was being a bitch. This time I wasn't. I was just shocked.

"Who is all of this for?"

"A few people." His eyes raised above and beyond my head. I turned to follow his line of vision to Nurse Jackie and Mandee over at the food table in the dining room. "They helped me with a few things."

The bell rang and then the door was pushed open. Sauntering in was Mel Richardson. My forehead wrinkled. Behind her was Cole, then Eli, and then was Nate.

Eli located me in the foyer right away and made his way over. The two men greeted each other in a half hug and hand shake.

"How are you feeling, Parker?" Eli asked. "I couldn't find you in the church."

"I was nearly in the back, not wanting to be seen."

"I was hoping you weren't alone. I had Mel take a walk to look for you." He pulled my hand in his. "I've expressed to James my feelings about the lack of sensitivity shown to you by him and his siblings." His tone was so warm, genteel. "There's nothing I can do professionally, but was sure to let him know my family and I would be here with you memorializing his father before I go over to the repass they're holding now."

My eyes swept over to Rut.

That's what this is...

I gazed over the foyer again and saw more people coming in. These looked like athletes.

"Thanks, Eli," I murmured, taken aback by it all, including the fact that these people were traveling just behind me from the church over forty minutes away and I didn't know.

He offered a final neck bow before stalking off. My regard returned to Rut. I was utterly speechless. Today had been a day of emotional constraint for me. Losing my grandfather was worse than losing my grandmother because I was older and more attached to him.

Love's Ineligible Receiver

But losing Jimmy was a hard hit on my emotions and psyche because I was pregnant and my hormones were soaring in this second trimester.

"Are you okay, Parker?" I turned to find inga. She wore an apron, and the look of concern in her eyes could mend scores of offenses.

"Mom?" Her eyes flew wide. I never called her that. She trained me otherwise. "inga!" I corrected myself. "How did *you* know about this?"

"Rut contacted me at school. I thought it was a nice gesture. I just hope the surprise isn't too much on you and the baby," she whispered.

Who the hell was this woman? The inga I knew was hard, direct, and temperamentally confrontational. And Rut. Since when did he care how I mourned Jimmy? Where was the selfish asshole?

My eyes closed and those stupid tears begin to fall.

Rut was on me first. "Those punk ass Wrights fuck with you?" he growled.

"Parker, breathe," my mother urged, rubbing my arm as I sobbed from the sadness of never saying goodbye.

I knew it was a foolish thought, but I struggled with the guilt of abandoning Jimmy. Just weeks after he was removed from his home, he died. And from what Mandee said her father had been told, none of his children were there when he crossed over.

I waved off the last guests to leave for the night. My mother and Nurse Joan were lifesavers, cleaning the post-mess left after the catering company packed their things to leave. I journeyed back from the side of the house where guests parked. There were close to fifty people here today. Everyone insisted I didn't lift a finger, including Rut, who left once he and inga were able to calm me after my emotional meltdown earlier.

The gesture of an informal memorial for Jimmy turned out to be a comforting one. It wasn't long as folks had to drive all the way back down into the city to be with Jimmy's family. Eli hosted it here, being sure I was at his side. He presented a brief yet moving eulogy from the living room. Then we all gathered outside where there was as many gold and blue helium balloons as there were people. An old teammate of his gave words of remembrance and we let our balloons ascend toward heaven as I hoped Jimmy had. He deserved rest from his heavy ailment and emotional torment over the years. Eli invited guests back inside for light refreshments before taking back to the city.

After I paced barefoot back into the house by way of the kitchen, I locked the doors. There were a few plates and cups my mother and Nurse Joan missed, so I collected them and walked toward the sink for the trash when I realized I wasn't alone.

"Oh, my goodness, Terrance," I breathed, dropping the plastic dishes on the island and grabbed my raging chest. "I didn't know you were still here."

I'd seen and greeted him on the way out for the balloon ceremony, but that was hours ago when the first round of guests was still here.

He leaned into the doorjamb off the hallway. "I was waiting for everyone to leave. They say that's when the grieved actually grieves."

I swallowed, smiling at the kind gesture. "Well, I wish you would have given me the heads up and not scared the crap out of me."

Terrance chuckled and moved toward a seat at the table Rut must have rented for today. "How are you? I've been busy in the preseason...haven't had the time to check in on you."

I raised my hands to my belly then gestured to the kitchen door where we'd had the balloon send off. "I've been quite busy myself, as you can see."

"You know, I had no idea you were pregnant until today."

My smile remained as my head shook softly. "You just said you've been busy."

"Now, I'm hurt."

"Hurt?" I echoed, expression fixed in a half smile, half astonishment. "We shouldn't use extreme intransitive verbs, Terrance."

I carried the cups and plates to the large trash can.

"I thought we were friends. Why wouldn't I be hurt?" I glanced over my shoulder to find his eyes on my rear. They rolled cunningly up to my face.

I snorted, being hit with a revelation before I returned to him at the table and leaned against it.

"Because we aren't friends."

"We've gone out before...texted before, too." His eyes roved up my black dress that didn't façade my belly much. "I've brought you flowers. Remember?"

"Yup." I nodded, smiling. Terrance's game was too thick tonight and pathetically weak. "And you may not have heard about my bundle of love here." I rubbed my belly. "But I'm sure you heard about Jimmy. A friend would have remembered he dropped those flowers off to the woman living with Jimmy. A friend would have called to check on her. And that's where we differ on the title."

"But I'm here now," he continued. "I'm here after everyone else has left. I want to comfort you."

"No thanks, Terrance."

"Ouch. This reminds me of the last time I texted you and you told me we shouldn't go out anymore because it was a conflict."

"*Oh*. So you got that text? You sure didn't respond."

His hand went to his chest. "I was hurt."

"Boy, do you hurt easily." I laughed. Terrance had to, too. This was bull and he knew it. And I wouldn't keep playing these games. I was ready for him to leave. I had other things to do before calling it a day. "I think you should leave before you get hurt again."

Terrance's eyes moved around the kitchen and into the family room.

"You know I was going to buy this?"

"Oh, yeah?"

He stood. "Yeah. But I didn't like the idea of living in someone else's dream home."

"Someone else?"

"Amare didn't tell you? He bought this house from Kyle Jameson, a *King*. They didn't want it anymore. You know this was their vacation home? Something modest. Their main residence would swallow this." His eyes continued to dance around. "But I see it's been painted." He shrugged.

My eyes went to the stark clean walls then down to the floors.

"And the floors were all done. Wood buffed and the carpets are all brand new." I knew this from documents left behind by the contractors. They were dated a week before I moved in. This place was purchased with intent. *More intent than my baby.* "Feels new to me." I shrugged cheerily. "C'mon. I'll walk you out."

I turned to leave, but before I hit the doorway, I peered behind me to see Terrance walking with his face toward the floor, shaking his head while chuckling. He got the memo. I wasn't interested.

"Thanks for coming out today, Terrance." He didn't stop once he passed over the doorframe. Terrance simply waved. "Get home safely," I called after him before closing the door.

Impatiently, I waited for him to pull out of the driveway then set the alarm. Next, I went around to each door of the house to be sure it was locked. I couldn't move fast enough. Finally, I trekked up the stairs to search for my phone. I needed to text Rut and say thanks. There were a few other things I needed to say and couldn't delay. But I had to get to my phone first.

The last I recalled, Rut had taken my purse up to my *ro*—

My belly filled with butterflies when I pushed open the door and saw long legs stretched across the bed. The sight of him reminded me of his grueling schedule. Rut had a game here at home yesterday and was still able to arrange this repass without me knowing. His shower shoes dangled from his feet as he lay on his back fast asleep. At first, I just gaped at him, observed his reposed state. I observed how one leg of his shorts was pushed up his hulking thigh. The hem of his T-shirt lay above his hairy, bubbled abs. My hands squeezed tightly into fists at the sight of his parted lips.

This was going to be difficult but had to be done. I just didn't know how. Forgiveness hadn't been a big deal to me; going back on my word always had. When Rut left me that night after finding out I was pregnant, I warned him not to go because I knew Parker. I didn't do re-entry into my heart very well. It had taken almost six years for me to let go of my issues with my own mother.

This was hard, so I decided to prolong it by showering. That could help fortify my courage. I turned for the closet and unzipped my dress to peel it from my frame. My bra and panties followed then I toed to the bathroom and into the shower.

By the time I was done, I felt less exhausted and apprehensive about what needed to be done. I tossed on a robe and went back out into the mostly empty room. As I drew closer to him on the bed, my body began to vibrate.

Soft nudges turning into heavy tugging had me shifting.

"Hey..."

That voice made my eyes flicker open. Then I felt the warmth of her touch on my thigh. My back swung up from the bed and I rubbed my eyes.

"Oh, damn. What time is it?"

"Close to nine."

I was tired as fuck. What was supposed to be me just closing my eyes for a few minutes until the end of the balloon-thingy turned in to me knocking the hell out.

I yawned. "Everything good down there?"

"Yup." I could still sense her standing over me so I didn't stand. "Everyone's gone. I didn't know you were here. I thought you checked out after bringing my things up here."

"I wanted to wait for them to leave before I snuck out. Didn't wanna look like an ass, dipping out during the ceremony." I finally dropped my hands from my face and took a deep breath. That's when I saw she was standing so close and with a robe on. Her hair was in one of those ponytails on top of her head and she folded her arms over her belly. A belly that I could finally see. My eyes swung back up to her face. "I'mma get outta here. Surprised Fats ain't hit me yet."

For a while, Parker ain't say shit. She just looked at me with a wrinkle between her eyes. Something was wrong.

"I owe you an apology." Parker took a deep breath and I could see her hands balled into fists under her crossed arms. And since when did an apology include squinting eyes? I couldn't front, she looked mad intimidating standing over me. "I've been cold to you these past few weeks."

She damn sure had, but I pretty much deserved it. Like she said, I was immature.

"You've been trying by calling me every day and making up excuses to stop by between your games." She rolled her eyes. "You even had Fats bring me here, to a place you bought with me in mind before we learned about the pregnancy. And today—" Her eyes squeezed and she began to cry, something I'd been seeing a lot of lately. The very thing that fucked up my soul when I had to watch and couldn't do anything about. Her body vibrated as she cried silently. "It's not that I miss him. I just... I started to care for the man while helping him out."

"It's okay to miss him, Park." I couldn't believe my words, but they made sense to me. "You lived with the man...gave him your all for years. You can miss him, baby." My hand made its way to her hip.

I gave her some time to calm herself. The tears stopped at one point, and her eyes went to the side of the room. She covered her mouth with her fist.

"My life was flipped upside down in one night it seems." She snorted. "I think it was shaken up a bit the night of Eli's party when I went home with a strange guy." Her face fell into her palms and she half laughed and half cried. "I had no idea what I was doing. I hadn't been so attracted to a man in years. And God, I thought you were so fine."

I smiled, wanting to say it wasn't just her opinion. What she saw was pure fact. But that would've probably earned me a slap.

Her head lifted, but Parker wouldn't look at me. "You were like a magnet. And then you kept coming by. And that's when I realized how lonely I was. I discovered you were an asshole, but you gave me so much energy...and inspiration." Another tear dropped while she was looking away. "You gave me so much life, I couldn't stop inviting you in. You were my 'me time.' Something to look forward to after I was done with my obligations for the day. I think I know what single mothers who are lonely experience. They work hard to take care of their children. But once the kids are tucked away, the house is shut down for the day, and the sun is sleeping, they need something for themselves. Companionship."

Parker turned to me and shook her head softly. "You were my companion. My retreat. My light when the sun went down. Yes, I've always wanted to be a mother, but I swear, Rut, I didn't mean to trap you. I *was* a taker, though. Just like every other woman you've come across in your life; I wanted something from you. But it was just your time, that's all. Eventually, I got exposure to your heart and learned who the real Rutledge Kadar Amare is. And then when I got that, I wanted more. I wanted your body. And..." Again, her head shook. "I'm sorry for being so mean. I'm sorry for dismissing you."

When the tears fell again, I stood to hug her. But then Parker pushed me away and I landed back on the bed. Before I could catch myself, she was breathing hard in my face. Her hot lips were on mine and her tears transferred to my face. She kissed me softly, pecking my lips. My eyes closed when her mouth opened. I received her tongue with a pounding chest. I couldn't tell you how my body got nervous this close to a woman's, but I knew it never happened before Parker Grayson.

As her tongue moved in my mouth, I felt intimidated. She was emotional and aggressive. That was some boss shit. That was Parker; a grown ass woman. When she leaned more into me, my shaking arm reached up and I grabbed the back of her head. Parker shifted closer and put one knee on the mattress. She pushed into me while twirling her tongue against mine, and before I knew it, she was straddling me.

Her hands were on my head, gripping my cheeks like I was precious to her. I roped her at the ass with my arm and pulled her into me. I could feel she was naked under her robe. That realization made my dick so hard and hot from all the blood rushing to it. I hadn't had a sniff of ass in over a month. I thought the month and a half I struggled through before her birthday was me growing the hell up. *This drought was a bitch.*

But is it what she wants?

Parker's ass twerking on my lap should have been the answer. Then her hands shot from my face and she whispered hard in my ear.

"I swear, I didn't plan this either," she panted loudly. "But it's been over four weeks for me."

She shimmied over me, making me open my eyes. I peeped her pulling her robe from her shoulders. When her arms were out, it slipped down to my knees. Parker was dead-the-fuck naked on top of me. I was just about to lean back a little to see her body until she pulled me back to her mouth. Then her hands went to my waist and her little ass scooted back on my legs to yank my shorts down. I lifted up enough so she could get them past my ass. The moment I sat back on the bed, Parker was shuffling closer.

Her hand went to my cock, stroking it between her pussy, belly, and hand. My eyes rolled to the back of my head, tongue laid in her mouth paralyzed from her massage. And Parker was fucking wet. My fucking word, her pussy was hot and slimy against me. I wanted in.

Shit...

I had no damn capes. But did pregnant people need one?

I tried talking around her busy lips. "You need a condo—"

"No!"

She lifted, grabbing my shaft from behind her. My arms went behind me to lean back while she handled her business. She danced on the head of me, trying to work me in. Her hands gripped my shoulder and head tossed back. My attention went to her face. It was tight as she bit her lip. Her body trembled, trying to sink down on me. Parker was wet, but fucking tight, too. She wasn't even halfway down my rod.

But her pussy moved over me, sponging me. I couldn't touch her, couldn't help because I didn't want to hurt her. Then her eyes blinked open and face relaxed. She moved faster, plunged harder. Parker grunted and her eyes rolled back before closing. I couldn't believe she was coming with just half my dick.

She moaned as she slammed into me, one hand leaving my shoulder and pressed down her chest, between her tits, and down. Her belly.

Oh, shit! Her belly...

It was there. It wasn't as big as I thought, but *that* definitely wasn't here the last time I had been. I started rocking with her, my shocked eyes going back up to her face. But her tits. They were bigger. I could see the veins of them through her skin. Her areoles were bigger...darker around her swollen nipples.

What. The. Fuck...

Her body was different. It even felt different.

My fuckin god...

My head fell back when I realized I was fucking a real ass, whole ass woman and not just a friend. That intimidation shit had heat flash in my sacs, pushing all sensation in that general area, and I bucked into her, taking from her like a damn well of life.

Fuck...

I'd gotten myself in some shit with this one...

Parker

"Graaaaar!" I roared, slamming my palms on the small folding table. "This my table! I'm the queen. You ain't heard about me, have you?"

"I guess I ain't," Marques, Rut's god-brother—his father's godson—chuckled sheepishly while scratching under his chin, admitted.

Blue Magic's "Sideshow" floated across the yard, bringing the best memories. My grandfather, a devout church goer, loved his gospel and seventies tunes equally. This was a nostalgic victory. I slapped the tabletop again, feeling the welcomed September breeze through my hair. "Parker G, baby. It's Parker G." I turned around in the yard and shouted, "Who's next?"

A few people around laughed. I was in Paula's back yard in Ewing, New Jersey. Finally, the day had come for Rut's college graduation and draft celebration party. It was also Kadar Amare's welcome home. I finally had the pleasure of meeting Rut's father, Kadar. He was... completely different from Rut. We met almost as soon as Rut and I arrived. He wasn't as tall as Rut. Neither was he as broad, but on the rare instance when he grinned, I saw "arrogant Rut" who charmed me panty-less. But Kadar didn't. Kadar pored over me, scrutinizing wordlessly.

Apparently, Kadar went to the *Kings* vs. *Giants* game last week, which was the day after his release. It was also the day before Jimmy's funeral. Kadar was sure to ask me why was I not in attendance. Befuddled, before I could pull a clean response from my head, Rut answered for me saying I was sick. That lie left me half grateful, half angry. I moved past it and gravitated to something familiar: kicking butt in *Connect Four*.

Today was more packed than it was for B-Rocka's repass. So many came out to celebrate Kadar's long-awaited release. There were people here of all ages but more older than younger compared to B-Rocka's repass. It was clear to me Kadar was a popular and connected man before his incarceration. So many of the older heads *looked* illicit and tenured on that side of the tracks.

But I was fine. Once I sat down for the first game, my attention narrowed.

"Parker G, huhn?" an older man, clutching a can of *Budweiser* asked.

I didn't see him coming but rebounded well. "The one and only!" I winked.

He wore an oversized white T-shirt and a scroungy military green cap. His eyes were yellow and glossy.

"Let's see what you working with, shawtie."

"What's your name and who are you to the gentlemen being celebrated?" I asked as I gathered the black pieces.

"I'm Uncle Tone-Tone." He chuckled. "Me and Reggie go way back."

My brows furrowed. "Who?"

He slapped his forehead, nearly knocking the hat from his head. "Damn," he swore underneath his breath. "Kadar, I meant. I went to school with that muthafucka."

"Oh..."

So that's Kadar's birth name.

I rubbed my hands together devilishly and the game commenced. Uncle Tone-Tone gathered the reds and I let him go first. Not even five minutes into it, I realized he was a great observer, mimicker. Uncle Tone-Tone saw I played the center and tried his hand there, too. The center was a great strategy but another was thinking ahead. I was always two steps ahead, which is how I won. I beat the poor man seconds before he realized the game was over.

I didn't realize we'd gathered a small crowd until they reacted to it. Even Paula, Rut's mother, was standing over the table cheering me on.

"That's right!" she yelled, holding her *Corona*. "That's my baby's special friend. Hahn!" she stuck her tongue wider than what should have been legal for a woman her age.

I was tickled by it and pumped my fists in the air. In my pompous act, I caught Rut's eyes on me. He, too, was drinking a *Corona* with a wedge of lime in the bottle. But Rut wasn't smiling. In fact, to say he was being celebrated, Rut's disposition was off today. If he hadn't stayed over at the house last night and rolled over to my back, taking me from the side, I would have been concerned. So, I ignored it.

"Auntie Paula," some young girl I couldn't see behind me yelled. "Uncle Kadar said he hungry. It's time to serve the food."

"Oh, shit!" Paula chirped over my shoulder. "Lemme go get this shit poppin'."

"I'll help," I offered, standing from my seat. I could feel my lower back stiffening from sitting too long.

"Aw, c'mon! I can't get a rematch?" Uncle Tone Tone trilled, feigning distraught.

"Sorry, Unc." I giggled. "Duty calls."

"You sure?" Paula asked with a low pitch and concerned expression.

I smiled. "Yeah, girl. I need to stand for a while."

She rolled her eyes. It made me wonder if Paula knew I was expecting. I'd been in touch with her over the months about today. She asked me to make a few things and to have Rut pay for it. Of course, I made what she requested and more without consulting her son on any of it. What I didn't understand was why didn't Paula have this event catered or at a hall. What was being celebrated—for Rut—was monumental. Why do a potluck in her back yard? But then I remembered where Paula and her family were from. Having this here in Ewing was likely as high class as some could imagine.

I followed her into the house.

"Ma!" Paula called out the moment we stepped inside the kitchen. "Kadar's ready to eat. Let's pull back the foil and serve these people."

"Can you tell me where the bathroom is?" I asked. "I'll be ready as soon as I'm done."

"It's over there, baby." Paula pointed to the same small hallway where Rut's basement bedroom was.

On my way to the door she referenced, I was met with a pair of familiar eyes on a less known face. Kadar was coming up from the basement with a few people following him. He nodded but didn't smile like I did when I cut past him for the bathroom. The man either saw what he liked or didn't like me at all. I brushed it off and went into the bathroom to relieve myself.

Over an hour later, we were serving the last of the long line in the dining room. My neck throbbed and back felt no better. When I scooped and dumped the last of the macaroni salad into a young girl's plate, I tossed the spoon in the empty aluminum pan and rolled my head over my shoulders with closed eyes. I took a few deep breaths as I did it, trying to loosen up.

My eyes opened to Kadar, standing at the opening of the dining room table, gaping at me. That's when I knew he wasn't attracted to me. The man just had a bone to pick. I smiled and stole my regard away.

"Rut ain't eat," he barked into the room.

"Why he ain't eat?" his grandmother, Annalise, chirped.

"I guess ain't nobody fixed the god's food." Kadar's eyes were stapled to me.

"Ain't hardly none left." Annalise observed the table.

"I got mad shit in the fridge." Paula noted. "I'll fix him something."

"Actually, I'll do it," I asserted.

"You sure? You ain't eat ya'self."

That's because I wasn't hungry. And I preferred fixing Rut's plate because he was at the start of the season and on a strict diet. I could spruce up his plate with a carb and fat or two but nothing near what his mother would do.

I went into the kitchen, found the stashed food, and was able to build him a healthy plate. By the time I went outside, it felt hotter than it was earlier. I stopped by the coolers and pulled him out a bottle of water, seeing he'd already had alcohol. Then I located him near the gate, sitting with a gang of people around him. Kadar was there, seeming to be holding court. As I approached, I noted Rut didn't speak or laugh at all.

"Hungry?" was how I introduced my presence to him.

Rut looked up at me and took the plate and water. With my hands empty, I decided to massage my neck, the cold hand thanks to the water felt amazing.

"You good?" I opened my eyes to find Rut's on me.

I took a deep breath and nodded, suddenly feeling sleepy.

"You eat something?" he murmured as the group continued in their talks. I shook my head, answering him as his eyes rolled down to my heeled feet. "You bring a sandwich? Chips?"

Again, I shook my head, partially annoyed from Rut thinking I'd do that again after seeing his mother kept a clean home. And partially from Kadar, clearly eavesdropping on our conversation. He didn't hide his concentration on our exchange though his son was speaking in a low tone for privacy.

He lay his plate on his lap and grabbed the back of my feet resting over a block heel. *God, his touch*, even in this heat, was heavenly. "You should probably take these shits off. You want me to get you a chair?"

Kadar's eyes were on me again.

I glanced down to Rut. "No. I'm fine."

"Aye!" I turned to see Uncle Tone Tone upon me, swaying while holding a small bottle of *Remy Martin*. "You ready for that rematch, Parker G?"

"She good, Tone!" Rut grated with short patience.

It made me feel uneasy. I could only offer Uncle Tone-Tone an apologetic smile. But his attention was elsewhere, on the opposite side of me. There was rumbling of surprised greetings.

"Aye!" a few people trilled at the incoming guests.

So many unfamiliar faces until my eyes settled on one I'd seen before. As one began a round of handshakes and manly dabs, working his way around the area near the gate, it dawned on me why I didn't recognize him right away. He wasn't clothed in an expensive, Italian three-piece suit. His wardrobe was far more relaxed in *Jordan* sneakers, long cargo shorts, a Notorious B.I.G. T-shirt, and a *Kings* baseball cap. His posture was much more relaxed than what I'd seen of him in the front office. Azmir Jacobs appeared to be ten years younger than what I'd known of him.

What was a supposed billionaire doing at a backyard party in nowhere, New Jersey?

Azmir stopped and gave special time to Kadar. The two hugged with both arms. Kardar buried his face into the taller man's shoulder, clearly emotional. Azmir spoke something over his head, much of which I couldn't make out.

"I told you thirty years ago, if you rocked with me..." Azmir murmured. Kadar nodded. "And you did. Now you're home to ya own house. Your family's blessed because of you, king..." I couldn't make out much more.

It was ceremonious. People all around cheered, awwww'd, recorded, and clicked away from their phones. I glanced down to Rut's empty chair finding his food and water on the seat. He stood, greeting one of the men flanking behind Azmir.

Paula charged through crying. By the time she made it to the men, they'd broken apart. Kadar's face wasn't wet, but his eyes were red. Azmir's expression was less emotional but light. She greeted Azmir with great reference before she took to Kadar's side.

Azmir Jacobs peered into the gathered crowd and shouted, "The king's back home, and we got a *King* at home. Salute!" he barked the last word.

The crowd shouted the salutation back and more. It was clearly a joyous occasion for this family.

I froze next to Rut when it hit me.

"*Those numbers he put up there were unparalleled. You heard the echoes of his abilities. He broke records in the drills. I believe Rut would be a great fit for the team.*"

"*Yeah. But a pain in the ass for my brand.*"

"*Not on my watch.*"

"*Yeah. Let's hope so.*"

"*I can guarantee it.*"

"*How so?*"

"*You know I'm familiar with his family.*"

"*He's a grown ass man.*"

"*He's an unbridled talent. You've dealt with those before.*"

Rut! He was the "Rut" Eli and Azmir Jacobs were discussing back in April. I swear, I didn't pay much attention to private conversations in Eli's office; I'd served during so many. The name was so informal and unflattering it hadn't dawned on me that I'd met a Rut—*that* Rut—the next month!

"Parker," Paula's raspy voice called over to me. She waved me toward her. "Come help me clean this shit up in the house."

Immediately, I ambled over to her. She looked down at my feet while drying her eyes as we walked toward the house.

"You still got them shits on," her vocabulary not much graduated from her son's. Then Paula grew closer, and her voice went lower. "I could have my nephew run over to the dollar store to get you some flipflops. Just tell Rut you need twenty dollars."

"For the dollar store?" I sputtered, trying to hold my full laughter.

"You just can't say where," she murmured.

I shook my head, chuckling. "I'm fine, Paula. I have flats in his truck."

We made it inside and Annalise sat at the kitchen table, playing cards with an older woman and younger guy. She smiled my way before sipping from her red *Solo* cup. My mind so cluttered with questions, I headed straight to the dining room to start cleaning. Paula and I worked together to get her kitchen and dining room cleared of food, plates, cups, and pans.

Later, I stepped outside with a cup of ice water. With one hand on my neck and the other holding my cup, I looked for Rut.

"Gray!" I heard him call, and when I glanced around, I saw Rut nearing me.

He walked deliciously close, towering over me. The muscles of his eyes were relaxed, totally unlike earlier. Maybe he'd had another drink and that helped loosen him up.

"Hey," I breathed, taking in his cologne mixed with perspiration.

"Always gotta play tough girl," he hummed.

"How'd you figure?"

Rut's hand went behind my back and he yanked a few strands of my hair back, causing me to wince. "You still in those heels after all these hours."

"I made Rayna take them shits off with the twins," another sultry baritone voice offered, walking up behind me. It was Azmir, eating from a plate of garden salad, similar to the one I'd made for Rut earlier. "Hey, Parker," he half sang, expressing familiarity.

My brain stammered. I didn't know whether to be turned on by the melodic bass of his vocals and undeniable good looks, or to be shocked he knew my name. Then when Rut's chin landed on the crown of my head, I could think clearly.

"Hi," I squeaked, teased by Rut's touch and scent all around me. "Nice to meet—" I got stuck again and blushed in embarrassment as he chewed his food. "I'm sorry. We haven't been formally introduced."

"That's because Rutledge here's been keeping you his little love secret." His eyes were to his plate, forking vegetables.

"Quit," Rut growled lowly over my head.

Just as Azmir had been unperturbed with his friend Eli's upbraids, his reaction to Rut's nastiness was a mild chuckle. "You still have more manners than that, duke."

"Park, this is *Div*—Azmir Divine Jacobs," he corrected himself.

"I think I knew that," I spoke to Rut, unable to meet Azmir's regard. In so many ways, I was daunted. I had an idea of what the man grossed. "I didn't know you two knew each other."

Rut kissed my cheek from behind, and whispered in my ear, "He and my pops were good...friends back in the day."

That statement seemed cryptic. Azmir's attention was still on his plate when I found the courage to look at him again. Azmir...good friends with a convicted drug dealer from Trenton, New Jersey? It made me think about the documentary the blogs had been abuzz about since the spring. The documentary that was recanted by midsummer. It was a laughable accusation: Azmir was friends with Eli Richardson, a legitimate businessman.

My eyes bounced around his attire, his b-boy stance. The men standing around him, trying to appear casual, but were clearly standing guard.

"*When I was nine, my pops got fifteen years Fed time for trafficking and distributing heroine. He don't know I know what I'm about to tell you. My moms don't even know I know, but I do. He worked for one of the biggest drug lords at the time. Dude came up in Brooklyn and worked his way to Chicago then Cali. My pops was one of his soldiers for years. He started out with dude and worked his way up to top dog in Trenton. Pops was making low-level millions.*

"*He got knocked. The Feds started down the chain in Trenton and worked their way up. When pop-dukes got his sentence, he made some kind of deal with the man at the top of the organization. Because they went way back, he asked the dude to look out for me. I wasn't there for the conversation, but between the two of them over the years, pouring this 'pact' down my throat, I get the 'General' was supposed to keep me outta the streets.*"

That documentary held a bit of truth to it. *Azmir Jacobs is the General*. He was a drug lord.

Suddenly, I felt winded. My hand went to my chest.

"You okay, Gray?" Rut's hold on me tightened.

My eyes closed and I licked my lips, fortifying myself.

"Yeah," I tweeted, anxiousness settling over me.

"Maybe it's the pregnancy," Azmir droned. "You're in your second trimester. Right?"

My eyes bulged and I snapped my neck to peer up at Rut. His expression was deadpan.

"You told him?"

Rut didn't answer, just gazed into my eyes. I'd never asked Rut who he told about the pregnancy, recognizing he was coming to terms with it himself while acclimating to the *League*. He also had the Emily Erceg obligation. And on top of that, his father had been released from prison—all in the same timeframe. It was a hard pill for the "prince of Trenton" to swallow: I got that. At this point, he didn't owe me much more than he had been giving.

Since the night of Jimmy's funeral, he'd been over a lot and had been asking questions about the baby's development, and if I stayed at the house, which room would be the nursery. He'd even texted me pictures of nurseries he liked. He'd been showing improvement and I wouldn't push him.

Azmir chuckled. "He better had told me or I'd've bust his ass."

Rut rolled his eyes, just as unperturbed as Azmir was with his disposition. These two were very much acquainted. It had all begun to make sense, this strange, cinematographic alliance. Still, I couldn't shake the feeling of anxiousness. Something felt awfully dangerous, and not in the hood element manner. I was from Waterbury, Connecticut. My mother may have raised me above my class, but we were in the same environment as everyone else there. This was something else entirely.

"How's he been treating you? First time pregnancies can be rough for both mother and fath—"

"So that's what we doin'?" Kadar rounded Azmir.

I didn't even see him coming.

Azmir didn't speak at first, perceptively catching the bite in Kadar's tone. It was confirmed by the glare etched into his hard face.

"Pops—" Rut tried.

Kadar's head whipped around to him. "I *knew* she was pregnant! Have you lost your fuckin' mind?" He paused as though he wanted an answer. "You wait to get to the *League* to get reckless and knock some broad up, Rut?"

"Kadar," Paula appeared, plunging herself between Kadar and me, as Rut had been behind me. "We gonna be grandparents; it's a blessing!" she pleaded with him.

"You knew, too?" Kadar's eyes grew wide as saucers. Ignoring Paula, he glowered over to Azmir with betrayal in his eyes before turning back to Rut. "You tell Divine and you ain't even tell me? So I look like a joke to you now?"

"Yo, Kadar," Azmir took him gently at the arm. "Chill. Your tone ain't necessary. It probably wasn't something he wanted to hit you with so soon."

"Don't fuckin' tell me to chill, man. Yo, Divine, this my fuckin' seed! I'm home now. You ain't got to speak for this clown."

"Clown?" Rut barked.

"Yeah. You let some experienced puss get ya damn head open the minute you sign a deal. I ain't never heard her name or no other female's name come from ya mouth. But all of a sudden, you get that first whack ass endorsement, you got a baby on the way?"

"Kadar," Azmir snorted, but I caught the authoritative ring in his tenor. "Easy. You talking to a grown ass man, not a nine-year-old kid. You don't know shit about their circumstances."

"Yo!" Kadar shouted so hard my ears stung. Around us, I could see a crowd drawing. "Divine, step the fuck off. This here between me and *my* son. You don't need to get involved in this. You been too involved. You probably the reason he on this sucka shit: not being the first draft pick, signing to fluke ass *Kings*, being the token nigga who signed to *Asé Garb*! You ain't see TB, The Flash or...StentRo fuckin' signing to a deal with them!"

Azmir raised his free hand in the air. "Cut every phone and camera out here!" One of his guys grabbed the plate from his hand. "If I see a second of this shit on the Innanet ever, you won't have a restful night until you see me," his voice dripped with viciousness to the guests.

"Oh, shit!" Paula cried out in a panic.

Azmir finally settled his eyes on Kadar, who in response, widened his stance.

"Fuck you 'bout to do?" Kadar challenged him.

People began to scatter all around, taking off for safety.

"Oh, shit!" Paula groaned this time. "Stop, Kadar! You just got home!"

There were several people who hadn't run for cover, still around echoing that same sentiment.

"Don't do it, Amare," Azmir warned.

His guys stepped closer to him. And in direct response, two men behind Kadar shifted to his side. One kicked out a blade with the flick of his wrist. My bladder nearly failed me when guns were drawn and cocked. The one most visible was Uncle Tone-Tone, striding out in front Azmir, pointing his pistol directly to Kadar.

My body was tossed defensively behind Rut's big frame. I peered around him, stunned into silence.

Divine shook his head. His eyes shooting bullets into my pops.

"We really about to do this? For what, Kadar?" He cocked his head to the side. "Haven't I held up my end of the bargain?"

"Seem to me you done a lil' too much, god."

"Too much? Like sticking by your only child, making sure *your* dreams came true?"

"I ain't ask you to do all that. That was your own 'better than everybody else' selfish way of doing shit. You ain't man enough to stand next to me. You ain't god-body. You ain't even worthy enough to call Allah the one and only messiah. You bow down to a blond-hair, blue-eyed devil. How the fuck you gone lead my family when you don't know who you are? Where you at, black man?" Kadar taunted. "*Asé Garb*'s black owned. So fuckin' what. My son bigger than that. He could go bigger than wearing a shoe for another man."

Whoa...

"Because Rut is *designing* a shoe. An un-fuckin'-precedented move in the history of their company. And they're paying him a shit load of guap to do it. Now, let me educate your ignorant ass on some other shit. That deal was made by his sports agency. Rut's engaged and particular about the brand he's building. He's the one who opted for the design deal and not just the traditional '*I'll wear your clothes for a few bucks*' which were the deals those other cats you just name did. My guy is an astute businessman in his own right."

He inched closer to Kadar and so did the men behind him. Divine raised his hand again. "Stand down."

And I let out a long quiet breath when the guns were dropped. Tone was the last to do it, and I would bet his pulling out on my pops was the biggest slap in the face. It reminded him of Divine's power. Tone and my father knew each other as kids. They didn't meet Divine until they were grown ass men.

But Tone dropped his pistol, and I was happy. I couldn't believe this shit was going down in front of Parker. I couldn't fuck with my father anymore. This solidified it.

"And as far as my beliefs go: my choices ain't got shit to do with me fulfilling my obligations to you and your family. For the record, I don't bow down to no man, especially none with those features. If you think that's what the Messiah looks like, you ain't been up on ya reading and can't call me out on shit. Rut is his own man. I haven't tried to convert him. That's not my role. He's what you made him."

"I'm what I've made me," I had to make clear. My pops' eyes were hard on me. And it hit me in that moment: he was just another man. He wasn't bigger, stronger, and obviously not wiser. He looked... angry. Mad. Just like he sounded when we talked on the phone over the years. The past few days I'd been stressing about this day. He'd said some shit after the game two days ago that made me feel he had a chip on his shoulders. He was just an angry man, and by the strains around his eyes, I believed I knew why.

"I get it. You just came home and you're overwhelmed by the success you didn't have a hand in. You did a heavy bid while life went on, on the outside with your input but not your work. Then when little things didn't go your way, you got mad." I snorted. "I got mad respect for you, pops, but this life coach shit gotta stop. I'm good."

This is what my therapist tried to warn me about. My father couldn't grasp my world enough to help guide me through it.

"You good—we good!" I tried to get him to see the big picture. "You're home. You gotta crib that's paid for. You gotta son, who could let you rest easy for the rest of your life. You ain't gotta worry about a job or how you're going to get on your feet. How many of your cellies got shit so sweet set up for them when they were released? You need to just chill. I don't get why you can't see that."

"You damn right, you don't, Rut. You don't get what it's like walking a mile in my shoes. I been up for fifteen fuckin' years! I leave my son out on these streets and have to depend on some other man, who could change like a flip of a coin on me, to raise my only son. You damn right, I'm mad! From a jail cell I had to play co-fuckin'-captain to my only seed. I tried to teach you what I could about the god-body in you since you was a pup. I gave you all I could, not knowing if I was gonna die or catch a long ass sentence. Lucky for me, it was just prison."

"And shit was taken care of. It was handled!" Why couldn't he see that.

"I can't tell. You out here raw-doggin and doing crazy shit! My lil' time with you wasn't enough. All those hours I spent feeding you knowledge and you still on some savage shit." That shit hurt. "I bet you ain't been keeping up with ya *120 Lesson*...ain't been out here building to grow either."

I shook my head, wrapping my arm around Parker's waist so we could go. I was a self-made man with the guidance of Divine. I had nothing to prove to him. "You don't know what I've been doing."

"Then what's today's mathematics?"

I froze. What the fuck was this? He was testing me? Putting me on blast in front everybody. I looked over at Divine who had been watching. Then my eyes went to all the god-bodies around. There were at least fifteen of them—old heads, too. I could just walk away, but it would mean he was right. And pops was wrong as fuck.

"Kadar, this ain't necessary," my mother cut in. "We here to have a good time."

I took a deep breath. This wasn't hard and I'd even do him one better: the month and date. "Born equality."

"Oh. We fancy, huhn? And?" he pushed for more.

This motherfucker...

Fuck it. I could play the game; my name was Rutledge Amare. Nobody pushed me into a fucking corner, and I wouldn't tuck my tail for no man. "Born is to be brought into existence physically, as well as, mentally. Physically through the mother's womb—*like my unborn child*—and mentally through Allah's mathematics."

"Yeah, and Born is going from being a slave of a mental power and death to the light of realization about self, too," he argued. "That only happens through the teachings of a true and living god. Born is also knowledge and understanding being manifested through god's wisdom. It's the completion of all things in existence." He gripped his chin, nodding with sarcasm. "But I'll give you that. Continue."

I shook my head. He wanted war. I'd fuck with him. "Equality is being equal in *all* things in existence like knowledge, wisdom and understanding. It's being equal in *everything*. It's the father's ability to deal equal with the life nourishing. It's truth and righteousness that is the father's teaching. *Equality's* the nature of the black woman."

He backed up and dropped his chin.

Yeah, nigga....

"Because that is her *limitation*. You're twisting it, son! You gotta come again." He laughed. "See, when you share *your* knowledge through wisdom, and bring forth an understanding, it only shows and proves equality. Knowledge, wisdom, and understanding: they're all being born to equality. She *can't* exceed it. She can only be elevated by god—*you*—to her fullest quality. And that happens by her uniting with god—*you*—to bring forth the understanding of the culture which *that* baby is."

He pointed behind me to Parker. That shit pissed me the fuck off. It was time to end this little game. I'd had enough. I pulled Parker into me by the shoulder and turned to walk off.

"Yeah... Just make sure you get right with culture and show the god more gratitude for holding ya angry righteous ass down while your son goes and gets understanding of his own seed."

As I held my new life in one arm, I didn't look back for a response.

"You were right, you know?"

My eyes opened regrettably as I lay in her lap, under a citrusy scent and over the slight aroma of her musk. That and the low vibrations of the truck was pulling me into a sleep.

"Right about what?"

"About his anger. He seems very alpha; alphas like to dominate even with far-reaching arms. It's hard to do that from prison walls. Although I may not agree with a lot of his ideology, it seems he's firm on his vision for you. Right or wrong: you can't knock a father with a vision."

"See what Dr. inga has to say about that."

She giggled over my head. "Lord, if I have a baby shower, I may have to have two. Two christenings, too."

"Two birthday parties...graduation parties and the whole shit."

Her belly shook when she laughed. I was too tired to laugh but enjoyed hers.

"Gray."

"Hmm?"

"I think I wanna know what the baby is."

I could feel her thighs tense under my head.

"You do?" she sounded surprised.

"I do." Then I thought. "Unless you had the ultrasound done already..."

"Not for the sex. I wanted to see if you wanted to..." She hesitated.

"I've been waiting."

Her belly grumbled. My face went hard and eyes went up to her.

"You ain't eat today?"

"You know what I had for breakfast." Parker was stalling the truth.

"What about at the cookout?"

Her attention went out the window or, at least, that's what she wanted me to think. "I didn't have time."

"You had time to kick ass in *Connect Four*, but you couldn't eat?" I sat up to look her dead in the eye. Parker was full of shit. "You know you's a bourgeois ass eater?"

"I'm not."

"Yes the hell you are. You talking about that pastor spoke about bloodline curses." I turned and looked out the other window. "That's one I'mma have to break with my kid. You can't be passing that shit on to it."

Then I felt her hand on mine in the middle seat. Parker's expression was a serious one. "I want to raise my child with Christian values. They were a secondary teaching in my childhood, with my grandparents becoming devote Christians in their latter years. Like your father, I have a vision for my children and their foundation. I choose Christ." I was still stuck on the plural she used. *Children?* "If you want to know the principles of Christianity, my church is hosting a new believers class on October third. It's after your *Titans* game but before the *Vikings*. We could go together."

"You know my schedule?" I smirked.

Her eyes narrowed. "I value your time."

I picked up my phone and went to the calendar app.

"I'll be with Emily that day."

I forgot all about the charity we were hosting together. It was supposed to be a couple's thing where Emily's organization was joining in with mine to do work in Connecticut.

"Okay." Her smile was just as small as her voice.

I reached for her hand and squeezed.

Parker's eyes returned to me. "If that's what you wanna do with the baby, I'm good with it. I trust your judgment, but we'll work out a date for me to check out the class."

Parker didn't smile this time. With a nod of her head, she turned back to the highway.

"Yo, Fats," I called into the front seat. "Let's hit up the first *B-Way Burger* we can when we cross over the state line."

When I thought that would have earned me a real smile, I was wrong. Parker never acknowledged it at all.

chapter twenty-two

"OH! HEY, RUT," INGA STOPPED ON her way out of the dining room as I let myself in through the front door of Parker's place.

I saw she had packing foam, used tape, and brown packing paper balled into her hand as she headed into the kitchen.

"Hey, Dr. inga."

"We bought accessories to decorate this fancy dining room set she bought." She smiled because we'd both been on Parker about getting some furniture in here. I stopped offering when I realized it had offended her. She said it was enough I bought the place: she'd fill it when she was ready. But I had a feeling she meant when she was decided. *On staying*. "Come on back." She continued through the foyer. "Parker's in her lab."

I took off my wet jacket. Just a few days into the fall, the temperature dropped like crazy and brought with it heavy rain today. As I passed through the house, it seemed like every time I came off the road I'd find myself here to relax. I didn't stay every night I was in town, but Parker damn sure saw me more than Sharkie did.

Parker made the wash room that was just off the kitchen her lab. It had a sink installed already and plenty of electrical outlets, making it work for her. The closer I got to the room, the louder the television sounded.

I saw her from the doorway perched on a bar stool at her workstation, watching TV from her laptop. I couldn't believe it was the Wil Cunningham show, the interview I just did with her two days ago. It went live today.

In the inset was a playback of the game that began my killer season. A season that had been bad for Jordan Johnson, which I hated.

Back in September, in a game against the *Colts*, the third down play called for Jordan to run a *Slant Route*. It was a route he had successfully run several times that day. But this time, Trent was under pressure and forced to throw off his back foot, causing the ball to sail. Jordan leaped high to snare it, but the Safety took out his legs and Jordan landed awkwardly on his shoulder. An MRI confirmed everyone's worst fear a repeat rotator cuff tear, which meant he was done for the season.

That shit still fucked with me. Watching the highlights of my time out on the field reminded me of the crazy imbalance of our performances this season.

And now, I was watching Parker watch it.

"*After struggling mightily since the loss of star wide receiver, Flash Johnson, early in the third quarter, the Kings are nearly in field goal range. The Kings have benefited from a couple key catches by rookie standout, Rut Amare. With twelve seconds left on the clock, the Kings have one—maybe two—shots to get into field goal range for a chance to win the game. With no timeouts left, all pass plays must be directed towards the sidelines. As Bailey breaks the huddle, Amare is lined up in the slot to his right. When the ball is snapped, Amare heads up field and breaks for the sideline. Miraculously, the defensive back whiffs at the tackle, and Amare turns it up-field and sprints forty yards for the touchdown to win the game!*"

The playback with the commentary from the game ended, the inset disappeared, and me at the desk with Wil took full screen.

"Big year for you, guy! Big year. It seems like just when the Kings started the season where they needed to prove to the world their winning wasn't a fluke, its franchise wide receiver was injured!" Wil cringed dramatically.

"But they had a ram in the bush, as the church folk would say." She smiled big and bright when she pointed to me. "As we just saw in the replay, you've been out there killing it on the green! That play against the Colts kicked it off. And that's all you needed to plant your feet firm in the League. We're only in October. So tell us... What can we expect from you this season?"

"You can expect me to be Rut: give my all to the game," I answered honestly. "It was a rough start to the season, I know you've heard the rumors with the shake up in the organization. The Kings brought on a new receiver coach to switch up strategy. That took some adjustments and I think we finally got it right. The team has gelled. Coach Brooks, her staff, Underwood—everybody's been working hard. You know... This is a game of momentum. You need those moments of opportunity to execute those great plays. The coaching staff's been preparing us since day one for them."

"And I'm sure bringing Brooks on was a huge part of that. How has she affected your performance?"

I laughed at first, thinking of the hell she put me through to prove her place in the organization. I thought of the full circle experience it had all been.

"She's made me a better player. I'm laughing because of the beating we both took to get me here. Apparently, she won. You know, Cunningham..." I sat up scratching my nose, scramming for the words to articulate myself. "Getting into the League grew me up, if you will. I had my own set of views and goals to perform my best out there amongst your TBs and The Flashes...even your Grants. But what I learned from Coach Brooks was to develop and focus on my own skill set and let them feed off of it."

"And it seems to have worked," Cunningham added.

"That," I laughed again. "and the fact I had a gang of women molding me since getting drafted. My therapist, Coach Brooks, and the mother of my child—"

"Excuse me?" Her mouth hung open.

"Yup. I'm expecting a little girl in February." I couldn't believe I finally put it out there.

"Are you serious?" Cunningham was acting like a girl, which was rare for her on camera.

I guessed being a parent herself had softened her.

"I better be, or her moms gots some explaining to do to my moms, who can't stop buying stuff for her already." Using my money, of course.

"Congratulations!" Cunningham cried, acting like a girl again.

But she could let it slip for this occasion. For my baby girl. It was actually comical.

I knocked on the doorframe. Parker's head whipped around.

"Hey."

"Hey," she whispered then sniffled. Parker wiped her nose. "Thanks for that." She pointed to the laptop.

"For what? Telling the world I'm having a baby?"

Parker took a deep breath, twisting her lips. That confused me. It was clear she was keeping something from me.

"I didn't know you were coming by tonight."

Me either, but she didn't have to say it. Coming here to Parker's place could feel the same as going to see her at Wright's. Only difference was at Wright's, I felt more welcomed.

"Just left a meeting by the stadium and wanted to check in on you."

"*Hotep Financial* is like...an hour away." She smiled. "I don't get the correlation."

"Emily and her people met with me, Elle, and our peoples today."

"About what?"

"About what she told me last night at the fundraiser we did."

Her forehead stretched. "And that is?"

"She's pregnant."

Parker covered her mouth and ran to the sink. I took long lunges inside to get to her. My hands went to her hair I pulled up from her face. After three hurls, she splatted all around the tub.

"Parker!" inga shouted behind us. "Are you okay?"

"She needs some paper towels," I responded.

She turned, taking off for the kitchen. I rubbed Parker's back.

"You good?" I asked.

Breathing hard, she nodded. inga was back with wet paper towels and a dry face towel. I handed the wet ones to Parker and she wiped her mouth. When she was done, she used the hand towel to dry her wet eyes then mouth.

"What happened, Parker?" inga asked the question I had in mind.

Still out of breath, Parker shook her head. "I'm fine. I'm going to go upstairs and wash up."

inga moved out of her way to let her daughter leave the room. I followed on her ass, all the way up to the master suite. Standing in the doorway, I watched Parker brush her teeth, wash her face, and pull her hair into a ponytail on top of her head. When she turned on the shower, I knew she was upset. *With me.*

"Did I say something wrong down there?"

Parker wouldn't even look at me. She started to strip out of her clothes. That sight ripped my body from my mind. Parker was sexy as fuck pregnant. I never thought I'd find pregnancy attractive, but Parker was life with a belly. Maybe it was because I felt a connection to her body in a new way.

"You gone just ignore me?" I asked, mad as hell when she stepped inside the all glass shower.

She turned to me. "No. I'm just thinking."

"About what?"

"About *this* adjustment. They've been coming so fast, I'm trying to keep up."

"What adjustment?"

"I don't know." Tears fell from her eyes. "Are you going to buy her a house, too? I know she can afford her own."

"Who?"

She rolled her eyes. "Emily."

"Why the fuck would I buy her a house?"

"Because of her baby."

"Her baby ain't got shit to do with me. She better work her shit out with Rick." When her mouth dropped, it hit me. "You thought I was sayin—"

Parker covered her face with her hands. Maybe she was embarrassed. She *should* have been embarrassed. That hurt.

"Yo, you think that little of me?"

"No."

"I can't tell. You accusing me of fuckin' Emily Erceg!"

"She's your girlfriend on camera."

"And? She's fuckin' her mother's ex!"

"Crazier things have happened." She gestured to herself. "I'm pregnant by you."

I scoffed. "Because we fuck."

"You fuck, Rut!" she yelled. "You!"

"And what the hell do you do?"

"I connect with one person on a physical level that transcends his level of maturity, clearly!"

That shit hurt, too.

"How did this turn into an 'attack Rut' show?" I pointed behind me. "You were just thanking me downstairs, then you hurl on me, thinking I got Emily, *of all people*, pregnant, and now I'm immature?"

I don't need this shit...

I walked out, closing the door behind me. How far I would go hadn't settled on me yet when I peeped inga in the doorway of the master suite.

"I wasn't eavesdropping but I was," she whispered.

I looked at her like she was an idiot. *Which one was it?*

"She's not saying what she really feels."

"Which is?" I had the damn time.

"Which is she's afraid you're free to be with whomever you want."

"She is, too."

inga shook her head and rolled her eyes. "Go get in there with her, Rut."

What?

"Why?"

"Because she's my daughter and will do this baby thing without you if you don't connect with her on a level she needs."

"And what's that?"

"Security. She needs to feel secure in a relationship with you. But she *will* settle for just sharing a child with you if you don't secure her."

"Why would she do that?"

"Because she thinks she's her mother: an idiot. Parker's way of putting on her big girl panties is accepting whatever you give her so long as you don't mistreat her. Proof of that is her staying here. She has a twenty-thousand-dollar trust left from her grandfather. If Parker wanted to be gone, she'd be gone," she was sure to keep her tone low. "She's here because it connects her to you."

When I didn't move from being on information overload, inga crossed her arms.

"She's not me. She's better. She believes in the romanticized aspect of love. Buried beneath the little inga role she's trying to play, that girl believes in the notion of partnership, commitment, and devotion between lovers." She pushed off the door frame to walk off. "Parker's pregnant and emotional. She won't tell you all of her needs, but you better figure them out and go handle it."

Rolling her eyes, she took for the stairs.

I was two steps behind her, closing the doors to the suite then yanking off my clothes for the shower.

love belvin

Parker

"These dope as hell." Rut stopped in the window of a jewelry store and pointed to a delicate bracelet with a name plate.

I sauntered next to him for a better view. The sterling silver piece had the words "Daddy's Love" engraved in beautiful calligraphy.

"That's adorable," I agreed.

"I wonder if they make that in platinum."

"Why? A baby doesn't need platinum."

Rut looked at me sideways as he held shopping bags in his arms. "Okay. Gold." He paused for a bit, I guessed, thinking I'd have a rebuttal. "I'mma go ask them what metals they make it in."

He sauntered on into the jewelry store, and I pulled my phone from my purse. As expected, I had text messages from Jade.

Jade: *I like the white, yellow, and turquoise ones.*

I rolled my eyes as I typed back.

Me: Of course you do. I only need one. I went with the turquoise one. Rut liked it.

Waiting on her reply, I watched people stroll by in the mall. The *Kings* were playing in a few days in London. Rut invited me along to attend. He and a couple of guys from the team planned to shoot over to France after the game, during their Bye week. Jade would be there, too, and suggested I bring a bathing suit in case we were blessed with warm temperatures while there. The problem was, I didn't have a bikini that fit. I hadn't been swimming in years and had put on a few pounds since. I needed something suitable for my upgraded hips and new belly.

Rut offered to bring me to the mall on his day off today. What was supposed to be a quick run in while I insisted Fats wait in the truck for us, turned out to be a miniature shopping excursion. I bought cute skinny jeans, a thin leather jacket, heeled boots for sight-seeing, and even a scarf to match.

It was actually fun shopping with Rut. He was like the compulsive diva girlfriend, who encouraged imprudent spending. And of course, he offered to buy whenever I dithered on something. I didn't let him spend a dime. I was doing well—not Rutledge Kadar Amare well, but better than I ever have. Not only was I full time in the front office now, but I got a contract with *DiFillippo's* restaurants across the country for a six-month supply of liquid soaps and lotions for their bathrooms. As small of a commitment that may seem, it was a huge task for me. I'd still been working virtually alone. Mandee had come up a few times to help fill that order, and even Jade once. But I hadn't found a commercial kitchen yet.

I shook my head as I leaned with one shoulder against the glass window. My phone chirped in my hand.

Jade: *And what about shoes? I got the cutest pair of Asé Garbs yesterday.*

Me: I just bought the Alexander McQueen booties I was telling you about. They're so much better looking on.

Rut hated them. He even sat with a nasty glower as I tried them on. But he knew not to complain. We'd been...strange. Our friendship had changed in many ways since our days at Jimmy's place. We'd remained lovers and comfortably so after he swore he would sleep with no one else three weeks ago.

After a nasty fight when he was trying to share with me Emily's team's decision for her and Rut to part ways after learning she was pregnant, and I thought he was breaking the news of impregnating her, he set the record straight. While on his knees in the shower, cupping my hips in his hands to feast between my thighs, he swore I'd been the only woman he'd slept with since meeting me—*other than that following weekend when Emily went down on him*. That irked my pregnant nerves for some reason, but he told me he wouldn't change that practice until we changed the rules for our friendship. And that worked for me.

No. I didn't care to rush into anything with Rut after coming out of the most peculiar, convoluted, and draining arrangement with Jimmy. I needed time to rebuild my identity as a real single woman. Yes. It was a humorous concept considering I was pregnant by another man so soon, but I was insistent on taking things one day at a time. And if that meant risking monogamy with Rut, so be it. Though I'd apologized for my response to his reaction of the pregnancy, I would not compromise *Parker* any more than I had with Jimmy. I was almost thirty and couldn't account for my twenties.

Jade: *Those booties are cute! I have to go. The big ogre is going off about the bikini I bought Ava Nese. RME! Can't wait to see you at the airport! I'm glad we can't travel with them to London. We can have our time without the guys.*

I laughed at that, wondering if Rut would be so protective over our little munchkin. My hand went to my belly.

RUT

I could stand there behind her for hours, watching Parker rub her belly. It was the only time I got a glimpse of the "sweet" Parker I met. She'd been lukewarm lately. I figured it was because she wasn't over me being angry about the pregnancy at first. But I'd been working hard to show her I could be better. And it had been hard dealing with that and managing my need of her. Being separated from Parker in training camp was hard for me. I was stressed out about this pregnancy, my pops coming home, Coach Brooks' bossy ass, and adjusting to the demands of being a public figure. I needed her for those weeks. The fucked up part of it was she was a part of one of the problems I needed her for.

Parker was my homie, lover, and friend since I lost B-Rocka. Lately, I'd been feeling like I lost a piece of her, too. I honestly didn't know what to do about it. Maybe it was the pregnancy. I didn't know. I still wanted her around me. When she agreed to come to Europe with me, I was happy as hell. Those premonitions of exploring the globe with her still happened every once in a while, especially when I ate her pussy. It was weird as fuck, but one of the many strange things in my life since I came to Connecticut. And I couldn't wait for our first trip.

I walked up on her and leaned down to her ear. "You should get butt ass naked in bed, and let me do that for you."

Parker didn't jump. She looked up at me and hit me with the

smile I'd seen a lot of lately. The one saying, *"you can do whatever you want to my body, but I won't say it."* It was one of my favorites.

"C'mon." I took her by the hand even though mine held her shopping bags. "Fats is gonna cuss *you* out," I teased.

She laughed as we started hiking it toward the entrance we were dropped off at. I browsed the window displays, looking at nothing in particular. When my attention went ahead, I groaned.

Walking straight toward us with a few of her girls, her eyes blew up before she sneered like an evil witch.

She tapped her girl to the right of her that I recognized right away. First, she whispered then she decided to get loud.

"Oh. That's her, huhn?" She stopped a few feet from us and her girls did, too. "Girl, I 'on't know why you fuck with him. Then again, I do. You snagged that nigga after that first endorsement deal. I ain't mad at you!" Chestnut Cherries, Brandee, and some other chick I didn't know stopped and the first two giggled like hyenas. The other one looked star-struck.

After shoving all of the shopping bags into one hand, I pulled Parker into me, feeling myself about to wig the fuck out.

"Man, don't come over here on no bullshit!"

"What?" Chestnut Cherries, who I couldn't believe would start nonsense, spit.

"Where ya boy at? Maybe he don't stunt like you do," Brandee sneered before her girl could finish her sentence.

Ignoring her, I replied to Chestnut Cherries. "You heard what the fuck I said. You wanna autograph, all you gotta do is ask."

She wanted to get new on me, I knew how to piss broads like this off.

"That'll be more than you ever gave, cheap ass!" Chestnut Cherries looked directly at Parker. "He use other girls to get you off—"

"*And* he don't give you no money!" Brandee shouted over her.

Chestnut Cherries continued while laughing spitefully, "I 'on't know why you let him raw dog you. He's a stingy nigga. Girl, you better lawyer the fuck up!"

That's it...

I tightened my hold on Parker and pulled her around them birds to go.

"Lawyer these nuts, bitc—"

"Aye!" Parker's hand flew to my mouth so fast, she kinda slapped me.

That added to my anger. I balled my lips tight to keep all the words I wanted to shoot at them chicken heads inside.

"Fuck you, Rut!" they began yelling behind us.

"I hope you break a mutherfuckin' leg or arm your next game!"

"Sucka ass!" They wouldn't stop, now drawing attention to us.

"I'm gonna ignore your ass in *Arch & Point* next time, nigga!"

Parker's legs kept up with my lunges until we were at the *Yukon* and I opened the door for her. When she was safely inside, I didn't mean to slam the door so hard. The truck rattled and I went over to the other side.

Damn!

Where's my cousin, Sheema, when I need her ass?

Parker

The entire truck vibrated when he slammed the cargo door, too, after tossing the bags in the trunk. My brows hiked and eyes coincidentally met with Fats from the rearview mirror. Rut threw his lengthy body inside with swift agility. His whole frame was visibly teeming with combustive energy. The man was so mad he couldn't face me.

One thing was for sure: I had never seen as much drama in my life as I did when with Rutledge Amare. Another thing made clear to me, even in the fit of his ire, he was embarrassed. We were out of the parking lot, turning onto the highway and he still hadn't looked my way.

I scooted closer, being sure to lean my breasts into him. I actually found the incident funny.

"Your old *Arch & Point* crew?" I murmured.

Rut didn't answer. My hand pushed onto his thigh and caressed it until going for the band of his sweat shorts. I found his resting member and wrapped my palm around it.

"They don't know you can be generous with the right twerking booty?"

Rut's head turned and his narrowed eyes met mine as I stroked him. I bit my lip from busting out laughing in his face. He was awakening from my efforts.

"You think this funny, Gray? You're pregnant. They coulda stressed you out...hurt the fuckin' baby!" his voice was gravely low.

But his eyes were softening as I shook my head.

"They would've had to upset me to hurt the baby, Rut. Do I look upset." He didn't answer. "Or do I look turned on?" I reached up and kissed his lips, loving the feel of him growing in my hand. "Now, answer me this..." I used the tip of my tongue to trace the seam of his lips. "Am I going to get that belly rub first..." I pecked his lips. "or do I have to earn it with a twerk? Because it looks like you're no longer welcomed in *Arch & Point*."

I coughed a light cackle, pausing my stroke on him.

Rut turned to me, pushing my arm to finish my fondling job and growled, "I'll fuckin' buy *Arch & Point* before that happens."

"Look at her go," Stroy teased Parker as she cleaned her plate.

She smeared the last of the cream of some sweet shit I couldn't pronounce then forked it into her mouth with a satisfied smile. And damn was she beautiful. Parker rocked a silk scarf, wrapped around the crown of her head with a fedora over it. It reminded me of the cutie whose phone I picked up at Eli's party almost six months ago.

"I remember them days," Jade shared. "I was eating my heart's content in my second trimester." Her eyes went into the bright blue air and her hand to her chin, thinking about it. "I just didn't burn off the calories as fast."

"I've already burned a few this morning," Parker's nasty ass smiled, still chewing her food. Her eyes swung over to me. "Oh, and I plan on working more off later," she told the whole damn table throatily.

That had everybody cracking up, loud as hell. It was a good thing we had sidewalk tables at *L'olive*. I tried to give her a nasty eye, but Parker wasn't bothered by it. Then my attention went to the row of houses around. It was a bright ass day in St. Tropez. The temperature was just perfect: not too chilly or hot. The breeze hugged us and the sun was gentle.

Parker's hand at my leg caught my attention. She was wiping her mouth.

"Don't forget the souvenir. There should be some shoppes down there to look in before we go."

Oh...

I glanced down the sidewalk. It was good she reminded me. I actually asked her to not let me forget to pick up something for Coach Brooks while we were out here. Me and the only female coach I ever had in any sport had developed a rhythm. Whenever she complimented me on a game—after tearing into my ass about it a few times

—I'd gift her something. To be real, it wasn't about tit-for-tat for me. I honestly had grown to like the lady. She and my therapist were like aunties, who didn't take my shit but would still remind me of the greatness in me. When I told my head doctor I was coming here after the London game, she told me not to waste my time bringing her back "a wasteful knickknack that would only collect dust." That shit had me dying.

I nodded at Parker to tell her I was ready then pushed back from the table.

"Oh, hold up!" Jordan barked, his one arm in a sling. "Before we move on to our next excursion, we gotta acknowledge the work." His wife, Cole, lifted her glass of sparkling water after he did. "TB, do the honors, preacher man."

We snickered at the table when Trent rolled his eyes. He switched his baby girl, Ava Nese, to the other leg then went for his glass. The group followed suit.

"The Wembley game was a W, but a mere one," he referred to the game yesterday against the *Jaguars* when we won by just three points. I may have been having a killer season, but it had been hot and cold for the *Kings*. "To the game that drives us, inspires us, and blesses us. May we do right by it. Let's evolve, take risks, and continue to change the game!"

"Here! Here!" Stroy shouted.

His two kids cheered, too. Kyrec, TB and Jade's son, hooted then yanked TB's arm to go himself. Cole and Parker stood at the same time. We were hitting the yacht in less than thirty minutes, so we had to shoot off to do whatever little shopping that had to get done before then.

The group broke away and Parker and I headed west and walked in and out of stores, looking for cool souvenirs. Parker was able to find little goodies for our moms, my pops, and Nurse Jackie in the second store.

"Let's go down a little further. The woman at the counter said there are more down there." She pointed down a much narrower road. It wasn't littered with bodies like the current one had been. I didn't like it because of the unevenness of it. It wasn't as flat as the main street. Parker must have seen my unease. She grabbed me at the arm. "Oh, come on, Rut. We don't have much time."

As I always did with Parker, I let her have her way. We started down the road for more stores. There were garbage cans against the brick buildings, no cars, but a stray cat zipped past. Parker didn't seem to care. She kept trekking on, looking into each building we passed.

"How you walk so fast in them shits, yo?" Already, I was annoyed.

Totally ignoring me, Parker slowed a little. Her eyes blinked and her hands flew to her face. "I forgot to ask the hotel to bring up the foot bowl to soak your feet tonight. Your trainer said every night until you get back."

"We'll handle it," I muttered then took her hand, wondering how she could think of something so random while walking down this glossy ass road.

Her body swung toward me a bit and she took a deep breath, scaring the shit out of me. "You should get Coach Brooks one of the string, banded bracelets with the metal plates on it. The one at that first shoppe had the nameplates that said *courage, dignity, hope,* and *power*." She smiled from ear to ear. "That's so her. Right?"

"Stop."

I dropped to one knee before she caught my command. Then I pulled her back to me by her calf, my eyes locked on the fancy bootie things she bought at the mall last week.

I heard her breathy giggle over my head. "What are you doing?"

I didn't answer, just went about the job of fixing the buckle of one of her high heeled boots. And by fixing, I mean making sure they were tight enough. Maybe that would make sure she didn't fall.

"This is beautiful, isn't it?" her voice was low, dreamy.

I didn't answer, but she knew what I'd felt. This was more than beautiful, and it wasn't because of where we were for me. It was because of the peace I felt having her with me. For real.

"First London, now St. Tropez. I can't believe we're in France—"

I popped up from my knee, squaring in her face when she froze. Then she took a deep breath and a step back like something had occurred to her.

"What's up?"

"You love me."

Whoa!

Her eyes bounced around and now she looked angry. Then she closed them tight and shook her head.

I stepped closer, worried. "What's wrong?"

She kept shaking her head. "That look in your eyes... I've seen just about all of your expressions, and maybe because we're in a new place, the revelation just hit me hard. It's not about the shoe. The house you bought me..." She pinched her nose. "It wasn't about the baby, I knew that. You bought it before we found out. But I never understood why until you looked at me. And it's not with anger from the stupid heeled bootie. It's because you have deep feelings for me. It's love, Rut."

My mouth moved as if to speak, but she raised her hand to stop me.

"That's the problem. You've never expressed what you felt about me—and I was okay with that. I didn't force you or have that expectation because you were twenty-four and wild. There was no way I expected you to acknowledge those feelings or act on them at your age or with your lifestyle." She licked her lips, looking away.

"I'mma grown ass man, Parker. I ain't never have a problem expressing my feelings." I put my hands in my pocket, switching the weight to my other leg. "Can't lie, though. It ain't been easy doing it since you moved out to the house. You've been different, Gray."

Damn, that was hard to say. It sounded like a bitch statement, but it felt good as hell to finally tell her.

Parker nodded, admitting to it.

"I fell in love with you." I almost choked on my spit. Parker nodded, making her words clear. "At Jimmy's, we were on a freefall." She shook her head, those long dark lashes meeting. "Getting to know the other person—consuming each other—exploring each other's opposing views without care." She squinted looking up at me. "Now, I'm afraid of falling any deeper. We've been so powerful together, we made a baby before we had sex." She chuckled to herself. "Imagine what more we can do if we just let go. I'm not sure you can handle that."

I took her at the shoulders and grabbed her into my chest. Her arms felt good on my back, gripping me. I whispered over her head, "My therapist lady told me I only chose chicks who were of a certain class because it's what I knew and was used to. It's been hard being with a woman who's wiser and more mature." My eyes rolled closed, hard to speak these words of truth.

"If I could go back to July twenty-fourth when we left the Brielle show, I would. I would be real with you and tell you I was scared. No, I ain't wanna be a father, and at that point in my life, I only wanted you. Nothing or nobody else. Then I would've held you tight and told you we'd get through it together, no matter how we sliced it. And then I would've taken the next few days to realize, because of what you were carrying in your belly, it meant I *have* more of you."

I could feel her shaking in my arms. "I'm sorry, Park. Sorry you fell in love with a man who's had a late start in learning how to handle your heart." My belly jumped and I skipped a damn breath when sharing, "But on everything I own, everything I'll ever be, I got you from here." I cleared my throat and vowed, "I'mma be that eligible receiver."

epilogue

Grayson Brianna Amare

February 20, 2019: 5:26 AM

7lbs. 6oz.
17.5 in.

Love's Ineligible Receiver

I LET US INTO THE HOUSE, SHARKIE'S PAWS TAPPING AT THE floor.

"Yurp!" I call out to his happy ass. He stops and turns to me. "Chill. A'ight!" I grumble.

inga comes out of the kitchen with her forehead wrinkled, drying a baby bottle.

"Oh, hi!" She finally smiles. "I didn't know you were coming today."

That shit snips my fucking balls, and I stand there looking at her like she's a damn fool. I couldn't give a shit she's been here, holding Parker down for months. She's a fucking mother and got a few years to make up for when Parker put her ass on knock off. inga's been cool as shit, but every once in a while I'm reminded of her poor views on men.

"Hell you mean, inga?" my father coming in after me questions. "This his family's house."

I don't need these two going at it today. They've already gone rounds in the past few months.

She freezes, giving him a hard stare. "Don't start, Kadar. I'm genuinely surprised. Parker said Rut was in D.C. for work."

"And he home now," my father pushes. "Is it a big deal he seeing about his family?" inga lifts her hands in the air, one palm opening in defeat. "C'mon, boy," he pats Sharkie's side. "We going out back for a run."

They take off toward the kitchen for the back yard. I go for the stairs, grateful that didn't get out of hand. I had enough shit on my mind and pops knew it. I flew into D.C. two days ago to present my sneaker design to the *Asé Garb* design team. I was supposed to stay two days to hit up a fundraising dinner Stroy was hosting for his organization, but I changed my plans and flew into Jersey late yesterday. I needed to kick it with my pops.

For over two months after that showdown at my moms' place, he didn't call and neither did I. It wasn't until the day after Christmas when my phone rang and it was him, telling me he was taking my moms to an alcohol rehabilitation program. He'd noticed her drinking beer with her breakfast and vodka with her lunch. Him being there with her every day allowed him to see how she had spiraled with her drinking that had been heavy for years. She didn't fight him on going much. Moms said she knew she was fucked up when I left for college. She was lonely and lost. Parker thinks it was because she didn't have any true responsibilities regimenting her life. She didn't work, didn't have a lover, and had no kids to get up and out for school every day. All she had was bingo and nice monthly stipends from Divine and me.

Since I arrived at the house in Ewing last night, we talked and politicked on some real shit. There were some things I had to get off my chest with my father. And then I learned there was some shit he had to share with me. Then we got up this morning, had breakfast at a favorite hole in the wall in Trenton, and continued up to Connecticut.

And now I'm here...

One of the doors to the master suite is open, and before I make it that close, I peep two of three of my favorite girls. This view is different. It's intimate and between mother and child. Parker's breast-feeding Grayson, watching her in her left arm. Then her attention goes to her right boob. I don't see anything, but apparently, it's leaking because she picks up a burping cloth—one of a bazillion new terms I've learned in the past eight weeks—and presses it to her areola for a few seconds before putting it down. Her attention goes back to the baby. And my pupils dilate at the sight of Parker's half naked body, sitting with crossed legs in the middle of the bed. The bright sun out is blasting into the room, making them both look angelic.

Well, Parker looks like a fucking vixen with swollen tits and a narrowed waist. Her shrinking pouch now hidden behind my baby girl is even cute on her. *Shit... This view is every-fucking-thing.*

She catches me.

Parker's eyes shoot up and land on me. After a few seconds, they narrow just slightly, something she does a lot lately.

"I didn't know you'd be coming today."

That shit burns me.

Love's Ineligible Receiver

Parker

She didn't sleep well last night, so I had to wake her to eat. My breasts were so full they leaked. I'm zapped, completely yet blissfully knackered. This little being is far more than I bargained for. I thought I knew the joys of having a child; I'd dreamed of it since I could conceptualize family. But nothing has prepared me for seeing a little human being, who looks like something I made. Grayson has a few of my features at eight weeks, but she's consistently looked like her father. She's been as demanding and hard-nosed as him, too. We've been warring over her sleeping in her bassinet since I brought her home. And because I've been so adamant, I've sacrifice much needed rest to battle with her. Last night was strange. She went down at her usual time, but what should have been the start of a night's rest turned into a catnap.

And now while she eats and sleeps peacefully, mommy leaks... from both breasts. I reach over and grab a burping cloth I keep handy and push into my nipple, which is absolutely useless. It'll stop for a few seconds, before the dripping begins again. I need to pump and by the looks of Grayson's little cheeks slowing, my hope of depleting during her feeding is now shot.

And I'll have to do it now—

My attention goes from a fully sleeping Grayson to...her sexy father. *My god.* My temperature spikes for a few seconds long as I drink him in. He's standing against the closed door of the set with his arms crossed, exposing the bulge of his biceps. And one leg's crossed over the other, revealing his erection. My spine shivers.

Motherhood brings the most bizarre changes. One is the tricks it played on my libido. In my third trimester, I had little desire for sex. Rut would be his usual needy self, always teasing, prodding my new body, and pulling down my panties. I complained little, understanding it was a part of my duties if I wanted to keep this thing monogamous. I put on my best efforts but had very little orgasms and was often left unsatisfied.

But, boy! Postpartum? Not only has my appetite returned, it's increased tenfold. It's been so bad I couldn't adhere to the six-week postpartum abstinence rule. Now, it's been poor Rut, who has to endure while I've taken what I've needed because he's so worried about "breaking something." The difference is he's been rewarded each time with a happy ending.

Rut has been present. The *Kings* didn't make it to the Super Bowl this year, but it had been a solid season for Rut. He's recorded more than eighty receptions, eleven hundred yards, and twelve touchdowns in a rookie season. He also broke the rookie record for the most average receiving yards per game. Because of all of this, Rut was the recipient of the *2018 Offensive Rookie of the Year* award by the League. And as soon as the season wrapped for the *Kings*, he had endorsement obligations to fulfill: a commercial to shoot and a sneaker to design. Next week will be the first of two grand openings for his sneaker boutique, *Rubber Soles*.

The man has been busy being a business mogul and being...devilishly *sexy*. I'm sure to school my face, something I've mastered over time with Rut.

"I didn't know you'd be coming today," I breathe, hardly able to hear the words leave my throat.

He grumbles something I'm sure is inappropriate as he pushes off the door and strolls into the room. To distract myself from his stimulating countenance, I go back to Grayson and gently pull my nipple from her. Her lips puckers adorably and tongue sucks the roof of her mouth with more fervor than it had my nipple. I prop her over my shoulder for a burp that comes virtually in seconds.

Her father is standing over me as I pat her tiny back for more. Although I have no idea what's going through his mind, I doubt it's what's going through my body. It's been insane, my insatiable appetite for Rut. And for him only. I've never been attracted to another man as I had Rutledge Amare. It's everything about him: his height, girth, sordid vernacular, surprising intelligence, and most appreciative, his resiliency.

Rut has undergone so many changes. Several women have stood ground against his misogyny and patriarchal world views. We've fought against twenty-five years of development until Rut saw his flaws and sought to change many of them...

He didn't agree easily to my name choice for our daughter.

Her middle name derives from B-Rocka. Brianna was as close as I could think could come from Brian. Rut appreciated that gesture. It's her first name he felt was a feminist sucker punch.

When I'm satisfied Grayson's belly is without excess air, I lay her on her side facing the bathroom. Rut's attention is on her as I place her burping cloth on the far end of the bed. Catching his attention on my way back, I take little time pulling down my shorts, rendering myself completely naked.

I refuse to waste any time with this. Rut wasn't supposed to be back here in Connecticut until tonight. At best, I would have seen him tomorrow. Excitement of his untimely presence is now pooling between the folds of my sex. I spread my thighs and lay back, but not before catching his eyes flash open with surprise. And I *love* that ability over him. Now down on my back, I'm peering between my legs at him, watching him strip out of his clothes.

Rut wastes no time taking to the bed and crawls up the mattress. The moment his mouth meets my core, all the wind is knocked from my lungs and my head collapses. His immediate actions warmed me. With Rut, I didn't have to hide my desires. As he's been doing since training camp last year, Rut's always ready to deliver on any of my needs.

Him diving just now to the depths of me is no different than three months ago when I decided on a living room set I desperately wanted but couldn't quite afford. Via text, I proposed he help out until I could repay him his portion. Without confirming, he went and ordered the set that was delivered three days later. He was that intentional with pleasing me. Or when it was time to have Grayson's ears pierced, with just few words shared of fear, he volunteered to be in the room with her.

His tongue swipes and dips inside of me. My back bows over the mattress in pure, tantalizing bliss. His big hands cup my waist, caressing my skin up and down. My hips burrow into his face, sex into his mouth. Greedy hands grab his head, grinding against it as I enjoy the pleasure of his tongue. I ride the wave of his yielding, his efforts, his vulnerability. His love. My hips lift more, spine curves more, head rolls onto my crown to the vista over my bed. It displays the glorious sun, winding trees, and dancing leaves. It mimics my world—or what could be if I just let go and flow with the treasure before me.

Lost in that view, time jolts still and everything moves in slow motion. I can isolate each pleasure point, feel the slither of his tongue on each inch of my sex. Sense the caress of his hands, and know I love this man from the depths of me. Knowing him for less than a year, I can't imagine the next chapter of my life without Rut. He's integrated himself into each corner of me. Filled me with a love and awareness of myself I've never known.

And without warning, I snap out of the trance into an unexpected orgasm shooting from my core, rocking my entire frame into a frenzy.

"Oh, baby!" I cry.

"Just like this," I can hear above my head as I suck her clit between my tongue and top lip. "We can do it forever. Just like..."

I keep going until she's back on the mattress. Pulling up on plank, I give her clit one last long and hard lick. Her whole damn body shivers. My dick is hard, damn belly is dancing, I'm so ready to be inside her. I run my tongue from her navel to between her big ass titties. My dick pressing into her opening, I check on Grayson before I plunge. She's still sleeping peacefully. They tell us all the time to enjoy the first weeks of her sleeping life. Being able to do this makes me enjoy every minute of it.

My head is pulled to face her mother's. Parker's eyes strain as though she's high. My mouth work could do that to her. I love every fucking minute of it, too. But I can also see the 'V' between them.

She licks her lips. "I want to be free with you again," she whispers, cupping my face. "I want to get back on the free-fall again." Parker pauses for a moment and I don't know what to say. "I got off. Even after I apologized for doing it, I stayed off the ride. I've been scared, Rut. That night, after the Brielle concert, my life took on a drastic change. You leaving me, me accepting my pregnancy, Jimmy being snatched away, my being kicked out, being homeless though I was given this beautiful house." Her tears arrive, and I just want to hold her in my arms to chase them away.

"That was a traumatic period for me, I realize now. Nothing had been familiar for so long. And when you finished camp, I decided to take whatever you gave me. I decided to stick around and accept whatever you offered, and not in the desperate way. In a very stubborn way, with just one condition of monogamy. I shut you out and I'm sorry." Crying, she reaches up and kisses my stained lips. "You're my familiar because you stuck around during my indifferent days. You gave me a home, accepted my mother and friends to help out, you nourished my body—even my postpartum body—while I've locked you out of my heart. You're now my familiar, Rut." Again, she goes quiet and stares at me.

Again, I don't know what to say.

"All these months I was avoiding the heartache of yet another man who didn't let me into his home with pure intention but circumstance instead. But you've given me so much more, and I want to try a new relationship with you."

My face goes tight. "What kind?"

Her body trembles then tears fall and she covers her mouth to hide it from me as though it's possible.

"I want to be your *gir*—girlfriend," she whispers so low I'm sure Grayson couldn't even hear it. "I think we should try it out. Just for a little while. We can see how it goes."

My dick is hard again, and this time with a fucking vengeance. I swivel my hips until I know I'm at her opening again and dive in. Parker jumps, sucking in a breath. I hold to see if she's okay. When her hips pull up, I know, and start driving into her. My mouth brushes down her lips to her neck where I suck. Then I move down to her boobs and lick her sweet nipples. She moans so seductively, pushing them into me. Her nails go to my back, scraping down to my ass. I plunge and plunge until I reach the ends of her.

And Parker must feel me there, too, because her damn pussy quakes around me. Her arms hold me in place, anchoring her while she throws it to me. I'm losing my mind trying to hold out for her. Her thighs move around me, her tits smack my face, warm milk squirting my eyes, nose, and mouth. And I'm in fucking heaven with liquids all over me.

Shit...

My balls go warm then jut. Quickly, I lift from her thighs, pulling my dick from her, and slam my body over to sandwich it. My body shakes like a damn fool as I bust between us. My damn feet curl as I bite into her shoulder.

"Rut!" she moans.

I pull my mouth from her soft skin. "Sorry." I try catching my breath.

Then I push up off my hands and arms to lift from her.

"That!" Her eyes are down her body.

I follow and see it.

"Shit!" I whisper as I stand to my knees.

"You have to either move up my body after pulling out or pull out faster!" Parker's annoyed as she takes inventory of my bullet game reaching underneath her belly button into her pubs. "This is how we got in trouble the first night," she groans.

I leave the bed as she uses my baby's burping cloth to wipe up her stomach instead of down. It takes me minutes to shower and brush my teeth. When I come back to the bed, Parker's up and dancing toward the bathroom. My attention goes straight to my pride and joy, laying in the same position. That gives me enough time to find some clothes in the closet to slip on. Doing that takes seconds, then I'm hopping into basketball shorts and switching the contents of my pockets.

I sit on the edge of the bed, the side Grayson's sleep positioner is.

Shit. She's beautiful. Parker thinks she looks like me. I only see Grayson, my baby. When we FaceTime'd my moms last week at the facility she's in, she said Grayson looks like my grandmother. My business partner, Jeremy, who visited her in the hospital says she thankfully looks like her mother, Parker. Divine and Jade thinks my baby looks like my pops. I don't care who she looks like. I just want her to be smart like her mommy and swagged out like me.

Parker comes out of the bathroom wrapped in a towel. She goes to the other side of the bed and pulls out the breast pump. That's when I hear little squeaks and snorts. Grayson's waking up. I go to lift her from the bed. Before I put her on my shoulder, I remember she needs a burping cloth. The one available to her before I showed should now be burned. Quickly, I carry her out of the room and down the hall to her nursery. I pluck a cloth from the drawer and toss it over my shoulder. Now I'm able to put her up there.

As we go back to the master suite, I'm rubbing her little back. Parker's pumping session is already in motion. She sits on the side of the bed while on her phone, letting the machine do its thing. I cop a spot next to her but on the floor, against the bed.

"Today's Trent's birthday?" Parker asks above us as I kiss Grayson, who seems to be very awake and moving. "They're having a private surprise party at *DiFillippo's* tomorrow! I completely forgot. Oh, god! I've got nothing to wear," she fake cries. "Jade told me about it a couple of weeks ago, but I've got baby cave brain. If I didn't just check *Facebook*, I would've never remembered. Are you going?"

"Were you gonna invite me?" I ask.

I pull Grayson's little fists to my mouth and watch her frown at me, sniffling.

Parker goes quiet for a minute. "Like... What do you mean?"

"You said you wanna be my girl. Were you gonna invite me as ya man?"

"Well... I assumed he told you about it."

"You just said it's a surprise party, Jade told you about it. She ain't got my number."

"But she could get it. You and Trent are signed to the same sports agency. You both have relationships with Azmir Jacobs. She could get your info if she wanted to."

"I ain't ask what she wanted. I asked about your intentions since you said you wanna be my girl."

There's another pause. I'm just fucking with Parker, but want to see how she comes out of this.

"I don't know what to say," she whines like a baby.

"I think she needs to be changed. She need a bath, too?" I'm prepared to handle it all.

Parker doesn't answer me, so I look up at her from over my shoulder. She's biting her lip, I can tell, stewing on what I said. I guard my face.

"You thinking 'bout what you gonna wear?"

Parker still doesn't answer me, and I know I might have gone too far. I reach into my pocket and put the box next to her.

Parker

His long arm reaches next to me, plopping a black velvet box next to my thigh. Dropping my phone on my lap, I grab the box. The springs are strong so it takes effort to lift the lid. My eyes are blinded by the brilliance of sparkly cushion-cut stone. If I didn't know the man handing it to me, I would think it's fake. That's how radiant it is. A flash of fear jolts my belly and my entire frame tenses.

I don't know how long I stare at it, but I can't find my tongue.

"What do you think you can find to wear with that accessory?"

His voice breaks my inner thoughts.

"*Wh*-When?" I stutter.

He peers up at me, our precious princess in his backdrop. "Earlier you said forever."

My mouth drops.

With my arms shaking and empty breasts being pulled into the suctions of the pump, I ask, "Is this..."

With a deadpan expression, Rut shakes his head.

All of a sudden I hear galloping just outside of the room. My face constricts and I see Sharkie chasing his tail out in the hall. Rut whistles for him, and his big body bolts inside the room. I'm ready to scream as he nears Grayson, but Rut holds out his hand, halting Sharkie's run just feet away.

"Why is Sharkie over?"

"I told you he needs to get used to being here. Shark's not a city dog. The resident groomer takes him out to the park, but that's just a few times a week. He needs to run every day."

Sharkie drops by Rut's side and rests on all fours.

That's when my shoulders drop, realizing how real this is. My eyes go to the box in my hand. "You're serious about this?"

With his attention back to Grayson, he murmurs, "I ain't that type of dude, but if getting down on one knee to prove to you I need you by my side to speed up my maturation process is what I mean, I'll run around the property butt ass naked. Hell... I'll run around *Hotep Financial*, that way with all my teammates and coaches watching."

I power off the pump and release my tender breasts. Then I lean over my lap toward his face.

Rut finds me there. "You need me to do that?"

I kiss his soft lips, my heart and eyes fill with so much joy I can't contain.

I nod my head. "I wanna do this. With you, and Grayson, and Sharkie, and maybe one more little Rut."

And his Coke bottle glasses. I fall head over heels each time he brings them when he stays over. I love taking them off and riding him. I know he can't see all of my features crisply, but he can feel me squeeze around him.

Rut sucks in a breath and his eyes close.

In a panic, I ask, "No more babies?"

"Nah." He exhales. "Maybe one more in a few years. It's just... I thought you were going to say no or maybe *in a few years* about getting married."

I shake my head as I laugh at him telling on himself. "No, silly. I can't imagine saying no."

"Good!" he huffs. "You'd be out your damn mind if you said no to all of this!" He gestures our current family.

I stroke his head, proud of his vulnerability. "I think I'd be crazy if I delayed you."

I can't resist kissing him again.

"So, about this Christianity thing…"

"What?" My brows hike. "The thing that ain't going nowhere? You better consult Trent on how to manage spiritual maintenance with the season's schedule because that's where your family will be until the Lord calls us home or Jesus returns for us. Don't miss the boat, Amare."

"*Shit.*"

The End

XXXX

#PenningWithoutParameters
🩶 #ImGonnaMakeYouLoveMe 🩶

~love acknowledges

Researcher: Shumethia S. — You've been absolutely amazing! I still can't believe you actually 'enjoyed' this project. Wowzers! I need to switch up my game. LOL! On to the next venture! And Christine and Christina (mother-daughter duo) – Thanks for helping me with the title for this book! Alan Manley of **Big Al Kicks** – I appreciate you lending your journey in the sneaker industry to Rut's character development. Your brain knows no bounds. Stay #Wild! (insider)

LBTR — Afi, Adrian, Angela B., Angela J.J., Artemysia, Ash, Ashleigh, Ashley, Ayanna, Ayo, Azaria, Bonita, Brittany, Courtney, Danielle, Dee, Deena, Deidre, Denise, DeVona, Diane, Diva Dee, Doresha, Doris, Erica C., Ericka M., Gail, Grace, Heather, Heidi, Hezie-Ann, Jasmine, Jessica, Kamashia, Karmen, Katrice, Katrina, Kay, Kendra, Kerry, Keyma, Kim, Kimmiko, Kita, Korei, LaKaya, LaKisha, LaLa, LaSonde, Linda R., Linda W., Lee, LeShonda, Levette, Malaika, Marshall, Michelle M., Michelle R.O., Michelle T., Mocha, Monique H., Monique N., Natoya, Nena, Nikki, Pamela, PJ, Rakia, Quan, Regina, Richell, Rose, Roslyn, Samona, Sharon L., Sharon F.W., Shaun, Sola, Sophia, Stacey K., Stacy M., Tabatha, Tamara, Tanisha, Tanya, Tara, Té, Teresa, Terri G., Terry H., Tesha, Tia, Tiffany, Tineka, Tonya, Tralaina, Vivian, Wendi, Yolanda P., Yolanda U., Yorubia, and Yvette H., you equal life! Thanks for being that core of support. ***Jemeka*** & ***Rita***, we fight (well, Jemeka and me), we laugh, we confer, and we do it all drama-free. I'm so grateful for you two. Seriously.

Love's Betas — Yorubia, you know you've been a tool for a headache and one of peace of mind, too. Thanks so much for taste-testing the soup. Sabrina SS, I appreciate you going the extra mile for me. Your support means so much! Shumethia, you liked this book! You said it and can't take it back! Ha! Thanks for having multiple roles in #TeamLove. I don't know what I'd do without you, which is why I hound you the way I do.

Christina C. Jones aka CCJ — Where do we go next? Thanks for your genius, creativity, flexibility, and friendship. You continue to make me a better human being. #Truly

Interior Artist: Cedeara Ardell McCollum — Thanks, baby girl, for the imagery you've designed for my books! Love you always!

Proof Reader: Tina V. Young — Simply amazing is God's creation of you. Thanks sooooo much for all you do. I can't say it enough. You're magic!

Editors:

Zakiya Walden of *I've Got Something to Say!* — Thanks for your brutal honesty. I so enjoy reading your edits, even the ones where you yell at me!

Octavia Frost of *Polish Your Pen* — Thanks for your bold willingness to step into the LB zone!

MDT: Time to level up! This is my promise...

Master, my *Jireh*, my *Rohi*, Psalms 119:114 (NKJV) "You are my hiding place and my shield; I hope in Your word." *Your vessel*

~other books by love belvin

Love's Improbable Possibility series:
Love Lost, Love UnExpected, Love UnCharted* & *Love Redeemed

Waiting to Breathe series:
Love Delayed & Love Delivered

Love's Inconvenient Truth (Standalone)

Love Unaccounted series:
In Covenant with Ezra, In Love with Ezra & Bonded with Ezra

The Connecticut Kings series:

Love in the Red Zone, *Love on the Highlight Reel, *Determining Possession, End Zone Love, Love's Ineligible Receiver, *Pass Interference, Love's Encroachment, & *Offensive Formations (*by Christina C. Jones)

Wayward Love series:

The Left of Love, The Low of Love & The Right of Love

Love in Rhythm & Blues series

The Rhythm of Blues & The Rhyme of Love

LOVE IN RHYTHM & BLUES series

The Sadik series

He Who Is a Friend, He Who Is a Lover & He Who Is a Protector

The Muted Hopelessness series:

My Muted Love, Our Muted Recklessness, & Our Reckless Hope

The Prism series:

Mercy, Grace, & The Promise

Low Love, Low Fidelity (Standalone)

~extra

You can find Love Belvin at www.LoveBelvin.com
Facebook @ Author - Love Belvin
Twitter @LoveBelvin
Goodreads: Love Belvin
and on Instagram @LoveBelvin

Join the #TeamLove mailing list to keep up with the happenings of Love Belvin here!

Made in the USA
Las Vegas, NV
18 April 2024